THE SUMMER UNITES

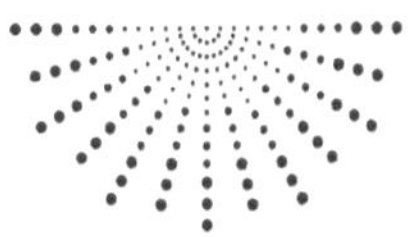

THE SUMMER UNITES

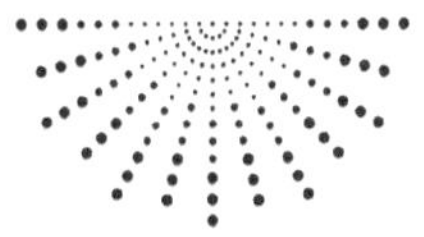

MARIE MCGRATH

ISBN: Paperback 978-1-956183-85-6
Library of Congress Control Number: 2022939221

Any references to historical events, real people or real places are used fictitiously. Names, characters, and places are products of the author's imagination.

Cover Design by Diana TC, triumphcovers.com

First Printing Edition 2022

Published by Creative James Media
Pasadena, MD 21122

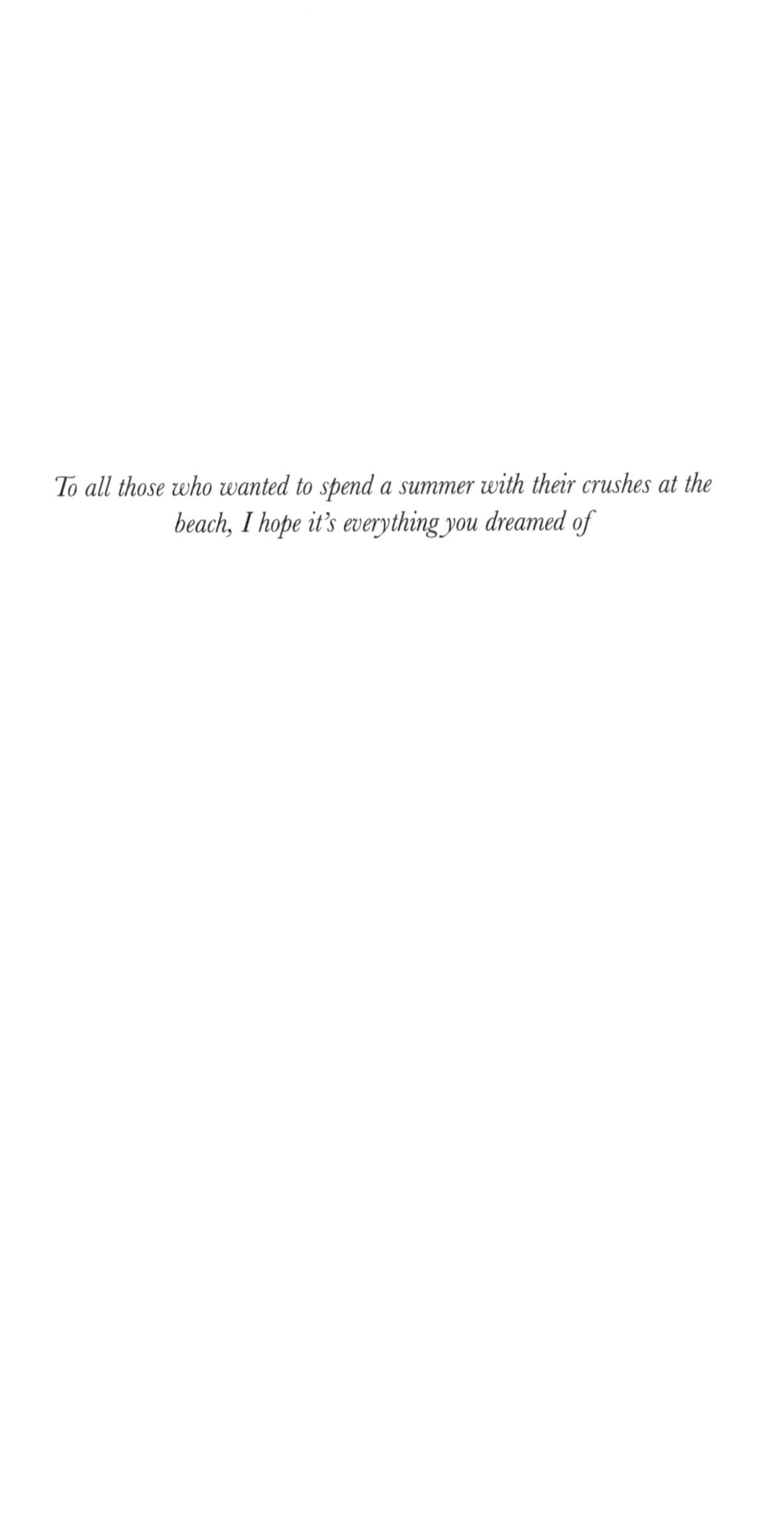

To all those who wanted to spend a summer with their crushes at the beach, I hope it's everything you dreamed of

CHAPTER ONE

RILEY

It was hard to believe how much could change in one year. I had two new best friends and a boy who was interested in me. Not to mention my parents were separated and talked more now than they had in several years. Of course, I also lived in a new state. Things were pretty great, and I had a feeling this summer would make it even better.

"Are you sure you have everything packed?" Mom asked for the hundredth time.

"Yes. I checked and double checked already."

Mom scrunched her nose and tapped her finger to her chin. "Tell me one more time what this house situation is."

I sighed. "Mom, we've been over this."

Mom-mom chuckled as she peered over her newspaper. "Jo, Riles is right. You've heard the arrangement ten times already. You've agreed, just let the girl get ready."

I smiled at Mom-mom; she still always looked out for me. Although, my mom did a better job of it after the fall fiasco. She made sure to ask what I was thinking as things changed between her and my dad. It was strange to be asked, but I was thankful that our relationship was on better terms.

"I know, but it will make me feel better. Just one more time?" she asked as she batted her eyelashes.

"It's Shelby's beach house. There are two wings, the one side has three bedrooms, and the other side has three bedrooms. Two of the bedrooms are fitted for multiple people, so realistically the one side will be ours, using bunk beds. The other side will be for the boys to pop in and stay on occasion. They can choose to all room together or to be in separate rooms. I promise to stay on the one side with Sophie and Shelby."

Mom smiled. "Good, even though I was your age once, too."

Mom-mom snorted. "Yeah, and we all know how that went."

"Momma! Riley will not make my mistakes." She winked at me. "She will make her own."

"You two are ridiculous, you know that? Who says I'll be making any mistakes? I don't even have a boyfriend."

Mom-mom's expression was like the cat who'd caught the mouse.

"What?"

She shook her head. "I don't think that will be true for long."

I exhaled. This topic was always up for debate. Everyone thought Randy and I were deluding ourselves. That we were in fact a couple in denial. While I could understand where they came from, I knew better. Randy doted on me like no one else, but he was still guarded.

He was never dishonest, but his family had hurt him— well, at least his father did. We were miles from where we started last fall, but the damage had already been done.

Even with the improvements his father had made over the last few months since the new year, Randy was always on edge—holding his breath for the other shoe to drop.

It broke my heart that he couldn't relax. That he couldn't just be a normal high schooler. Maybe, this summer would help him see that.

"If you say so, Mom-mom. I'm focusing on fun with Sophie and Shelby this summer. It's my first full summer in Honey Cove and I can't wait. I've barely seen the cove since we moved here and us girls are in a good place."

"That's a great point, Riles. See, Momma? Riles has her head on her shoulders, she isn't like me."

"Thank the lord for that, Jo."

I chuckled.

Mom put her hands on her hips and scoffed. "Oh yeah? Well, I got my spunk from you!"

Mom-mom eyed Mom suspiciously, then shook her head. "I'll let that one go." She turned in my direction. "When do you leave?"

I slid my phone from my back pocket. "Shelby is picking me up in about two hours."

Mom-mom clapped her hands. "Just enough time to swing on the porch with us."

Mom opened the fridge and pulled out a large pitcher of iced tea. "Some iced tea to go with it?"

"Sounds perfect," I said.

The porch swing was my favorite place to sit; I would miss it this summer. I plopped on the swing with my mom-mom.

She pushed off the floor and set us adrift. The creaking of the chains lulled me as we steadily moved through the air.

Mom brought out a small tray with three glasses of iced tea. She carefully handed us each one and then sat on the small porch chair close to the swing. She took a long drink, smacked her lips, and sighed. "There is nothing like iced tea in the summer."

"Amen to that," Mom-mom said.

"I'll miss you two," I said.

"Despite my anxiety, you'll be having too much fun to remember us. Plus, it's only for a little bit and we will still see you. Your dad is coming to visit, too, remember?" Mom asked.

It was so strange to think about their arrangement now. Last summer they weren't even speaking, and now he was visiting on long weekends and during breaks at school. I tried to not overthink it. Mom wasn't sure where things were going with them. She said they would always love each other, but she wasn't sure they could ever be *in* love like they were before things went south.

"I know. I'll come home when he's here. Shelby already promised to drive me home, or someone can come get me. It's not like the house is that far."

"I'll let you know when he picks a week. He's still shifting some cases around as much as he can, but it'll be in June."

I took a sip of my tea, letting the liquid cool my throat. "Okay, whichever, Mom. We don't have any set plans except to just enjoy the summer." A slight breeze picked up as we swung. "What will you two do without *me*?"

"Party!" Mom-mom said as she wiggled her eyebrows.

Mom laughed. "Since when have you partied, Momma?"

Her right eyebrow rose. "Oh, I know how to party. I may be old, but I'm not dead."

"Momma! I don't want to think about that."

I giggled. "You two are crazy. Mom, you'll probably work, come home, and plop on the sofa to read. Mom-

mom, you'll be playing pinochle and attending your gardening meetings."

"Maybe so, I guess you'll have to wait and find out," Mom-mom said.

"I guess I will."

We stayed on the porch for a little longer before I escaped to my room. Shelby would be here in a little over an hour and I wanted to make sure to be ready and waiting for her arrival.

My clothes managed to fit in a wheely suitcase I had used as a carryon last summer. Shelby assured us that there was a whole laundry room at the cove house we could use. So, even against my better judgment, I downsized my wardrobe choices.

My phone dinged the special sound reserved for only one person. My stomach fluttered even after all this time. Randy had sent me a text, *Hey, superstar. Are you ready to start this summer adventure?*

Absolutely! I can't wait to see the house. I have no idea what to expect.

A massive house. It's the Rowe beach house. You know extravagance is guaranteed.

All accurate. What time are you heading to the house?

I have my shift at Morgan's until four. I'll stop by my house to pick up my bag and shower then head that way. You'll be there before then, right?

Yep. Shelby is supposed to get here in about an hour. Then the three of us will settle in.

Sounds good. I can't wait. 😊

Me either.

Need me to bring anything from Morgan's for dinner tonight? Shelby hasn't answered how stocked the house will be.

Hmm, good point. I can ask her when she gets here and let you know. Either that or we can order pizza. Are there many places for food at the cove?

Not too many and not depending on the time of night we order.

I will never get used to not being able to order food whenever I want.

I can't even imagine that. Did you honestly order food after midnight?

Once and it was worth it. I returned the phone back to the nightstand and plopped on my bed. Everything was packed that I could think of: my chargers, laptop, clothes, my summer reading books, *everything.*

I'll have to take your word for it. Break is over. Don't forget to let me know what Shelby says. See you soon.

It never ceased to amaze me how thoughtful Randy was of others. No one else had even mentioned food for tonight, but him. I doubted anyone would have thought of it until we were faced with the dilemma. How he managed to be such an amazing person with all he went through still surprised me. He was special, I just wished he would realize that.

CHAPTER TWO

SOPHIE

Burnt popcorn from the machine invaded my senses and burned my throat. I plugged my nose. "Who left the machine on for too long? That reeks. We must clean it before we make any more." I peered over the side of the machine. "Thankfully, there isn't much left in the bottom."

Drew grimaced as he tried to not breathe. "Wasn't me. I haven't been on snacks all day. Did you ask the new trainee?"

Sasha had started almost a week ago and while she was perky and great with customers, so far she had not mastered the machines as easily as I had. "Haven't seen her."

Drew used his hand to cover the headset to avoid interference with mine. "Sasha, Sasha, Drew. What is your location?"

Her voice flowed through my headset as if she stood next to me. "Had to run to the bathroom. I'm headed back to the snack station now."

My eyebrows rose. "Guess that answers your question."

Drew chuckled and put his index finger to his nose. "Not it."

I sighed and pretended to glare at him. "No fair! I'm not the one she's shadowing."

"True, but you're the most recent hire before her, so you get to do the dirty jobs."

"Oh, is that so? I'll remember that later," I said as I smiled devilishly.

"That's cheating. You can't withhold stuff in our relationship because of work stuff, it's in the rules."

"What rules?"

Drew inched closer. "The rulebook that we discussed."

My hands settled on my hips. "I didn't discuss any such rules."

He stroked his chin. "No? Well, I'm enacting it now. Work hierarchy can't be held against me in our relationship."

"Watch me."

He shifted his arms around me as he held me close to him, face-to-face. "What a pity. I had plans for the first night at the cove house."

Sasha rounded the corner and we separated. She grimaced as she got closer. "What's that smell?"

I eyed Drew telling him with my expression that I wasn't giving up yet. "That would be the popcorn machine. It burned."

"Oh rats. I thought I could let it go and run to the bathroom. I guess I can't."

I shook my head as Drew backed up. "It's picky. The kettle should be dumped once it's done to prevent the kernels from continuing to cook, especially if it doesn't switch to warm. It happens, don't sweat it. Just be careful." I grabbed the trashcan from under the counter. "We must empty it out and clean the kettle from the burned parts, then you can make more to fill it up. I'll help until my shift is over."

Sasha smiled. "Thank you. I really do appreciate it. I'll get it next time."

"I know you will."

Drew winked as he rounded the corner and disappeared. We both only had twenty minutes left in our shift before Courtney came to take over. Courtney had been given the opportunity to have her first shadow— Sasha. No matter what happened, she stayed positive.

Sasha had already emptied the popcorn in the bottom. "Are you ready to head on your vacation?"

I laughed. "I'm ready to get away in between my work shifts, but I don't know if I can call it a vacation when I will still be here a few days a week."

"I'd call it a vacation. It sounds like so much fun. My parents would never let me do something like that."

"Honestly, I'm surprised my mama let me." And that was the truth. After all the trouble I had been in during the spring, I was sure Mama would have me on a tight leash until I turned thirty. I guess I proved she could trust me.

"Well, enjoy it for us all who are stuck with a boring summer."

"I'm sure you'll find a way to make it interesting. You'll be here. And shifts here are always full of new experiences."

"That's for sure, especially if I can't figure out this machine," she said as she hit the kettle a few times.

"Courtney can show you again when she gets here. She's actually the one who taught me to use it."

"Really?"

"Yep, and if I can learn, so can you."

Sasha put the last scoop full of popcorn into the trash.

We worked in silence to clean out the burnt kernels in the kettle and wiped it clean once they were removed.

We high fived, just as Drew stopped in front of the counter. "You ready?"

I looked around the counter for any of my belongings. "See you in a few days, Sasha. Don't sweat it too much." I walked next to Drew and stopped. "I need to grab my keys from my locker. Meet you out front?"

"I'll be the cute guy waiting in the idling car."

I winked. "We think highly of ourself, do we?"

"You know you think I'm cute." He kissed my forehead and patted my arm encouraging me to hurry up.

I giggled and sped toward the locker room. It was vacant as I entered, grabbed my lanyard with my house key, clocked out, and headed to the front doors. I waved to Sasha as I walked through and was bombarded by the sticky heat.

Just as Drew said, he waited in his car idling by the front. He peered over his sunglasses as I walked out and whistled, wiggling his eyebrows suggestively.

Heat crawled across my cheeks. "Oh, stop it. I look ridiculous in my uniform. That's not sexy."

"You look good to me regardless of your uniform."

Gawd, he's so sweet. How did I manage to have a boyfriend? Out of all my friends, I didn't expect to be the one with a boyfriend. I figured I'd be alone forever, but Drew wiggled his way into my heart and now that he was there, I didn't want him to ever leave it.

I walked around to the passenger side and got in. "Are you ready to drive to the cove house?"

"I will once I finish packing after I drop you off at your house."

"Boys! How do you manage to wait until the last minute? I have been packed for like two days."

He shrugged. "It's not rocket science trying to pack for the beach."

I rolled my eyes. "No one said it was hard, but you have to make sure what you want to wear is clean, do laundry if it isn't, and then put it all in the bag."

"Easy peasy. Twenty minutes tops."

I laughed. "Maybe for you. Anyway, you remember I'm going with the girls, right?"

"I do. I just need the address and I'll be by later."

"Not too much later, right? I think we're all hoping to have dinner together to break in the first night."

"I'll be there a little after you. Don't worry, okay?" He reached across the console to hold my hand. The warmth enveloped it. "How are your hands *always* freezing? You need to ask your doctor to check your circulation."

"My circulation is fine. They'll be warm soon." He always complained about their temperature, but he never let go.

With one hand, he pulled into the neighborhood, drove past his house, and parked in my driveway. He left the car on and followed me up to the front door. No matter what he always walked me to the door.

He leaned closer until our lips touched. He kissed me gently, only lingering for a few seconds, before leaning back. "I'll see you soon."

I nodded and watched as he walked back and then drove away.

The door opened with no resistance, then I placed my keys on the hook by the door. "Mama, I'm home."

"I'm in my bedroom."

I kicked my shoes off and walked to her room.

She stood in front of her full-length mirror, adjusting her black pencil skirt. "How was work, Soph?"

I relaxed onto the edge of her bed. "Good, although

the trainee burnt the popcorn in the machine. Had to empty it and clean the whole thing twenty minutes before the end of shift."

Mama giggled. "That sounds lovely." She scrunched her nose. "I hate the smell of burnt popcorn."

"You and me both."

She faced me. "Are you all ready for Shelby to get you on the way to Riley's?"

"Of course. I had my bag packed two days ago. I just need to add my phone charger and it'll be all done."

"I can't believe you'll be gone almost all summer."

"It's not all summer. I'll be back and forth for work. I still have to do my movie theater shifts."

Mama twisted her thumb ring. "Speaking of going back and forth, I wanted to show you something."

I cocked my head to the side. "I'll be safe, Mama. Shelby and Drew promised to drive me when I need it."

"I know they did, and I know they'll stick to their promise. But I still have something I want to show you."

"Okay," I said, dragging out the word.

Mama exited her bedroom and headed for the front door.

"Outside?"

She ignored my question and kept walking. She propped the front door open and stopped on the front porch.

"What could you—"

"Tada!"

My body froze and my eyes widened. There was no way I could be seeing what was in front of me—Rowan exiting a purple Jeep.

"Is that …?"

"Yours? Yes, it is!"

My jaw slackened. "You bought me a Jeep? For real?"

Mama nodded as her smile deepened. "You had a rocky start this spring, but I'm so proud of your hard work at the movie theater. You've found ways to get there and not complain that you can't drive. I thought with you going back and forth from the cove house that you should have something to drive. Rowan helped me find a gently used one a couple towns over and picked it up for me today so you wouldn't see it!"

I squealed. "I love it!" I rushed to the driver door even though I only had socks on and ran my hands over the steering wheel, then gripped the leather. This was mine? I never expected Mama to buy me a car. I figured if I ever wanted something to drive, I'd have to buy it myself.

I exited the car and squeezed Mama in a bear hug. "Thank you, thank you, thank you!"

She chuckled. "You're welcome, Soph."

"What in the world?" Caleb asked from behind the door. "Why is everyone shouting?" He peeked around the door.

"Mama got me a Jeep!" I shouted.

He moved closer and eyed me and then Mama. "You bought her a Jeep?" He threw his hands up in the air. "Great, just great. I don't want to have to drive a *purple* Jeep."

I crossed my arms. "Who says *you* will be driving it?"

"Who do you think will inherit it?"

"Not you!"

Mama chuckled. "Okay, enough you two. Sheesh, no one is inheriting anything now, but Caleb you will be in it at some point."

My eyebrows shot up. "What?"

"Well, another bonus with you being able to drive is that you can take Caleb to school next year. You both will be in Honey Cove High, and I won't have to worry about him walking in the bad weather."

I glared at him. "You are *so* lucky. I had to walk regardless of the weather."

"I'd rather walk."

Rowan chuckled as he gripped Mama's shoulder. "Caleb, you say that now until it's time to do it. Having a ride to school from a senior could be cool."

"Not when it's your sister," he muttered and trudged back into the house.

Rowan tossed me the keys.

"Thanks."

He nodded and kissed Mama on the forehead. "I'll go check on Mr. Mopey."

Mama smiled as he disappeared into the house. True to her word they were taking it slow around me. After the spring fiasco and my two drunken episodes, Mama went on dates with Rowan and only brought him around occasionally. We had only been on two outings since then and both times, Mama checked in to make sure I felt comfortable. She also tried to incorporate memories about my dad more instead of hiding the moments she remembered him. If she had a difficult day, she didn't hide it anymore. Instead, we talked about it, and she used it to see how I was feeling, too.

"Riley and Shelby won't believe it!"

"Well, you're about to find out. I think that's Shelby's BMW."

I looked where Mama pointed and beamed. This made the summer ten times better.

CHAPTER THREE

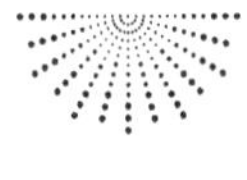

SHELBY

The aroma of Chef Frank's cooking invaded my senses. I would miss his meals while spending the summer at the cove house. I knew how to make food, but Chef Frank and his wonderful pasta would not be something I could manage on my own.

I inhaled deeply. "You need to bottle that alfredo sauce and sell it. It's so addicting."

Chef Frank chuckled. "Why thank you, Shelby. Unfortunately, my cooking skills are for the Rowes and the Rowes only."

"What will I do without you?"

"It's only a few months, you'll manage. Plus, if you need help you can always video call me and I can help you out a little."

"True. I hadn't thought of that."

He tossed the fettuccine noodles into the alfredo sauce and swirled it around a few times, then plated it.

My stomach gurgled and my mouth drooled. "My last meal. I am so savoring this for as long as possible."

"I could make you some to take with you, if you wanted."

"I ... no, that's okay. Maybe later in the summer though when I come back for a founders' meeting or something."

He nodded and wiped his hands on the dish towel. "If you change your mind let me know." He walked from the kitchen as I carried my plate of pasta to the dining room table.

I plopped in the nearest seat, took a deep breath, then plunged my fork into the yummy goodness. I had just shoved a large spoonful in my mouth, when the click-clack of heels echoed.

Ugh. What were my chances that my mother wouldn't be looking for me?

"Shelby?"

Apparently, zero.

"In the dining room, Mother."

The click clacking sounded for a few more steps until she appeared in the doorway. "When are you leaving?"

I checked the time on my phone. "Not for another three hours or so. Sophie doesn't get off work until later. I'll leave a little after she gets off work, go to her house to pick her up, then pick up Riley."

She pursed her lips. "I see. Well, remember that you have responsibilities to maintain this summer. Several festival meetings and founders' meetings, of course. You can't let those slip just to have a summer of *fun.*"

I knew she didn't like the idea of me at the cove house most of the summer. She didn't think that summers should be wasted at my age doing frivolous teenage things. It was a time to learn the business or learn more about running a household or whatever other outdated foolish notions she deemed important.

She had at least stopped scowling when I said Riley's or Sophie's name, which I supposed was progress, at least for her. I, however, had hoped she would be further along in her acceptance at this point. She merely tolerated my choices, even after the spring festival had proven that I could manage the company, my responsibility, and have a life.

My father had been pleased with the results. Most of the companies had seen an increase in their profit margins and more people were continuing to stay with the companies or visit Honey Cove. Overall, the festival had been enough of a success to warrant a summer one.

"I won't forget. I'm bringing my laptop so I can work on things from the house. I have my schedule programmed into my phone so I will get notifications and reminders about upcoming meetings. I'm excited to do another festival. I want it to go well. No need to fret."

"I'm not fretting, Shelby. I am doing my duty in reminding you of yours."

"Right, well, you have accomplished that."

She nodded and straightened her posture. "Well, I will see you when you visit."

"Thank you, Mother."

Her eyebrows drew together. "For?"

"For you and Father allowing me to use the cove house and to invite friends for the summer. I want you to know how much we appreciate it."

"Oh, well, sure. Just don't break anything and remember to keep it nice."

"Of course."

She turned on her heels and left.

I stifled my giggle, she couldn't accept kindness, no matter how hard I had tried to give her some. It was sad that she was so warped from her past she didn't know how to handle it. Maybe someday she wouldn't have such a tough exterior.

I returned to eating my pasta before it got cold. Then I had to finish up my list before picking up the girls. This summer would be like no other!

The familiar cherry blossom trees blew in the slight breeze as I followed the winding driveway of Penny Brooks. Riley's mom-mom had become a sounding board for me. I talked to her more about things that mattered than my own parents. If I wasn't sure of my intentions for something, I asked her. I couldn't imagine Riley's family not being in my life.

Riley sat on the front porch steps with her bag behind her. She stood as I parked my BMW.

I got out and walked to where she waited. "Are you ready?"

Riley grinned. "I'm *so* ready. I feel like I drank ten espressos. I can't sit still."

I laughed. "Well, it's time to go, so you can take a breath."

Riley looked around me to the front seat of the BMW. "Where's Sophie? Didn't you pick her up?"

"Well—" I was silenced by Sophie's Jeep in the driveway.

Riley's mouth hung agape. "Who has a purple Jeep?" Understanding dawned on her expression. "Is that Sophie?"

I nodded.

She squealed and bounced in place. "Her mom got her a Jeep? That is so cool! Oh, I'm so jealous."

Sophie parked next to my car and stood on the seat to peer over the top of the Jeep. "What do you think?"

"It's amazing! When did you get it?"

Sophie beamed. "Today! Mama surprised me when I got home. Isn't she beautiful?"

"Oh yeah."

I elbowed Riley. "So, you have a choice. Are you riding with me or Sophie?"

"Well, it is beautiful, but I'll stick with the plan. I can ride around in the Jeep any time now."

"True." I peered at her bag. "I unlocked the trunk if you want to put your bag in there. Then we can go."

"Sounds good. I just have to let my mom and my mom-mom know I'm leaving, and we can get on the road."

I sat back in my car, adjusting the radio as I waited. Sophie danced on the driver's seat in her new Jeep to a tune I couldn't hear. We would have so much fun this summer.

Riley settled into the passenger seat. "Ready to go. Don't let me forget my mom wants me to text her when we get to the house."

"Sure. I need to do that, too, even though my mother probably won't answer me."

"I'm sorry. Has she gotten any better? It's been months since the spring festival."

"Unfortunately, her progress is minimal. I don't know that she will ever be a touchy-feely mother who has a close relationship with her only daughter. I don't keep my hopes up that she will ever be that kind of person. I'll settle with her not manipulating things and being somewhat supportive of who I surround myself with."

"Well, don't give up on her, maybe she will surprise you."

"Maybe." I passed Sophie's Jeep and headed for the main road. "Anyway, we should be at the house in about forty-five minutes and then our summer can officially begin."

"I can't wait. I never went to the beach for the summer like this before. I had vacations here and there, but I usually stayed in the city. This will be so different."

"Ha! You'll be a beach bum yet!"

"I don't know about a beach bum, but I can't wait to go running in the mornings and just relax in the sunshine."

I grimaced. "Only you would be excited about *running* on the beach. I, for one, plan to do no cardio on the beach. I'll lay out and soak up the rays, maybe get in the water every now and then."

"To each their own." She leaned closer to the window and stared. "Oh, before I forget, Randy wanted to know if he should bring anything for dinner tonight at the house. Will it be stocked?"

My eyebrows rose. "I hadn't even thought of that. No. We keep it empty after the season. Yeah, we will need something. Tell him to bring something simple. Maybe a frozen pizza?"

She nodded and pulled her cell out. "I'll let him choose whatever, although frozen pizza would certainly work."

"Tell him thanks for me. I'll go tomorrow to get food to stock the fridge and pantry."

"Sounds good. All sent. He said it was no problem." She shoved her phone back in her pocket. "Is Luke coming tonight?"

"Yep. I think we have everyone staying tonight. Are you nervous with Randy being in the same house? My stomach is in knots every time I think about Luke and the summer."

Riley grinned. "Yes and no. I don't think it's hit me yet. You haven't seen him since he was here for Easter, right?"

"Nope, and while that trip was nice, we never discussed

a future together. We focused on getting to know each other more." Oh, how I had wished we were more. For someone I despised at first, I couldn't help but daydream about what it would be like to kiss him. Or what he would do for a date. I didn't know if that was stupid or delusional, but I had a hard time focusing on anything else when he was around.

"That's good, though. Friendship is a good foundation for a relationship … or so they say."

I chuckled. "Are you trying to convince me or yourself?"

She smiled. "Maybe a little of both."

"Well, I have heard that bit of wisdom, too. I mean look at Drew and Sophie. Those two are inseparable now. I think it helped that they were friends when they were younger."

"Maybe." She exhaled with a dreamy expression. "I want what they have. So, content with each other. It's so obvious they are together. They are free to express their feelings whenever."

I snorted. "Sophie doesn't express her feelings all the time."

"Well, maybe in her own way. But they can if they want."

"You can't express your feelings to Randy? You two are like half dating."

"I know. It's been nine months since he told me how he felt and kissed me that first time. I just don't know why we aren't more at this point."

"Have you told him that?"

"No."

"Are you planning to?"

"No. Yes. Maybe. I don't know."

I fiddled with my steering wheel cover. "Not that you've

asked my opinion, but I think you should. Randy has always been receptive to how others are feeling, especially when it comes to you. I don't think he would want you to feel something and not be able to tell him."

"You're probably right, but what if it changes everything?"

"Isn't that the point?"

"I guess you're right. Either way something would be changing."

I understood Riley's hesitation. Telling someone what you felt about them, regardless of the scenario, was hard. It made you vulnerable and that vulnerability gave someone an opportunity to disappoint you or hurt you and at least in my experience, it usually happened.

Like with Luke, I could have told him about my feelings at Easter break. We had spent time together as much as we could during the break, but we both avoided the topic of a future. He went to boarding school; did I expect us to become a couple with that kind of distance?

Now with the summer and us all staying in the same house, would it change? I hoped for Riley's sake that things would change for her. She deserved to be happy and so did Randy, but I wasn't sure it was in the cards for me.

Our conversation faded as we both listened to the radio, and I continued to contemplate the signals Luke had sent. Soon enough I parked the BMW in the driveway of my family's cove house. Sophie pulled up next to me and I killed the engine. It was time to start the best summer of our lives.

CHAPTER FOUR

RILEY

My eyes widened as Shelby parked her BMW in the driveway of the cove house. It was better than anything I could have imagined. The exterior had been painted teal with white trim. A white staircase led up to the door closest to the driveway. A beautiful wraparound porch with several different colored Adirondack chairs littered throughout was the first thing I could see.

I inhaled a sharp breath. "Wow. This is amazing, Shelby. If my family had this place I would never leave."

Shelby giggled. "You get used to it after a while."

Sophie honked then parked next to us.

"I would never get used to this. And that porch! Oh my."

"I know where you'll be this summer."

If I had any control over it, I absolutely would be on that porch all summer. It was beautiful. Porches were already my kryptonite, but this one at the beach, this was something different.

Shelby skipped up the stairs to the front door. "All

unlocked. Do you want to take a tour of the house first or get the bags in?"

"Tour!" I shouted.

"Tour!" Sophie said.

"Tour it is."

We hopped up the stairs and followed Shelby inside. The air was warm and stale, most likely from being sealed off for most of winter and spring. Past the door was a grand room. In an open concept style, was the main sitting area, kitchen, a dining table, and a door I assumed was a powder room. The walls were painted a light-green, the flooring a light-ashy wood grain, and white trim.

"As you can see this is the main living space. My mother didn't want small boxy rooms, so she insisted on an open floor plan. I think she just did it to make a statement with her décor." Shelby moved closer to the door I had noticed when we entered. "This is a powder room, only a half bath. The full baths are upstairs near the bedrooms."

Sophie's eyes widened. "I can't imagine having a place like this. It's bigger than my whole house."

Shelby shrugged. "Money is power to a Rowe, you know that."

Sophie smirked. "Wanna share some?"

"Want to see the bedrooms?" she asked instead.

"Duh, I have to pick the best bed," Sophie said.

I giggled.

They walked back toward the front door to a hidden staircase, if the front door was open, with Shelby in the lead.

I waited a little longer, taking in the main area before following them up the stairs. At the top was a smaller, den-like area full of couches and armchairs. The décor was a mix between modern and beachy. Shelby's mom would have probably considered it beach chic or something ridiculous. But at least it looked comfortable, which is what I always cared about anyway. On either side of the den were the set of bedrooms.

Shelby pointed to the doors close to the staircase. "These are the rooms that are better for the boys." She opened all three doors as I peeked in. The paint colors were all pastel. A pastel blue, yellow, and salmon covered the walls. Two of the rooms had a large Queen or King bed, while the third bedroom had two sets of bunk beds. "Plus, they are a little smaller on this side and the bathrooms aren't as big."

Sophie laughed. "They wouldn't need the space anyway."

"Exactly," Shelby said and continued to the other side of the den. "These are for us. I didn't know if you'd want to stay in the bunk bedroom or if all of us should have separate rooms."

"I don't mind sharing a room," I said.

"Same," Sophie added.

"Well, bunk bedroom it is then."

"I call a bottom bunk, though!" Sophie shouted and ran toward the door.

I shook my head. Personally, I didn't care, top or bottom bunk, but apparently Sophie couldn't imagine being on the top bunk. I followed Shelby into the bedroom and took in the room that would be ours for the next twelve weeks. It would be strange to have constant company.

As an only child, I never had someone else my age share a room with me or even be in the same house. It wasn't until I had sleepovers with Zoe and Madison that I had even known what that was like. This would be even more than that, six of us in this house, but two of them falling asleep mere feet from me for the whole summer.

It would be an adjustment; I only hoped that we didn't mind being near each other all the time.

This room was a pastel-purple with gray accented furniture. The flooring was the same as downstairs and all through the hallways. The back wall with the bunk beds up against it had been accented with a black and white designer wallpaper—the design reminded me of Paris or some posh location. To the right of the room was a door that opened to the bathroom, which was shared with the bedroom next to it. The door on the left had a decent walk-in closet with enough shelves and rods to hang clothes up. It even had a built-in section to store shoes.

Sophie plopped on the bottom bunk closest to the bathroom.

"Riley, do you care, top or bottom?" Shelby asked.

I shook my head. "I'm good with either."

"You decide top or bottom and which side," Shelby said.

"I can sleep above Sophie."

Shelby studied my expression. "Are you sure?"

"Yep. It's not like I'll never leave the room. It's just to sleep at night."

"Okay, looks like we have it all set then. The boys can fight over their rooms if they want. Let's get our stuff from the car. I at least want to be unpacked or close to it by the time the boys arrive."

"Good thought. I don't need Randy to see me unpack everything."

Sophie's eyebrow rose. "And what exactly would he see that you are embarrassed of?"

I glared at Sophie. "Nothing unusual, Sophie. But a girl has a right to privacy."

Shelby snatched a pillow from the bunk bed and

launched it at Sophie's head. "Leave her alone and let's go unload. Luke said he wasn't that far behind."

We had come so far in less than a year. I was proud of us. If someone would have told me last fall that I would have been friends with the most popular girl at high school *and* we were all going to live together with three boys this summer, I would have said they were crazy. Not just because it was the furthest thing from reality, but even if I had wanted to, I never imagined my mom would have let it happen.

Alas, here we were.

The other two had already headed downstairs, but I wanted to take one last look and then snapped a photo for socials to send to Zoe and Madison. They couldn't believe my mom had let me go either.

By the time I had returned outside, Shelby had pulled my bag from her trunk. "Thanks."

"No problem. So does it meet your expectations?"

"Meet them? No. Far exceed them? Yes. You really don't use this house that much?"

"Nope. Mother and Father send clients here with their families. I think we stayed for a week when I was younger and they had just bought the place, but otherwise no. They don't believe in taking time to just enjoy things. If they can't further extend their connections or enhance the business, then it's time wasted."

"I'm sorry, that's awful. I assume you never went on any family vacation trips either then?"

"You'd assume correctly."

I gave her a meager smile. "Well, that all changes now! You can spend a summer having fun."

"That sounds nice. Even when I was friends with Tabitha and Priscilla, we didn't go with each other on vacation. So, this whole thing is new for me."

My arm settled around her shoulder as I drew her a little closer. "Well, I may have gone on vacation with my parents, but this is new for me too. An adventure we can all enjoy."

"I sure hope so."

With that, we trudged up two flights of steps, bags in hand, and went to work unpacking. Sophie finished first and only used two drawers in the closet to fit her clothes. I was done a little after her, hanging up a few dresses and then folding the rest and storing them in the drawers.

Shelby, on the other hand, had filled up two rods with hanging clothes and at least three drawers and still had one more bag.

My eyebrows knitted. "Didn't you tell *us* we could do laundry here? You have clothes for like three weeks straight before you need to clean anything."

"What? This isn't that much. I need options. Who knows where we'll go and what we'll do. My wardrobe is too far away to be caught by surprise."

Sophie shook her head. "That's insane. Do you expect to go to a Gala event or something? I don't even have that many clothes in my whole closet at home."

Shelby shifted her weight to her other foot and rested her hands on her hips. "I still must go to the founders' meetings. I can't go in jeans and a T-shirt. My mother would absolutely kill me. They all dress business casual at the least."

"Fine, you get a pass because of the meetings, but the rest is still a bit much," I said.

Sophie wiggled her eyebrows. "She's just overpacking because of *Luke*."

Shelby began to retort back, when a loud knock emanated from downstairs, followed by footsteps.

"Hello? I know you're here. The lights are on and vehicles in the driveway. Where is everyone?"

Shelby's cheeks reddened. "He's here."

"Speak of the devil," Sophie said and smirked.

My stomach twisted for her. Shelby was smitten with Luke, and this was their chance to figure out what they had, if anything together. I wanted to see her happy, she deserved it.

"We're upstairs unpacking, be right down." She stood and practically ran from the room and down the stairs.

"Someone's excited," Sophie said.

"You're not excited to see Drew?"

"I saw him all day today."

"And?"

Sophie wiggled on the bed. "Fine. Yes, I am excited, but it's different when you see him a lot."

"Must be because you two are a couple. I still get butterflies every time I see Randy. Doesn't matter if it's in the hallway at school, or at Morgan's, or we go to Over Easy's."

"I still get flutters, too, but I don't know, maybe I'm just not like that like you are."

Sophie might not admit it, but I had seen her get ready for dates with Drew and had caught them in the hallway at school when they thought no one was looking. She might deny being a romantic, but her eyes told a different story.

"We better go downstairs and say hello." I checked the time on my phone and my messages. Nothing from Randy yet, but he should be leaving soon and bringing food with him. "When does Drew get here?"

"Soon. He texted me like thirty minutes ago that he left."

We descended the stairs and found Luke and Shelby

standing near each other in the hallway by the door. At our arrival, they stepped back a few steps.

I stifled a giggle; it would only make Shelby embarrassed if I drew attention to it in front of him, but I would ask her later what they had been discussing. "Hey, Luke," I said.

He smiled and walked toward me, giving me a hug before saying, "Hey, Riley." He did the same greeting to Sophie, who nodded. "Shelby said I'm the first guy to arrive?"

"Drew will be here soon," Sophie said.

"Nice. I'll put my bags upstairs then and wait to see what they want to do." He eyed Shelby. "Want to show me the way?"

She smiled and nudged him past us up the stairs.

Sophie puffed air from her mouth like a tire deflating. "Thank god I'm in a relationship."

I snorted. "Why's that?"

"Because if I had to watch you two all summer and be alone, I would poke my eyeballs out."

"Gee, thanks."

She linked elbows with me. "No offense."

"Some taken."

She patted my arm. "What? You two are all cute and stuff with your beginning relationships but being forever alone and watching that is hard."

"I know."

She crinkled her nose. "What do you mean by that? You and Randy are cutesy together."

"Yes, we are. But we aren't a couple. It's hard to watch you and Drew and know that I am technically not with Randy. He could date someone else if he wanted to, and it wouldn't be cheating. I can't even count how long it has been as an anniversary because we aren't dating."

The familiar knot in my stomach took precedent. I hadn't meant to spill those thoughts, at least not yet, but I supposed I could no longer control them. It had been a long time since Randy and I had been honest about our feelings for each other. I understood he had familial obligations, but at some point, weren't we worth more than his worry about what I thought of his family? Didn't he trust me enough to let me all the way in? Didn't he want to be a couple instead of whatever it was that we were doing?

"I was wondering when it would bother you."

"What do you mean?"

She smiled and strode to the sofa then sat. "You've been incredibly understanding, Riley, but everyone has their limit."

"Do you think I'm being ridiculous?"

"No. It's been a long time, and I've told you this before, but his reasons don't make sense anymore. You two have spent quality time with each other and discussed important things for almost a year. You two have always been honest with each other, if you aren't happy with how things are anymore, then tell him."

"I don't want to pressure him about his family. It finally feels like he is in a better headspace regarding his dad."

"It's not pressuring someone if it's how you feel, and he is supposed to care about how you feel. If things are good, then why not try. The worst thing he says is he isn't there yet and then you know."

She made sense, yet the pit in my stomach when I thought of the conversation didn't ease. Too many what ifs ran through my mind. What if he decided we should just be friends? What if he decided to pull back altogether? What if I wasn't a good match for him anymore?

I wanted more, but I also didn't want to end up with less.

Our conversation was interrupted when Drew arrived.

Sophie smiled and squeezed my hand. "We can talk more later. I won't forget."

I nodded, but secretly hoped she would forget. If I had the conversation with Randy, I needed to be ready for less, and I knew I wasn't ready yet.

Randy was the last to arrive, which was fine, except everyone seemed to couple up, which left me to stew in my feelings about him. By the time he walked through the door with his duffel bag and a couple plastic bags, Luke and Drew had claimed the two bottom bunks of the bunk bedroom on the opposite side of the house.

Sophie and Drew sat on the couch opposite me, snuggled together, while Shelby sat at the kitchen counter and Luke stood on the opposite side, leaned over, discussing something in hushed tones.

Randy shuffled through the door. Drew and Luke went to help, while I stood and walked to where Shelby sat.

"Dinner is here!" Randy shouted.

"Good, I'm starving," Sophie said.

Randy chuckled. "Well, it's the raw ingredients of dinner anyway."

Sophie moaned. "Are you telling me we have to cook it?"

"Unless you want to eat frozen pizza and a salad that's not put together."

"Soph, I can make it," Drew said.

Randy held up another bag. "I also brought chips, pretzels, and popcorn."

Sophie's eyes widened. "Ooh, now you're talking."

Randy tossed the bag to Sophie, who tore into the bag like a bear who hadn't eaten in three months.

Drew shook his head as he took the pizza box and headed to the oven to preheat it.

"I'll show Randy around upstairs," I said.

Shelby sat back in her seat. Her eyes gleamed with mischief.

Randy winked at me, sending zings that went all the way to my toes. How even when I felt unsteady, did he manage to make me feel like that?

Randy followed close behind up the stairs.

"Luke and Drew chose to stay in the same room with bunk beds. They both took bottom bunks," I said.

Randy shrugged. "That's fine. I don't care if I'm top bunk. I've had to do that with my sisters so nothing new."

I smiled. "I'm a top bunk, too."

Randy dropped his bag and grasped my hand. "Yeah? Great minds."

"I didn't think you'd ever get here."

He inched closer, then pulled me into an embrace. "Missed me?"

I nodded into his chest, acutely aware of his warmth underneath the cotton T-shirt.

He squeezed me harder then kissed the top of my head. "I missed you, too, but I'm here now and we have all summer. You want to head back downstairs?"

I nibbled the bottom of my lip. "Did you want to unpack first?"

"Nah. I'll do it later. Let's go head downstairs. You'll want to keep an eye on Sophie before she eats all the snacks, anyway."

I laughed. "So true."

He laced his fingers with mine and nudged me toward the stairs. We walked hand-in-hand back to everyone else.

Drew peered into the oven, while Sophie sat next to Shelby chomping on chips. At the sight of me, she raised an eyebrow.

I shook my head to quiet her, and she nodded.

Shelby listened as Luke continued to talk.

"It should be about ten minutes until the pizza is ready," Drew said.

Shelby surveyed the room until she made eye contact with Randy. "Did you happen to bring paper plates? We could use the plates in the cabinet, but then we have to do dishes."

Randy smiled. "Yep. I came prepared."

"You are awesome," she said.

Randy and I went and sat on the couch.

"Did you have a good drive here?" I asked.

"It wasn't bad. It's been a while since I've driven down here so it was nice to enjoy the scenery and all."

"It's definitely beautiful."

"Do you want to take a walk after dinner?"

I nodded. "That sounds nice. Do you know where you're going down here?"

"I should be able to figure it out. If not, we will be lost together."

My stomach fluttered at the thought, if only that pizza would hurry up.

CHAPTER FIVE

SHELBY

I couldn't stop staring at his mouth. The more Luke talked, the more I wondered what it would be like to kiss him. Would he go slow? Would he claim my mouth with the passion I felt as he entered a room? Would his lips be soft and gentle? Or plundering?

I pinched my thigh. What was I thinking? We were surrounded by all our friends, and he was telling me some story about something Paul did at school. I had no idea what he was saying, and when he expected me to respond I wouldn't know what to say. Had I mentioned that we were surrounded by our friends? It wasn't like he would act on anything—even if there was anything to act on—in front of them.

My head spun. How would I focus on anything going on this summer if within the first hour of his presence, my brain was consumed by thoughts of kissing? We weren't even there. If *there* was even our destination. Easter was a far cry from confessing feelings.I needed to focus on something else.

"Will you save some chips for us?" I asked Sophie.

She stuck out her tongue. "Do you want some? All you have to do is ask."

"I don't, but others might."

Sophie huffed and sat the bag on the counter. "Well, have at them. I didn't eat before we left and before that I was at work. I'm just hungry."

Drew chuckled. "The pizza will be done soon, you'll make it."

"I might not. I might faint from nausea."

I rolled my eyes. "Extra food is going on the list. I can't take your dramatics over food all summer."

Sophie smirked. "Am I getting to you already?"

"No."

She wasn't. My annoyance was from the thoughts that continued to swirl in my brain about Luke. He sat across the room now, near Riley and Randy, but every time I snuck a peek, he managed to make eye contact with me.

This was bad, like apocalyptic bad.

Sophie squinted and tapped my head. "What's going in there? You look intense."

I shook my head and mouthed, *not now*. I would tell her in our room, but I couldn't risk it when everyone was together. What if he heard?

The stove timer beeped until Drew turned it off and checked the pizza. He placed it on the trivet and then said, "Ready. Come and get it."

Sophie launched off her stool, grabbed a plate, and cut the pizza.

Riley and I both stared, while Randy shook his head and Luke raised his eyebrows.

After she placed her pieces on the plate, she faced us. "What?"

Riley gave me a knowing look. "You'll be the last to know about dinner this summer."

"What? I didn't take all the pieces."

"Yet," Drew said.

She glared at him and slapped his arm playfully.

He shrugged then handed everyone a plate.

We each took two slices and then sat at the dining room table.

Luke sat next to me, and Randy sat next to him. Across from Randy was Riley, then Sophie, and Drew.

I raised my water bottle and everyone else raised their cups. "Before we eat our first meal together here, I just wanted to say how lucky I am to be spending the summer with the five of you. I think I can speak for us all when I say that a year ago, this is not what I expected to do with my summer, but I am enormously grateful to have each of you in my life and to enjoy this house and summer together."

"Here, here," Luke said and winked at me.

Everyone else raised their cups then took a drink.

"Dig in!" I said then sat to eat my own pizza and chips.

My heart overflowed staring at the friends I had in my life. I was used to being alone and keeping people at arm's length. It was nice to let them in and to share our lives with each other. I had no idea what I was missing until Riley and Sophie let me see what friendship could be and Luke broke the walls around my heart.

"What should we do after dinner?" Sophie asked with her mouth full.

Everyone looked to me to answer.

"I don't know. We might have some board games in the hallway closet. I don't have to be the deciding factor. What do you all want to do?"

Riley peered at us. "Randy and I are taking a walk after dinner."

"What kind of games, Shelby?" Luke asked.

"I'm honestly unsure. We could also use the smart TV to stream a movie or something."

"I'm okay with anything," Drew said.

Sophie shrugged. "I'll check the closet when we're done. Maybe we can find something in there."

We all ate our slices quickly, it appeared Sophie wasn't the only hungry one tonight. I would need to figure out a good list of groceries for us for the week and figure out who was staying for how long—a task I could do in the morning.

Surprisingly, Drew was the first to finish his pizza and throw away his trash. He scrolled through his phone on the couch as he waited for everyone else to finish.

Of everyone here, I knew him the least, but I hoped that I could learn more about him this summer. Sophie and Drew didn't get together until practically the end of the school year, so even though we all had lunch together, he wasn't with us long.

Randy and Riley were done next, followed by Sophie. Luke and I were done last, which was okay. I grew up eating slowly and politely, as any proper lady should. And well, habits like that were hard to break.

Sophie rubbed her hands together quickly. "Where's the game closet?"

I pointed to the door closest to the TV. "Whatever we have to play should be in there."

Sophie opened the door and peered inside. "Scrabble, Life, Monopoly, Pictionary, Uno! Let's play Uno."

"You don't want to play Scrabble?" Drew asked.

"With you?" She scrunched her nose. "Definitely not."

He chuckled. "Chicken."

She crossed her arms. "I am not, but that doesn't sound fun right now."

"I'm okay with Uno," I said.

Sophie peered at Luke, and he nodded.

She jumped up and down, grabbed the game and brought it to the coffee table. Pushing the sofa a little closer and then the large chairs, she claimed one for herself then shuffled the cards.

She eyed Randy and Riley at the dining table. "Are you sure you two don't want to play?"

They nodded.

"I'll play when we get back if you're all still awake."

I checked the time on the microwave: *8:00*. Did they expect to be out that long?

Sophie eyed me, too, clearly thinking the same thing as she wiggled her eyebrows.

I covered my mouth with my hand to stifle my laugh. Riley would kill us if we made a scene.

Riley turned to Randy. "I'll be right down and we can leave. I want to grab a little zip up in case it's chilly."

He nodded and shoved his hands in his pockets. I couldn't put my finger on it, but something was nagging at him.

Randy and I had become closer this past year, too. While we always dealt with each other for the founders' meetings, we never confided in one another until this past January. He had been a good sounding board for me trying to get through to Riley.

In the end, like Luke, Randy understood what it was like to be a founding family in Honey Cove. There were only five families in that position, and unless you lived it, you never truly understood the kind of pressure we dealt with.

Before I could ask Randy what was bothering him, Riley bounded down the stairs carrying her dark gray hoodie. "We'll be back later. I have my cell in case anyone needs me."

"Bye," Sophie said from the couch, still focused on shuffling the cards.

Drew waved, as did Luke.

"Bye you guys. Be safe," I said.

They nodded and left, Randy's hand on the small of her back as he let her lead.

A smile tugged at the corner of my lips. Those gestures were how I knew Riley was important to Randy. I only hoped he realized she needed more before it was too late.

We all took a seat around the coffee table as Sophie dealt us our hands. It had been a while since I played Uno. When I was younger, my mother had hired a nanny to take care of me. She ordered me around, of course, but the day-to-day duties were relinquished to the nanny. Playing with toys, giving me a bath, that was never something my mother did. I had had many nannies in my lifetime, but the one I was most fond of was Lucy. She was young and kind. No matter what my mother said or did, she made sure I was heard and respected the way a child should be.

She had bought a pack of Uno cards for us one week during the summer. I had a cold and felt miserable. My mother didn't believe in infecting everyone else, so she had ordered me to stay in my room. Lucy was the only one who came in and out.

She had propped me up in my bed, pulled over my nightstand, and used a folding chair for herself. She taught me to play Uno that week. We must have played it a hundred times over the next few days, but she never complained. She never made me feel like a burden. Oh, how I had missed her when she left.

"Everyone knows how to play, right?" Sophie asked.

"Yep," Luke said. "I played it at boarding school, surprisingly."

Drew nodded.

"Good, then I won't feel bad crushing you all."

Drew rested his hand on Sophie's. "You don't have to be so intense. It's just a card game."

"I know, but I like to win."

I giggled. "Everyone here knows that. I'm sure Luke even knows that at this point."

He waved me off. "I don't mind; it keeps things interesting."

I cocked my eyebrow and he just shrugged.

A smile broke out on his face and the flutters in my stomach increased. *Yep, apocalyptic bad.*

CHAPTER SIX

RILEY

His fingers were laced with mine as we walked. In my other hand I held my flip flops as we walked along the beach. It wasn't like the big beaches. There wasn't sand and water for miles, but the cove had enough of the beach to walk on and still have the smell of salty water.

The breeze twisted my brunette hair as it passed over us. Randy had led us to the right when we exited Shelby's house. It wasn't long before we found a beach access at the back of the house that led to the ocean.

My ears were filled with the sound of waves crashing on the shoreline. We didn't talk; we didn't have to. We just walked. I focused on the squishing of sand beneath my toes and the waxing gibbous moon. There were too many clouds to see the stars well enough, but the light from the moon still managed to break through.

He was the first to break the silence. "I can't believe this is the summer before our senior year of high school."

"Me neither. It's nothing I would have ever pictured."

"Hopefully in a good way."

"Of course. You know that."

He nodded. "It's always nice to have a reminder." He squeezed my hand.

"When must you go back to work?"

"I took the rest of this week off, but Saturday morning is my next shift. I'll stay at home for a few days while I have some of my dad's company meetings to deal with, then I can be back for another several days."

"That'll be nice to have a week, though."

He smiled. "I hope so. If you don't get tired of me."

I inhaled sharply. "I couldn't get tired of you."

He laughed. "We'll have to see. We've never spent this much time together before."

My stomach lurched. I apparently wasn't the only one who had thought about that. Did it mean that he was worried about what would happen? Or was he just bringing up the obvious?

"Will your sisters miss you not being at home?"

"Possibly. Emma won't care. She's focusing on field hockey camp and tryouts all summer. Jade might. She's still young enough to miss her big brother."

I smiled. "We should invite them to the house one day. Maybe do something with them?"

Randy's fingers tensed in my hand.

Had I said something wrong?

Then just as fast, his fingers relaxed. "Yeah … maybe."

My nose scrunched. His response was off. Did he not want me around his sisters? So far he had only been to my house. He had met my mom and my mom-mom, but other than a few times in the parking lot when I saw Emma, I hadn't met anyone in Randy's family. "Are you okay?"

"Yeah, of course. I'm tired."

I didn't believe him. There was something he wasn't telling me. Could he be embarrassed of me, and I had gotten the whole situation wrong?

I shook my head absentmindedly. That couldn't be it. He had always been honest with me. He probably was just tired from work, and I was overanalyzing everything because of my own issues.

He let go of my hand and waded up to his ankles in the water, then kicked a little at me.

A drop or two landed on my arm and I screamed, "Don't you dare."

His expression grew mischievous. He kicked again before I could run too far. He went to splash again, but this time I kicked as hard as I could at the water toward him.

His khaki shorts darkened where the water landed. His eyes widened. "Game on."

I screamed and ran down the beach. Even with my speed, Randy kept up somewhat, getting me a few more times before I stopped to breathe. "Truce?" I asked.

He stroked his chin. "Hmm for now."

"Deal."

We kept walking farther from the house.

"Do you know when your dad is coming yet?"

"Nope. Mom said he's still moving meetings around so he can come for a little longer. It'll be this summer, but who knows when in June or if he will make it another month."

"Are you excited to see him?"

I shrugged. "You know how it is. Of course, it's nice to see him once he gets here, but it just feels like borrowed time when he visits. It's not real life. He is basically on vacation and at least when he visited and I was in school, he only dealt with dinners and right before bed. Mom is still unsure what they're doing. It all just feels like too much limbo if you ask me."

He nodded. "That's understandable."

I sighed. "I don't want to discuss them. All I ever do is

think in circles about their relationship and us as a family. It never improves and I'm starting to get dizzy."

He laced his fingers with mine again. "I'm always here for you, you know that, right?"

"I know." Which was true. I did know that. I knew that he probably *would* always be there for me. He was a good listener and was honestly fairly wise for his age, but did those things equate to a relationship? No. Sure they were parts of a good friendship, but it wasn't everything, and that's what worried me.

We reached the end of the beach and turned around. "This place is pretty amazing. I didn't know what to expect, but I think it'll be perfect for a run."

He laughed. "Always thinking about running, aren't you, superstar?"

"Not always, but you know running is more than just running to me. It's like breathing."

"I know. I'm only teasing you. I think it's impressive. You're so dedicated. You don't worry about what others are thinking or what pressure they place on it. You do it because it's what you want to do."

"Maybe." To be honest, I hadn't thought of it like that. "Do you want to come with me tomorrow morning?"

"That's okay. I'll pass this time, maybe later this week." He pulled out his phone and checked the time, then placed it back in his pocket. "We should hurry back. It's been like two hours out here."

"Really?"

"Yep … time flies."

The downstairs was dark when we arrived. From outside, though, I knew the light was on in the girl's room. The boy's room wasn't visible from the back of the house by the beach.

Randy locked the door behind us and then walked up the stairs. I followed close behind. We stood in the middle of the hallway, halfway between both of our rooms.

I hadn't thought about saying goodnight. It was one thing to say goodnight outside of my mom-mom's house when he would have to drive home. It was something else entirely when he would sleep on the other side of the house.

Randy leaned close and kissed my cheek so fast, if I had blinked I would have missed it. "Good night, Riley."

My hand settled on my cheek where the whisper of his lips had been. "Good night, Randy."

He turned and went to the bedroom. He paused before he went inside, then opened the door and closed it.

When I could breathe again, I walked to my room and closed the door. As I figured, Shelby and Sophie sat on their bottom bunks in pajamas talking until they stopped as I entered.

"Ooh someone is blushing," Sophie said.

Shelby tossed a pillow at her head. "Leave her alone or she won't tell us what happened."

I rolled my eyes. "Nothing happened. We went for a walk, we came back, we said goodnight. End of story."

"Mm-hmm," Sophie said. "And Drew and I aren't a couple."

"Soph, believe what you want, but we truly didn't do anything. If anything, I feel like he pulled away from me while we were walking."

Shelby's eyebrows knitted together. "What do you mean?"

"We were discussing his sisters. I had asked him if they would miss him while he was here this summer. Then I had offered for us to pick them up and do something together, but he hesitated before saying maybe. I don't know, maybe I'm imagining things, but his response didn't seem like he thought it was a good idea."

Shelby averted her gaze to the floor. Did she know something I didn't?

"Did you ask him about his response?" Sophie asked.

"Of course, but he said he was tired."

"Then maybe he was tired." Sophie patted the bed next to her, so I sat. "I know you, so I know you're thinking that maybe this is a sign he isn't into you the way you want him to be. But a guy who is just *friends* with someone doesn't agree to spend a summer at a beach house and to go on cute little walks on the beach at night. That's like couple material."

"Maybe, but Sophie, something was off about his response. I mean it's been months since that English project together and I've never been to his house."

Sophie shrugged. "I've never been to Drew's. Not since we were kids."

"Has he spent time at your house?"

"Well, no. Other than to pick me up."

"See? Randy spent my birthday party at my house, and he had dinner with my parents when my dad visited in October. There have been several times he has been inside the house, yet I've never met his parents. I've never formally met his sister Emma and never met Jade. Isn't that strange?"

Sophie shrugged.

"Shelby? What do you think?" I asked.

"I think he's always been guarded when it comes to his family. There are several years of rude comments, dirty looks, and judgments that have been placed on the Walkers. That kind of experience isn't forgotten easily."

"I know that, but does he truly believe I would be like that?"

"I don't think it's about you though, Riley." She sighed. "Some things are hard to change when they become habit. Randy has become an expert at hiding his family to protect them. If people don't interact with them, they can't learn things to hold against them. It's not so much about you as it is about his inability to let go of that pattern," she said while never meeting my gaze.

Sophie nodded. "I think Shelby is making a lot of sense. It's hard to change behavior. I think we've all seen that in our own experience one way or another. But ultimately, Riley, if you feel like more is happening, then think about having an honest conversation with him. You always say he answers your question if you ask. It's a good time to ask."

I stood. "Yeah … maybe." I stretched and forced myself to yawn. "I'm getting in my pajamas. I want to run in the morning so I should probably go to bed."

"Okay," Shelby said.

"Want company?" Sophie asked.

"Sure, if you can keep up."

Sophie glared. "You're on."

I grabbed my clothes from the closet and closed myself in the bathroom. As I got ready, Shelby's explanation twirled in my thoughts. It was a logical explanation. It made sense that it should have nothing to do with me, except I still couldn't unclench my stomach like before a really big test or right before the big drop on a roller coaster. And if I couldn't unclench, then something else must have been going on.

CHAPTER SEVEN

I was the first one awake in the house. It was silent and peaceful. The sun was barely up, and this was the perfect time for me to do some work and make a grocery list. With only the light from my cell phone, I grabbed my things and took a shower.

I wasn't sure when Riley and Sophie would get up to take a run, but in case it was soon, I wanted to be ready. I applied light makeup, and braided my dark-brown hair, then headed downstairs.

If I had been home, I would have had Chef Frank make me breakfast and a caramel macchiato, but since I wasn't, I would have to make do with what we had in the house.

Rifling through the cabinets, I managed to scrounge up a box of cereal that would go bad in a month, some protein bars, and K-cups for the Keurig—at least I could have caffeine.

I brewed the coffee and sat at the counter with my laptop open. I needed to make a decent grocery list. Everyone was staying the whole week, except for Drew, who had to leave mid-week for a shift, then would be back later that night. Overall, all six of us would need food for all three meals for the six days. The meal prep ideas alone could take me another hour. I didn't know how anyone planned for this many people for this long. I needed to get Chef Frank a thank you gift card or something when I got home. He did this for us all the time and we never thanked him for it, even if it was his job.

By the time the first set of footsteps were on the stairs, I had managed to write out the general things to stock the house—condiments, chips and other assorted snacks, spices, and bread. When everyone woke up, I would figure out what most of us wanted for certain meals. I had absolutely no idea who skipped breakfast and who would be okay with sandwiches for lunch.

Luke plopped himself on the stool next to me and leaned over my shoulder. "Who makes a grocery list on their laptop?"

"I do. It's easier to organize."

"You can do that on apps on your phone and then you can take it with you."

I knitted my brows. "I can take this with me, too. I could email it or print it and then cross things off the list."

"For someone so in the know about so many things, I'm shocked you want to go paper and pencil with a grocery list."

I crossed my arms. "Are you going to help me make it or critique my use of technology?"

Luke chuckled. "Someone is feisty this morning."

I wiggled in my chair. "I'm not feisty. I'm focused, there's a difference."

He tugged on a strand of hair near my ear. "If you say so." He leaned closer to survey the list.

His cologne infiltrated my senses. I used to think he

wore too much, but once I got to know him, his scent was intoxicating. I missed being this close to him. I could even smell his shampoo. He must have been fresh out of the shower.

Don't even go there, Shelby. That thought will ruin your thought process all day.

"You need vegetables and fruit. We can't live off snacks or we'll gain like twenty pounds this summer."

"I know that, Luke. I was filling in what I know everyone will be fine with. I have no idea if people want bananas, apples, grapefruit, or kiwi. I mean there are a lot of choices."

"Fair enough, but no one will have anything to eat if there isn't something in the house."

I sighed. "I know, but I want everyone to be satisfied with what's here. It's our first week together."

"Start basic. We could always pick up more if we need to. The store isn't that far away."

"True."

He smiled. "See? I have good ideas."

I rolled my eyes. "Okay, so basics. Bananas, apples, lettuce for salads, some ground beef and chicken breasts, a few frozen pizzas, what else?"

"How about some spaghetti noodles, boxes of mac n' cheese, bacon, sausage links, eggs, and then drinks."

"Okay, we're getting there. Slowly."

Riley bounded down the stairs. "Good morning." She stretched as she stood in front of us wearing a sports bra and athletic pants. "Whatcha doing?"

"We're working on the grocery list. Anything you absolutely *must* have?"

Riley grabbed her ankle and held it. "Hmm, Frosted Flakes and trail mix of any combination."

"Frosted Flakes? Really?" I asked.

Luke chuckled. "Frosted Flakes are awesome." He nudged my shoulder. "We can't all have a personal chef, Shelby."

I gasped. "I eat boxed cereal, too."

Riley raised an eyebrow. "Sure ya do, Shelby. What kind?"

"My mother picks it, so it's usually something high in fiber and protein."

Riley burst out laughing.

"Why's that funny?"

"You're seventeen, not seventy."

"It's not like I get to choose."

Luke smirked. "So, choose here, no one else will tell you what to buy."

"Fine. I'll get two boxes so we can all have some."

Riley checked her phone, then shoved it back in her workout pants. "Sophie needs to hurry up or I'm leaving without her."

"Why don't you wake her up?" Luke asked.

I snorted and Riley laughed.

"Am I missing something?"

"You don't *just* wake up Sophie," I said.

Riley nodded. "She isn't exactly the nicest person to wake up. I wouldn't be surprised if she punched someone accidentally because they tried to wake her."

Luke's eyes widened. "Good to know. I officially won't be waking her for any reason this summer."

"Wake up who?" Sophie asked as she jumped off the stairs before reaching the bottom. She, too, was dressed in athletic pants, but she had a tank top instead of just a sports bra.

"You," Riley said. "Let's go. Today is supposed to be so hot."

Sophie rolled her eyes. "Don't get your panties in a bunch. I just need to stretch."

Riley had moved on from stretching to running in place. "I'll be outside. Make it quick."

Sophie sat on the floor and touched her toes as she counted. When she reached twenty, she leaned to her left side, then her right.

"Soph, what do you absolutely need to survive the week, foodwise?"

"Uh, I don't know. What do you have so far?"

"A lot. You don't have something you always eat or crave?"

She stood and started stretching out her arms. "I guess strawberries. I eat them during the week, at least while they're in season."

"Is that it?"

"I think so. If I change my mind, I'll text it to you."

"I'm going in thirty minutes or so, make sure it's not too late otherwise it will go on the list for our next trip."

Sophie nodded then waved. "See you later."

Luke scooted my laptop closer to him and scrolled through what we had. "I think this is a pretty good start."

I eyed him, forcing myself to ignore how close his arm was to mine. "What about you? Anything you want?"

He shrugged. "I can go with you to the store if you want."

I gulped. "Ah, sure. That would be good."

A trip just the two of us? I knew I needed to expect us to spend time together and I wanted to, but I hadn't expected it to be this soon already. My stomach kicked up like I was on a roller coaster with too many loop-de-loops.

"Should we ask Randy or Drew?"

Luke stroked his chin and then nodded. "I'll go see if

they're up. If so, I'll see if I can get an idea of what they want. I'll be back."

He turned and headed for the stairs before I could respond. I took a deep breath while I waited for him to return. This would not be easy.

Relax, Shelby, it's just Luke.

We were friends. I could spend a morning near him, and it not be a big deal. Friends went grocery shopping, right? No big deal at all.

The boys had been awake when Luke went upstairs. He texted me their list and I added it before we hopped in his hunter-green Audi and headed to the store.

"I could have driven," I said for the tenth time.

"It's fine. I like to drive and my trunk is bigger than your BMW. Not to mention you're trapped in the driveway."

He had a point. It would be easier to get our list in his Audi than in my car. I hadn't even thought about that until he said it. Albeit, I never picked up groceries from the store. Our staff at home always did that.

I fiddled with the radio trying to get a station to tune in instead of all the static. When nothing seemed to work, I sighed.

Luke chuckled, then switched his radio to Bluetooth and started streaming some playlist of pop songs through the speakers. "Better?"

I nodded. "Thank you. The static was grating on my nerves."

"So, how have you been? Tell me something I don't know yet," he said.

Something he didn't know? We texted and occasionally

talked on the phone after he left for Easter. What had happened he didn't know about?"

I shrugged. "Mother seems to have lessened up a little bit."

Luke faced me briefly, before returning his gaze to the road. "That's good. I mean they did let us all live at their beach house. That has to be something, right?"

"It's a step. Hopefully, it'll get better with the summer festival."

"I'm sure it will. From what I continue to hear, my dad was impressed with you both on his return from the festival."

I smiled. "Thanks, it means a lot. Randy and I made a good team. I hope we do as well this time."

"You will and this one will be easier because you've done it before. I'm excited to be home to see it."

"Yeah?"

He nodded. "I'm glad to be here for the summer. I can't remember the last time my summers haven't been filled with camps or events to occupy the time in between boarding school."

"I know what you mean. It will be a time to relax." It still surprised me how similar our lives were; then the familiar pang hit my stomach reminding me of the guilt I still carried for judging him in the beginning. I had always thought he was arrogant and full of himself. He was a kind soul and nothing like what I had expected.

Luke patted his steering wheel to the beat of the song and kept eyeing me.

With each passing glance, my hands turned clammy, and my stomach fluttered. "Do I have something on my face?"

"What? No. Why do you ask that?"

"You keep glancing over here."

"Oh." He glanced again. "Sorry, I'm just getting used to being around you again. It's nice."

I smiled as heat crept to my cheeks. "It's nice to see you, too."

He pulled into the grocery store, one of those big chain stores, a far cry from Morgan's Market at home. After placing a sun visor in the front window, we got out and he locked the doors. Armed with my list, we headed for a cart and started in the produce section.

I stared at the bananas and grabbed some that had just turned yellow and set them in the cart. Luke added a carton of strawberries, while I stared at pineapple on sale. I nibbled my lip, unsure of how to tell which one was ripe.

Luke eyed me warily. "You okay?"

"I have a confession. I … I don't know how to tell if a pineapple is ripe."

Luke grinned. "That's easy. You see the leaves making the crown of the pineapple?"

I nodded.

"If you pull one and it easily comes out, then the pineapple is ripe. If it's hard to pull it, then it's not ready yet."

"Really? I never knew that."

"Yep. My mom loves pineapple, so I learned early how to pick the best kind."

"Oh, nice." Luke's family had a lot of money like mine, yet he had more memories of doing stuff with his family than I did. It was strange how we could have such different upbringings in similar circumstances.

Luke eyed one pineapple in the back, tested it, then placed it in the cart. We left the produce aisle after getting apples, salad mix, fresh avocados, tomatoes, and cucumbers for salad.

"Should we get some stuff from the deli?" I asked.

"Can't hurt. Probably should get cheese and some deli meat in case we all want sandwiches or something for a quick lunch."

"Good idea, although no idea what everyone would want."

Luke walked to the deli counter to scroll through their choices on the screen. "They have their brand of turkey and ham on sale. Why don't we get like a half a pound of both and a pound of cheese and then if anyone wants something else, we can put it on the list for next time."

"Okay, that works."

Luke keyed in the order and added his number to be alerted when it was done. "All set. They'll text me when we can pick it up."

I pushed the cart forward down the next aisle.

Luke walked close by, our arms brushing together every now and then. "So … any plans for when we get back?"

"Nope."

"We should go to the beach. I mean … if you want to, that is."

I smiled. "Sure. I'll want to eat something before we go, but that sounds nice."

"I can make brunch for whomever is still at the house."

"Oh? Like what?"

"I could make breakfast burritos. The avocados, bacon, eggs, and other veggies would be perfect for them. We still need tortillas."

My stomach grumbled at the thought. "That sounds delicious."

He smirked. "See? I'm good for something."

"Hmm. I don't know. We haven't tasted them yet; it could be awful."

"Is that so?"

"Yep, wouldn't want to give you a big head before the

results are even in." I startled when he poked me in the side. "Hey!"

He chuckled. "That's what you get."

I raised an eyebrow. "I'll remember that, mister."

"Good, there's more of that if you keep it up."

"Is that a threat?"

Luke smiled devilishly. "That's a promise." Then he winked and strolled away with the cart.

What did I get myself into?

CHAPTER EIGHT

RILEY

Five minutes after I left the house, Sophie joined me on the stairs. "It's about time."

She waved me off. "We can't all be morning people."

I giggled. "Grouchy, are we?"

"No." She sighed. "Fine. I didn't sleep well. It takes me time to adjust to a new bed." She ran in place. "You know where you're going?"

I nodded. "It's not that hard to follow the beach until you get to the end and then turn around."

"Lead on."

I took off at a jogging pace. Sophie stayed with me effortlessly. It was strange to feel the squish of sand beneath my sneakers instead of pavement. With blacktop there was a spring to my step. It forced my foot away from it. With the sand, I felt like it tried to swallow me.

Sophie had the same struggle as her face contorted with every step.

"Let's keep a slower pace today. I want to talk anyway."

Sophie nodded. "Are you feeling any better since last night?"

"Sort of, I guess. It doesn't feel as all consuming, but I still don't know what I'll actually do about it. I hate this. I want things to be easy and straightforward."

"I'm sorry."

"It's not your fault. It's no one's fault. I just need to get the courage to do something about it instead of analyzing it."

"You'll get there, give yourself time."

"Thanks, Soph. I know I get repetitive with my complaints. I appreciate you listening anyway."

"Duh, loser. Not to mention after what I put you and Shelby through this spring, I owe you both."

"Good point. I don't feel bad anymore."

Sophie nudged my arm. "How do you think Shelby is doing at the store with Luke?"

I giggled. "She's probably losing her mind. I know I would be."

Sophie's ponytail swished with her pace. "You both need to go on dates and sort out your feelings." Sophie gasped and stopped suddenly. "Do a double date!" she shouted then caught back up.

"I'm not doing a double date. That would make everything so awkward. Not to mention how are you supposed to talk about feelings in front of the other couple. I don't want to talk about things with Randy in front of an audience. I mean would you have wanted that?"

Sophie scrunched her nose. "Okay, no. Bad plan." She cut toward the water.

I followed behind her. The sand was firmer near the water, but not too wet that we sank. I could get used to running on the beach. It used different muscles. It pushed me to be better.

Before I knew it, the end of the beach was before us.

We stopped on the rock marking the boundary and watched the waves roll in.

My phone beeped in my pocket. I pulled it out to see a text message, *Your dad will be coming at the end of June. 23rd to the 30th.*

"What is it?" Sophie asked.

"My dad is coming the last week of June to Honey Cove."

"That's a good thing, though, right?"

"It is, I just wonder how this will go. He only came down at Halloween and then briefly in March. This will be the longest he has visited since we moved."

"Do you have to go back for the whole week?"

"I don't know that *have to* are the right words, but I probably will unless something happens."

"Well, I can bring you home when you need to go and if something goes down, I'm only a text or phone call away to come steal you back to the cove."

I smiled. "Thanks." I returned the phone back into my pants pocket and nudged Sophie. "Race you back."

Sophie wiggled her eyebrows and then took off running. "Too slow!" she shouted several paces ahead.

I laughed and bounded after her. We both knew I'd win, but it didn't stop her from trying. It was nice that some things never changed.

Sand fell from our shoes with every step. "We should take our shoes off on the porch. They won't get wet with the covered deck."

"Good thought," Sophie said as she toed off her right shoe. "I hate the feeling of sand underneath my bare feet."

I nodded because I never had that experience. We

didn't go to the beach often when we visited my mom-mom.

Luke and Shelby sat on the couches eating something when we entered.

Randy and Drew were on the chairs with an empty plate.

"Luke made us breakfast burritos," Shelby said.

"They're amazing," Drew said.

Luke smiled and fist bumped Drew. "Thanks, man."

Shelby made eye contact with me, rolled her eyes, then subtly widened her hands by her head.

Luke poked her in the side. "I saw that. My head is not big from the comment."

Her eyes widened before she giggled.

How cute were they? He could read her mind, which was as good a sign as any for how they would be together.

"Grab some and come join us," Shelby said.

"I'm taking a shower first, it got hot out there," I said.

"Same," Sophie added.

"Well, hurry up, we were discussing what to do tonight."

"Oh?"

"And …?" Sophie asked.

"I suggested we have a bonfire on the beach," Randy said.

Sophie rubbed her hands together. "That sounds fun. I didn't see fire pits though."

Randy shrugged. "We could build one; it isn't that hard. If we got a metal can and then dug in the sand to set it in there it would be a makeshift one."

"There are quilts and blankets in the closet. We can use that to sit on," Shelby said.

"I'm down," Sophie said and ran up the stairs.

"Hey! No fair, I said I needed a shower."

She stuck out her tongue and kept going.

"I guess I'll wait then." I walked to the kitchen and grabbed a plate. I assembled a burrito and then sat at the counter.

Shelby came to join me while the boys kept chatting.

"How was the grocery store?" I asked.

Shelby's cheeks reddened. "It was good. He was helpful."

"That's all? Your cheeks are as rosy as Rudolph's nose."

"He was flirty, but nothing too crazy."

"Mm-hmm. Were you snarky Shelby or soft and approachable Shelby?"

She gasped. "I'm not that snarky toward him anymore."

"If you say so." I winked. "It's cute. I think he likes your snark anyway. I mean he has seen enough of it. If he thought it was an issue I think you would know that by now."

"True. To be honest, I can't focus around him. It's like my brain is full of images of me kissing him or him kissing me."

"Is he a good kisser in your daydreams?"

She nodded.

I giggled. "Well, why don't you test it?"

"I don't know. Although, if we keep this up for too long, I won't know what's real and what's not. The daydreams are intense."

"Get it, girl!"

She slapped my hand. "Quit that," she said as she fanned her cheeks. "I need to contain it. He can read my face and I don't want him to know that … At least not yet."

"What about you? When's the last time you two kissed, like *really* kissed?"

I shrugged. "I have no idea. He doesn't kiss me on the lips as much as he holds my hands or holds open the door. I wish he would kiss me. I almost forget what it was like the first time."

Shelby sighed wistfully. "Boys are dumb."

I took a large bite of my burrito. "Amen to that."

"Promise me something."

"Hmm?"

"By the end of this summer, we both will have figured out what we are doing with the guys in our lives." She outstretched her hand.

I shook it. "Deal."

Summer was a long time. It was barely mid-June. We had plenty of time to sort things out and she was right. It was the place to do it. If not now, then when? During the school year? Would we waste what time we had before we went to college? No, it needed to happen … even if I wasn't sure of the answer.

CHAPTER NINE

SOPHIE

After my shower, I wandered downstairs, only to find that Drew was the only one in the living room. "Where is everyone?"

"They all went to figure out the bonfire situation."

"Oh. You didn't want to go with them?"

"Nah." He stood and closed the gap between us. "I wanted to stay here with you." He swept his arms around me and gazed into my face.

I pressed my damp head onto his chest and listened to the steady rhythm of his heartbeat. *Thump, thump. Thump, thump.* We stood there like this as our bodies synchronized. His touch could ease me in a way no one else could. "You're the sweetest."

He bent his head touching his lips to mine in a slow kiss.

I kissed him back, goosebumps erupting over my skin as his kiss turned more passionate than gentle.

He broke the kiss and smiled. "I had selfish intentions."

"Fine by me."

He chuckled. "Want to sit on the deck out back?"

I nodded.

His arm slid from my back to my hand, then entwined our fingers. He kissed my knuckles as we walked, then slid open the French doors to the back patio.

I inhaled a sharp breath. On our tour, we never checked out the back part of the house. Down below was a large in-ground pool, complete with a diving board and a section near the shallow end that had a seating area. "Is that a hot tub built into the pool?"

Drew followed my stare. "Looks like it." He wiggled his eyebrows in a suggestive manner. "That could be fun."

I slapped his chest playfully.

"What?" he asked and smirked.

Like the front porch, the back part of the porch had chairs to lounge on. I chose the sectional's chaise to lay out on. Drew snuggled next to me, but not too close that we would sweat to death in the humidity.

"This place is so nice," Drew said.

"It's like too nice. I can't stop comparing it."

"Same. I knew Shelby's family had money, but this is crazy."

"You haven't seen anything until you've seen her guest house and then her house. Let me tell you, my jaw nearly hit the ground," I said.

"Really?"

"Really. It's bigger than my whole house and that's just the guest house."

"Jeez."

"Yeah, but I must say I judged her too harshly. I spent too much time thinking she was this girl with all this money and no soul. I was wrong."

"That's normal. She didn't exactly interact with kids like us at school. What else were you going to think?"

I shrugged. "Maybe, but being her friend taught me I can't know a lot about someone by what I think I see."

"True." Drew twisted the end of my hair around his pointer finger. "Are you having a good time, though?"

I peered into his eyes. "Absolutely. I could sit with you like this forever."

"That could be arranged."

"I don't think everyone would want to see that the whole trip."

"Eh, they can avert their eyes."

I giggled. "You are full of surprises."

"I must be to date you."

I leaned my head on his shoulder.

"Not to kill this vibe, but did you bring your SAT book?"

I groaned. "Really?"

"Did you?"

"She got to you, didn't she?"

"Who?"

"Mama."

He nodded.

"So typical." I sighed. "Yes, I brought it, although I don't know how much it will help. I do well in classes when I apply myself, but those standardized tests suck. They trick me and I've never been a natural at them."

"That's what the book is for. It gives you tips and tricks to the test. Plus, you practice the problems and get used to the way they're worded. It'll help."

"Ugh. That sounds awful and a total buzzkill to the perfect summer."

"It doesn't have to be. It'll be like when we studied for your energy test. I have ways to make it fun."

"So, you'll be my tutor then?"

"If you're nice to me."

I planted a big sloppy kiss on his lips. "Does that suffice?"

He pulled me closer and whispered, "That's a start."

The air tickled my neck. I squirmed to fight the urge to giggle, but it was too late.

He saw my expression and knew it tickled. This time he blew on my neck as he held me close so I couldn't move.

"Drew!" I shouted. "Quit. It." I writhed in his arms, trying to break free from the chills it sent down my spine even on an incredibly warm day. I gasped between uncontrollable laughter as he continued to tickle me.

With a smug expression on his face, clearly satisfied with his torture, he stopped.

"I'll get you back for that, Drew Abbott."

"I'm counting on it."

I growled.

His composure cracked as he laughed hard. When he finally stopped he said, "Okay, okay. I'll stop for now. Why don't you go grab your book and come back? We can work on one of the sections for just a little bit and then go help them figure out the bonfire. Work then play, how's that sound?"

I blew all the air from my mouth, creating a raspberry sound. "It sounds like something Mama would say, but I'll cave."

"Good, now get going."

I stuck out my tongue and stood. I hated when he was right about things like that. Unfortunately, I didn't have the time to screw it up the next time I took the SAT. I was late as it was. Most of my class had concentrated on their spring score for colleges. Since I had screwed up several things this spring, it's not a surprise that the SAT was part of that.

If I wanted to get into Duke, I had to fix my score. And I had to do it at the end of the summer before applications were due. Nothing like a little pressure to motivate me to figure it out.

CHAPTER TEN

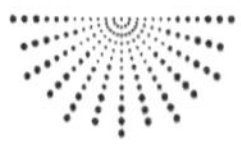

SHELBY

Luke and Randy scouted the beach ahead of Riley and me. They had serious expressions as they pointed and gestured with their hands.

I giggled. "Look at those two. They look like they're trying to solve a Calculus problem or something."

Riley followed my gaze. "This is serious business!" she said with a straight face and then devolved into laughter.

Randy planted his feet, faced the house, and then squinted. "I think right here is perfect. You are still in the house boundary and can see the rocks off to the side. What do you think?"

Luke nodded as Randy spoke.

"I'm fine with wherever. If you two think that's the perfect place, then go for it."

The boys high fived.

"Someone has to stand here so we don't lose the position while we get supplies."

I cocked my head. "Are we really doing this now? It's gorgeous today and we could spend time on the beach instead."

"Yeah, bathing suits, water, sand. Perfect combo," Riley said then winked at me.

I stifled my laugh. I knew Riley had noticed what I was saying. We wanted to spend the day relaxing, not necessarily digging a hole for a bonfire hours away.

Luke's eyes widened as he met my gaze.

Randy chuckled. "Luke, it sounds to me that the girls don't want to do any physical labor. What do you think?"

Luke stroked his chin, a mischievous glint in his eye. "Randy, I must say I think you're right." He kicked his sandals off and placed them on their *perfect* spot for the bonfire. Then he lifted his orange tank top over his head and set it on his shoes. He inched closer to me.

My heart felt like it would leap from my chest cavity as my brain processed Luke's sculpted chest. My eyes darted between Riley and Luke, who kept getting closer and closer. "What are you doing?"

Luke said nothing but smirked. He sent a silent signal to Randy, who had followed suit and was now getting closer to Riley, with a nod of his head.

Oh, crap.

I realized what their intentions were too late when Luke lifted me off the sand and straight over his shoulder.

I screamed and kicked my legs. My arms slammed onto Luke's back as he jogged toward the ocean. "Luke Warrington, don't you *dare*!" I twisted my neck to get a view of Riley, whose screams could rival my own.

"No, no, no, no, no!" Riley screamed.

Luke waded a few feet into the water until it reached his mid shins before he dropped me fully clothed into the waves.

Before my head dipped below the water line and the waves rolled in, I held my breath, then tried to stand. Off balance, I stood and glared at Luke.

Riley was experiencing a similar emotion, while the boys laughed and then bolted away from the waves.

"You are so dead, Luke."

He winked and ran toward the beach house.

I stared at Riley. "I can't even believe they just did that."

Riley wiped at her face then took her hair tie from her wrist and put her hair into a messy bun. "I don't know how, but I am so getting them back."

"Same here, but first I need to change."

Riley nodded and waded from the water with me.

"What chickens. They totally bolted. Luke's lucky I was caught off guard."

"Those two are dangerous together. I never thought Randy would do it."

I laughed. "I'm not. Why wouldn't they want to be flirty and drop us in water? It's like when a guy pulls a girl's ponytail. They can't help themselves."

"Psh, we aren't in middle school."

"True, but on one hand it made Luke take off his shirt, so I can't say I'm unhappy about that. Did you see his abs?"

Riley's cheeks reddened. "No. I wasn't looking at Luke, I was dying that Randy carried me like a sack of potatoes over his shoulder and dropped me in the water."

We walked up the back steps to the porch. Drew and Sophie sat on the sectional discussing a book when Sophie burst out laughing at the sight of us both. "What the heck happened to you two?"

Riley crossed her arms. "Luke and Randy teamed up to dump us in the water and then ran off."

"Didn't they come back here?" I asked.

Drew shook his head. "We haven't seen anyone since brunch."

Riley raised an eyebrow. "Where did they go?"

"No idea, but I'm getting changed; then they can figure out the bonfire on their own after that."

"Agreed." Riley faced Sophie. "You coming to the beach?"

"In a little bit. I need to study for at least an hour before I go have fun."

She nodded. "Well, you know where we'll be. And if you see the boys, throw a pillow at them."

Drew hid his smirk behind his hand, while Sophie giggled. "You got it."

I pushed open the French doors and gasped at the chilly air hitting my wet clothes that stuck to my body. "I so dislike being trapped in wet clothes. At least I'm not wearing skinny jeans though. They are the hardest to get off."

"It's still uncomfortable."

We waddled up the stairs and into our bedroom. I sifted through my bathing suits and decided on a black one piece with cut outs around my belly and across my back.

"Should I wear a big floppy hat or sunglasses?" I asked.

She stopped looking at her own suit choices. "Hmm. Both."

I put them both on my head and then carried a cover up and switched into flip flops instead of sandals. I sat on my bed and scrolled through my phone as I waited for Riley to finish getting ready. No new texts, but my mother managed to email me several reminders of daily to-dos. *Don't forget to watch your carbohydrate intake. Shelby, make sure you're moisturizing before bed. Make sure you hang up your clothes that need to be dry cleaned.*

It went on and on. Did she think I magically forgot what to do because I no longer slept in the same house? Not to mention, why would I have brought clothes that needed to be dry cleaned to a beach. Even if I was going somewhere fancy that would be ridiculous.

"What's wrong?" Riley asked.

"My mother. It's not really anything wrong so much as just overprotective and ridiculous. She hasn't asked me how it's going but she continues to email me ridiculous reminders at her stream of consciousness. It's getting seriously out of hand."

"Reminders like what?"

I turned the phone so she could see.

She clasped a hand to her mouth. "Moisturize?" She giggled. "Really?" She shook her head. "That's kind of sad, though. She can't just ask you things, she has to pretend to send you reminders."

"Pretty typical. She might not disapprove so openly of who I spend time with anymore, but she doesn't know how to show positive emotions. I'm not sure she even knows what they feel like anymore honestly."

"I'm sorry, that sounds awful." Riley added a turquoise cover up over top of her pastel-blue two piece, then twirled. "Do I look okay?"

"If you mean will that outfit make Randy drool, then yes."

She blushed. "He won't drool."

"He will appreciate your toned body thanks to the running you insist on doing every day for your mental health." I tapped her shoulder. "It'll turn his head, trust me."

"It's not too much?"

"Nope. It's perfect."

"Okay, let's do this."

"I'll meet you by the back door. I want to grab a few of the towels for when we're done in the water to lay on."

She nodded as I left our room. I closed the door and

then walked to one of the hallway closets by the stairs. After the third try, I found the right one and picked out two massive towels, then headed for the back porch.

Riley stood by the stairs chatting with Sophie and Drew when I emerged.

"All set. Let's get our beach on." I headed down the back stairs and surveyed the beach looking for Luke and Randy. If they were still out here, they weren't in plain sight. "Do you see them?"

"Nope. I keep looking over my shoulder in case they sneak up on us. I might be in a bathing suit now, but I don't want to get dropped in the water again. Once a day is plenty."

"Never is more like it."

We walked to the edge of the sand before it dropped and became damp. Dropping the towels on the ground and removing my hat, I then walked to the water. I waded in inch by inch, letting the water seep all the anxiety from my body. I closed my eyes and surrendered to my other senses. I could smell the salty ocean in the air mixed with the remnants of my perfume. The water swirled around my feet as it rushed the shore and then receded.

Once the water reached my waist, I stopped standing and allowed myself to float through the water, keeping my head above the waves.

"This is the life," Riley said.

"I was thinking the same thing. It's so nice to just relax and enjoy the waves without rushing to a meeting or having someone hover over you."

"Or to do homework."

"That, too. I feel bad for Sophie. I don't mind school, but it is the *last* thing I'd want to do at the beach house."

"You and me both. I brought my summer English

books to read but I guarantee I'll leave those packed away until the last minute."

I snuck a peek at the beach to see Luke and Randy were digging in the sand. Luke looked my way and waved, then got back to digging with Randy.

"Looks like the boys returned to do the bonfire."

"I hope it's hot and takes them a while."

"Someone holds a grudge."

Riley glared in their direction. "No, but I don't like surprises. So, what will we do to retaliate?"

"I'm not sure yet, but we will think of something." I readjusted my sunglasses after a wave. "Let's just relax and enjoy, you know they'll eventually show up in the water and then there goes the silence."

Riley giggled and shut her eyes, floating along with me. It was only our first week at the house, but I already knew this is exactly what I needed this summer.

CHAPTER ELEVEN

To my dismay, it took less time than I hoped it would for Luke and Randy to finish digging the hole.

I groaned. "They're already putting away their shovels."

Shelby peeked an eye open as she floated in the water. "Already?"

"That's what I'm saying. It was supposed to take them *hours* to pay them back for their crude behavior."

"So, now what? Obviously, that backfired."

"I don't know, but here they come." I braced myself for the running and the splashing, but somehow I still managed to get hit with more water than I wanted to.

Luke and Randy chuckled about something as they floated near us.

Shelby pretended to not even notice them, which was more than I could manage.

Randy had taken off his shirt again to get in the water and all I could notice was his body and how much I wanted to touch him. Why couldn't my brain have real thoughts besides what he looked like? It was ridiculous.

"Your bonfire spot is complete," Randy said.

Shelby didn't budge.

"Your highness," Luke said.

That got her attention.

She scowled. "Riley, I feel like there's this buzzing. Do you hear that?"

I giggled. "Yep, two large bees, right around here." Then I slapped my hand down hard in front of the boys, splashing the salty water right into their faces.

Randy's eyes widened and Luke looked like war was about to begin.

Maybe I hadn't made the best choice in payback.

Randy shifted closer to me, as I tried to do the opposite.

"Bees?" Luke asked then glanced at Randy. "I think if we're bees then maybe they should feel the sting."

Randy's expression shifted into an orneriness I had never seen before.

"I think you might be right," Randy said.

Shelby looked at me like I was dead meat, too, then shifted her body to try and get away from Luke.

I placed my hands in front of me. "Whatever you're going to do, don't."

Randy's grin widened. "Oh, so now you can hear us? Tsk tsk tsk. Too bad, I can't stop what you already set in motion. That wouldn't be fair, would it?"

I eyed Luke, who was getting closer to Shelby.

Before I realized, Randy was close enough to wrap his arms around me and tickle my side with zero mercy.

Luke was trying to dunk Shelby, which was an even worse idea.

She splashed water toward him mercilessly as she shouted, but my own laughter drowned her out as I struggled to catch my breath.

"Stop! Okay, stop. I'm sorry."

Satisfied with his torture, Randy stopped and eyed me. "Truce?"

I growled. "Truce, for now, when you can't torture me with tickles or water."

He chuckled. "I doubt it was torture. We slaved away digging the bonfire and you ladies floated. I think you've had lots of relaxing time."

"Pfft." I reached up and pulled my hair from its messy bun and worked to redo it.

Something shifted in Randy's gaze and little fires exploded under my skin. Why was he looking at me like that? "What?"

He shook his head. "You just look so beautiful."

I rolled my eyes. "Really? My hair is crusty from the salt and sand, and I probably look like a drowned rat."

He shook his head. "Never." His hand settled over mine before he used it to pull me toward him. The heat of his skin on mine warmed me. Then, he lifted me up as he twirled us around.

I laughed, despite the surprise, and relaxed in his arms.

"There she is." He brushed my cheek with his finger. "I love it when you laugh."

A grin broke across my face. The air felt charged, like in a lightning storm. Who knew that even with all our time together, it could still feel so new?

Laughter broke our gaze as we shifted to see what state Luke and Shelby were in.

Shelby's hair laid wet off the side of her head, while Luke shielded his eyes as sprays of water came toward him. Both had wide grins.

Those two were just dying to tell each other their feelings. It was so obvious in the tension. He made excuses to touch her, while she made excuses to glower, a true sign that she was simmering with emotion beneath the surface.

Randy chuckled. "That seems to be going well."

"I think so, too. They'd be so cute together."

Randy's gaze lingered on my face, before we floated over toward them. They paused on their splash fight once we were close enough.

I raised an eyebrow at Shelby. "Did you win?"

Luke smirked. "I think it was a tie."

Shelby crossed her arms. "Not if I had been allowed to continue."

"Want to dry off?" I asked her.

"Sure. The ocean has gotten a little congested."

Luke snorted. "Is that so?"

Shelby flipped her hair out of her face, sending a spray of water droplets toward Luke's face.

Randy chuckled as he and Luke picked up another conversation.

"Those two are dangerous together," I said.

"I'll say. It's like the pranks and all have gone up ten-fold."

"Mm-hmm. Sophie's lucky. Drew would never do that."

Shelby giggled. "True but can you imagine him doing it anyway? He doesn't seem the type."

"Maybe, or maybe that's what he wants everyone to think. He did play truth or dare with girls in middle school. That takes guts."

Shelby laughed. "Or stupidity." She tossed a towel to me, and we both shook them out over the sand. Once it was as flat as possible, we laid down.

"Think they'll be out here soon?"

Shelby glanced at her phone's screen. "Hmm, I don't know. It's getting late to get all messy then get ready."

Tonight, we would all be together for the fire, and I couldn't wait. I propped my arms up on the towel to get an unobstructed view of the boys in the water. They were trying to catch waves and body surf in, but it didn't look like they were doing well.

It was nice to see Randy have someone to hang out with. He was always with Sophie and me, which I liked, but it didn't give him any guy time. Their friendship would be good for him.

I laid back down and relaxed as the sun warmed my skin and dried my bathing suit. This was the life.

We all gathered around the campfire. The night was perfect. Sophie and Drew cuddled into each other as they sat on the blanket. Randy sat a few feet from me, while Shelby and Luke sat across from us. Everyone had moved on from the attacks of the afternoon.

I stared at the sky, taking in all the constellations and the silence besides the sound of the fire crackling as the wood burned. The day on the beach had ended when the boys had gotten out and asked about dinner. Sophie and Drew had started down as we went up to the house.

Shelby straightened and cleared her throat. "Who wants to make this bonfire interesting?"

I raised an eyebrow. "Interesting how?"

"Like someone tell us a creepy story or something."

Sophie rolled her eyes. "A creepy story? What are we at camp?"

Drew chuckled. "Soph, relax. It's just a story. I'll protect you."

She leaned away and faced him. "Protect me? I don't

need protecting. I won't be scared anyway. I didn't expect Ms. Big and Bad to suggest a *creepy story*."

"Well? Who's interested?" Shelby asked.

Randy stood. "I'm in and I want to go first." He surveyed the faces around the campfire and when no one objected he began. "Well, it's said that in this exact cove ten feet over there,"—he pointed toward the rock outcrops —"the founding families came ashore."

Shelby groaned. "This story? Of all the stories you could pick, you choose this one?"

Randy chuckled. "Yeah, why not? Riley hasn't heard it."

"Well, I certainly have," Luke said.

"I want to hear it," I whined. "If you've all heard it, then I want to know about it!"

Sophie gestured with her hand. "Well, go on then."

Randy nodded. "Anyway … the founding families came ashore just over there. It's even said that instead of five founding families, there was actually a sixth. The sixth family, Stewart, was only represented by an ailing man in his late forties. It was an odd thing to travel at such an age in those days. Some say Charles Stewart came to America to avoid his wife and children. Some say he was avoiding the authorities in England. Either way he arrived with our ancestors in the cove."

Randy moved closer to the fire. "In the beginning, times were difficult for our ancestors. They had little food left from the voyage and they were unaccustomed to dealing with life by the ocean. No one knew how to fish or farm … except Charles. They were forced to depend on him to survive. And at first he did help. He built them nets and showed them how to go farther inland to plant. But people grew restless with his delinquency. He no longer helped when they asked, and he wouldn't share his rations with anyone."

Randy leaned forward. "The other five families grew tired of Charles and his antics. They devised a plan. They would sneak up on him during his nightly stroll. Trap him in his own nets and launch him into the ocean," he said, his voice much lower.

I gasped. "That's terrible."

Sophie giggled and shook her head.

"On the infamous night, the head of each family had been given a job to accomplish. Some were to be on the lookout for anyone else, while others had to hold the net to be ready. It's said that on that night it had been overcast, hiding the full moon. Charles arrived on the beach just like he always did, when they hit him over the head with a nearby rock. Once he was out cold, they wrapped him tightly in his net and drug him toward the deepest part of the cove. Before casting him into the water, they weighed the net down with rocks."

When Randy suggested a story, I hadn't expected it to be laced with murder.

"When his body hit the water, they watched and waited for a while to be sure it didn't resurface."

Sophie rolled her eyes and Shelby snorted.

I grimaced. "Great story."

"Oh, but it's not over." He leaned closer to the fire, letting it illuminate his features. "It wasn't long after their planned attack that those in the five founding families started hearing and seeing weird things. Mirrors cracking, cold spots in the middle of the heated day, and objects disappearing. Then a small girl from the Tate family had taken a stroll on the beach. She said she heard a voice whispering something, but wasn't sure what it was, until the whispers turned to screams."

I shifted on the blanket.

"The little girl disappeared that night, but not before leaving a warning. Those in the founding families, if they walked on this beach during a full moon, they, too, would see Charles Stewart again and never be found."

Luke clapped. "Bravo man. Seriously, my father could never get through it all with a serious face."

Randy grinned. "Well, it's true." He nudged my arm. "Want to take a walk on the next full moon?"

I slapped his arm. "Definitely not!"

Everyone erupted into laughter.

"Yeah, you all think you're funny. Just because you've heard the story before doesn't mean that crap isn't true, or things happen."

Sophie giggled. "Well, at least we all aren't part of the founding families. You'd be safe. Only Shelby, Luke, and Randy wouldn't be."

I looked up at the moon; it almost looked full, which meant any day we'd have a full moon, and I knew for sure I wasn't taking that chance with anyone. "No thanks. When we have our full moon, we will all be safely locked away in the beach house. No moonlight walks for any of you."

Luke chuckled. "Thanks for the concern, but I'd be fine."

Randy nodded. "Me, too." He plopped back down on the blanket. "Anyone else want to tell a story?"

"And follow up that?" Drew asked. "How could we ever do such a good job?"

I shook my head. "How about no more creepy stories. Why would we want to scare each other when we still have to go back to the house in the dark? That doesn't sound smart if you ask me."

Randy's eyebrow rose. "I haven't seen you this freaked out since Halloween."

Sophie burst into a fit of giggles. "Oh man, that was a good night."

Shelby frowned. "I haven't heard this story."

I glared at Randy and Sophie. "Trust me when I say it was a night full of those two preying on my inability to handle horror. They made me go to some stupid place whose whole purpose is to scare."

"It was called Terror Town," Sophie said.

"Either way, I passed out from one of the stupid haunting houses."

Shelby clasped a hand to her mouth. "You didn't."

"Oh, she did," Sophie said.

"I'm pretty sure the deal was never to talk about it again though."

She shrugged. "Randy brought it up, not me."

Randy smiled and winked at me. "My bad."

"Mm-hmm. I think you both just enjoy scaring me."

Drew looked at Sophie. "You weren't scared?"

"Me? No. I love those things, who do you think suggested it?"

He laughed. "Good to know."

"We should have gotten stuff to make s'mores."

Luke pulled packages from behind his back. "Your wish is our command."

I clapped my hands together. "Yay! You two thought of everything. Thank you."

Luke held out his hands, palms up. "Wasn't me. It was all Shelby."

"Well, regardless, toss those marshmallows over here."

Shelby handed everyone a poker to roast the marshmallows.

I grabbed mine and two marshmallows, then stuffed them onto the end.

Randy cocked his head. "I didn't realize you were such a s'more enthusiast."

"Of course, I am. Aren't you?"

He shrugged. "I suppose I don't mind them, but they're not in my top ten."

"Even though it has chocolate? I figured you'd enjoy that."

He snatched a small piece of the Hershey bar. "I do, but the whole melty marshmallow part is not."

I leaned closer to the fire and held my marshmallows overtop. The fire crackled and sizzled. I shoved my two marshmallows right into the flame and hoped they would catch on fire. I pulled them out gently, then returned it when it didn't have a flame.

"You like them burnt don't you?" Randy asked.

"Is there any other way?"

He shook his head, but a grin still plastered his face.

I surveyed my friends as we all gathered around the fire. Each of us focused on the boy that we were interested in. It was funny how that happened. If anyone would have told any of us that this is how we would spend a summer night, I think we would have told them they were crazy, Sophie especially. And yet, it felt right. All of us were smiling and laughing, even though we weren't all coupled, we vibed.

Randy scooted closer to me on the blanket. "What are you thinking about?"

"What says that I am?"

Randy gave me a knowing look. "Your face is all scrunched up. You must be thinking about something."

"I was just thinking about how happy I am that we're

all together and having a good time. I think it'll be a good summer."

Randy's smile reached all the way to the corner of his eyes. "It is nice, isn't it?"

I nodded.

My marshmallows were finally the perfect level of char that I had hoped for, and I slid them onto the graham cracker and added my Hershey bar. Pushing down on the crackers, the marshmallow oozed out and onto my fingers. I took a big bite. The marshmallow stretched off the cracker, dripping down my arm. Some stuck to my cheek.

Before I could wipe it off with my clean hand, Randy's thumb came close to me. He held the bottom of my chin with this other hand, then swiped his thumb across my cheek. I stared into his gaze as his eyes bored into me. They flashed with emotions I couldn't read, and then the heat from his touch was gone. His hands back in his lap.

The butterflies in my stomach whirred to life as the heat beneath my cheeks where he touched me grew into full on wildfires. I would have been worried about the redness of my cheeks if it weren't for the bonfire. At least this time I could blame my blushing on that instead of how he made my body react.

I focused on eating the rest of my s'more while I tried to push the feelings down, but the harder I pushed the more they bobbed to the surface. How long could I go without confronting them?

***

Couple by couple, they disappeared from the bonfire, leaving Randy and I as the final two.

He stoked the fire with a large stick, while I had stolen the covers from Shelby and Sophie to wrap around my shoulders. It wasn't that it was a particularly cold night, but more of a protection from the incessant bugs that I knew would bite me. I should have doused my whole body in bug spray—a lesson for next time.

After getting the fire to perk back up, Randy sat next to me, leaned back, then rested his head on his hands as he stared up into the sky.

It was important to do the same, so I leaned back and rested next to him. The air crackled with the things unsaid. I didn't want to be the first to break the silence, so I focused on what constellations I could recognize. I didn't know many, but I had at least learned Orion's belt and the big and little dipper. I squinted but found it difficult with the light from the moon. It would be better when we had a new moon, several weeks away.

Randy faced me, his eyes boring into the side of my face. "You seem tense."

Could he read me that well? "Oh, I was just thinking."

"Thinking again, huh?"

I rolled to my side to face him. "I don't want to ruin the day."

He knitted his eyebrows. "Why would something you're thinking about ruin the day?"

I fiddled with my shirt and looked away from his gaze. "I … I've been thinking about things between us."

"Okay."

"I've been wondering why we aren't a couple yet."

He exhaled and faced the sky again. "I just want to get things with my family under control."

"I know your family has put pressure on you. I don't want to add more pressure, I really don't, but it just feels weird that we aren't a couple. It's been like nine months since you told me how you felt about me, and I told you I felt the same. I just … do you not want to be a couple anymore?"

"Riley, I still like you. Everything I've learned about you has made you more important to me. I just want to get it right as a couple and I don't think that would happen if we were a couple now."

My chest tightened.

"Can you understand that the timing still isn't, right?"

I wanted to shout and say no I couldn't. I wanted to yell and push to get my way, but I didn't want to lose him. "Yeah, of course."

He laced his fingers with mine and squeezed. "Thank you for understanding." He kissed my cheek and laid beside me, falling back into silence.

This time instead of the air crackling with the tension of not saying something, my chest felt heavy, and my eyes prickled with tears. Thankfully, the darkness shielded my feelings, and for that I was grateful. I just had to wait it out and understand his situation was difficult. I could do that. I *had to* do that.

CHAPTER TWELVE

SOPHIE

I sunk into the seat of my Jeep at the end of my first summer shift at the theater. This wasn't just the first shift I've had since staying in the beach house, but it was also one of the first ones in a while I wasn't working with Drew.

It was strange. We had our work rhythm. It was like he knew when I was out of something at the snack counter and would bring it before I even had to radio him. And when he was at the podium, I knew when he needed help or to escort someone to their seat. Without him, the shift went slower.

Courtney and Sasha had worked with me. Poor Courtney still struggled trying to get Sasha up to speed, but it wasn't going as well as she had hoped. I wasn't sure what to say to help her, but I would tell Drew about it. He had experience with several shadows at this point, maybe he had more tips for her.

I stuck the key in the ignition and started the Jeep, allowing the nice cool air conditioner to cool me off. The theater wasn't warm, but the short walk outside was enough to have me sweating in my long pants and shirt.

I would drive back to the cove house, but first I wanted to stop at home. I found a good radio station and cranked it up, then pulled out of the parking lot. It would be about thirty minutes to my house, and I wanted to soak up all the time in my Jeep. I had only driven it a handful of times since Mama gave it to me a week ago. It was surreal that it was mine, but it was absolutely perfect. I loved the purple exterior, my black seats, and the Honey Cove pendant that hung from my rearview mirror. I wouldn't change anything about it.

The driveway was empty, except for Rowan's Porsche SUV. I frowned. Why was his vehicle here and not Mama's?

I parked my Jeep next to his and hopped down. I fiddled for my keys when Rowan walked out the front door. I stopped and stared. My body froze. "Is something wrong? Are Mama and Caleb okay?"

"Oh, yes. Sorry, I'm sure this is a strange sight for you."

I nodded.

"They're fine. Caleb went to a friend's house and your mom should be home in about an hour."

"Oh." I squinted from the sun. "So, what brings you here?"

I took in his expression and outfit. He still wore gray dress pants and a dark red golf-like polo. His mouth was spread into a flat line, not frowning, but also not smiling. For nothing being wrong, he didn't seem to be all that happy, either.

"I wanted to talk to you. I was hoping we could chat before your mom gets home."

My breath caught. Since the spring, Mama hadn't

forced us to be alone since he drove me to the theater. Had she grown tired of waiting for me to be okay?

He eyed me warily. "She doesn't know I came over early. She mentioned you might stop by after your shift. I thought it might be one of the only times I could chat with you."

I twisted my keys around in my hand. "Oh, um, okay." What could he want to discuss with me? My stomach flopped as I walked closer and sat on the front step.

"Do you want to walk? We could walk and talk if that makes you more comfortable."

Did I want to walk? I didn't know that anything would make me feel less uneasy. This was strange. I didn't know what he wanted, and I didn't know how I felt that he orchestrated it without my mama knowing.

"Okay. Let me change my uniform first. We can walk to the playground."

He nodded.

I opened the front door and jogged to my room. My mind whirled as I sorted through the clothes I had left at home. I found a pair of denim shorts and a graphic tee. I put flip flops on and walked to the door. I had an overwhelming feeling that whatever he wanted to talk about would change everything.

He waited where I left him and gave a weak smile when he caught sight of me.

I pulled the door shut and started down the sidewalk.

He followed closely by me, walking not quite at my side.

I gulped. "So, what's up?"

He shoved his hands in his pant pockets. "Your mom and I have been dating for about eight months and I know you've only known about it since April, but I wanted to be up front with you."

Where was he headed with this?

"I love your mom. She makes me laugh and smile every second I'm around her. She's so independent and yet she makes me feel needed. She's an incredible woman."

I smiled. "Yeah, she is."

"I don't pretend to know what it's like to lose someone I love. I haven't lost more than one grandparent in my life and that is nowhere close to the loss that you and your family have endured with your dad. I also don't pretend to know how someone heals from that, and I would never want to disrupt that process."

I trained my gaze on the blacktop as we walked. I didn't want to talk about my dad. I didn't want to end up crying from the unexpected mention of him either. I dug my key into my palm to avoid the tears that wanted to escape.

"Your mom is fiercely protective of you and Caleb; she hasn't told me everything that happened in the spring with you. I know that you weren't ready to be around me much, but I wanted to let you know what I was thinking."

He stopped talking as we approached the playground. I sat on the swing, and he stood near the other. "I-I want to ask your mother to marry me."

My eyes widened and I kicked off the ground to move the swing. He wanted to marry Mama? Wasn't that too soon?

"But, Sophie, I don't want to do anything unless I have your permission."

My heart pounded in my chest. He was asking me for my blessing? Would he not do it if I said no? "What did Caleb say?"

Rowan made eye contact with me and kept it. "I haven't told him. I wanted to talk to you. I know you were older when your dad died. I can only imagine it feels differently for you than it would for him."

"Oh."

"So, what do you think?"

"I don't know, honestly. I didn't expect this to be the topic of conversation."

"I'm not rushing you, but I wanted you to know it's on my radar. I also want you to know, though, that I want you to feel comfortable with it all first. I won't ask her unless I know you're okay with it."

I stood and pretended to check the time on my phone. "I will think about what you said, but I should head back to the cove house. I'll text her later."

"Sophie, are you sure?"

I nodded and sped walked back to the Jeep. If he had tried to follow, I couldn't tell. I hopped in my Jeep, started the engine, and left my house before he could return. On the way out of the cul-de-sac, Rowan sat on the swing.

My stomach ached the way it did after eating too much candy, only this time I had no candy. I knew Mama was happy with Rowan. I knew Caleb liked Rowan. I didn't mind him for Mama so much anymore. I recognized that he was a decent man, and he did look out for her. But did I want him to live with us? Would she change her last name? Would she be Faye Ashburn? Would they move in together in a bigger house? Would she have to take down photos of Dad?

How could I ask her about all those things without giving away what he wanted to do? How could I pause without upsetting her? I know it hurt her last time when I stalled the relationship between him and me. She had tried to get us to meet and spend time together, but I had been so upset about my dad I couldn't accept anyone else coming into our lives.

I still wasn't sure I was ready for that. I sighed and focused on the road. There wasn't going to be an answer tonight and I needed to stop acting like that would change.

CHAPTER THIRTEEN

SHELBY

"How much longer until we get there?" I asked.

Randy chuckled. "You're worse than Riley."

I crossed my arms. "Well, when I agreed to let you drive, I wasn't aware that there was no radio. I can't go so long in silence."

"There isn't silence right now. We're talking aren't we? Or am I imagining that?"

I straightened my gray pencil skirt. "No. You aren't imagining it, but I'm still feeling like a five-year-old who can't wait to get out of the car on a long road trip."

"Twenty minutes and we will be at the meeting. Relax."

"Fine." I looked around the cab of his F150 for the hundredth time. "So, have you been enjoying the beach trip?"

"Yeah, it's been nice. The house is great. I can't remember the last time I felt like an actual high schooler. It makes everything feel so normal."

I nodded. In Randy's situation, he became less and less like a teenager as he took control of his family's company.

My father still ran the business. I was only given some leeway, especially with the festivals, but with Randy's father continuing to drink, he had to step up or the company would go under. I couldn't imagine that kind of pressure.

"I'm glad you're liking it. Has it been weird to bunk with Luke and Drew?"

"Nah. They're both pretty cool. It's a shame Luke doesn't go to Honey Cove High."

"You can say that again. Things would be so much easier."

"How's that going?"

"I was going to ask you that."

He knitted his eyebrows.

"I mean … does he talk about me?"

"Not really. I don't think we're all close enough to share that. You girls are closer than we are right now. I think we each feel connected to each other, but only through one of you."

"That makes sense but doesn't help me. I keep wondering what he's thinking. As every day passes I can only focus on the set amount of time we have before he goes back to school. I mean it's almost the end of June."

Randy tapped his steering wheel. "I think the only way you'll know what he's thinking is by asking him. Luke is the closest with you in the house. He might open up to us eventually, but do you really want to wait that long before you do something?"

"No. That could take all summer."

"Exactly."

I hated that Randy was right. I didn't want to waste time that we could be spending together. One of the hardest parts about starting something with Luke is that the time we could be around each other always had an expiration date. He would go back to boarding school and wouldn't be home until Thanksgiving. That was a long time to have a long-distance relationship. Would it even work if we had barely been together? I wasn't sure, but the probability seemed poor.

"So, will you stay at the cove house while Riley goes home to see her dad?"

"I will for some of it. I have a few shifts at Morgan's during that time. But I figured we could work on festival stuff while she's busy, so I'll be back, just unsure exactly what days."

"That works. I hope she's okay."

He cocked his head and then refocused on the road. "Why do you say that?"

"She just seems all twisted about her dad's visit. I don't think she knows whether or not to be happy he's here or wonder what it means for her parents. It just seems hard for her, like living two lives that don't meld well together."

"Oh. Yeah, but she does miss him."

"Of course. I hope for her sake the trip is more about her and doesn't ruffle any feathers. She doesn't need any more drama."

He nodded but something about his posture changed when I mentioned drama. Had something happened between them I didn't know about?

I thought back to the past week and nothing seemed out of place. Riley also hadn't said anything, so maybe I had imagined it. Either way, I didn't get a chance to dwell on it much longer because we pulled into a parking space outside of the meeting.

I shifted into business mode, hopped out of his truck, then straightened my clothes. "You ready?"

"Yep. You have the folder right?"

I held it up and he gave me a thumbs up. "We've got

this. I doubt they'll even focus on us for long since they already know what we can do."

He shrugged. "You know how the founders' council is. Those men are so fickle, well at least the loud ones."

"True, but my father mentioned there was more important business information for the meeting than just the end of summer festival we're throwing. All we're doing is getting approval for the big-ticket items and then moving ahead with setting it up."

"Well, let's head up. I want to get this meeting done and over with before the entire day is gone."

"You and me both. The beach is calling my name."

"I'd say that went rather well, don't you?"

Randy smiled and loosened the tie he had worn to the meeting. "No one argued and we got approval, I'd say yes."

I beamed. "Best one yet. Now we just have to get the vendors and all set up for the event."

"We'll get there, we always do. I wouldn't worry about it too much."

"Oh, I'm not. I'll relax while you drive. Maybe I'll even take a nap. That's the beauty of being the passenger."

Randy chuckled. "How was the conversation with your dad?"

"Okay mostly. He reminded me that Mother wanted me to check my email daily and make sure to respond. I also was warned to keep the house in top shape." I rolled my eyes. "Can't ask me how I am, but reminders about their *property* is all they can manage."

"At least they ask something, right?"

I lifted one shoulder. "If they're going for the bare minimum parent duty award, sure."

"Not that I don't agree with you, but at least they aren't standing in your way. It does seem like they've come a few steps in your direction. That's better than going backward."

"True." My phone chirped, alerting me to a new text. I unlocked the screen and checked my messages. It was from my Aunt Delilah. She had sent me a photo of her standing in front of a massive tree. I squinted. Was that a sequoia tree? I guess it made sense since she was traveling around the Pacific Northwest. Beneath the photo she texted, *Miss you.*

I texted her back, *How's your trip?*

Amazing! I am loving it out here. It's not for everyone obviously. The rain is hard to get used to, but the trees are beautiful. I don't want to go home.

When's the trip over?

We have another week before I head back home.

I smiled. She was traveling again, and I was so happy for her. She had come to Honey Cove to visit us around Christmas. In her own words she had escaped from her life because she had essentially dropped a bomb on it. Her boyfriend had been married and was a client of the company she worked for. She eventually went back and discussed things instead of running, but she ended up getting a job offer from a separate company in California. Now she was rocking it and had even been able to go on this trip with some of the partners to stake out new clients.

Hopefully, you soak it all up by then.

If not, I'll be back. How's your beach adventure?

Good! We've been in the house about a week at this point.

Any good dirt?

Aunt Delilah! You're bad.

Hey, I might be older than you, but I'm not dead. You all are teenagers in high school, I can't possibly believe any stories of a G-rated nature.

Well, believe it. No one is hooking up or doing anything crazy.

What is the fun in that? Have you and Luke made out yet?

No.

Why not?

I don't know how to initiate something with him. I don't know what he's thinking.

Shelby, haven't we discussed this before? You must ask the poor boy if you want to know.

What if he wants to be friends?

Then you'll have your answer. But I saw you two at Christmas. There were sparks even when you couldn't stand the poor boy. I say you two go out on a date and feel things out. He's probably waiting to see what you're feeling.

I could do that. Go on a date and just see how things were, just us, no pressure from anyone else.

That's it? Just go on a date?

Yep. You're at the beach. Go on a picnic at the beach and then go swimming in the ocean after. After that you can go back to the hot tub and relax.

Do I tell him how I feel?

That's up to you. Read the vibes and then decide. Let me know how it goes, I need to head out. I love you and talk soon!

She made it seem so easy, but she had to be right. She had so much experience with guys, and I knew she had had several boyfriends, so it's not like she didn't know what she was discussing. Mother would never discuss flirting with me. It wasn't important because in her eyes marriage and dating was only for certain families and at that point it would already be arranged.

I placed my phone in the cup holder and closed my eyes. I had plenty to think about and the perfect place to do it. What else would I do in the car with no radio?

CHAPTER FOURTEEN

SOPHIE

I parked my Jeep in the driveway and hurried inside. Riley, Luke, and Drew were the only ones left at the house. Shelby and Randy should have been finished with their founders' meeting by now and on their way back, but I needed to get this out now. I couldn't hold it inside.

Riley looked up from the couch. "Hey, Soph … woah, are you okay?"

Drew and Luke came in from the back porch. Drew's gaze took in my expression, and he sprinted to my side. "What's going on? Come sit."

I let him guide me to the couch next to Riley, my hand entwined in his. "I had my theater shift. Which by the way, Courtney needs help with Sasha."

Drew nodded. "Courtney texted me shortly after your shift ended. I've given her some ideas, but that can't be what your expression is from."

"No. Of course not. I decided I would head home after the shift to check in on Mama and see how things are going. Instead of her being home, Rowan was at the house all by himself."

Riley's eyebrows knitted. "That's odd."

"I thought so, too. At first, I thought something had happened to Mama or Caleb, but Rowan said he found out I would be back and possibly stop in at the house so he wanted to see if he could catch me before Mama got home."

Drew squeezed my hand, a knowing look in his eyes. Had he already figured out what had happened?

"Rowan and I walked to the playground in our neighborhood, and I sat on the swings. He talked about how important Mama is and how much he cares about her and our family. Then he … he asked for my blessing to marry her. He doesn't want to ask unless I'm okay with it."

Riley gasped.

"My head is swimming. How do I even begin to sort out what to do?"

"You don't need an answer yet," Riley said.

"I can't leave him hanging for forever."

"Well, no. But he had to know asking you wouldn't result in an immediate response. If he has any inclination into the type of person you are, you wouldn't make that decision lightly. If anything, he probably asked you now *because* it would take you some time."

"Maybe, but what I want to do is ask Mama about things and I can't. I can't ruin a surprise for her." I stood. "I'm going upstairs. I-I don't want to bring the mood down."

"You're not going—"

My eyes pleaded with Riley.

She stopped and nodded.

I gathered my stuff and headed up the stairs. I collapsed in the den on the large L-shaped couch. I shoved a pillow over my head until there were soft steps on the stairs. I didn't have to look to know who it was.

Drew sat next to me and moved me toward him. He settled his arms around me and just held tight, rubbing my arm up and down in a steady rhythm. He waited, not pushing or prodding me. He knew I needed the time.

I sighed and peeked out from the pillow.

His eyes were closed as he held me.

"I don't know how to separate the past from the here and now. I know deep down that Rowan is a great guy. He would take care of Mama and Caleb. He would protect them and put them first. Mama is happy with him. I can see it in her face when she discusses him or when he calls or texts her. He focuses on her needs, and she deserves that. She's been a widow for too long."

Drew eyed me warily. "But?"

"But I can't get past the fact that if she married him everything would change. Dad would continue to be a memory. Would we stay in that house? Would she change her name? I have so many questions."

"That's normal to wonder. I think you would experience that even if your dad was still alive and they had divorced. No one is saying you must have all these answers and handle it perfectly. No one expects that. But I think it's worth noting that you have grown since he first arrived. You would have flat out refused a few months ago and instead you're tearing yourself up about the best solution."

"I guess."

"You don't give yourself enough credit. Just think about it for a few days. Relax and enjoy the day. Why don't we head to the beach and enjoy the beautiful weather?"

"Yeah, maybe."

He squeezed me tight, then nudged me off the couch and winked. "I'll put my suit on and I expect you to have yours on too when I'm done."

I huffed, but it was hollow. I wasn't mad. I was more frustrated that I couldn't come up with the best answer to Rowan's proposal. Drew was right, I needed time not to dwell on it so I could decide how I felt about the whole ordeal. The more I scrutinized the situation, the cloudier it would end up being.

The room was dark and cold. Shelby kept the air conditioner on frigid for the day so it would be refreshing from being outside. Personally, it always felt cold.

My bathing suit from the day before had dried while hanging up in the bathroom. I grabbed the sherbet colored two piece and quickly changed, then I snatched my black cover up and scurried from the room and down the stairs.

Riley still sat on the couch reading a book. She peered over the top as I approached. "Going to the beach with Drew?"

I nodded.

"Nice. It'll be good for you to go and relax."

"That's what he thought, too."

She smiled. "That's why I like him. I don't need to say anything; he already knows."

I stuck out my tongue. "Whatever. We should run tomorrow morning."

"Can do. If you decide you want company in the water, let me know."

"You can come if you want, we aren't making it an exclusive thing." I looked around the room. "Where's Luke?"

She shrugged. "He disappeared again when you two went upstairs. I assumed he went back down to the beach."

"Oh, okay. Well, you know where we are. Get changed and come hang out with us. Shelby and Randy will be back in a bit."

"I know. They both texted me about the meeting. Should be here in about a half hour."

"Plenty of time then."

She shoved her bookmark in her book and closed it. "Okay, okay. I'll get changed and meet you down there. Drew is already outside."

"See you soon." I skipped to the door and saw that Drew sat on the bottom stair of the back steps.

He grinned. "You look gorgeous. Have I said that today?"

"Oh, stop. I do not. This is an old bathing suit."

He pulled me close, wrapped his arms around my waist and drew me in for a slow kiss. "I don't care if it had cartoon characters on it. You're beautiful."

My cheeks reddened.

"You ready?"

I nodded and we walked hand in hand to the beach. I pulled off my coverup and dropped it into the sand. He did the same with his T-shirt. His chest would surprise most people considering he gave off major nerd vibes with his shaggy blond hair and black-framed glasses. But underneath his shirt was a toned chest and arms. Nothing like a body builder or even Randy and Luke who obviously worked out frequently, but Drew was still nice to look at.

"You must stop looking at me like that if you expect to go swimming."

I giggled. "Look at you like what?"

"Like a piece of meat."

I feigned shock. "Me? I would never."

"Yes, you would and are. It's all over your face."

I didn't try to hide it anymore, he was sexy to me, but it was even more fun to make him squirm, at least a little.

He growled. "Soph, seriously."

"Okay, okay. Let's go swimming."

We waded into the water to cool off. It didn't take long in the sun before I was sweating, but the water still had a little chill to it. By the time we left the house in August, it would be warmer.

"Thank you for recommending this."

"No problem."

"I really don't know what I did before we were together. You help calm me so quickly."

"You managed."

I laughed. "Not well. Do you remember me at that party?"

He shuddered. "I do, but I try not to. That wasn't my favorite night of you."

I swam closer to him. "What is your favorite night with me?"

"That's easy. Our first official date. I waited so long to kiss you; I couldn't believe I was actually doing it."

"You're so sweet. Is that seriously your favorite night?"

He nodded. "What's yours?"

"The day at the spring festival."

"We weren't even a couple then."

"I know, but you were present. It was nice to relax around someone. It was like I had been stuck underwater for so long and that day was like coming up for air. I could finally breathe again."

Drew twisted the purple corded bracelet around my wrist.

This time I leaned in and kissed him first on the lips and then trailed to his ear. I got lost in the feeling of the salty water on my mouth as I kissed him.

Splashes of water jolted me back to the reality that we were in the water in broad daylight.

I pulled away from him to see Riley wading through the water with Luke not far behind.

"I found Luke and thought we could all enjoy the sun and water," Riley said. Drew's back faced her. She mouthed, *sorry* and winked.

I smiled and waved off her apology. "The more the merrier. It's a beautiful day."

"Hey, Riley," Drew said as he adjusted his glasses on his nose. He floated closer to Luke to talk about something I couldn't hear, while Riley chatted about the plot of her book.

Even though I didn't plan to read it or care about the book, it was nice to just be around the people who I cared about. Things were right with my friends and boyfriend, now I just had to sort things out with my family.

CHAPTER FIFTEEN

RILEY

The plan had been to wake up early with Sophie and run on the beach. Instead, it had turned into a stormy day with thunderstorms dispersed in between rain showers. Either way, I couldn't run outside.

Once everyone had woken up and gotten breakfast, we planted ourselves in front of the TV and streamed movies. This was our fourth one. The boys had convinced us to watch Marvel movies in order.

"The second Iron Man is so much better than the original," Drew said.

"What? No, it's not," Luke retorted.

Drew looked to Sophie to break the tie. "Oh no. I'm not going there. I don't even know what's happening let alone to come up with an opinion on which one is better. This movie isn't even over yet."

I hid my giggle behind a pillow.

Luke looked to Randy. "What do you think?"

He held his hands up. "I think Iron Man is overrated."

Drew gasped and held a hand to his heart. "Who is

better than him?" He squeezed his eyes shut. "Please don't say Captain America."

"No, that's not who I was going to say."

Luke faced Randy.

"The Hulk."

Drew and Luke both stood.

"Seriously? The Hulk. I can't believe you just said that. That answer is worse!"

I rolled my eyes and made eye contact with Sophie.

She made a goofy face at me then pretended to pass out. She mouthed, *Boys are weird.*

I nodded.

The boys continued to banter, when suddenly the lights went out mid movie.

Sophie smirked. "Well, well, well, looks like we won't be able to finish the movie today after all."

"It might come right back on," Luke said.

Shelby peered out the back doors to look at the sky. "I doubt it. The sky is black. No one will be out to fix the power until this storm passes and who knows how long that'll take."

The boys sighed.

"Now what?" I asked.

Shelby used her phone's flashlight. "I'll look for some candles to light, then we might have to play a board game or something."

Luke stood and crossed the room to Shelby. "I'll help you look."

Shelby smiled at him as longing flickered over her expression. I doubted he noticed, but Sophie and I certainly did. Ever since we had arrived here, we caught the glance she gave him when she thought no one was looking.

While they looked, Sophie and I scoured through the game closet.

"Find anything good?" Randy asked.

"Not really," Sophie said.

"We have the games from before, but they aren't the best games to play with six people. Anyone have any other ideas?" I asked.

Sophie winked then asked, "How about truth or dare? It'll keep things interesting while the storm rages."

Drew groaned. "Really? Truth or dare?"

Sophie made chicken noises at him. "Is someone a scaredy cat?"

"No, but I figured you would be scarred from that game for life after before."

"Me? No. Maybe you were."

"Why don't we see what Luke and Shelby suggest when they get back," Randy said.

I nodded. "That sounds safer."

Sophie pouted. "What a bunch of babies."

Shelby carried an armful of candles with Luke trailing behind her. "Who is a baby?" She placed them around the couches and kitchen, then used matches to light them.

Sophie crossed her arms. "Everyone but me."

I rolled my eyes. "Sophie wants to play truth or dare."

Shelby wiggled her eyebrows. "Ooh, that could keep things interesting."

Sophie pumped her fist in the air. "See? At least Shelby is with me."

"Well, if we play then it has to be nothing illegal for the dares and not trying to purposely hurt anyone's feelings," Randy said.

Sophie sighed. "Fine. Who's in?"

Drew chuckled and raised his hand.

"Fine," I said and pulled a throw pillow onto my lap. "But if someone ends up crying, I blame you, Sophie."

She outstretched her hand to shake. "Deal."

I slapped her hand away.

She laughed. "How should we determine who goes first?"

Shelby plopped on the sofa across from me and raised her hand. "I don't mind going first but remember whoever asks someone the question can't be asked the question in turn. So, if Sophie asked me a question, I can't ask her one right back."

We all nodded.

Sophie rubbed her hands together quickly. "Shelby, truth or dare."

"Truth."

Sophie stroked her chin as she thought of a question. "Do you have a nickname we don't know about?"

"Shelly welly. My aunt thought it would be fun when I was younger and irritate my mother. She definitely irritated my mother more than it bothered me."

"Shelly welly? Where'd she get that one?" I asked.

"No idea. It didn't last long." Shelby surveyed the room, then stared at Randy. "Randy, truth or dare."

He sighed. "Dare"

Her eyebrows rose. "I dare you to take one of the frosted cookies. Put ketchup and mustard on it then eat it."

Randy grinned. "Done."

We watched as he went to the kitchen using the flashlight on his phone as his guide. He created his cookie masterpiece then ate it all in two bites.

I grimaced, that sounded like an awful combination. Of course, I hated mustard so there was that, but even so, ketchup on a frosted cookie? *Barf!*

"Drew, truth or dare?" Randy asked.

"Truth," he said as he leaned against Sophie.

"The power to shrink yourself or to hear someone else's thoughts?"

"Shrink myself, all day. Hearing people's thoughts is a lot of responsibility, plus if you can't control when you hear them, that could get pretty loud." He eyed me. "Riley, truth or dare?"

"Truth."

"Do you like New York City better or Honey Cove?"

"Hmm. That's hard. Do you mean like the infrastructure and development or everything like how my life was in each?"

"The development of the actual place. The location, not necessarily the relationships or connections you had."

I covered my eyes. "New York."

Sophie threw a pillow at me.

"What? He said location, not people. I lived there for sixteen years; the city is in my blood. I haven't even been here a year yet."

"So?" Sophie asked with a pouty face.

"Well, I enjoy Honey Cove, and the sights are growing on me, but New York has its own cool things. More stores and restaurants. There isn't just one grocery store and there are tons of movie theaters. You don't have to go to a whole separate city for certain luxuries. I like the fresh air and openness here, but I grew up with skyscrapers and lots of noise, too."

"I guess you're off the hook."

I stuck out my tongue. "Just being honest. Sophie, truth or dare?"

"Dare."

"Of course. Okay, I dare you to run outside right now, stand in the rain for one minute, and then come back."

"That's it?"

"Yep."

She kicked off her flip flops and ran out the door. She ran down the stairs into the rain, waited, then came back in—drenched from head to toe.

"At least try to make it difficult."

Shelby giggled. "Let me get you a towel before you soak us all."

Sophie shook her head and body like a dog coming in from the rain. "You don't want water everywhere? Why not?" She did it again, harder. "This is fun." She took the towel Shelby offered and rubbed it over her hair. "Let's see who hasn't gone yet. Luke, truth or dare?"

"I'll start with truth."

She tapped a finger to her chin. "What's the best piece of gossip from your boarding school?"

Luke smirked. "This one guy from down the hallway from my room is dating a girl from the sister boarding school, her roommate, *and* a girl back in his hometown. We can't wait for it to blow up in his face."

Shelby's eyes widened.

Randy shook his head.

Sophie gasped. "The girls have no idea?"

"The roommate knows he's dating the other girl, but I don't think the girl at home and the original girl at the sister school knows anything about the other two."

"That's just awful."

Luke nodded. "He thinks he can get away with it. His family is from California with lots of money. I don't think he would care even if he did get caught."

"Someone should tell the girls."

"I'm sure they'll find out sooner or later. You can't exactly hide that forever. My guess is it'll blow up this summer when he's home and his phone never stops going off from the girls at school."

"True."

"Hmm, how about—" Luke stopped when the power kicked back on, followed by the TV. "Do we still want to play or finish the movie?" Luke asked.

"It's getting close to dinner time, so why don't we pause both to get dinner ready while we still have power. Never know when it'll go back off," Shelby said.

Sophie nodded. "I can help if someone tells me what to do."

"I'll set the table when it's time," I said.

Shelby, Luke, Drew, and Sophie headed to the kitchen, leaving Randy and I alone.

"That could have gone so badly without your rule."

"That's why I made it," Randy said.

I played with the fabric of the pillow, running it through my fingers. The rain came down in sheets. I knew if I laid in the bedroom, it would lull me to sleep with the steady rhythm of it hitting the windows or the roof. I had put on a good face with everyone gathered for a rainy-day event, but I felt about as happy as it appeared outside.

My insides were raging their own storm. I told Randy I was fine, that I could handle being patient and waiting, but every day that passed since our conversation, I felt like I had lied.

I couldn't wait. I wanted to be his girlfriend. I wanted to count the days we were together as days as a couple. I didn't want to wonder if someday he would just decide to be friends or if we would waste our last year before college never being official.

Drew and Sophie were happy. They could kiss whenever they wanted to. Every step they took, they made as individuals and as a couple.

It wasn't that I expected much to change between us, but it was getting to a point that I wanted the title. I wanted the comfort of knowing that I was as important to him as he was to me. I wanted the world to know it, too.

"I need to talk to you about something," Randy said, pulling me from my thoughts.

"Oh? What about."

"I'm going back home for a few days. I need to attend some meetings for the company and then I have a shift or two for Morgan's."

I twisted the corner of the pillow. "When would you get back?"

"Not before you'll be back home to see your dad."

"Oh. Okay."

He peered into my gaze. I supposed he was trying to read my expression and decide if I was okay. "I can visit you at the house before I come back to the beach if you want?"

I wasn't sure what I wanted. My dad and Randy got along at Halloween. I wasn't worried about that, but was this a good time to assess what I would do about our situation? I could take the time and evaluate how to approach him again and what I would say if he repeated his reasons.

"I can text you and let you know. I'm unsure what Dad has planned for when he visits."

He nodded. "That's fine." He pushed a stray hair from my face. "Want to set the table? I can help."

"Sure."

We stood and headed for the silverware. I welcomed the mindless chore. If he stared at my expression for too long I knew he could read what I was thinking. He had always been intuitive like that. For once I didn't want him to be, not until I had my plan.

CHAPTER SIXTEEN

I wrung my hands together as I waited for Luke at the bottom of the stairs. After our rainy movie day, we ended up alone before bed. I summoned all the courage I had and asked if he wanted to hang out as just *us* today.

He had agreed, but now that it was here and I was waiting, I wanted to run. The picnic basket was packed with various kinds of sandwiches. I had gotten up early to buy them at the grocery store. There were individual sized bags of chips and pretzels. I had also packed a parfait for dessert, which was in the cooler with the drinks.

My foot jiggled to the beat of my heart—fast and loud.

Luke bounded down the stairs in a navy-blue swimsuit, white T-shirt, and a hunter-green baseball cap.

Heat crawled up my cheeks. He looked good. How would I make it through this and keep my hands off him?

His gaze met mine at the bottom stair and he smiled. "I'm all set. Do I need to bring anything?"

"Nope." I patted the basket and cooler. "I've got it all packed."

"All prepared and ready to go. Hmm, where could you be taking me?"

"To the beach. I have the towels by the door. We can go out the back."

He nodded.

We both reached for the cooler, our hands brushing each other's.

"I can grab this," he said.

"Are you sure?"

He flexed his right arm. "You see these muscles? Of course."

I giggled. Of course, I saw his muscles. I couldn't stop staring at them or at his lips, which enticed me more every time he smiled. Those hazel eyes pulled me into the warmth like a blanket on a chilly day.

He lifted the cooler off the floor easily and waited for me to lead the way.

I had to force my feet to move and to break the trance his body had me in. This was ridiculous. How did I swoon so hard after he had irritated me so much at first? I was a Rowe. I didn't need to lose my head over a boy, even if he was Luke Warrington.

"We must walk a little bit on the beach. I hope you don't mind."

"Not at all when I have such beautiful company."

I blushed. "What are you trying to butter me up for?"

He feigned hurt. "I can't pay you a compliment just because?"

"I don't know, can you? You Warrington men know how to woo the ladies to get things."

"Is that so? Well, the way that I hear it, the Rowe women know how to bat their lashes and sashay away to do the same."

I gasped. "I do not do that."

Luke laughed. "You did at the Christmas ball. It was extremely convincing."

"Well, that was different. Mother told me I had to make it appear we were dating, and you did the same."

"I never pretended, Shelby."

My eyes widened. "You did at first, didn't you?"

"I was persistent because of the arrangement, but anything I ever said to you wasn't because of our parents. I don't believe in being disingenuous just for social gains."

I thought back to all he had said during that time. There were several moments he had complimented me, and I had assumed it was for show, because that's what we were told to do.

"But that doesn't really matter now that you cracked your walls, and I could see you're just a big softie."

I poked him in the side. "Watch who you're calling soft."

We walked a ways down the beach to avoid seeing anyone in case they wanted to go swim. I didn't want to see anyone else except Luke today. It was time we saw how the chemistry could be if we tried acting like a couple.

"Here we go."

He placed the cooler on the ground and helped me spread out the blanket for us to sit on. I placed the basket in the middle, then we sat.

I tucked my feet underneath me and sorted through the basket. "I brought several hoagie options. I wasn't sure what you would pick. There's turkey, ham, roast beef, and Italian."

"Roast beef, please. That sounds delicious."

"I also brought chips and pretzels. The cooler has our drinks and a dessert."

He raised his eyebrows. "What's the occasion?"

"No occasion. I thought it might be nice for us to spend time together."

He grabbed pretzels and a soda, then unwrapped his hoagie. "I like what you're thinking."

I chose an Italian hoagie and unwrapped it. "It's a great day, too. The storms took away so much of the humidity. You can breathe out here without it feeling thick."

He took a bite of his sandwich, a piece of lettuce dangling from his chin.

I giggled. "You, uh … You have something on your face."

He wiped his cheek, completely missing the lettuce.

I leaned forward and wiped his chin with my thumb. I tried to pull away, but he caught my hand.

His fingers were cold from the cooler, but instead of cooling me off, they heated everything up. He stared into my eyes, not blinking.His gaze was intense and full of emotions I didn't know how to read, and then he let go, breaking the contact and taking another bite of his sandwich.

My body was frozen, unable to process that moment.

"I guess I need more etiquette classes so I can eat a hoagie properly without making a mess. That's what I get for only having meals with boys who don't care about appearances like that while at school."

"I can't imagine attending an all-boys boarding school."

He shrugged. "You get used to it. Besides, some of our classes are with the sister school, so it's not entirely all boys all the time."

"What was your favorite class this year?"

"Not really a class so much as a teacher. I had Mr. Simmons for AP Government. He always made things interesting and connected it to us so that we cared about what we were learning."

"That makes sense."

"What about you?"

"I enjoyed my AP Psychology class this year, but the teacher was pretty dull. She has taught this class for the last ten years and knows what she is talking about, but she's so monotone. If it wasn't for the content being interesting, I doubt many people would take the class."

"I don't get that. Why would someone continue to do something if they don't find it interesting?"

"Some people don't have the choice, I suppose."

He took another bite. "If you could do anything this summer what would it be?"

"Anything?"

"Yep, anything. No limits."

I couldn't say my real answer, which was to kiss Luke and ask him to be my boyfriend. So, what else would I want to do? "Maybe go to an amusement park."

"That's it?"

"Yeah. My parents never took me anywhere like that. Father was always too busy, any time of year, and Mother wouldn't spend a day with random people sweating to death on roller coasters."

His eyes widened. "Have you ever gone to an amusement park?"

"Nope."

"Ever ridden a roller coaster? Water ride? Gone on vacation?"

"Unless you count coming to the cove house maybe once or twice a vacation."

"Oh no, that's a tragedy. You can't be seventeen and not have gone on a roller coaster. That's absurd."

"It is what it is. I can't exactly change it."

Luke set his hoagie down on the paper. "That's it. We're visiting an amusement park this summer."

"What? No. We're here all summer."

"So? We can go on a day trip to Carowinds, it's not like one is that far."

"You mean it?"

"Absolutely, even if no one else wants to go. I'll take you. I just couldn't live with myself if I didn't take you on your first roller coaster."

I smiled. I tried not to read too much into his statement. I would do something like that for a friend, regardless of any romantic feelings I had for them. "Then you have a deal."

"Good. I hope you like heights because I'm dragging you on every ride we can manage to fit in with all the lines."

I laughed. "Heights aren't a problem for me."

He winked and finished his hoagie. "That was so good."

"I'm glad you liked it. I found them at the grocery store we went to when we first got here. I wasn't sure which one you'd want."

"Roast beef was an excellent choice. I enjoy a good honey ham sandwich, too, but honestly can never go wrong with a hoagie."

"Good to know."

"What about you? What's your go-to food?"

"Pasta."

He chuckled. "You didn't even hesitate."

"Nope. I have Chef Frank make me pasta all the time."

"Anything goes or …?"

"Fettuccine Alfredo. I could eat that every day if Mother let me and I wouldn't gain like a hundred pounds."

Luke eyed my body as I sat there. "Well, you haven't gained anything like that now. I wouldn't know you secretly had a thing for pasta."

My eyes widened. "And what pray tell do I appear to eat?"

He shook his head. "I'm not touching that question with a ten-foot pole."

"Smart man."

He leaned closer. "For the record though, you can eat whatever you want, you still look amazing."

Heat crawled up my cheeks. "Thanks. You don't look half bad yourself."

His eyes rounded and his smile slowly built. "Is that so?"

I gulped and tried to nod.

He closed the space between us on the blanket. He sat close enough to touch but remained far enough away that I had to imagine our legs touching, our arms embracing one another, and his lips on mine. My breathing came in pants as I tried to control my feelings.

I caught a glimpse of his eyes, and something wriggled around in them that I hadn't seen so openly before. It seemed like desire, but then it flickered until it was masked.

"Should we test out that dessert?"

I took a long drink of water trying to ease the desert that had located itself in my mouth and throat. "Do you like parfaits? I found a strawberry mousse layered with blueberries, raspberries, a layer of Greek yogurt, and topped with strawberry sauce."

Luke licked his lips. "That sounds so good and refreshing."

I dug out the two parfaits from the cooler, handed him a spoon, and focused on eating the dessert, instead of his proximity to me. We ate them in silence.

He tossed his trash in the bag I brought with and then kept it open for me. He stored it back in the cooler and removed the remaining hoagies to place them in the cold.

"That's a good idea, thank you. I hadn't thought about the ones we wouldn't eat."

"It's a trick I learned from my mom. She always had beach picnics or picnics in the middle of the summer and would store them in the cooler after we had picked through what we wanted to eat." He shrugged. "Nothing special."

I twisted the edge of the blanket between my fingers. "Do you want to take a swim?"

"Sure." Luke stood and pulled his shirt up and over his head, tossing the hat on top. He walked to the water as I stared at the sun gleaming over his broad shoulders.

Focus, Shelby. You need to have the talk with him.

I pulled my own coverup off and headed for the water, lagging a little behind him.

He stood several feet ahead of me and up to his waist in the water. "Come on in. It feels good once you're in."

A shiver traveled across my body. "It might feel good when you get used to it, but it's chilly at first."

"Nah, it's perfect temperature." He kicked the water toward me.

Water droplets landed on my legs, as I stood only ankle deep in the waves.

A devilish grin spread across his face.

I held one hand up in front of me. "Don't you do it."

"Do what, exactly?" He kicked again, but harder this time.

"Luke, I'm serious."

He inched closer and kicked again.

I turned my body to the side and twisted to block some of the water. "Luke," I warned.

He leapt toward me, arms stretched around me, and

nudged me farther from the shore. "You'll thank me after." Then he pulled us into the wave as it broke, reaching clear to the bottom of my bathing suit top. He released me as the wave passed.

I gasped at the cool temperature. "Oh, you are so in trouble."

He winked. "You have to catch me before that happens."

I crossed my arms. "You think you're so clever." I punched my hand into the water, sending droplets all around.

His eyebrows rose and then he was splashing me as hard as he could.

I turned my face away and splashed him as hard as I could back, just like when we had first gotten here.

Water flew all around me, some from him and the rest from my own actions. Before I knew it, my long, dark brown hair, clung to the side of my face while the rest flopped to the side in the massive bun I had erected on top of my head. "Time out," I said while placing my hands in a T position.

When I stopped splashing, so did he.

He shook his head to disperse most of the water from his hair.

I pushed what I could from my face and tucked the rest back into my bun unsuccessfully. I pulled the scrunchie from my hair, letting the tangled mess cascade over my shoulders. When I met Luke's gaze, he was watching me. "What?"

"N-nothing." He moved closer and grabbed a piece of my hair, moving it away from my face and behind my ear, hovering before he withdrew his hand.

I closed my eyes and forced the words from my mouth. "I think we should date and see what happens." I took a deep breath and held it as the blood roared through my ears. My heart pounded as I waited for what he would say. I didn't dare open my eyes. If I did, I could see his rejection or something else and I didn't want the thought to shatter, not yet.

Luke grazed my cheek with the outside of his hand. "I would like that."

My eyes popped open to take in his expression. "You would?"

He smiled. "Are you really so surprised I could be interested?"

I shrugged, then averted my gaze at the water moving around us. "Maybe?"

"Hmm, maybe my flirting isn't as on point as I thought it was."

I laughed and relaxed my shoulders at the unexpected humor. "How come you didn't ask me out on a date sooner then?"

"I certainly thought about it, especially after the night we spent together on New Year's Eve." He ran his hands through his wet hair. "But with me going right back to school, and the fact I couldn't promise spending much time together except maybe Easter, I didn't think the timing was right."

I gazed into his eyes. "And now?"

He moved closer to me in the water. "I still think boarding school could be a problem, but we have two more months of summer to see if there is something real between us." He grabbed my hand and raised it from the water as he held it. "At least on my end, I think we could have something real."

I grinned. "I'm glad to hear you say that, because I think so, too."

He dropped my hand letting it hit the water and then

splashed me. "Well, let's see what else the day can bring."
He winked and waded from the water.

I didn't have a clue what he had planned, but I
followed him anyway, the butterflies soaring around my
stomach.

CHAPTER SEVENTEEN

SOPHIE

My phone sat on the bed in front of me. I toyed with the idea of calling Mama and secretly discussing things about Rowan, but every time I managed to pick it up and click on her contact, I couldn't do it. How was I supposed to bring up Rowan without her suspecting something? I needed to know what she felt about him and if it was even something she wanted.

Maybe she never wanted to get married again. Maybe she didn't plan to marry until Caleb and I were older.

I shook my head. Who was I kidding? Mama liked Rowan, maybe even loved him. The way she seemed after being out with him and talking to him on the phone, was the same buzz I felt deep inside when Drew and I spent time together and made out. It was a vibration sent out in waves and only detectable by those who experienced it—a recognition of deep feelings.

I sighed and picked up my phone again. Even if I didn't talk to her about Rowan, I still needed to check in. I clicked the contact card and waited until she picked up. "Hey, Mama."

"Hey, Soph. How's the beach?"

"Really nice. The weather has been pretty great, minus a few days so far. How are you and Caleb?"

I could hear dishes shuffling in the cabinet in the background. "We're good. You know how your brother is. He's absorbed into videogames. I think he's enjoying having more control over the TV in the family room, but otherwise he seems to be the same."

I laughed. "He better not get used to it. I'm still coming home in a few months."

Mama laughed too. "You two are silly. You both have TVs in your room and yet you fight over the one out here."

"It's about power, Mama, not the TV."

"I know. So, what's up? I'm surprised you're calling."

"What? I can't call home without there being something?"

"You can, but you usually don't."

"Fine. I was letting you know I'll be home in two days. Riley's dad is coming to Honey Cove from New York City, and she didn't drive to the cove house. I figured I would drop her off at her house, maybe stay for dinner, and then stay at the house for a day or so before heading back to the beach."

"That would be nice. I miss you and I'm sure Caleb does, too, even if he won't admit it. Maybe we can even have a nice dinner the second night before you head back."

"Sounds good, Mama. I love you."

"I love you, too."

"See you soon."

"Be safe, sweetie."

I placed the phone on the nightstand next to my bunk bed. Laying back on my pillow, I stared at the wooden bottom of the bunk above me. When I got home maybe I could find a way to talk to Rowan. If not, I would come up with a different plan.

I exhaled and headed for my clothes. It was time to get in pajamas and relax before bed. No doubt Riley would wake me up early wanting to go for a run. She had become addicted to her morning runs when the weather cooperated. I didn't know if it was the sand, or she just wanted to keep pushing herself, but she seemed more obsessed with it than when she was at home.

I settled for purple with white polka dot pajama bottoms and a baggy school spirit wear shirt. Pulling my covers back, I plopped down and snuggled underneath the blankets, as Shelby and Riley came into the room. "You two coming to bed already?"

"Yep," Riley said.

Shelby nodded.

I raised an eyebrow. "I figured you would stay out all day and night with Mr. Warrington."

Shelby's cheeks flushed. "We spent a lot of time together."

"So, how was it?"

Riley sat across from me on Shelby's bed, while Shelby stayed closer to the bathroom door.

"It was good … We decided to go on a date."

Riley and I cheered.

"That's awesome, Shelby," I said.

"It's a start. I don't know what will happen."

"Who cares? You at least get to explore how you both feel."

Riley nodded. "Shelby, she's right. This is the best scenario."

"So … what'd you two do?"

Shelby smiled. "We started with a picnic and then once we got in the ocean, I blurted it out and he agreed to see what would happen. He even said he thinks there could be something real between us."

I clapped. "And?"

"Then he thought it would be fun to come back and go in the hot tub. Then we joined you all for dinner."

I wiggled my eyebrows at her. "Anything *steamy* happen in the hot tub besides the water?"

Riley giggled. "Soph, that was a terrible pun."

"Psh, I thought it was fabulous." I faced Shelby. "Well?"

"No. We kept it G-rated for your information, not that it's any of your business."

"*Yawn.* You could have at least used the fiery atmosphere to spice things up. You seriously just soaked in the hot tub?"

"We talked. I asked him about boarding school. He asked me about Honey Cove High. We don't really know what it's like to be around each other all the time."

"There's nothing wrong with that. When do you go on your date?" Riley asked.

"Probably in a few days."

Riley hung her head. "Oh, when I'm at home?"

"Most likely. I don't want to leave when you're all here, but don't worry. I'll tell you all the details when you get back."

"You better," Riley said.

I rolled to my side. "Are you excited to see your dad, Riley?"

"Yeah. It's been so long, but it's also so weird. I never know how to incorporate him into our life in Honey Cove. Our routines are so different and when he's here it feels strange. I don't know if that makes sense."

"Sure, habits are built over time, when he isn't part of it, it can be strange to still do them," Shelby said.

Riley looked at the floor and played with the bed covers.

"What else is going on?" I asked.

"What? Nothing."

I folded my arms. "Nope. I don't buy it."

Shelby glanced at me as if asking a question.

Riley sighed. "Okay, okay. I guess I'm happy for some time away from Randy to figure things out."

I sat up. "Did something happen?"

"Well, after the bonfire, we talked about things."

"The bonfire? That was days ago."

She fiddled with her fingers. "I know, but I didn't know what to say about it, so I kept it to myself."

Shelby sat next to Riley on the bed and patted her leg. "You know you can tell us anything, right?"

Riley nodded. "I just didn't want to say it out loud because then our conversation was real, and I didn't know what to think."

"Okay, so what happened?"

"I told him that I wanted to see us be together. Like really together as a couple and he simply stated the timing wasn't right. He wanted things to be right with his family so it didn't mess us up. I said I could understand and do that. Only now I don't feel like I can. You two are moving forward with your guys and I feel stuck. I like Randy so much it hurts to think of him not being around, but I hate this spot we're in now. I want us to be a couple and to be able to feel more connected. I want to meet his family and I want that label as silly as it sounds because I know it's just a stupid word."

"Don't say it's silly. You're allowed to want and feel what you do and that doesn't have to be diminished by anyone or anything."

Shelby nodded. "I think it's a security thing for you. I

don't think you doubt how he feels about you, but it gives your relationship the security to flourish. There isn't a question of changing feelings or how others view your relationship."

Riley nodded and swiped at her eyes. "I … I think I love him. I would do anything for him, but it just feels like that's denied when I can't say he's my boyfriend. We have a year before college, and I don't want that to be wasted. Liking each other and being together are different and I feel like it limits our relationship. We can grow as friends without being together, but not in a relationship."

"Those are all valid concerns, Riley." Shelby sighed. "I wish he didn't focus so much on his dad's transgressions and instead focused on how you two being together can make him stronger. I see it in founders' meetings. He acts like the whole thing lands on his shoulders. He doesn't need to bear the brunt of his father's actions solely on himself. Not to mention it will be a lifelong struggle for him. Timing like that will never be perfect."

"So, what do I do?"

"I think you're doing it," I said. "You're thinking of how you feel and deciding what you want. You can't control Randy, but you can control you. No matter how you feel about him you must decide if you're okay being in this spot. If it doesn't change, can you handle being in between even with someone you might love? If it's a yes, then okay, you let it keep happening. If it's a no, then you must tell him that and let him know it can't happen. Then it'll be his turn to decide if it's something he can change or wants to."

Riley covered her face with her hands. "Why does this feel so complicated? We care about each other, why can't that just mean we're a couple?"

"Life is complicated, unfortunately," I said.

"Well, that sucks."

Shelby gave a weak smile. "Things will work themselves out. And if Randy doesn't realize the amazing person you are because of his family turmoil, then he's an idiot to miss out on a relationship with you."

I nodded. "And I'll beat him up."

Riley giggled. "You must stop threatening to beat him up. First, I don't know that you could actually be successful in that action and second is I don't want him hurt."

I held my hands, palms up by my shoulders. "Just putting it out there."

"I know and I appreciate the support, I just wish it wasn't even an issue." She stood and walked to the dresser. "I'm getting changed then going to bed. I don't want to dwell too much on it. I'll know better once I'm back from the week at home and then maybe he will think clearly or change his reasoning."

"I hope so," Shelby said.

Riley grabbed clothes and headed into the bathroom.

"What is he thinking?" I asked.

Shelby shrugged. "He can't see the forest for the trees, I suppose."

"Uh?"

Shelby giggled. "He is so focused on his family and their legacy; he can't see what he's missing out on. It doesn't have to be an either or situation, and yet that's what he keeps making it." She sighed. "I can understand his side of it, though. He feels responsible for his family's legacy and the workers at his family's company. I used to feel that as well. I mean I still do, but I realized my happiness makes me a better person *for* the company and the community. Everything doesn't have to be perfect for us to have a relationship to make us happy, but he hasn't learned that yet."

"Well, he better figure it out. Do you think she would move on?"

"Maybe. Only she can answer that."

"I—"

Riley exited the bathroom, a cheerful expression plastered on her face. "Bedtime. Soph, want to run tomorrow?"

I groaned. "Sure."

Next time, I needed a best friend that wasn't such a morning person.

CHAPTER EIGHTEEN

RILEY

"You are absolutely the designated driver this school year," I said.

"Is that so? I'm not driving twenty minutes out of the way to pick you up and then head back to school. That's a whole hour of beauty sleep I wouldn't get," Sophie said.

"Psh. I've driven you to school plenty of times."

"Yeah, the last ten minutes or so. That's not a hassle."

"Fine. Then you'll drive when we go somewhere on the weekends. I love this Jeep." I closed my eyes and let the wind rush over me from the open roof and doors. "It's such a summer vibe."

Sophie grinned. "I can't disagree there."

We drove past Morgan's Market and usually my stomach fluttered as butterflies swirled from the chance I would see Randy as I drove by, but today, my stomach sank like a pile of rocks dropped from a bridge.

It had been good to tell the girls the other night about what had happened between us but announcing what had happened cemented more of my feelings and that somehow made things worse.

I couldn't pretend that I had all these large feelings for Randy and yet we weren't together. If I watched Sophie or Shelby be in a relationship like that, I would tell them they were being naïve and he was playing games. And I knew with everything in my heart that Randy wasn't doing it on purpose or even based on me, but it didn't dull the ache I felt that we weren't more.

"Will your father be at the house when we get there?"

I checked the time on the dash of her Jeep—4:00 pm. "He should have arrived in the airport at two, so, yeah, as long as nothing was delayed."

She nodded. "That'll be good then. You won't have to wait for him to get there."

"Yep."

Sophie eyed me and then refocused on the road. "What's on your mind? Randy or your dad?"

I sighed. "Stop reading my body language."

She laughed. "Can't help it. You're radiating doom and gloom vibes."

"Mostly Randy I suppose. Just thinking about what we talked about two nights ago. I have no new epiphanies, so I didn't want to drag the mood down."

"You don't have to feel guilty for saying something. If you're going through something then it's normal to share it with friends. If you don't want to share, that's fine, but I'm not docking you friend points if you mention it more than once in a week or even in a day."

I smiled. Sophie always knew how to lighten the situation even when the weight on my chest was too heavy to lift. "You're the best friend ever."

She winked. "I know." She turned up the radio and we belted a few pop songs before pulling into the long driveway at my mom-mom's house. As Sophie parked, the three of them were sitting on the porch, sipping something out of a glass. If I had to bet, it was probably Mom-mom's sweet tea.

I shifted in the seat. "You're staying for dinner, right?"

"I can as long as you want me to."

"Of course."

She nodded and turned off the Jeep.

I grabbed my bookbag from between my feet that was stuffed with a few things and hopped out.

We walked toward the porch.

"Hey, Riles and Sophie," Mom called.

Sophie waved as I bounded up the stairs.

Dad opened his arms and I went in for a hug. "Hey."

"Hi, Dad. How was your flight?"

He let go and held a hand over his stomach. "Bumpy. The turbulence wasn't the best, but I'm glad to be back on the ground now."

"Me, too."

Mom-mom rose from the porch swing. "Shall we head inside? I can get started on dinner. Sophie, I hope you're staying, too."

"Of course, Mrs. Brooks. I wouldn't miss your cooking."

Mom-mom laughed and patted her on the shoulder. "You're my favorite."

Sophie beamed and I rolled my eyes. Mom-mom managed to tell Sophie and Shelby that every time it was just one of them, but they ate it up anyway.

We all trailed behind Mom-mom and Sophie into the house. They went to the kitchen, while Mom, Dad, and I hovered in the hallway a little longer.

"Are you getting taller?" Dad asked.

"I don't think so. I haven't gotten taller since like seventh grade, Dad."

He stroked his chin. "I don't know, you seem taller."

Mom rolled her eyes. "Beau, maybe you just shrunk."

He gasped. "I did not shrink."

She tapped his back. "Then your posture sucks because you don't look as tall as normal."

He crossed his arms. "Well, I see where this is headed."

Mom stuck out her tongue.

Were they *flirting*? I oscillated between the feelings of disgust and amazement that after everything they could flirt with each other, although I didn't want to see it.

"Anyways, I have a surprise for you, Riley," Dad said.

"A surprise? What is it?"

Mom and Dad exchanged glances that told me she already knew what it was.

"Zoe and Madison will be here in two days to visit and will leave the day I do on Sunday."

I squealed. "They're coming *here*? Oh my god. Those little buttheads, they didn't say anything."

Zoe and Madison were my best friends from New York. While we didn't talk every day like we used to, I would forever consider them best friends. We had too much history between us for it not to be like that.

Mom giggled. "That was the point. We told them not to say anything. We wanted to tell you."

I twisted the strap of my bag around my finger. "Does that mean we must stay here the whole time, or can I take them to the cove house for a day or so?"

"That's up to you, sweetie," Mom said.

I looked at my dad. "But you'll be here. If we go to the cove, then I would see you for less time."

"It won't be the only time I'm here again, but that's up to you. You have my blessing to go, though. I know you'll want to go to the beach and show them your friends and all. I don't mind that. We can still spend a day together before they get here."

I hugged them. "You're the best, thank you."

Mom kissed the top of my head.

Dad beamed. "You've earned it and we figured you were overdue in seeing them."

Mom linked arms with me. "Shall we go check on Sophie and Mom-mom in the kitchen?"

I nodded and walked arm and arm with her.

Sophie was rolling out dough while Mom-mom watched carefully.

"Whatcha doing?" I asked.

"Sophie is helping me to roll out the peach cobbler dough."

My stomach grumbled. "Yum. I can already taste it."

Sophie stared with great intensity at the dough and rolling pin.

I moved closer to her and then poked her in the side while she focused.

Her gaze met mine and she glared. "I'm concentrating, Riley."

"I know, that's what made it fun to do."

Mom-mom shooed me away from her. "Don't bother her. I don't want uneven dough for the peach cobbler."

I saluted her. "Aye aye, captain."

Mom elbowed me. "Riley how about you help by setting the table?"

I groaned. "Okay." The plates were kept in a large China cabinet off to the side of the dining room. Mom-mom had several designs she used, but since this was family, we would use the most basic design—simple roses and vines that circled the outside. After placing the five plates, I went to the utensil drawer and grabbed enough forks, knives, and spoons for us and placed them on paper towel napkins. We didn't need anything fancy.

Mom and Dad disappeared from the kitchen, so I went

to Mom-mom and Sophie when I finished. "Need any more help?"

"The pork chops are in the oven, but you can cut up some vegetables for a salad."

I grabbed cucumbers, tomatoes, green bell peppers, and carrots to cut up. "So, did you know about the surprise, Mom-mom?"

She grinned. "Of course. Your parents can't keep secrets from me."

Sophie's brows knitted. "A surprise?"

"Yep. Zoe and Madison, my friends from New York, are coming down for a visit. I was thinking of bringing them to the cove house to meet everyone."

"That'll be so fun. The boys will be outnumbered."

I laughed. "Yes, they will. I think you'll like them. Zoe is a lot like you."

Sophie winked. "You sure you want double?"

"I can take it."

"You say that now, but we will see."

I tossed a piece of cucumber at her head.

Mom-mom gave me a death glare, while Sophie ate the piece I threw.

"No throwing food in my kitchen."

I hung my head like a scolded toddler. "Yes, Mom-mom."

She cracked a smile and shook her head. "You two go ahead and relax. I'll call when dinner is ready."

We headed for my room to wait. I hadn't seen my parents on our way. Where could they have gone off to?

Dinner had felt like normal, with us all seated at the table, talking and eating. Sophie had just left, and I sat swinging on the porch too full to get up and do anything. Three helpings of peach cobbler and I was regretting it.

Mom-mom peered from the screen door. "Want company?"

"Sure," I said as I patted the space next to me.

She carried two large glasses of the sweet amber liquid.

I slowed the swing and took a long swig of the sweet tea while she sat. When we were situated, we pushed off to get our usual rhythm.

"I've missed you, Riley bug."

I snuggled next to her. "I missed you, too. I can't believe we're in the last week of June already."

"Summer is like that. You blink and it'll slip from your fingers."

I stared at the horizon as the sky filled with deep oranges, pinks, and purple. The sunset was never more beautiful than in this exact spot on the porch swing.

"Are you enjoying the cove house?"

I nodded. "It's gorgeous, Mom-mom. So big and the beach is right there. I never thought I would be a beach bum. I never cared about going to the beach when we lived in New York, so it's so strange. I love running on the beach."

She held her arm next to mine. "You're getting darker in the sun. Make sure you're using sunscreen."

I giggled. "I know, Mom-mom."

"You laugh, but it's not just the health of your skin that it damages, you also look older over time. Take it from someone who didn't pay much attention at your age to my skin care routine." She pointed to her cheeks and forehead. "Now look at all the sunspots and wrinkles I have."

"You're still beautiful, though."

She squeezed my leg. "Bless you, child, but it could have been better. Is everyone getting along living together?

I can't imagine it being easy with six different people and personalities in a tight space."

"So far it's working. We all do what we want every day, so we aren't always together. Just depends on our schedules, too."

"That sounds nice." She cocked her head. "How are things between you and Randy?"

My face paled before I could control it. It didn't matter, though, because she caught every moment of my reaction. There was no point in hiding it. "Depends on how you look at it, I suppose."

"And how do you look at it?"

I sighed. "Things could be better. I tried to ask why we weren't a couple yet and he said the timing still isn't right. I don't know how to still understand that and reconcile my feelings and needs."

"I like that boy, but as I'm a little biased, you must listen to your heart. If it's saying something you need to follow that."

"What if it leads me somewhere he isn't?"

"If that boy lets you go, then he doesn't deserve the enormous heart you have. No matter who he is."

I leaned my head on her shoulder. "Thanks, Mom-mom."

"You're welcome, darlin'. Just remember no one is ever more important than what *you* need to be happy."

The condensation on my glass dribbled down my hand. Her words swirled in my head as we moved back and forth. The crickets became louder as the sun continued to set. By the time I returned to the cove house, I would have to make my decision and plan, but for now, I tried to soak in the moment before I blinked and it was over.

CHAPTER NINETEEN

SOPHIE

After dinner at Riley's, I headed home in the Jeep. I had planned to arrange a day to pick her up, but with her friends coming from New York, she would drive them. I wasn't sure how I felt about meeting the infamous Zoe and Madison. Of course, I had heard many stories over the previous months since I met Riley, but it was intimidating to meet friends she had for almost a decade.

I wasn't trying to compete, but the thoughts crept in and preyed on my insecurities. What if they didn't like me? Would it matter to Riley at this point and change our friendship? I thought I could confidently say that no it wouldn't, but I'd be lying.

The house lights were on, and in the driveway was Mama's SUV and Rowan's Porsche SUV. He was visiting, which had me all fluttery from nerves. On the one hand I could try and sneak in the conversation I wanted to have with Mama, but on the other, I had to interact with him around my family and I wasn't sure I could be convincing given the situation.

Shadows danced in front of the windows as someone

inside moved. If I had to guess, I would say everyone was in the family room watching something on TV. Caleb generally unhinged himself from his videogame console when Rowan was around.

I hopped out and grabbed my bag from the backseat before entering the house. As predicted, Mama and Rowan sat on the side of the couch closest to the door, while Caleb lounged on the oversized armchair.

"Hi, honey," Mama said as she stood to hug me.

"Hello," I replied.

"Aw, man," Caleb mumbled.

"Dweeb, aren't you happy to see me? You can relish in my awesomeness."

He rolled his eyes. "I'd rather you be at the beach. I can have the whole house to myself."

"Enough, you two. Five seconds and you're already bickering."

I giggled. "Not bickering, just flexing my authority."

"Well, go flex your authority in your room to drop your stuff, then come back out."

I nodded and walked to my room. I breathed in the familiar scents of my perfume and moisturizer. It felt nice to be home, even though I thoroughly was enjoying the getaway. There's something about my bed in my bedroom that evoked a different feeling to me, though. I placed my bag on my bed and headed back to the family room.

Mama had moved from the couch, and I assumed she was the person making noise in the kitchen.

I stooped below the TV's line of sight and went into the kitchen.

"How was dinner with Riley?"

"Good. She found out her friends from New York are visiting soon."

Mama faced me. "Oh, how fun. I'm sure she was so excited. When will they be here?"

"In two days. She's bringing them to the cove house for a night or so to meet everyone."

"Oh my, five girls in one house? That will be something."

"Yeah, definitely." I pulled out a chair and sat.

Mama studied my expression. "Are you worried about their visit?"

"No. Maybe. Is that dumb?"

"Not at all. But I've seen you two spend time together on numerous occasions and you have nothing to worry about with her old friends coming here. They will go home and you'll still be her friend."

How did she know what bothered me about the situation? Was that a mother's intuition or was I that obvious?

"Want to sit and watch a movie with us?"

"Sure." What else would I do? It felt too weird to stay in my room while everyone was spending time together. Not to mention, maybe I could find a way to talk to Rowan alone.

Mama didn't fall asleep until the last twenty minutes of the movie.

Rowan draped the royal-blue and gray Afghan over her when it happened.

We finished the movie and Caleb told Rowan goodnight before he headed to his room.

This was the perfect time to do it.

Rowan stood and walked to the door. "Goodnight, Sophie. Tell your mom I'll call her tomorrow."

"Wait." I stood and stopped a few feet from him. "I was wondering if I could talk to you." I leaned in close and whispered, "You know, about what you asked me before."

He peered over my shoulder to look at Mama.

I gestured outside and he nodded.

The sun had set and the sky was dark. The moon was unobstructed by clouds. It was the perfect night to look at the stars, but I didn't want to go down that rabbit hole. It would lead to thoughts about my father and if I was going to have this conversation with Rowan, I couldn't think about that.

I sat on the front step and kicked at a clump of dirt with my sneaker. "I'm sorry I kind of bolted the last time we talked."

Rowan sat on the step next to me but kept a good distance away. "You don't have to apologize. I asked because I wanted to know how you felt about it. And I got my answer."

"Not really. It took me off guard mostly. I hadn't expected us to talk about that. I honestly never thought of Mama getting married again. It's not something I planned or even considered. So, when you asked, my head spun with all these questions, and I didn't know how to resolve that."

"That's okay. To be honest, I expected it not to be a resounding yes."

"It's not a no either. I haven't really decided one way or the other. I feel like I need to know some things first."

He turned to face me. "Anything you want to ask, just go for it."

He had no idea how dangerous that statement was, but lucky for him, I didn't plan to ask anything crazy. "Have you ever been married before?"

"No, and your mom is the only person I have ever thought of marrying."

"If I said yes, what's your idea of a timeline?"

"Nothing set in stone. Of course, I'd want to marry your mom, but I don't have a date set and it would depend on her comfort level, too."

"Okay. So potentially it would be a semi-long engagement?"

"Yes."

"Would you move in with Mama before the wedding?"

"Depends on you and Caleb and how you feel about it, along with what your mama wants to do."

My lips twisted to the right as I contemplated his answers. So far they were better than I could have hoped for, but it didn't fully assuage the sinking feeling in my stomach when I thought it could happen. "Do you think you would want to move if you got married?"

"Not necessarily." He combed his fingers through his hair. "Sophie, I'm not going to do anything that you, Caleb, or your mom wouldn't all agree on. I don't want to upset any of you or tread on the life you've all recreated after your father died. Faye is fiercely protective of you two. She would do anything for the both of you over her own happiness and needs. If you or Caleb felt uncomfortable with a decision, I want you to know you can tell her or even me. I want us to be a team. I'm not here to replace anyone or anything."

"I can tell Mama really likes you. She's happier since you've been around."

Rowan smiled. "She makes me happy, too. And Caleb is hysterical."

I smirked. "Don't tell him that; it'll go to his head."

Rowan chuckled. "I'd like to know you better, too. I

know I've said that before, but I do mean it. When you're ready of course."

I nodded. "Maybe we can start there?"

"Absolutely. Just tell me when and where." His shoulders relaxed and the lines on his forehead weren't as creased. He truly meant what he said.

I needed to remember that when I doubted what things would be like.

Clearly, he wanted everyone to be comfortable with the situation. If that didn't say everything about his character, then I didn't know what else would convince me. I could do this for Mama. I could get to know him and then decide. I owed her that much.

"How about in July? I have a few shifts at the theater, and I can sleep over here so we can do something."

"July is perfect." He glanced at his watch and stood. "I should head home." He walked toward his SUV. "Thank you for considering this. Goodnight, Sophie."

I waved. "Goodnight."

When he had pulled out of the driveway, I went back inside and locked the doors. Mama still laid on the couch. I shut off the lights and TV and headed for my room. All the driving and stress had made me tired. Tomorrow would be a full day of family time and I needed all the sleep I could get. By the time my head hit the pillow, I was already slipping off to sleep.

CHAPTER TWENTY

SHELBY

My heart practically leapt from my chest. Luke was waiting for me downstairs, while I finished getting ready. No one else was at the house but us, which should have been weird, considering we were discovering what we were to each other, but didn't. There was a natural comfort in knowing I was here with Luke *alone*.

What wasn't comfortable was the idea that this was our first official date after announcing we wanted to discover what this was between us. I knew he planned to take us to an amusement park since my confession, but beyond that, I had no idea what he expected or planned.

I smoothed the front of my peach-colored cotton tee. I also wore my only pair of denim shorts—a piece of clothing I had to smuggle into my closet because my mother didn't approve of denim. Not ever.

Luke said I needed to dress in an outfit I could essentially play in, so a pencil skirt or sundress didn't sound appropriate. He also warned me against wearing flip flops, so I had to pull out my sneakers I used to workout. I stared at my reflection one last time, before heading downstairs.

Luke waited by the door. He wore a pair of gray khaki shorts and a light-turquoise t-shirt. As he turned he smiled, the blue tint of his hazel eyes sparkled. "Are you all set to ride some rides?"

"I think so."

He rubbed his palms together. "Let's head out then. I'll drive."

I followed behind as he walked to his hunter-green Audi, while I locked the door.

His arms intercepted me as I reached for the door handle. He held it open and waited as I climbed in. "Thank you."

He bowed like he was part of the help and then got in, too. "You're welcome, madam."

I giggled. "Madam? What are you, forty?"

"No *madam*. Got it."

"Does that usually work?"

He wiggled his eyebrows. "I don't know; you tell me."

"No. No, it doesn't," I said, suppressing a laugh.

"Aw, man. I had a whole scenario planned on, now that won't happen."

"I hope you're kidding."

Luke smirked. "Of course." He fiddled with the radio stations until he found one that played classic rock. He backed out of the driveway and headed for the highway. "Okay, so even with our early start, there's no way we could ride everything at Carowinds today. So, what do you think you'd want to ride the most? Roller coasters? Or do you want to do the carnival type rides like the big boat that goes back and forth shooting you high into the air like a pendulum?"

"Honestly, I have no idea. I've never been, so maybe we do what you like and once I go on a few we can see."

"That works. This will be so much fun. I still can't

believe you've never been to an amusement park. That's like a crime against humanity."

"That's definitely not a crime against humanity."

"Okay, well a crime against you."

"Possibly, but I've told you before, my parents are just different. That's not their focus."

Luke glanced in my direction. "I know, but my parents have a lot in common with yours and they just aren't like that."

"Well, I'm sure they married for love and family, not just to be a perfect couple to the public regardless of their initial feelings for each other."

His brows drew together. "What do you mean?"

"My mother wanted to marry into a well-to-do family. It didn't really matter who it was as long as their social standing was adequate for her ambitions. I guess they care about each other enough to tolerate a marriage and have me, but it doesn't give me the warm fuzzies like a marriage should."

"That's so crazy."

I shrugged. "It is what it is. How'd your parents meet?"

"They actually met at the dentist."

"The dentist?"

He nodded. "I know, it's a crazy story, but true. My mom was getting her teeth cleaned and had sat in the waiting room for her appointment. My father left his appointment, tripped over the rug, and literally landed in her lap."

I gasped. "Oh no."

"Oh yes. He was mortified; he said he tried to stand as quickly as possible, but he couldn't get a good handle and laid in her lap a little longer than he had wanted. When he finally stood, she had burst into a fit of giggles. She was laughing so hard she didn't even hear her name called. She went in for her appointment and he waited to try to figure out a way to apologize and make it up to her."

"How do you recover from that?"

Luke smiled. "When she finished her dentist appointment, he sat waiting for her and as she exited the door he stood and asked if he could buy her coffee and a meal to say sorry for practically laying on her. She had surprised the heck out of him and said yes. Later he asked her why she ever said yes to a date with him, and she told him she liked a man that could make her laugh."

"That's so sweet."

"It's definitely a good meet cute."

I scrunched my nose. "How do you know that term?"

"Hello? I watch romantic comedies, remember."

"Right … well, I like it. My parents have nothing like that. They went to high school together and got together later in college. How boring is that?"

"Maybe it's more than you think it is. Have you ever actually heard the whole story?"

"Well, no. Mother doesn't talk about it past they got together. I doubt I could ever hear the actual story unless my Aunt Delilah told me. She would tell me the little details."

"You should ask her sometime then."

"Yeah, maybe, at least we both know how it feels to be an only child. Did you ever wish for siblings?"

"Sometimes, but honestly I enjoyed having my parents' attention on me and doing things. They were busy, so I can't imagine them splitting their time with more than one child."

"That makes sense."

"What about you?"

"I wanted siblings. I used to wish that Aunt Delilah could be my sister instead of my aunt. She always told me stories and would take me on trips. She was the perfect companion when I felt lonely around my parents. On the other hand, I'm glad no one else was subjected to the kind of expectations and responsibilities I had."

"Is it getting any better?"

"Somewhat. Mother still watches me like she's waiting for me to screw it up, but at least she doesn't vehemently disagree anymore. If she does, she doesn't voice it, which works for me at least. I still wish we could have some kind of relationship where I could talk to her about things. I end up talking to Mrs. Brooks more than I do my own mother."

He reached across the console and squeezed my hand. "You've always got me, too."

I smiled. "I know. You've helped me see a lot of things."

"I'm glad I can help."

"So, what's your favorite ride at Carowinds?"

"Hmm, I like most of the roller coasters. I don't think I have just one ride I'd go on like a hundred times until my legs fell off."

"Why roller coasters? Is it the speed?"

"Nah, that part is cool I suppose, but I'm more in it for the view."

I crinkled my nose. "The view? That makes no sense."

"At the top of the first hill on any roller coaster. I don't clamp my eyes closed. Instead, I look out in every direction, as far as I can and I take it all in. It's like the same feeling I get in the middle of a body of water. It reminds me of how tiny I am in this world and of the beauty we all go too fast to pay attention to."

I smiled. "I like the sound of that."

He nudged my arm. "You'll have to tell me if it's worth it when we get to the top of your first roller coaster."

I laughed. "So, what's something you've never done?"

Luke stroked his chin. "Hmm, I've never gone bungee jumping."

I raised an eyebrow. "Is that something you would do?"

"Probably not. I don't mind the heights, but free falling to your death with nothing but a bungee cord and harness to protect you doesn't exactly sound like the best plan to me."

"Fair enough. I don't think I'd ever do that either. I'm not really a thrill-seeking type of person."

"If you could spend your evening in any season doing anything, what would it be?"

"Spring and sitting in a nice comfy chair with the sun streaming in the window, the breeze blowing through, and reading a book."

"I didn't have you pegged for spring."

"Which season did you think I'd say?"

"Fall or winter."

"I like them, too, for their own reasons, but spring is the best. The sixty-degree weather feels like a heat wave after winter and it's like the ultimate optimistic season in my opinion."

"Optimistic? Can a season be optimistic or pessimistic?"

"I think so. You have similar weather in fall, but it feels different after coming down from summer. The temperatures are cool, and we grab blankets and coats and huddle in front of bonfires, which are nice. But those same cool temperatures in the spring are a chance to break outdoors after being shut inside and it triggers plants to grow and the growth of life. It feels like the best way to explain the hope of mother nature."

"Interesting. I wouldn't have thought of it that way, but you have a point."

I smiled. "I don't think I've ever said that out loud before." I stared at the car radio. We had already been on the road for about an hour. "How much longer do we have until we arrive?"

Luke glanced at the dash and then to me. "About forty-five more minutes."

I nodded and watched the scenery blur. It was strange that I could feel equal measures of calm and anxious when I was with Luke. It was like this was supposed to happen, but then I would consider the possibilities or if he kissed me and my nerves cranked up the dial.

"I'm happy you agreed to come with me." Luke glanced toward me every few seconds.

"Me, too. I like spending time with everyone but it's also nice to just spend time together, just you and me."

Luke grinned. "You know I like the sound of that."

"The sound of what?"

"You and me."

My cheeks flushed. We kept dancing around our conversation. I guess we were intrigued to see how this would turn out. Would we have chemistry? Or should we just be friends? I hoped it was the former because I couldn't imagine just being friends. Just the sight of him made my pulse quicken. How could that reaction turn into just friends?

"Don't be nervous. It'll be so fun."

I gulped for air. We stood in line for my first roller coaster. Luke had told me the name, but I couldn't remember it anymore. The only thing I could focus on was the enormous line that spread before us and the high rise of the first hill. The purple track soared up until it sped down and zoomed into two loops. From the ground, it stood taller than any trees I had ever stood next to. My stomach was no longer anxious about the proximity of a certain boy, but instead cringed inward from the unknown of the coaster and not having control.

"Yeah … sure."

Luke chuckled and gently turned my face toward his. "Focus on me for now. When we get to the seats, then you can stare at the coaster. We still have about ten minutes in line, so no sense in panicking before you even get on the first one."

"Maybe." Only staring into his relaxed expression did nothing for my nerves, it merely replaced one bundle of nerves for another.

"So, do you have your colleges all picked out?"

"You mean to apply to?"

He nodded.

"I guess. It has always been understood that I would go to somewhere impressive being a Rowe. Duke, of course, is at the top of the list with it being my parents' alma mater."

"You don't sound that excited about the prospect of going there."

"It's not that, necessarily." I moved forward as the line made progress. "It's more that when life decisions are made for you for so long it feels less your choice and more just something you do. I don't want college to feel like that. I should be excited about my college decision, you know? When you constantly have no other options, it just feels off."

"Duke is a good school, though; you could do worse being forced to go somewhere."

"I know. It's not even about that. I just want to choose what makes me feel good. What about the other prestigious schools in the country? Like Columbia or UNC?"

"Do you think they would let you choose somewhere else?"

"Knowing their history, probably not." I shook my head. "But I don't want to talk about that. It makes me sad to think about leaving Honey Cove High and the friends that I've made this year. It was different thinking about college before. I was fine with the escape, but now, I don't want to leave just yet."

"I don't want you to, either."

"You'll be leaving before then. You'll have to finish your senior year in Georgia."

"I don't want to think about that, either."

Finally, the line moved ahead for us to sit on the coaster. Luke moved into the row first and I sat next to him. He helped me push the bar over our lap and secure it before the park's employee double checked it.

I gulped with the click on the coaster as we sat back waiting for it to go forward.

Luke reached across my lap and grabbed my hand. "It's okay. I've got you."

My eyes were clamped shut as the coaster clicked forward. The *click clack click clack* as we climbed up to the top resonated with my heartbeat. I forced my eyes open as we neared the end before the drop. Luke said it was his favorite part and I had to see what he meant.

I faced Luke, whose eyes were locked on me. He smiled when I met his gaze and then we both viewed the surroundings. The sky felt closer, like I could touch it if I reached just a little farther. I soaked it all in until I lurched backward in my seat as the car sped forward.

Luke shouted a hoot of excitement as we fell. The

sensation of my stomach in my throat was shortened by the sudden looping and then twisting and turning.

"What do you think?" he asked.

"When I can feel my fingers again, I'll let you know."

Luke laughed and squeezed my hand back.

Just as quickly, the ride returned to where we started and then we had to climb out. Luke proffered his hand to help lift me, then he pulled me in close as we stood on the platform. His head dipped down and angled to the side. I found my own head mirroring his angle, until my eyes fluttered close as his lips met mine. It was the slightest brush of skin and then it was gone.

I blinked several times. His arms were still wrapped around me. Did that just happen, or did I imagine it?

"Wh-what was that for?" I choked out.

Luke pulled his arms away and shoved his hands in his pockets. "I couldn't resist anymore. I've been wanting to kiss you for weeks."

More blinking. "You have?"

"Yes."

And the next thing I knew, I had pulled him closer by the front of his shirt. In no gentle way our lips met, this time with passion and fierceness. His lips were soft, which contrasted with his intense kisses and caused zings to erupt all over, like firecrackers being ignited.

Someone coughed near us.

We pulled apart, gasping for breath.

"I'm sorry, but we need to get the next group on the platform. You need to exit to the left."

"Oh, right, sorry man," Luke said and then guided us toward the exit with his arm draped over my shoulder.

My brain fumbled over what to say and do. It had barely processed being able to put my feet one in front of the other.

I had kissed Luke Warrington. Not once, but twice! I couldn't believe it. It was so surreal I was tempted to pinch myself, and then I remembered, no felt, his arm over my shoulder, brushing my skin as it wrapped around the other side.

Once we were back in front of the coaster's entrance, he spun me toward him so he could gaze into my eyes. "That was … intense."

I nodded because words still weren't my forte at the moment.

"Should we get in line for another?"

I nodded again.

He chuckled. "Are you okay?"

"Yes, just processing."

He smirked. "Okay good. I know I'm a good kisser but didn't think I was *that* good that I had rendered you incoherent."

I glared. "So cocky."

He nudged my elbow. "Nah, but I just wanted that spark to come back. I'm not used to you having nothing to say."

"Then let's get to the next ride." I tried to muster all the attitude and snarkiness I could, but my mind was fuzzy and all I wanted to do was know what he was thinking and better yet, kiss him again.

CHAPTER TWENTY-ONE

RIILEY

The piece of bacon dangled from my mouth as I shoved my foot in my running sneakers. Today I planned to spend all day with just my dad. It had been his idea and I couldn't be more excited for it to actually happen. I loved days when we would go to Central Park in New York before I moved with Mom. I couldn't even remember the last time we did that.

"You ready, Riley?" he asked from the doorway.

I checked my laces and stood. "Yep. You sure you want to run to town?"

"What, you join a track team, and you think I'm too slow for you?"

"I don't know. I thought it was more that I haven't seen you run in a long time."

"Well, I'll have you know I have started running. I had to do something to occupy myself when I got home from work."

I tilted my head. "I guess we will have to test that out then."

I bent to touch my toes as I stretched. My turquoise

athletic shorts stuck out and tickled my nose. It was supposed to be a muggy day, so I went for cool athletic gear, instead of my regular black athletic fit capris. Instead of just a sports bra, I wore a white tank over top. It felt strange to run with my dad and only have on a sports bra.

He copied my stretches and then held open the screen door.

"What kind of pace do you want?" I asked.

"You set it and I'll keep up."

"You got it." I pulled the headphones from my pocket and put them in my ears. Once I found my running playlist on my phone, I hit Play, and took off. To my surprise, my dad stayed in pace with me, although his shirt had a distinct sweat stain covering most of the front and he breathed harder than I was when I glanced in his direction. But he didn't complain or tell me to slow down.

When we reached the city limits, I slowed and took out my headphones. "Has it changed much since you lived here?"

Dad gulped air like he had been deprived of it for too long. "Yes and no. The main businesses like Over Easy's, Morgan's, they all seem exactly the same. Maybe fancier technology at check out, but otherwise it looks and feels the same."

"That's what Mom said when we moved here, too. It must be weird to be in a place that seems exactly the same, and yet everything is so different."

"A little, yes. It takes me back if I'm not fully paying attention. Like getting shifted into auto pilot when you do a mundane task."

"Did you like growing up here?"

"It wasn't bad. I like New York better. It's bigger, louder. I can hear myself think there."

I giggled. "I miss the noise, too."

He smiled. "It is definitely quieter here."

"Is there anything you miss about Honey Cove?"

"I feel nostalgic being here, but I don't know that I miss anything about Honey Cove that makes my heart ache. It feels more like I can appreciate what I had here, but ultimately would still choose the path I did to leave and move to New York."

"Gotcha."

He stopped walking. "I do miss you and your mom, though. I think about you two all the time. I was an idiot last year."

"Yes you were, but I don't think things can just shift back now."

He sighed and walked ahead. "You're right, but I wanted you to know that I've thought a lot about what I did, and I would take it all back."

"Everything happens for a reason, right? That's what you used to tell me anyway."

"Maybe you're right. You're in a great place at school and with the track team. I'm happy you're thriving here."

"Ha. Thriving? I don't know about that. I would have done what I needed to anywhere, Dad, but I do love living with Mom-mom. The countryside has grown on me although I do miss skyscrapers."

"Enough to visit?"

My eyes widened. "You mean come to New York? When?"

He shrugged. "I'd have to arrange it with your mom, but maybe Thanksgiving or Christmas? Everyone could come if she wanted, but it'd be nice to go on a trip to Central Park."

"You remember."

"Of course, I do. You're my little girl. I loved those trips as much as I gathered you did."

I nodded.

He elbowed me and pointed toward the park. "Want to go in there and walk around? It's not the same, but it could be nice."

"Sure. I know a bench we could sit on."

He smiled and followed behind me as I walked ahead.

The place was technically Randy's. The familiar pang bolted through me as I thought of him. After the talk with everyone this week, I had decided. When Zoe and Madison left, I would find a time to tell him that I wasn't okay with waiting endlessly. I wanted to be together now and if that wasn't possible, then maybe we needed some space from each other.

The bench loomed in my view. "Here it is."

We sat and stared out into the green space before us.

"Are you excited to see Zoe and Madison?"

"Oh my gosh, yes. It's been so long. I can't believe you all arranged it without me finding out."

He chuckled. "That's not difficult when we live in different states."

"Fine. I take it back." I laughed. "So, when you were my age what did you used to do?"

"Do?"

"Yeah, for fun."

"Well, I liked to golf and hang out with my friends. My parents had a large estate out of town limits. We would use that house to spend time in the pool or play games like foosball and billiards."

"What were they like?"

"Who?"

"My grandparents. Mom told me a little about the disagreements they had when you two left together, but what were they like? Were they always so hardened?"

He stroked his chin as he sat, his left arm stretched

behind me. "I like to think that they weren't but for some things they were. They expected greatness in their household. They had worked hard to get the money they had made, and they wanted me to do the same. I could have been rich if I merely conformed to what they wanted. When I chose differently, I crushed the possibilities they had held for me."

"Do you regret it?"

His eyes widened. "Leaving for New York with your mother was the best decision I ever made. The money would have made some things easier in life. Not struggling as hard, but it would have come with the price of never having you, having to love someone else, and I would never take that back. Not ever. You know I mean that, right?"

"I do." I meant it now. In the fall I wasn't so sure. It had seemed easy for him to stop talking to me and ignore that he was missing two thirds of his family. I had thought he had traded us for his job aspirations, and I wasn't sure how I could forgive that or release the anger it caused, but we had come farther since then. He still had more to atone for, especially with Mom, but I could see that he had made mistakes. He was a human, too, and I sometimes forgot that. "What was the dumbest thing you did as a teenager?"

"Dumbest, huh?" He placed his arms on his legs as he hunched over. Suddenly he sat straight. "I've got a good one. I was about fifteen or so and I had this buddy who lived on a farm. He had so many acres. His farm was a big supplier around here for produce and livestock. One night the four of us—me, him, and two other boys—went to the barn where they kept their equipment. Most of us had learned how to drive tractors by then. Even I did in a limited capacity."

"Uh oh," I said as I clasped a hand over my mouth.

"We decided to take out the tractors to the farthest part

of his farm. There was a shallow pond that flooded every year, with lots of rocks. It wasn't prepared for crops, so we used it as a hang out spot. After a particularly large group of storms, we headed out a few hours before dusk. My buddy drove us out there and the rest of us crowded into the cab or rode on the back where it was hitched to a trailer." Dad shook his head. "There was a massive puddle and we got the great idea to drive through it. Go mudding if you will. So, he revved her up and started to run her through, but the puddle was deeper than we expected. It had merged with the pond, which on a shallow day was at least eight feet deep."

"Not good."

"So, he kept her going and we got somewhere near what we thought was the middle when the water poured into the cab of the tractor. The guys in the back had already been shouting and hopped off when the water went over the trailer. We had made fun of them, until this moment when not only was the water coming in rather good, but we could no longer move forward in the water. We had to climb out. He had to tell his dad and they had to pull the tractor and the trailer out when the water had receded. We were in so much trouble."

I shook my head. "Yep, that would definitely count as stupid."

He shrugged. "We were boys. We didn't think about the consequences. Most boys that age don't."

I giggled. "What happened to you?"

"We were grounded and the tractor had been damaged, so we each had to pay what we could. My parents then paid the difference from their pocket. That summer I had to work off my debt to them doing whatever they needed to be done. Anything I *earned* was merely a payment to them."

"Ouch."

"Mm-hmm. Thank goodness you didn't do anything like that."

"Yet." I winked, then burst into a fit of giggles. "I'm kidding. I don't know how any of you thought it was a good idea. I wouldn't do something like that."

He patted my shoulder and smiled. "Want to walk to Charlie's and get some ice cream before we head back to the house?"

"That sounds perfect. It's starting to get warmer out anyway."

He used his thumb and pointer finger to pinch his shirt away from his chest and then fan it. "You're telling me. I feel like I was in a puddle."

I giggled and sprang to my feet.

Charlie's wasn't far from the park, but it was in the opposite direction of the house, adding more distance to our adventure.

"So, how are things for you?" Dad asked.

"Good. I'm glad we're out for summer, although I can't believe June is almost over. It's going so fast."

"I'm afraid that only gets worse. As I get older, the years seem to fly by."

"Great, just what I want to hear."

He chuckled. "How are you and your new friends, Sophie and Shelby?"

"We're good. We honestly are a lot closer than I thought we would be in such a brief time."

"I'm glad to hear that." Dad scrunched his face to make it all serious. "And what about you and Randy?"

"We're still just friends, Dad."

His expression was puzzled, trying to decide if that was the truth or not.

I held my hands up in surrender. "Honest to god, just friends. We aren't a couple."

"And why is that? I could tell the way you two looked at each other at Halloween there were feelings. Isn't that what you want?"

"It's something I would want but hasn't happened yet."

"Well, if he hurts you, you let me know. I'll fly down and teach him a lesson."

I patted his arm as we walked up the street outside of Charlie's. "I'll keep that in mind, but as I told the other person who threatened to bodily harm him, even if we don't work out, I don't want him to be hurt."

"You have such a big heart, you know that?"

"Yeah, yeah, yeah. Let's get ice cream."

He saluted me and then waited for me to walk through the doorway.

I welcomed the mint-green walls and black and white checkered floor like I welcomed a family member. I drummed my fingers against the counter as Dad surveyed the options. "Are you unsure of what to get? We always used to get the cookies and cream sundae."

Dad grinned. "You mean the sundae I barely had any of?"

I nodded.

"You and your mom love that flavor. I didn't eat much because it's not my favorite."

My eyes widened. "That's why you never complained about us eating it all."

"A dad has to have some tricks."

"Well, then what is your flavor?"

"Chocolate and peanut butter."

I scrunched my nose. "Really?"

"Yep. Your mom always liked to share ice cream. She doesn't know how to not eat my ice cream, so I had to adjust my flavors. She doesn't like all the chocolate, but I love it."

"I never knew that."

He shrugged. "Parents have their secrets, too."

"I'm beginning to see that."

He waved the young boy behind the counter over to us.

I recognized him from school but couldn't remember from what class. I guess I needed to do a better job of paying attention to those around me.

"We will take a medium cookies and cream sundae and one medium chocolate-y peanut butter sundae."

"Any toppings?" the boy asked.

He looked at me for reassurance, but I shook my head. "Nope. That's it." He pointed to the booths. "Why don't you grab us a table and I'll bring it over when it's ready."

"Okay." I strolled to the nearest booth and sat. The parlor wasn't that busy inside. One couple waited to the side of the counter, but no one else sat.

I found a few napkins and wiped my forehead. Sweat had gathered there from the run and then sitting in the summer heat. Today would have been gorgeous beach weather. I wondered how everything at the beach house was going. But more importantly, I wondered what Randy was up to. He had said he would text or call me to meet up for dinner at my mom-mom's or do something with my family, but so far he hadn't.

Dad sat and slid the sundae over to me. He dug into his sundae faster than any time I had seen him do with us. It was strange to realize he had never complained because it wasn't the flavor he wanted. I had always enjoyed that memory. It was like a token to who he was with us because he was willing to sacrifice his share for us. Was that what it was like to get older? Things we thought our parents went out of their way to do for us, was just a trick of fate?

"What should we do after Charlie's?"

"I don't know. Why don't you pick?"

He tapped the spoon to his mouth. "Maybe we could stream some movies?"

"That works for me."

He smiled and dug back in.

I took an occasional bite as the thoughts swirled. I needed to find a way to push them out while I still had time with him. Soon he would be getting back on a plane and flying to New York. And then who knew how long it would be before we were in the same state again. I was determined to focus … and eat my sundae.

CHAPTER TWENTY-TWO

The sun reflected off the pool water right into my eyes. It was so intense I had to borrow a pair of Shelby's sunglasses just to avoid a headache. Riley was spending the day with her dad and Randy was busy working. So, for the first time this summer it was just Shelby, Luke, Drew, and me at the cove house.

I waded into the pool as Shelby and Luke floated near each other a few feet away. I kicked hard at the water, splashing them both.

Shelby faced me and glared. "What was that for?"

"You looked hot," I said and winked.

She narrowed her gaze. I would pay for it later, but I didn't care. It had the desired effect I wanted. "So, why aren't we at the beach today?"

"Rip tide," Drew said as he got in behind me.

Luke nodded. "It wouldn't be good to be in the water and today is one of those days you should be in the water if you're going to be outside."

"Gotcha. Well, what do we want to do in the pool? We haven't used this the whole time so far."

Shelby tipped her hat up to glare. "Why must we *do* anything? Can't we just get on some floaties and relax?"

"What are you, forty?"

"Why must I be forty to want to float?"

"Because we should be playing a game or making a whirlpool."

Luke chuckled. "Make whirlpools often, Sophie?"

I made a face at him I reserved for Caleb. "No, I'm just saying."

"We could play chicken," he suggested.

"Chicken?" Drew asked. "That's not exactly a fair advantage, compared to you, I'm going down."

Luke flexed his arms. "Nah, you'd be fine."

"Sure, I would. You just want us to lose."

"What is chicken?" Shelby asked.

"Do you ever have fun in a pool, Shelby? I mean next you'll tell me you don't know what Marco Polo is."

"I know what it is … I just haven't played."

I gasped. "You've been sheltered more than I expected."

She shrugged.

"Chicken is when you sit on someone's shoulders and then push the other group until the person sitting on top falls off," I said.

Her eyes widened. "No thanks. I don't want to soak my hair."

I giggled. "You didn't just say that."

"What? The chlorine is harsh. I hate the feeling of pool hair."

"Mm-hmm sure."

"Well, we could play Marco Polo," Drew said.

I shrugged. "Okay."

"Sure," Luke said.

"Yeah, it's better than getting knocked off someone's shoulders."

I moved my finger to my nose. "Nose goes. Not it."

Drew and Luke were quicker than Shelby.

"Oh great," she said.

Luke eyed her warily. "Just so we're clear you know the rules of the game, right?"

Shelby glared at him and then at us all. "Yes. I close my eyes; I shout Marco and y'all shout Polo. I try to find you based on that. No one can get out of the pool, but you can go underwater and all. Once I tag you, you're it."

"Not bad," I said. "I guess you aren't as sheltered as I thought."

Shelby stuck out her tongue then got to the edge of the pool at the last step. "I'll count to ten once I close my eyes, then you're all going down."

Luke chuckled. "I'd like to see you try but carry on."

She crossed her arms and shut her eyes. Once shut, Luke waved his hand near her face to test it. When we were satisfied, we all lunged in different directions from her.

There wasn't much time to talk strategy as she had already gotten to eight when we stopped moving. At ten, Shelby launched into the pool sending waves in every direction. "Marco."

Drew went first, "Polo."

Shelby snapped her head in the direction he had been as she swam toward him.Drew was pretty agile and dove into the opposite end closer to where she counted.

"Marco."

"Polo," I whispered.

Shelby angled to the right. "Marco?"

"Polo," I whispered again.

Luke used my second Polo to flatten himself against the side of the pool.

"Marco?"

We all shouted, "Polo."

Shelby half turned as her head bobbed above the water.

Luke took a deep breath, sank to the bottom, and then swam over to the other side avoiding her moving legs. I was impressed; it was a good strategy.

"Marco."

"Polo," I said again.

This time, Shelby turned like she could see. Without warning she launched herself in my direction. I tried to swim away, but she was too fast and tagged my foot.

"Aha!" she said and opened her eyes. "And look who I caught. Sophie. You're it now." Her expression was smug.

I narrowed my gaze. "Lucky start."

"I guess we'll see."

"We will see. I know their strategies. You must beat that and my superior skills."

Shelby giggled. "Well, get to counting. Oh, and make sure you're over there to start. Wouldn't want to cheat your way to a win."

Just for that, I splashed toward her, hard. The water launched toward her until it soaked some of her hair that floated down from her bun.

She splashed back, which turned into me retaliating. Soon, we were splashing each other, and the boys joined in. For them it wasn't a big deal, but for Shelby and me, our hair was sopping wet and clung to our face. I tried to move it from my eyes but wasn't successful.

"Okay, okay," I said, wiping off the water dripping down my face. "Shall we get back to the game?" I moved to the spot Shelby stood and closed my eyes, counting to ten and then swam into the water.

When I played this game as a child, my cousins always tried to use the water to hear where people had moved. If they could feel the water's movement or hear it bounce off someone, they knew where to go. I strained to hear the vibrations as they did to no avail.

Eventually I caught Drew, but I think he had let me win, sensing my growing frustration.

He kissed me after I caught him. A quick kiss, nothing too crazy. He wasn't big into making out in front of anyone and I was the same way. I didn't think it was necessary to kiss someone's face off in the company of others. Personally, I didn't need to see a full on make out session, so I supposed I remembered that when I was around others, giving them the same courtesy I'd want.

We played a few more rounds, until Luke had decided to go inside and get a snack.

Drew had followed, leaving us by ourselves.

I peered over my sunglasses at the door, making sure we were alone. "It's about time they left. I never got a chance to ask you how your date went."

Shelby's face reddened.

"Oh my god! Something happened, didn't it? You're as red as a cherry."

Shelby looked over her shoulder, like she wasn't sure she should say in case they came back. "We might have kissed …"

"Might have? Kissing isn't something you *might* do. You either kiss or you don't."

She rolled her eyes. "Yes, we kissed."

I floated closer to where she stood. "And?"

She sighed dramatically and fanned herself. "It was better than I imagined."

"Oh, do tell."

"We went to an amusement park since I had never ridden a roller coaster before. We had just gotten off the coaster and he gazed into my eyes and then his lips brushed against mine. It was short, nothing crazy. I felt awestruck and asked what that was for. He told me he had wanted to kiss me for weeks and couldn't resist anymore."

"Aww. That's cute."

"Something came over me and I pulled him toward me and kissed him harder this time. We made out on the coaster platform until an employee asked us to move."

I giggled. "I'm sure that was awkward."

"Yes, but I didn't care. I couldn't believe we finally kissed."

"I'm happy for you."

"I'm happy, too. We had a momentous day on the rides. We went on the big swings and the carousel. We rode several roller coasters … and kissed when we could."

"That sounds so cute."

Shelby gasped. "Are you saying that *relationships* are cute? Oh my, how things have changed."

I splashed her. "Hush. You two have been dancing around the idea for months now, it's just cute to see it go somewhere. Now we just have to help Randy and Riley."

Shelby sighed. "I don't know if that will happen. Randy seems stuck on his idea of it not being the right time. I don't know what he's thinking."

"He better figure it out before he hurts her, or I'll hurt him, even if she says that isn't what she wants."

"Well, we have to let them figure it out. If we push too much it could be bad."

"Maybe, but what if it works?"

Shelby eyed me warily. "And what if it implodes? I don't think we have a good position to do much about the situation. Riley and Randy are both stubborn and will do what they do. We must respect that."

"Fine. I won't nudge, but I will react if he acts like an idiot."

Shelby giggled. "Fair enough. I'll help you."

"I wonder how she's doing at home with her dad. I hope things are going well."

"How did it seem when you were at dinner?"

"Fine. They talked like normal. Are you nervous about meeting Zoe and Madison tomorrow?"

"A little. I'm not sure how they'll react to what I did last year."

"I wouldn't. That was a long time ago. You're practically a different person now."

She shrugged. "Friends hold grudges for their friends. It's the natural order. I would be prickly to someone for the two of you. I wouldn't blame them for doing the same to me."

"Yeah, but Riley won't let anything come of it. You should know that."

She smiled. "Yeah, of course."

I didn't believe her. The smile didn't quite meet her eyes. She was worried, but I'd look out for her. She didn't deserve any slack from anyone for the fall. That was plenty of time ago and if anyone forgot that, I'd remind them.

CHAPTER TWENTY-THREE

SHELBY

My head pounded as I stared at my laptop. The pool had been a nice break, but now I had to work on the festival again. With Zoe and Madison coming to the house, I wouldn't have time otherwise. I needed to finalize the vendors, call the companies, and figure out supplies. I couldn't believe there was only six weeks left until the festival.

Luke leaned close, bathing me in his cologne.

I closed my eyes and drank it in until he pulled my hair. "Ow!"

Luke chuckled. "You looked too serious."

I glared at him. "I'm trying to focus. I need to call the tent and chair rental place. I have people who want to set up at the festival like last time to call back. Too many emails to return."

"Bleck. Don't they know it's summer vacation? You should come back outside with us."

"I can't."

His lip stuck out as he pouted like a toddler.

"How attractive."

Luke grinned, revealing that cute little dimple. "Why thank you."

"It's called sarcasm."

He twisted the ends of my dark brown hair around his finger. "Can I help?"

"Not really, except maybe go back out to the pool and let me focus."

"Must I?"

I faced him. "Why?"

He pouted again, this time exaggerating even more. "Drew and Sophie are all kissy kissy, couple-like out there. Not exactly that much fun. Plus, he's helping her study for the SATs again."

I narrowed my gaze, focusing on his hairline to avoid the cuteness of his dimple and those smoldering hazel eyes. "Do you promise to be quiet and not distract me?"

He made an x on his chest and then raised his right hand. "Absolutely. Scout's honor."

"You can't say that if you were never a scout."

"Who says I wasn't?"

My brows rose. "You weren't … Were you?"

"Yes." He crossed his arms, annoyed, then burst out laughing. "No. I wasn't, but I had you going didn't I?"

"Ugh. You are *so* not going to behave, are you?"

He shrugged, then walked toward the cabinets.

I redirected my gaze to my screen but couldn't help watching him dig through the cabinets. I wasn't someone who generally was bothered by background noise, but ever since we kissed, I felt like we were similar to magnets. When he entered a room, I gravitated to him. Most of the time I sensed him before I actually saw him. I didn't know that could even happen. I had read it in books, but it was happening, at least for me.

Luke abandoned the cabinets and went searching in the refrigerator.

"What are you looking for?"

He swirled around. "I thought you were working?"

"I am, but you obviously are having difficulty. I couldn't exactly ignore it."

He wiggled his eyebrows. "Just looking for a snack. Don't you worry. You go back to all that festival stuff."

I shook my head as he spun around. He was laying it on thick. I had to admit, if I didn't have to actually make progress, this mood would be infectious. I had never seen him like that. He had let loose. Letting everything have that double effect, the actual message and then the one he was implying. So much flirtation.

My cursor blinked in the same spot it had since he walked in. I hadn't been able to add or delete anything.

The refrigerator door closed, and the cabinets opened again.

What on earth?

I peeked over the top of my laptop.

Luke reached into the top cabinet and pulled out a tin of peanuts. He avoided my gaze as he walked to the stool next to me and plopped himself down. He peeled back the protective layer and dug into the peanuts.

When he did look my way, he smirked as he popped one peanut into his mouth at a time.

The information on my screen was blurry; I was forcing myself to stare at it so intently that it was no longer clear. This was ridiculous. I switched tabs to my email and scrolled to the oldest email. I strung words together until it was coherent enough to send. Then I went to the next email. I continued until a peanut flew at the side of my face.

I turned toward Luke, whose face was giddy with excitement and orneriness.

"You did *not* seriously just hit me with a peanut."

"What if I did? What would you do?" He wiggled his eyebrows at me like a dare.

I snatched a peanut from the tin and launched it at his face.

The peanut bounced off his nose and hit the floor.

Luke's eyes widened and then he lunged toward me.

I hopped off the stool and ran.

His fingers found my side and tickled.

I collapsed to the floor in a fit of giggles as he kept tickling me. "Okay, okay. Truce?" I gasped. I had ended up lying flat on the floor as he hovered over me.

Luke paused tickling to stare into my eyes. Something flickered through his expression before he leaned down and kissed me. It was more intimate than the others. His lips lingered like there was no hurry to move. It didn't matter that Drew or Sophie could walk into the room. The only important moment was the kiss.

His hand settled over my hip as he kissed me, the skin igniting from his touch. My body was alight from the sensations—the cool hardwood floor contrasted with his touch.

My chest tightened as he rose, his gaze lingering on my face. He outstretched his arm to pull me to my feet.

"Thanks," I whispered. My cheeks were flushed. If I thought I had been distracted before, I now broke that threshold. My thoughts raced as I replayed his touch and the moment over and over.

We both sat at the counter in silence. Was he thinking about that kiss, too? Was he replaying it? I had considered him to be a good kisser already, but that kiss … that kiss was laced with more. Could he feel it too?

My phone vibrated on the counter, and I turned it over to see a number. Although I didn't recognize it, I answered anyway.

"Ms. Rowe?" the person asked.

"Yes. This is she."

"We would like to discuss your order for the summer festival."

"Ah, yes." I covered the speaker of my phone. "I'll be back."

He nodded as I turned to the front door and sat on the porch. The distance relieved my mental fog but reminded me my to do list was massive and business hours were slipping away.

CHAPTER TWENTY-FOUR

RILEY

My leg jiggled as I moved it up and down waiting for the vehicle that brought my best friends from New York City. I hadn't seen them in almost a year. I used to see them every day for hours on end at school and then on the weekends when we spent most of it together.

The screen door screeched as Mom-mom joined me on the porch. "How far away are they?"

I unlocked my phone's screen for the tenth time in the last sixty seconds. "Ten minutes out was the last they sent."

Mom-mom sat beside me on the step. "Then they'll be here soon. Why don't you help me make a pitcher of peach lemonade to welcome them when they get here?"

"Okay." I followed her into the house, even though the farther I got from the porch, the more antsy I became. My body was alive with buzzing and jitters. What if things were different somehow? What if they had moved on past me in my absence and they felt like *I* was different?

I shook my head. This wasn't helping. I would make myself crazy.

Mom-mom grabbed the pitcher from the cabinet and

pulled ingredients onto the counter when a horn blared through the house.

I startled, and then my eyes widened. "They're here!"

She laughed and waved me out. "Go. I can finish up here."

I didn't need to be told twice. I made it to the bottom of the stairs when Mom had parked and walked to the trunk while Dad, Zoe, and Madison exited.

I screamed and wailed as I ran to them and squeezed in a group hug. "I can't believe you're both here."

"Right?" Madison said.

"I know you explained what this place looks like, but I don't think you did it justice. That *city* if you can even call it that was like a blip and we left," Zoe said.

"That's what happens in the country, Zoe. I told you that."

Zoe rested her hands on her hips as she sniffed the air. "What's that smell?"

Mom placed a suitcase on the ground. "It's called livestock, Zoe. You best get used to it."

"I think it's nice," Madison said.

I smiled at them both. "Let's head in. I'll show you my room and we can catch up."

They each grabbed their bag and followed me inside to my bedroom. I opened the door and held my arms wide, like I was a real estate agent showing it to clients. "My bed is here and over there is my closet. Oh, and I can't forget this is where I sit to do my work."

Madison smirked. "Nice, when did you get your real estate license?"

I laughed. "You are seriously always on my wavelength." I plopped on my bed as they settled into the room. It felt so good to have them here. Like a little piece of me that I hadn't realized I had lost or dropped. They looked the same, and more importantly, things *felt* the same already.

Zoe crossed her legs as she sat on my desk chair. "This used to be your mom's room? I can't even imagine her living in this town."

I snorted. "Yep. Her home for as long as we've been alive."

Madison eyed the walls and my décor. "Was she sad to see it all disappear and you redo it?"

"I don't think so. She didn't say anything at least."

"Still so wild." Zoe eyed my books and makeup sitting on my desk. "So, when are you taking us to this beach house? I can't wait to see what it looks like."

"We can leave in a little bit. I figured you would want a break from being in the car before we drove to the house."

Madison raised her hand. "Yes, thank you." Madison swatted at Zoe. "Plus, I'm sure Riley wants to spend a little more time with her dad. We didn't even meet your mom-mom yet."

I gasped. "Crap. We must do that or she will be upset with me. She's super excited to meet you two."

Madison clapped her hands on her leg and rose.

Zoe had barely moved.

Madison grabbed her arm and pulled her to her feet. "Come on, lazy butt. We have people to meet." She leaned in close. "Plus, I can't wait to see the rest of this house. It's amazing, so farmhouse chic."

I giggled. "Well, it is on a lot of land, Madison. It kind of fits with the area."

"I know, but I'm so used to clean, hard lines and modern design. This is refreshing. Not to mention its authentic. When people at home do it, it seems tacky, like they're trying to be country in the completely wrong environment."

I stared at Zoe, who was ignoring Madison as she stared at her phone. "Since when did she go to design school?"

Zoe peered up from her phone screen. "Don't let her fool you. She's spent the first part of summer binge watching HGTV. She now thinks she knows what she's talking about because she's watched a hundred episodes."

Madison glared. "I don't *think* I'm an expert. And what about you? You've binged watched Grey's Anatomy for the fifth time and are already on season seven again. It's been like two weeks off from school. You act like you have a medical degree."

I beamed. "It's so good to have you two around. I've missed this."

They moved closer for a hug. We all embraced and then headed to the kitchen.

I pointed out the rooms as we went, Madison's eyes glinting in the afternoon sunlight. Her expression appeared to approve of the décor. Maybe she had been watching *too* much HGTV.

Mom-mom stood behind her large kitchen island as she stirred the peach lemonade. "Hey, girls." She wiped her hands on her jeans and came over to hug each one.

"This is Zoe and Madison," I said as I pointed to each of them.

"It's so good to finally meet you two. I've heard so many stories over the years. We should have had you girls down here before now."

Zoe rested one hand on her hip. "I completely agree. I've been saying that to Riley for a while."

"How was your flight?" Mom-mom asked.

Zoe huffed. "Tragic. I was stuck in the middle seat between an old guy who snored the whole time and a businesswoman who used the plane ride to be on the phone. And when I say she projected her voice, she *projected* her voice."

Madison rolled her eyes. "Ignore Zoe. She wouldn't know what they did. She was passed out the second she put in her earbuds."

Zoe squished her eyebrows together. "How would you know? You were chatting up the cute boy in the seat next to you." She faced me. "Madison had the lucky seats. She sat on the aisle, the middle was empty, and the boy had the window seat. She flipped her hair so many times I lost count."

Mom-mom's eyes widened. I shook my head and mouthed, *totally typical.*

They bantered more than an elderly married couple, but it was joyous to me, like a favorite song you played repeatedly. It was home.

"Did you get his number?" I asked.

Madison sighed. "Unfortunately, no. He ended up having a girlfriend. He was flying to visit her."

"You didn't tell me that," Zoe said.

"You didn't ask."

"Bummer, Mad."

"Oh well, it's not like it would have worked anyway. I mean seriously what were the odds that he even lived near us?"

"True, although you could test out that long distance relationship life."

"Uh, no thanks."

Mom-mom poured three glasses of peach lemonade. "Here, why don't you girls take these and go relax. I'm sure you have a lot of catching up to do."

I nodded and then led us to the front room. It was more formal than anything. I rarely even came in here, but it was guaranteed to be quiet and private. The couches were fluffy from rare use and the sun poured in through the windows.

"So, besides binge watching TV shows, what have you two been up to this summer? I feel like we've barely chatted since school ended."

Zoe played with the tassels on the pillow she held. "This is pretty much the highlight of my summer. Mom wanted me to get a job or do some kind of camp thing, but I put it off and missed all the deadlines."

"And she didn't whine about it?" I asked.

Zoe's parents were … different. Her dad worked in the stock market and was usually at work, while her mom was a teacher. They both felt any time should be well spent, which certainly was not best spent sitting on a sofa watching TV. But what made them weird was that Zoe was always allowed to discover her own interests. They didn't put any preconceived notions on her besides working hard. If she wanted to pick up ballet, they got her lessons. If she decided to quit two days later, that was fine too. I had never understood it.

"Nope. She left me alone. I blame it on the schoolyear she had. She was moved to the third grade from first and was too distracted with that and my little sisters to worry about me."

Zoe also had twin sisters, Maggie and Mandi, who were *oopsies*. Her mom hated that Zoe called them that, but what else was she to expect when they had kids more than a decade after she was born.

"Aww how old are they now? Like three?"

"Nope just turned four."

"Four? Wow."

Madison giggled. "You should have seen them the other day. They pulled Zoe's makeup out of her bag and had it all over themselves and her mirror."

"Yeah, real funny. It took me three hours to clean it all up."

"You should have put it up higher."

"They should have stayed out of my room."

"That's like saying New York is quiet and still. It will never be true."

Zoe stuck out her tongue.

"I miss those two," I said.

"They miss you, too. They ask where you are. They always say, 'Where's Whywi?'"

"Aww. What do you say?"

"That you moved. They don't ask as often anymore. I show them pictures of you here when I can, they seem to kind of understand."

I never realized how much of their families I took for granted. I had been friends with them for so long that their parents and siblings also felt like family. I had made connections with all of them, and their absence made me ache, too.

"Riley," Mom called from down the hallway.

"I'll be right back." I wandered until I found her in the kitchen sitting at the dinner table with my dad. "What's up?"

"I think you should get started on your trip to the cove. It looks like a bad thunderstorm might roll in. We would feel better if you were already at the house before it started."

"Oh, okay."

Dad stood and walked to me, pulling me in for a hug. "Be safe, Riley. Text one of us when you get to the house."

"I will, Dad. Are you sure it's okay that I leave before you go back? When will you return to Honey Cove?"

"I'm sure. You deserve some time with your friends.

I'm hoping to make it back by Labor Day. But don't worry about me, okay?"

I nodded and hugged him tighter.

Mom gave me a hug, too.

"Where's Mom-mom?"

"She should be out in her garden I think."

"Okay, I'll tell her bye on our way out." I waved one more time then went back to the front room. "We're leaving now. My parents are worried about the thunderstorm that is supposed to roll in. They want us there before we get stuck in it. So, let's get your stuff and get going."

"Wahoo. Time for the beach!" Zoe shouted.

Madison rolled her eyes. "Do you even know what a beach is like? I mean have you ever really been?"

I giggled. "Let's get in the car before you two start bickering again."

"Aye, aye," Zoe said and saluted me.

We trudged up the stairs, grabbed our stuff and headed outside to my Impala. I started it then rolled down the windows. "You might want to give it a minute or two. It's roasting in there."

They dropped their bags in the trunk.

"I'll be right back. Need to say goodbye to my mom-mom."

They followed me around to the other side of the house. Sure enough, Mom-mom was bent over her flowers, digging in the dirt. When she saw us, she rose, pulled off her gloves and wiped her hands on her pants. "Heading out?"

I nodded and gave her a hug.

Zoe and Madison said goodbye.

"You girls be safe." She gazed at Zoe and Madison.

"And you two make sure to come back and visit. You're welcome any time."

"Be careful what you wish for."

Madison shooed me. "Oh stop, we are awesome."

Mom-mom waved as we walked away and around the corner.

"All right let's get this car on the road. I can't wait for you to meet everyone." Which was mostly true. I wanted to know what Zoe and Madison would think of Sophie and Shelby, and vice versa. I also wanted them to meet Randy, but with how things were for us right now, I wasn't sure how it would go, and that was always a scary feeling.

CHAPTER TWENTY-FIVE

SOPHIE

The cushions squished as I sat. The back deck had become our spot. Whenever Drew and I wanted to be alone or just wanted to step away for a bit, we came here. The view was incredible, and the outdoor sectional was my favorite place to sit.

The deck was adorned with Adirondack chairs in the back and the front, but only the back had this sectional. The cushions were dark-red and the rest was a dark wicker material.

"I never get tired of this view."

"Me neither," Drew said as he stared longingly at me.

I launched one of the pillows at his head. "Quit being corny."

He shrugged and chuckled. "What can I say? It's true."

"Whatever. We have serious things to discuss."

His demeanor shifted as he settled near my feet on the sectional. "What's wrong?"

"When I was home I ended up talking to Rowan one on one again."

Drew's eyebrows rose above his black-rimmed glasses, then dipped back down. "Oh? How'd that go?"

"I guess it was better." I fiddled with the purple, corded bracelet Drew had bought me. "I asked him about his plans in terms of the house and us."

"And?"

"He seemed to respect that we had a say in it all, too."

"We as in your mama or you and Caleb, too?"

"All of us. He wanted me to know that he cared about how we felt and wouldn't push anyone to do something that wasn't comfortable."

"At the risk of being wrong, that sounds like a good thing, right?"

"Yes, it's a good thing, but it doesn't clear things up for me. Sometimes I wish he would do the evil villain thing I expect him to do and then make my choice easier."

Drew leaned closer, his blond hair shifting into his face. "It would be easier, but it's also not likely to happen. I don't see Rowan tramping on anyone's wishes and turning out to be the evil kidnapper here."

I knew Drew was right, but it was the one area where logic seemed to halt, and irrationality took over. "I know that somewhere, I do …"

"But it still doesn't feel easy." Drew stood and pulled me up with him. He led us to the deck railing to stare at the water. "This situation is like the shore in front of us. It's weathering, erosion, and deposition at its finest."

I scrunched my nose and eyebrows. "It's *what?*"

He chuckled. "The sand on the shore takes years to be created. Rocks must be weathered slowly but consistently by the waves repeatedly, to be carried here and then deposited in large quantities making the beach."

"Okay. How is that the same?"

"You're expecting this situation to be like when a

hurricane comes to the shore and wipes out the beach in a day. Quick, fierce, and tumultuous. In reality, it's like the processes of weathering, erosion, and deposition. They are slow, steady, and persistent."

"You're such a nerd."

Drew glared. "Are you listening?"

"Yes, yes. Go on."

"Rowan is steady and persistent, but not aggressive. He loves your mother, and I would suspect he cares about you two as well. He is steady in his presence and is letting those feelings build without trying to overwhelm you. He isn't about the short wins. He is slow and steady. He wants to marry her and be in the family. He's not going to blow it by irritating you, which would irritate your mom. *And* the analogy works regarding your feelings about it, too. Don't expect to wake up one day and have a magic answer. It takes time with these things but look how far you've already come. You used to scowl around him. You wanted nothing to do with him, regardless of how anyone else felt about it."

"It still doesn't always feel great."

"I'd expect that. You delved into your feelings about your dad and him only this past spring—two months ago. Give yourself time. According to his answers he is expecting you to take some. So do it."

The wooden railing under my fingers was gritty from the trail of sand blown around as I rubbed my hand across. "So, slow and steady?"

He nodded and leaned close as his arm slipped around my waist. He pulled me close and just held on as my body relaxed in his arms. We stood like that forever, just staring at the water and holding each other close.

Shelby bustled around the kitchen.

"Who made you Susie Homemaker?" I asked.

"No one, but they'll be here any minute," Shelby said.

Luke chuckled. "You do look funny. Who would have thought a Rowe with a private chef could cook?"

Shelby glared at him, then poked him in the side. "Hush it."

He smirked.

Randy shook his head as he sat off to the side of the counter. He had been quiet since he had arrived. I had almost expected him to be a no show arriving only thirty minutes before they did. Something was going on, but I didn't know all the details. I only hoped Riley was okay.

The oven dinged. Shelby, who was halfway across the room, stopped in her tracks. "Ugh, of course."

I hopped down from the stool. "Relax. I can pull it out. It should be done right?"

"Yes. I followed the recipe exactly from Chef Frank. The lasagna should be perfect."

My stomach gurgled at the thought. Shelby had arrived arm deep with grocery bags to make tonight's dinner. Luke had been roped in to help carry everything else.

Lasagna wafted from the open door of the oven. I inhaled a deep breath before I pulled the casserole pan from the oven and placed it on the trivets Shelby had set out. It bubbled around the edges.

"Well, private chef or not, you can make all the meals now," I said.

Drew grumbled. "Did I not make good meals?"

"Of course, but can you *smell* this? I could do a swan dive into the whole pan."

"Let me know how that works," he said.

My phone vibrated from my back pocket. I pulled it

out to see the text from Riley scroll across the screen, *We're here.*

"They're here."

Shelby's face paled. "Oh crap."

Luke placed his hand gently on her arm. "Relax. You're trying too hard."

"What he said."

The door creaked and a flutter of voices emanated through the open doorway. They were here and my stomach decided now was the perfect time to cut and run. Riley strode in first, carrying the bag she had brought home with her. Behind her were Zoe and Madison. They looked the same as the pictures Riley had shown us.

Zoe had a short pixie cut. Her hair was almost black, and she was the same height as Riley. She slouched in her dark-washed, distressed, high-waisted denim shorts and jade-green, lace cami. Her shoes were black combat boots —a strange choice for the beach in my opinion.

Where Zoe's style had rough edges, Madison's style was delicate and feminine. Her hair was golden blond and curled sitting a couple inches below her shoulders. She wore a white mid-calf cotton dress with pink flowers. The puffy sleeves were off her shoulders and the chest was bunched together. She wore nude sandals to pull it all together.

It was strange to think these two girls were Riley's best friends before she moved here, not to mention that all three of them were best friends. Their styles were all so different, but the same could have been said about us too. I wondered if they were sizing us up, too? Did they think we seemed out of touch with who Riley had been?

Riley met my gaze and beamed. "We're finally here. I thought we would catch that storm, but it only ever trailed us."

I smiled. "That's good."

Shelby held out her arms like a grand hostess. "Welcome! Dinner is ready, I hope you all like lasagna."Shelby eyed Zoe and Madison, no doubt making the comment more toward them than us. We had already told her our answers.

Zoe spoke first, "Lasagna works for me."

Madison nodded and hovered closer to Zoe. Was she shy or quiet?

Everyone moved toward the tables, Riley hesitated before sitting next to Randy. Something was up.

Shelby deposited the lasagna dish in the middle of the table with a knife and spatula next to it to help everyone grab their piece. While we had waited for it to cook, Drew had whipped up a salad and Luke had made garlic bread.

"Now that we are all seated I'll introduce everyone," Riley said. "This is Zoe and Madison," she said as she pointed to each girl. "Zoe and Madison, this is Shelby, Sophie, Drew, Luke, and Randy."

Everyone smiled at each other with that awkward school-picture-forced-smile. We took our turns passing around the food and grabbing what we wanted.

"Who made dinner?" Riley asked.

"We all helped," Shelby said.

Madison dug her fork in the lasagna.

Zoe took several bites before she said, "This is really good, and I've had my fair share of lasagna."

Shelby's cheeks flushed.

"So, what's everyone been up to?" Riley asked.

Luke cranked up his charm as he grinned and stared at Shelby. "I took Shelby to her first amusement park. She rode a roller coaster."

Riley's eyes widened. "You've never been before?"

Zoe stopped mid bite. "Like ever? Aren't you like super rich?"

Riley went pale. "Zoe!"

Shelby laughed. "Yes, I am, but my parents never really took me to places like that."

"Wow! That's crazy. We go to Coney Island every year," Zoe said.

"That's what I told her. So, of course, I had to take her," Luke said.

Riley faced me. "What about you, Sophie?"

"Nothing exciting like that. I went home after I dropped you off, then came back after I spent the day with Mama and Caleb."

"Has Riley shown you much of Honey Cove?" Shelby asked.

Madison took a sip of her water and then said, "We saw a drive thru version of the town on the way here."

A mischievous glint passed through Zoe's gaze. "We saw a place called Morgan's Market." She faced Randy. "That's where you work, right?"

Randy, who had been pushing the salad around his plate, looked up. "Yeah." Something flitted across his face and was replaced with a smile—a forced one at best. "You should have gone in and gotten a proper tour."

Riley didn't meet Randy's gaze. What was going on?

Zoe stared him down in a challenging way. It was as if she dared him to do something she could call out. "Maybe you can give us one before we leave?"

My eyes widened and I caught Drew's gaze. He shrugged in response and went back to his lasagna.

I couldn't help feeling like I was missing a big part of the story.

Randy either didn't pick up on the expression or didn't care. "Sure."

Riley glared at Zoe. "I don't think there will be time. You two aren't here long."

"So, what do you think of our small town so far?" Shelby asked.

"I expected more tractors," Zoe said.

Madison choked on her water and then glared.

"You have to excuse Zoe. She never had a filter installed at birth," Riley said.

Luke chuckled. "Those are the people that have the most fun, though."

I laughed, too. "He has a point. We get that a lot though."

"I rather like it," Madison said.

"Of course, you would. You've never been completely into New York City," Zoe said.

Madison stuck out her tongue at Zoe.

So, she must be shy. Madison clearly had no problem telling Zoe like it is.

"Zoe is a diehard city girl. The subway is in her veins," Riley said.

"So were you, unless that's changed," Zoe said.

"She's still more city than she is country. She still complains about the no noise thing," I said.

"Yeah, what is with that? How am I going to sleep?" Zoe asked.

Madison giggled. "With your eyes closed and laying on a pillow."

My eyes widened. Yep, just shy at first. I liked her. Honestly, I liked them both. Zoe was refreshing. You knew where you stood. And Madison clearly had a sense of humor I could get behind. This visit wouldn't be so bad after all.

CHAPTER TWENTY-SIX

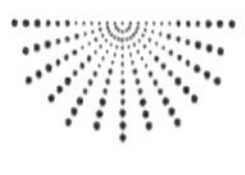

RILEY

Dinner had been one of the most awkward ones I had ever experienced, and it wasn't for the reasons I had expected.

Randy seemed distant. He perked up a little when Zoe teased him, but he wasn't carefree like I had grown to know and love. What I hadn't told anyone was our text conversation.

I pulled my messages up, starting with his, *Hey, my shift is almost over. Want me to swing by afterward?*

No. My dad surprised me and Zoe and Madison are coming for a visit. I just want to spend time with my dad alone while I can. He is giving up some of the visit for them.

Oh, okay. What about tomorrow?

It's fine. I'll see you back at the cove house.

He never answered that text and hadn't texted me since then. If I had to bet, I was sure his behavior had something to do with that, but what I didn't understand is why it was a big deal. I had never met his parents and yet my wish to spend time with my family alone wasn't received well. It wasn't fair.

Sophie bumped my elbow on the way up the stairs. "Everything okay with you and Randy?"

So, I wasn't the only one to notice. *Great.* "Yeah. We just didn't see each other the last few days. I think he's giving me space to hang out with Zoe and Madison."

Sophie nodded, but I could tell she didn't fully believe it. That girl was too attuned to people's moods. Sophie passed me on the stairs as I slowed down for Zoe and Madison.

"This place is amazing," Madison whispered.

"Right? I couldn't believe it, either. I would never go anywhere else in the summer if my family owned this," I said.

"Can she adopt me?" Zoe asked.

I rolled my eyes. "You're too much. I'm glad everyone understood your humor. That tractor joke wasn't funny."

She shrugged. "I thought it was."

"So, there are two bedrooms no one is using on our side of the house. You both could share a queen or king size bed, but the other girls and I are in the bunk bedroom. If you want to be in there, I can sleep on the floor, and you can take the spare bunk and my bunk. It's up to you two."

"I don't care either way. I'll let Zoe decide."

"Let's just stay in the same room, but you don't have to sleep on the floor."

"Please, I don't care. It's not like there aren't a million blankets I can steal and make a bed on the floor. Shelby probably even has an air mattress somewhere if I really wanted it."

Madison eyed me warily. "You sure?"

"Of course. It's only a couple nights. It's not like it's the whole summer." I led them down the hallway to the room we had chosen. Sophie was the only one in there so far. "Hey, we're all going to sleep in here if that's okay?"

Sophie smiled. "Of course. I don't care. Should we stay up and have a girls' night?"

"Ooh, that could be fun." I faced Zoe and Madison. "Are you two too tired to stay up a little more? I know you've been traveling all day."

Zoe tilted her head. "Do you remember what I'm like at all? It's only nine o' clock. I'm usually up until the sun rises."

I feigned shock. "How could I forget? Of course, it's practically noon for you, but Madison is not such a night owl."

Madison settled a hand over her hip. "Are you calling me a grandma? I can stay awake."

Sophie burst into a fit of giggles. "You are hilarious. We need you around all the time."

Zoe sulked. "What about me? I'm funnier than she is!"

"Oh, you can stay, too. I love the humor from you both. Yours is just a little different."

"Well, I guess it's a girls' night then. Think Shelby will join?" I asked.

Sophie didn't hesitate. "And miss stories about you from New York? Definitely not."

My cheeks heated. "Um, who said anything about stories of me? That's not what I meant."

"Nope. You already agreed to staying up, so too bad."

Zoe rubbed her hands together as she toed off her shoes. "I like this idea. You share about Honey Cove stories, and we will share about New York."

Sophie outstretched her hand. "Deal."

Zoe shook her hand and smiled.

"What the heck? Now I'm outnumbered?" I faced Madison. "Won't you say no?"

Madison shrugged. "I want to hear the stories too."

I crossed my arms. "Well, that's just not fair."

Shelby opened the door and strolled in. "What's not fair?"

"Those three are ganging up on me."

Shelby's eyes widened.

"Don't be so dramatic, Riley. We are just swapping Riley stories," Sophie said.

Shelby's shoulders relaxed. "Oh, that's it?"

I nodded.

"Then that sounds fun!"

I growled. I should have known better. Of course, they would bond over stories of *me*. "I'm getting changed." I grabbed my pajamas and hid in the bathroom. Maybe I could avoid the first story if I stayed in here long enough?

When a chorus of laughter erupted from the other side of the door, I bolted out. "What's going on?" Instead of stopping, it only caused the four of them to erupt in more giggles. I scowled. "Will someone clue me in?"

Sophie barely stopped and faced me. "Zoe was telling us about the time you got caught on a patch of ice walking home and practically skated trying to keep your balance. Then eventually fell on your butt."

My gaze narrowed at Zoe. "That story? Why do you love that story? My tailbone was bruised for like three weeks."

"Because if you had the vantage point I did, you would have died of laughter too."

"I hardly doubt that." I opened the door and went to the hallway closet, snatching all the blankets I could find and dragging them back to the room. When I returned they had calmed themselves.

Shelby wiped her eyes, Sophie sat on her bed, Madison sat crisscrossed on the floor, and Zoe lounged on my top bunk.

"Are we all done laughing at my expense?"

Sophie shrugged. "I suppose so. Did Shelby tell you she kissed Luke?"

I gasped, my eyes widening. "You didn't tell me that! I asked what I missed."

Shelby launched a pillow at Sophie's head. "Well, you asked when everyone was sitting together. Was I really going to gush about our kiss in front of him?"

"Okay, fair enough." I arranged the blankets on the floor for my makeshift bed. "How was it?"

Shelby's cheeks reddened. "Amazing."

"Are you all coupled up here?" Zoe asked.

"Zoe!" Madison shouted.

Zoe shrugged. "What? It's an honest question."

I giggled. "Don't have enough of a boy pool in New York anymore?"

"Of course, but maybe a country boy could be an interesting fling."

I rolled my eyes. "Yes. Drew and Luke are both off limits."

Sophie tilted her head. "Why didn't you include Randy in that?"

I sighed. "Well, I would hope she wouldn't go after Randy, but he isn't exactly off the market."

"He isn't on the market, either," Shelby said.

"I suppose."

Shelby and Sophie exchanged glances, while Madison and Zoe got their bunks ready for bed.

"So … where did the kiss happen?" I asked.

"After we got off the first roller coaster."

"That's so cute. Did he start it or you?"

"Who cares?" Zoe asked. "Have you seen him?"

I giggled. "Zoe, you're seriously shameless."

Shelby laughed. "He started it, and then I started the make out."

My eyes widened. "That sounds like an interesting story."

"Oh, it is," Sophie said.

"I missed all the good stuff being at home." I needed the whole story, but I would let Shelby off the hook for now. Later when Zoe and Madison went home I would ask. "Should we have a beach day tomorrow?"

"Yes!" Zoe and Madison said in unison.

"I've got to work on the festival, but you guys go ahead," Shelby said.

"Soph?"

"Drew and I are leaving for a town date. You three have fun."

I had hoped the five of us could hang out more, but at the same time it would let me catch up with Zoe and Madison in person. There were things that were just easier to discuss when you were together—and I could use a good beach day with my best friends.

CHAPTER TWENTY-SEVEN

SHELBY

My papers, journal, and laptop were scattered around me, like someone walked into Staples, bought a whole bunch of office supplies, and exploded it everywhere.

Randy squinted at a line of text near the bottom of the paper he was holding. "That's really how much they're donating for the festival?"

I checked the value he referred to. "Yep. I couldn't believe it either. Mr. Tate left my dad a voicemail yesterday and told him he wanted to personally donate money for some of the operating costs. My father told me he must be angling for something, but he can't figure out what it is."

"Maybe he's trying to buy his way back into the center of everything."

"Most likely or to connive Priscilla into importance. Who knows?"

He leaned back into the sofa cushion. "Do you ever miss hanging out with them?"

My eyes widened. "That's a question I never expected to be asked."

"I know what you've said about them both in the past, but they were around you for a large portion of your life. I was simply curious, even with the negative things they caused."

"Honestly? No. Priscilla and Tabitha were never really my friends the way everyone here is. They didn't care about my feelings or wants or needs. They used anything I was going through as a weakness to weasel into or elevate themselves through my pain. If they helped me with homecoming or any kind of recognition it was for their personal gain through association."

"If you couldn't have separated yourself from their negativity, do you think you would have still tried to be Riley's friend so much?"

I placed the papers next to me and studied his expression. "What's this really about?"

"I'm just curious, knowing how negative they are and can be, would you still try."

"It depends, I suppose. I wanted to be her friend more than theirs so I would have found a way to separate myself."

Randy sighed.

"Is this about someone else? Like maybe you and Riley?" Randy's expression remained blank. "How is your family doing?"

"They're fine. Emma and Jade are enjoying the summer playing outside and being with their friends. Momma is doing well. She has her book clubs and takes care of the house."

I arched an eyebrow. "And your dad?"

"He's … drinking on and off."

"Even with the increase in business he hasn't cooled it?"

He shook his head. "Habits are hard to break, I suppose."

"Have you tried talking to him about it?"

"No. You know how founding men are. Do you think your father would want you telling *him* what to do?"

"Well, not necessarily, but I've tricked him into agreeing with my perspective and made him think it was his idea."

"My dad wouldn't listen to me about that. He would tell me it wasn't my place. He was the man of the house, and I should mind my own business."

"He doesn't hit any of you, does he?"

"No. Not at all; he just drinks and becomes sloppy. He doesn't focus on work or his responsibilities. He isn't abusive."

"So, what's the connection with Riley then?"

He ran his fingers through his hair. "You saw how she reacted to Sophie's drinking. She was hurt and it scared her. How can I bring that negativity around her? I can't guarantee that my dad would cooperate if I took her home. He could be drunk or on his way to being drunk and how would that be fair to her? It's not her dad. She shouldn't have to deal with it."

"Maybe not, but you should let her decide what she can handle and what she can't. Sophie's drinking was different. It affected Riley because it was out of the blue. Sophie got wasted on our watch. She had never been like that before. It was surprising and then hurt when she wouldn't let us in so we could help with *why* she was drinking in the first place."

He shook his head. "It's just not right. I can't do it." He ruffled the papers in front of him. "Let's get back to this. Forget I said anything, okay?"

"Sure."

I wanted to say *no*. I wanted to tell him he needed to get over this fear because he was wasting time with a girl he deeply cared about. I wanted to say that Riley was a big girl and would tell him if she couldn't handle it. But at the same time, it wasn't my place.

Randy didn't talk much about his family and shaming him into thinking his feelings were silly wouldn't motivate him to change it. So, I left it alone.

"When you were home, I called the tent rentals, the blowup obstacle course rentals, and started going through the applications for the booths. We have dozens of new applicants. I don't think we will be able to take them all."

"How many new ones?"

"At least twenty. I stopped counting after that."

He rubbed his chin. "There's no way to accept them all? The booths were a hit and we pulled in new customers from it."

"We sectioned off the same amount of space as last time and that had been almost completely used. If we cut down on the size of some of the booths, we still can't fit everyone in that space."

"Let me see what I can do with getting more space for the booths. We can put the amusement rides on the other side of the park this time and free up that space for booths."

"Okay. Whatever you want to try, I'll go with it. We must answer them soon, though. So, I would say by the end of the week, we need to know how many booths we can add and then start responses."

Randy jotted a note in his notebook. "Okay, what else is top priority?"

"We need to finalize the look for the punch cards. I took what we did last time and added a few spots that wanted to join. I also added summer details to the paper."

I pulled up the mockups on the screen and turned the computer to face him. "What do you think?"

He leaned closer and studied the image. "Can we swap these two stores and make the beach ball a little bigger?"

I made the adjustments. "Like this?"

"Yes. Perfect. I say order them."

I laughed. "I'll send them to my father's secretary. You know he always wants final approval."

"Of course. So, what will he say when he finds out about you and Luke?"

My eyes widened. "Surprising me twice in one day. I must be off my game."

Randy chuckled.

"I don't know what he will think. He's from a founding family, so I can't see him caring all that much. Obviously, he will remind me of my responsibility to be discreet and not cause any waves in local gossip. Mother wanted us to date for the ball anyway, so I can't see them saying no."

"Does that bother you that they don't really know him?"

"Not really. My parents have never been involved in that way. I can't expect what has never happened. Would it be nice to have parents that were focused on other things? Absolutely. But that isn't Thaddeus and Vivian Rowe."

"True. Aren't you worried about him going back to boarding school?"

"No … Okay, maybe a little, but I'm not focusing on it. We have eight weeks left of summer vacation and I don't want to waste it."

A smile formed over his face. The first one I had seen since Riley came back from home. "That's an awesome outlook. I hope it works for you two."

"Thanks." I glanced at our to-do list and the few things

we had checked off. "We have a lot more to finish before we can stop."

He rubbed his hands together and waited.

He was a hard worker, kind, and loyal. I hoped Riley and him figured out their dilemma before it wrecked how they felt about each other. They both deserved happiness, I just didn't know if their timing was right.

The boys had decided to escape from the cove house to give us girls some alone time. I didn't know if they were secretly afraid of Zoe or Madison, but they seemed too eager to disappear.

Not that I cared. It was fun to have a girls' night. And I rather liked Zoe and Madison. If they had lived here, I could easily see us all being friends.

Sophie nudged my elbow. "What's for dinner tonight? Chef Frank give you any more amazing recipes to try out?"

"I was thinking we could have pizza instead."

Riley giggled as Sophie's jaw slackened. "Sophie, there's still leftover lasagna in the fridge."

She crossed her arms and frowned. "I'll just have pizza."

Zoe and Madison skipped down the stairs.

"Did I hear pizza?" Zoe asked.

"Is that okay?" I asked.

Zoe rubbed her hands together. "Yes, as long as it's cheese and pepperoni and not some floofy cauliflower nonsense."

I giggled. "You won't find that here."

"Good, because there's a line and that would cross it."

Madison rolled her eyes. "Didn't you tell me your mom made you one and you loved it?"

Zoe gasped, while Riley stifled a giggle. "Mad, that is a trade secret." Zoe tried to keep her face stern, but quickly broke.

We all laughed.

"I'll preheat the oven and put some chips in a bowl while I wait. Why don't you all go have a seat on the couches? I'll be right out."

Sophie, Zoe, and Madison headed for the couch.

"Thank you. I can help you know," Riley said.

I smiled. "I know ya can. I'll be right in, though."

She eyed me then moved a little closer. "What do you think about them?"

"I can see why you're all friends. I'll be sad when they leave."

She relaxed and grinned. "I know, they fit in so fast."

I shooed her out of the kitchen, then set up the oven for the pizza. With how much Sophie ate, I put two pizzas on pizza pans, then emptied a regular bag of chips into a bowl. Then, I did the same with tortilla chips and some dips into smaller bowls.

"What's the subway like?" Sophie asked Zoe.

I placed the chips on the coffee table.

"Dirty, smelly, claustrophobic."

Sophie wrinkled her brow. "Riley, you told us it was fun. That sounds horrible."

"Zoe is dramatic," Madison said. "It can be fun, but it's also public transportation, so it's as weird as those who take it are."

Sophie laughed. "Okay, that I can imagine. What's the strangest thing you've ever seen on the subway?"

Zoe dipped a chip into the salsa. "Probably this one guy dressed up as a clown on the bottom half and a punk rocker on the top half. He was playing an air guitar and tap dancing at the same time in these enormous green shoes. So weird."

I widened my eyes as I sat. "That sounds bizarre."

"It was. I got out of there fast. Creepy clowns are a no, especially when their top half doesn't match."

Sophie looked to Madison. "What about you?"

Madison tapped a finger to her chin before she lifted up and tucked her legs underneath her on the couch. "This woman was staring at one of the advertisements, talking to herself. Like full on conversation, then she talked about the ad, too."

Sophie shivered. "Okay, so maybe the subway isn't as glorious as it seemed."

Riley laughed. "It's a must though if you're in New York. *And* you don't have to wait until you're sixteen to take it. So, the freedom is cool."

"Okay, fine. But you can walk anywhere in Honey Cove and that's free," Sophie said.

The oven beeped, and I stood to put the pizzas in. Their conversation floated to me in the kitchen, but I only caught snippets. What was clear, was that Sophie would *never* be venturing into a subway at night. No matter how glamorous she thought it was.

I set the timer and joined them back on the couch. The conversation had shifted to Madison asking Sophie about her brother.

"He's obnoxious. He'll be a freshman this year and he thinks he's so cool. I can't wait for his bubble to pop once he enters the door. Bottom of the food chain again."

Riley launched a pillow at her head. "Leave Caleb alone. He means well."

Sophie rolled her eyes. "You say that because he hits on you every time you're over."

Zoe and Madison laughed.

Riley scoffed. "That is not why. He's only fourteen. He doesn't know any better. Were we any better when we entered high school?"

Sophie crossed her arms but didn't answer.

"Pizzas should be done in twenty minutes," I said. "Why don't we play a game?"

Sophie leaned forward. "Truth or dare?"

Riley and I groaned and said, "No," at the same time.

Zoe and Madison exchanged glances.

"Trust me. You don't want to play with her," Riley said.

"So, what else is there?" Sophie asked.

"Never have I ever?" Madison asked.

"Sure," I said. "Don't we all need a drink though?"

Madison giggled. "Not unless you play the alcoholic version. We could just start with ten fingers. The person who gets all their fingers down first loses."

"Okay," Riley said as she adjusted her place on the couch.

Sophie and Zoe nodded.

"Riley, why don't you go first?" Madison suggested.

She sighed then stayed still while she thought of something. "Never have I ever been to New York."

Sophie and I narrowed our gazes as we put a finger down.

"Oh, so it's like that then," Sophie said. "Never have I ever lived in two different towns."

Riley stuck out her tongue and put down a finger.

Zoe went next. "Never have I ever busted my butt on a patch of ice."

Now it was Riley's turn to glare, while the rest of us cackled.

"Never have I ever taken the subway," I said.

Sophie smiled, but the other three put down a finger.

Riley was losing so far with three fingers down, while most of us only had one.

We all stared at Madison for her turn. "Oh, never have I ever kissed someone with tongue."

Sophie smirked as she put a finger down. Clearly she and Drew had done more than she gave us details about.

"Hmm. Never have I ever wet myself in public," Riley said.

Zoe and Madison put fingers down.

Sophie raised an eyebrow. "Oh, do tell us those stories, please."

Zoe shrugged. "Laughed too hard and my bladder was full. You can imagine the rest."

Sophie nodded, then looked at Madison.

She sighed. "Well, fine. Mine was less like that. Scary movie at a public theater. One of those jump scare scenes and next thing I knew, I had peed myself."

Zoe giggled. "I forgot about that one."

Madison's cheeks reddened. "Yeah, yeah. Honestly, it is what it is."

"Never have I ever stayed up for twenty-four hours," Sophie said.

I put a finger down, but no one else had.

"Never have I ever lived in a tiny town," Zoe said. That got Riley, Sophie, and me.

"Never have I ever joined a sports team," I said.

Zoe, Sophie, and Riley all put a finger down.

"What do you play, Zoe?" I asked.

"I played softball briefly in middle school. Nothing since."

I couldn't see her playing a sport. She seemed too tough around the edges to be on a team.

"Never have I ever stolen something," Madison said.

Zoe and Sophie put down a finger.

I gasped. "What did you steal, Sophie?"

She giggled. "It's stupid, but I took an extra piece of candy at the store once. Nothing crazy."

"Oh, okay."

Riley looked at Zoe. "And you?"

"Chapstick." She shrugged. "My lips were in dire need."

Riley shook her head. "Stealing now, are we?"

Zoe smirked. "Stop being such a goody two shoes. As if you've never done *anything* bad."

Riley held up her fingers. "Well, clearly I've never stolen!" She exhaled then said, "Never have I ever snooped through someone's phone."

Madison put down a finger, but no one asked whose phone.

"Never have I ever sent a sexy selfie to someone," Sophie said.

Madison put down another finger.

Zoe and Riley could catch flies from how wide their mouths hung agape.

Zoe elbowed Madison. "Who did you send *that* to? And why didn't you tell me?"

Madison's cheeks went a whole two shades redder. "Someone I met online."

"And?" Riley asked. "Name? Age? Do you two still talk?"

She shook her head. "He was older, in college now, but it was while he was a senior. I didn't mention it because nothing ever happened."

"What did you do in the picture?" Zoe asked, her eyes narrowed.

"Nothing crazy. I pushed my boobs together more, wore a tank top, showed a lot of cleavage."

"Oh," Zoe relaxed. "That's all?"

Madison rolled her eyes. "Yes, and it counts, but no, I wouldn't do it again."

Riley shifted. "Why did you in the first place? I'm honestly surprised you would."

I had to be honest, I was surprised, too. Madison seemed like the opposite, like if someone had asked, she would have flat out refused.

"It was a while ago. I liked him, thought it would get his attention."

Zoe shook her head. "I'm glad it didn't. That's the wrong way for a guy's attention."

Madison pursed her lips but kept silent.

It was Zoe's turn again, and currently Sophie and Riley were tied with the most fingers down, only having five left. "Never have I ever gotten sick from drinking."

Sophie put down a finger and groaned. "Thanks to a month ago, otherwise I wouldn't have."

"Never have I ever *enjoyed* running," I said.

Riley and Sophie put down a finger and smirked.

The oven beeped. "Ooh, pizza time!"

We all looked around at each other's hands.

"Looks like you lost, Sophie."

She growled and then frowned. "Fine, but rematch later."

I giggled and headed for the kitchen to take out the pizzas. Sophie was too competitive; I didn't think it was in her to know how to win gracefully.

I pulled the pizzas from the oven and placed plates on the counter. We ended up streaming a movie while we ate, which was fine by me. Sophie would get revengeful with the game now that she had lost. I certainly didn't want to see that.

CHAPTER TWENTY-EIGHT

Our beach day had been a blast. We floated among the waves and played chicken to see who would dive or jump over first. We got entirely too much sun and had laughed until my cheeks hurt. I had missed spending time with them.

It was nice to see them bond with Sophie and Shelby, too. Our dinner together had been good for all five of us. Today was the last full day with them before I had to drive them back tomorrow.

Last night before bed, Shelby had suggested we have a pool party cookout. Zoe and Madison had agreed, and the boys had said they would use the grill to make us food. Luke had driven Drew and Randy to the store this morning and picked up hot dogs, hamburgers, buns, and other barbecue sides.

I glanced at Zoe in front of the mirror in the bathroom. "Are you ready yet?"

Zoe turned around one more time. "I can't decide. This bathing suit or the green one?"

I rubbed my temples. "I told you I liked the purple one,

but you pick. I'm going downstairs."

Madison had already left the room in a navy-blue one piece, a large, white, floppy hat and a white cover up and I had decided to wear my new coral bathing suit with my mint-green cover up.

I hopped down the stairs, two at a time.

Shelby glanced up from her laptop as I came down. "All ready?" She scrunched her face. "Where's Zoe?"

"Changing her bathing suit, *again.*"

"Still? I thought she narrowed it down before I left," Madison said.

"Nope. Where are the boys?"

Shelby jerked her thumb toward the back. "Setting up. Something about checking the propane tank and complaining about the floaties they had to blow up."

I giggled. "How big?"

Shelby's smile turned mischievous. "A large flamingo and a couple rafts."

"Oh, no wonder. I'll go check on them."

"Suit yourself," Shelby said as she got lost in her laptop again.

I squinted against the reflection of the sun off the pool water. Just as Shelby had said, they were huddled around the pool, each with a floatie, attempting to blow them up.

"She's crazy—" Luke said, before he saw me, then his cheeks reddened ever so slightly.

I chuckled. "Are we complaining about the floaties?"

They all nodded with the floaties dangling from their mouths.

"We've been trying to blow them up for ten minutes," Randy said.

Drew's cheeks were reddened, and his eyes were about to roll behind his head.

"Why don't you look for an air pump?"

"We did," they said together.

"Oh. I guess that wasn't successful?"

"That'd be right," Luke said as he assessed his progress. He had gotten stuck with the flamingo, which was at least a foot bigger than he was and had only managed to blow up one leg so far. This would take him all day before he was done.

Randy was the only one who was almost done with the float he was working on.

"Can I help with anything else?"

They shook their heads.

"Okay. I'll go get the beach ball from inside. Want any drinks?"

"Water," Drew said, exasperated.

"Luke? Randy?"

"I'll take a sweet tea," Randy said.

"Water," Luke said.

"You got it. Coming right up."

I bolted up the stairs and back into the air conditioning.

Shelby lifted her gaze once more. "Are they still alive?"

"Barely. Drew looks like he might pass out from his floatie. Randy is the only one even close."

Sophie's eyes widened. "I'll go help him. Poor guy."

"I told them I'd bring them drinks. Soph, he'll be happy to have help. He looked rough."

She nodded and exited through the French doors, when Zoe came down the stairs. She ended up in the purple bikini, like I told her. "Nice of you to join us."

She stuck out her tongue and hopped from the last step. "Are we all ready?"

I tossed her the beach ball. "Take that out and we will be."

She caught it with ease. Then Madison headed out with her toward the pool.

I peered over Shelby's shoulder as I rounded the counter. "What are you so preoccupied with?"

"Stupid emails for the festival. They came in this morning and unfortunately are urgent. If I don't deal with them now, I have to do it later. I know I won't want to, so I'm doing it now in case. Is that okay?"

"Of course. We'll be outside."

She nodded, lowered her gaze, and then her fingers flew over the keys as she typed her email.

I grabbed two water bottles and an iced tea, plus a water for me, then headed back out.

Zoe and Madison were ogling over the pool railing at someone. If I had to guess, they must have seen some boys on the beach. Zoe only had that expression when she saw a cute boy she couldn't help staring at.

Sophie had finished the float, while Drew gulped the water I brought him.

Randy only nodded at his sweet tea as he pushed the float into the pool.

Luke had paused on the flamingo. "Where's Shelby?"

"She had to finish a few emails for the festival."

Randy's eyebrows knitted. "She didn't say anything. I'll go check if she needs help."

I tried to say she would be out shortly, but Randy had already bounded up half the stairs, his white and blue bathing suit crinkling as he moved. Things still felt prickly between us, and I hated it. I wanted things to be like they always were. Or at least get those butterflies from the looks he would give me when I caught him looking in my direction. I hadn't caught him staring at me in days and it sucked.

A huge splash sent water over the sides of the pool and onto my feet and flip flops.

Zoe had dive bombed into the water and soaked Madison in the process.

Madison shed her hat and cover up and dove gracefully into the water after her. The splashing was quick and aggressive. Madison was in the middle of trying to dunk Zoe's head under the water when Randy returned with Shelby.

"Finally," Luke said as he pushed the last plug into the flamingo. He launched the float into the pool and almost landed on Madison's head, which caused the war to terminate briefly.

"Let's all swim!" I shouted and kicked the beach ball into the pool, too.

Drew and Sophie jumped in on the deep side and then claimed two of the rafts, floating near each other.

I waded in using the stairs on the shallow end and Randy placed his feet into the pool near the deep end.

Hmmph. At every turn he was avoiding me. It was final, I had to talk to him about everything once they left. I couldn't push it off. I hated how we passed by each other's thick tension surrounding our events. It's not how I wanted us to be.

Luke did a cannonball right next to Sophie's raft, sending a tidal wave over her and Drew.

She scowled and pushed water off her raft, while Drew shook his blond hair out.

Luke snatched the beach ball and tossed it at Randy, who spiked it back at him. Luke hit it again, this time toward my end of the pool.

I scooted forward and hit it back. Before I realized, we were all hitting the beach ball around the pool as we floated in the water.

Shelby had climbed onto the flamingo and played, too.

All eight of us sat in the water and played. I could have never imagined our time would turn out so well that everyone would welcome Zoe and Madison. I had the best friends ever.

Their bags surrounded the back of my Impala as I helped load them into the trunk. I couldn't believe that we had already spent forty-eight hours together and it was time for them to go home.

Zoe loaded the last bag in the trunk, and I slammed it shut. They waved to everyone on the deck one last time before we all got in and started the car. "I can't believe I'm taking you two to the airport already. This was way too short."

Madison pouted. "Right? Why didn't we do a week? That would have been more fun."

"It was a surprise trip meant to be short. We couldn't spring ourselves on her for a week," Zoe said.

"Of course, you two could have. I wouldn't have said no to that. Even if we had gone back to my mom-mom's."

"Next time. Although, we've been down here, so now you must come back to New York to visit," Zoe said.

"I might be visiting my dad around Christmas. I miss the lights and all our traditions in a big city."

"Really? You aren't lying?" Madison asked.

I shook my head. "My dad mentioned it when he was here. I'm not sure if it'll be just me or if Mom is going, too."

Madison clapped her hands. "Well, I don't care who comes as long as you're on the plane."

I laughed. "I'll see what I can do. My parents seem to

change every month, so by Christmas who knows where they'll be."

"True." Madison wrinkled her nose. "Are they all lovey-dovey around you again? When they picked us up from the airport, Zoe and I thought we saw them holding hands and staring into each other's eyes. It looked too teenagerly for me."

"I don't know. Mom likes being back home even though she won't one hundred percent admit it. I can tell she doesn't want to move back to New York. As for Dad, unless he got a new job and looked for a house here, I don't see him necessarily moving, either. How are they supposed to have a long-distance marriage permanently?"

"That sounds seriously awkward."

"Tell me about it. I leave them to sort out their feelings. If I don't see and hear the fighting and it doesn't affect their relationship with me, then I leave them alone."

"Parents are weird. Who separates, moves hundreds of miles away, and doesn't fully get divorced?"

"You're asking the wrong person. If you find an answer, let me know."

Madison giggled.

I adjusted the volume of the radio and searched their expressions. "But you guys had fun?"

Madison nodded.

"Yes," Zoe said.

"Good. What did you think of Shelby and Sophie? Are they what you pictured?"

Zoe tilted her head. "Yes and no. Sophie's humor is a lot darker than I had pictured, but I absolutely love it."

"And if I'm being honest, I was concerned about how Shelby would be. She seems like a completely different person than the one you told us did all the sabotaging," Madison said.

I smiled. "Shelby has been a surprisingly great friend. I honestly think about her from the fall and her now as two completely different people. So much has changed since then. Plus, she really didn't *do* all those things. You remember her mother orchestrated it."

Zoe stretched out in the backseat. "Still. For how much money her family has and her social influence, she is down to earth."

"Definitely. Maybe it's the whole small-town vibe that changes those at the top?"

Zoe snorted. "Yeah right. Most families with money like that and clout with neighbors are stuck up. Didn't you say her mother was the exact opposite?"

"Yeah."

"So, Shelby is just the outlier."

I shrugged. "Maybe. Maybe not. Honestly, what if all the popular kids in all the schools are living this double life and we just don't know because they never get the chance to show it? I mean other than Priscilla Tate, the youth of the founding families are chill. I mean Luke and Randy aren't stuck up."

Zoe fanned her face. "Luke is *hot!*"

Madison swung around to face Zoe. "Zo, that's practically Shelby's boyfriend."

"So? He isn't here. I'm not stealing him, but I can appreciate a good-looking guy. I mean damn."

I giggled. "Since when are golden boys your type?"

"Since they look like that."

Madison rolled her eyes. "What's up with you and Randy? Things felt colder than Antarctica."

Zoe leaned between our two seats. "Yeah. I mean based on what you had told us about your *relationship* I expected more sparks or sexual tension, but you barely looked at each other."

I gripped the steering wheel tighter. "He was just giving me space to spend time with you two."

"Likely story, Riley. That was not about us. That was about you two," Madison said.

Zoe nodded. "And to be honest, you deserve someone who flaunts you and thinks about your feelings and he wasn't giving me that vibe."

"He has a lot going on, you guys."

"Why are you defending him so intensely when you know you aren't happy with things?" Madison reached for my shoulder. "We are your oldest friends. You may be good at lying to them or to yourself, but we aren't so easily fooled."

I sighed. "Okay, fine. We aren't in the place I want for us. But that boy who surprised me with peach rings and made grand gestures is still in there. He's just going through a time with his family."

"You don't even sound like you believe that when you say it," Madison said.

Was she right? Of course, I knew the cute gestures and chivalry were still a part of who Randy was, but it had been a while since I'd seen it. I was more against my belief that his family was the only obstacle between us. "I do believe it, but I don't like it."

"Then do something about it," Zoe said.

Madison's gaze pierced my side as I focused on the road. "There are a lot of great guys out there. It doesn't mean they should all be boyfriends. He obviously knows how to treat a girl. No one is debating that, but it must work for you two, and if it isn't then maybe it's time to move on."

"We spend so much time together. How will that work if I try and it doesn't happen?"

"You will figure it out when and if it happens.

Worrying about it before the scenario is even real isn't going to help," Madison said.

"I have a plan. I've had a plan for days, but it still doesn't feel that great to risk everything."

"You won't know until you do it," Zoe said.

The plan was simple. I would ask him to reconsider on the Fourth of July. It had to work with the exuberant atmosphere and the jovial nature of the holiday. And if it didn't, I had no idea how I would handle that.

Zoe drummed her hands on the back of Madison's seat. "Let's crank up the radio, then dance and sing it out until we're at the airport. It's been too long, and I don't want the trip to end on a sad note."

I smiled and cranked up the volume. It had been a long time since we belted out anything together. Not to mention it would feel good to release all my tension.

CHAPTER TWENTY-NINE

SOPHIE

The pale wood stared at me as I lay awake. Today was the Fourth of July and as with every year, it never got easier to remember that soon after this day, my father had died. I never wanted it to tarnish the festivities of this holiday, but it did. So, here I lay, staring at Riley's bunk above me.

I was never the one awake first, but as I peered over to my right, the lump that I knew to be Shelby was still and rose and fell in time with her breathing. I kicked the covers off and stood. I needed to move around, or the feelings would consume me.

This day was different. I was determined to make it different. I was with my friends. I had a boyfriend, and we were all at the cove house. I wouldn't let something that would happen at the end of the month ruin today, even if it was hard not to think of him on this day.

My father loved the Fourth of July. When he wasn't deployed, he would buy all the fireworks Mama would allow. He set them up and once night fell, he launched them all in a sparkling show. It was the best, until his absence made it the worst.

Downstairs was silent. The lights were off and the curtains pulled close. Apparently, I was not only the first one awake of the girls, but the guys, too. I grabbed the soft blanket from the back of the couch and walked out the back French doors to my favorite sectional.

The cushions welcomed me like a hug from an old friend. The air was already warm and humid, but the blanket was more for comfort than for warmth. A slight breeze sent goosebumps over my bare legs from my pajama shorts. For now, the air felt good since my body was in a deep freeze from the air conditioning. Until I thawed out, I couldn't exactly *feel* the humidity the way I knew it should be.

Cuddled up in the blanket, I stared out at the open beach. No one was out there as far as I could tell, but soon, the beach would have endless crowds as everyone gathered for fireworks on the water. It would be the first time I had witnessed fireworks on the beach, but I was excited to spend the time with my friends. We all needed a good night to relax and unite in the excitement.

Riley hadn't been herself in days since her friends left. I couldn't tell if it was because she missed them or because the Randy drama was more in her face now than ever. And Shelby was so entranced by her to-do list for the end of summer bash, that she hadn't gone to the beach in days, either.

The French door sliding open startled me. I turned and smiled. "Hey you."

Drew smiled back as he combed his fingers through his blond curls. "You're up early. You okay?"

I patted the sectional next to me. "I'm okay."

He surveyed my expression. "I was wondering if it would bring up feelings of your dad today."

I never understood how he could read me so easily. "You are incredible, you know that?"

"Nah. I just know your expressions, Sophie." He pointed to my face. "And that is the look you get when you're thinking of your dad."

"If you say so. You're the only one who notices it then."

He plopped on the sectional next to me, then snatched half the blanket. "Maybe. Maybe not. Most people don't stop and take the time to pay attention to what people are doing. And sometimes even if they do, they don't say it."

"Well, yes. I was thinking of my dad. It was always his favorite holiday."

Drew chuckled. "I remember the year where his fireworks backfired. He had gotten one of those big ones that shot in the air and exploded high up with all the colors like at Disney."

I clasped a hand over my mouth, recalling the memory.

"He had gotten it too close to that tree, and when it exploded, it lit the tree on fire."

"Mama was so mad. She had always warned him about that."

"Thankfully, he had a fire extinguisher and managed to get the fire out before the tree ignited more."

I shook my head. "Mama almost banned all the fireworks the next year because of that."

He poked my cheek. "There's that adorable smile."

I covered my face with my hands. "You're so good at that. You must teach me your mind tricks."

"No mind tricks. I just—"

"Know me. Yeah, yeah. I know."

"Well, what are we doing today? It sounded like the three of you had some big plan for tonight."

"Nothing crazy … at least for us. We're going to walk on the beach and get a good spot for the fireworks."

"Gotcha. What about until then?"

I shrugged. "Not sure." My stomach growled.

Drew's eyebrow arched. "Is someone ready for breakfast?"

"Probably. I didn't feel hungry when I came out here."

Drew stood and then pulled me up with him. "Let's go fix that. The smell of breakfast will wake everyone up anyway."

I waited as I watched him walk toward the door. His hair flopped around in the slight breeze. He wasn't classically handsome, but he was sexy to me. And the fact that he knew what I was feeling and could help calm me down if I needed it was an even bigger bonus.

"Are you coming or just going to stare at me?" Drew asked without turning around.

"What? How …?"

He faced me then and winked. "Omelets or French toast?"

"French toast, you mind reader."

"I'll get the eggs and spices if you can grab the bread for me."

I nodded and headed to the bread box. I didn't understand why we had to keep it in a fancy box in the dark. At home we just kept it on the counter and it never got moldy any faster or slower than in a box.

I held up our half remaining loaf of bread. "Should we use it all or save some for lunch?"

"Is that our last loaf?"

"Think so."

"Let's use it now. We can do something else for lunch. Maybe use the tortillas for quesadillas or something."

I placed the bread on the counter, then hopped up as Drew compiled his French toast concoction to dip the bread in. "So, what do you want to do before the fireworks?"

Drew dropped a piece of bread in the egg and spices. "I'm good with whatever. Do you need to practice your SAT prep more?"

I groaned. "Can't I have one day that I don't have to worry about SAT prep? My scores are already getting better on the practice tests."

"They are, but you still have a few more sections of your book. Summer will disappear before we know it and your mom will kill *me* and *you* if you don't get a decent score this time."

"I'm well aware. I remember the discussion quite vividly, however, it's a national holiday. Everyone is off for the Fourth of July. Can't I be off, too?"

Drew glared at me over his glasses. "I suppose you can play hooky. But only until midnight, then back to work."

I giggled. "What am I, Cinderella?"

"You're seriously such a smart ass. No. You'd hate the big frilly dress and the glass slippers."

"Touché. But the midnight deadline seems a bit much."

"It's not about midnight. It's an expression."

I stuck out my tongue. "I know. I just wanted to rile you up."

He pretended to glare at me. "I'll remember that."

I closed the gap between us and hugged him from behind while he finished dredging the bread.

Someone coughed from behind us.

I turned.

Luke stood by the counter. "Sorry. I didn't mean to interrupt."

"You're fine. Drew is making French toast for everyone."

"I thought I smelled cinnamon."

Drew faced us. "Didn't I tell you the smell would wake everyone up?"

I waved him off. If he thought he was always right, I'd never hear the end of it … even if he had a knack to be right at least eighty percent of the time.

Luke sat at the counter. "Can I help?"

Drew shrugged. "Maybe some eggs and bacon or sausage? Just to let everyone have a choice."

Luke hopped down and strolled to the fridge. "Extras coming up. Oh, and happy Fourth of July."

"Happy Fourth," I said.

I moved to the stools to give them room to work. They moved around each other with ease. A carefully crafted routine since living here. I supposed I hadn't noticed the boys getting closer, too. We had figured it would be a time for us girls to get closer to each other and to our respective guys, but it made sense they would become friends after sharing a room together for so many weeks.

Luke elbowed Drew as he said something I couldn't hear clearly.

Drew's shoulders moved up and down as they always did when he laughed.

I smiled. Drew could use friends that were guys. Plus, if they got along it would make it easier for us to all hang out when they became an official couple. Who knew, maybe sparks would be flying for more than just the fireworks tonight.

The salt from the water clung to my hair and knotted it as I tried to pull the scrunchie out. "When will I ever learn to keep my hair down in the ocean? Trying to brush out all the knots is absolutely the worst."

Riley giggled as she unwrapped the bun she had made with her own hair. "It honestly doesn't matter. Salt water just does that. Unless you keep your head out of the water, it's kind of pointless. Plus, I hate my hair wrapping around my neck. It makes me feel like I'm being strangled by seaweed."

"Seaweed?"

She stared at me. "What? It's long, and in the water I can't tell what it is."

"That's just sad, Riley. Your hair isn't slimy. At least I hope it's not."

"Oh, whatever. You got freaked out the other day when you thought my foot was a fish in the water. You should be able to tell the difference between human skin and a fish's scales."

"Fine. We agree to disagree." I sighed and stared at my reflection in the mirror. Half of my hair was now out of the scrunchie, but even the sections that had escaped, it was still a rat's nest. "This is hopeless."

Shelby strolled into the bathroom with a small bottle. "Here use this. It'll detangle your hair enough for you to run a brush through it. Use a little more in the shower before you shampoo, and it'll be better."

The bottle was purple, with some name I couldn't pronounce. "Thanks."

Riley snagged the bottle and studied it before she sprayed down her hair.

"Leave me some."

She tossed her hair over her shoulder. "I can't help that I have long, luscious locks."

I rolled my eyes. "You're ridiculous. My hair is only shorter than yours by like three inches."

"Three inches is a big deal."

"Well, how do you plan to wear your hair tonight anyway?" I strolled from the bathroom. "Shelby, will we be *on*, on the beach? Or are they setting up like a platform?"

Shelby glanced up from her phone. "It should be on the sand. I doubt they'd construct anything. Everyone wouldn't fit anyway."

"Ugh, well there goes that outfit. I planned to wear my platform sandals with the black netting on the front."

Shelby tapped a finger to her chin. "Yeah, those won't work, but the rest of the outfit doesn't have to change just because you can't wear those. Pick regular flip flops and whatever you had planned up top."

"Hmm maybe. The sundress looks better with those sandals."

Riley exited the bathroom and brushed my shoulder as she walked by. "Drew won't care. He will think you're beautiful regardless."

My cheeks heated. "What makes you say that?"

"I see the way he watches you. You could probably wear sweatpants and a sweatshirt, with your hair piled on top of your head and he would still find you attractive."

I rolled my eyes. "Totally not true."

"I must agree with Riley on this one, Sophie. He's totally head over heels for you."

I waved them off. "We've been dating for less than six months."

"But you've been friends since childhood. That changes an actual relationship."

I crossed my arms. "We had a significant gap there."

"Doesn't matter. You two are so connected." Riley smiled. "We say it because we think it's cute. You don't need to be defensive. It's nice to see you with someone who is so devoted to you."

It was still hard to get used to hearing about my relationship from others, let alone being comfortable with our feelings being out there for others to see. So, instead, I changed the subject. "What are you two wearing?"

Riley pointed to an outfit on the dresser. "I didn't bring anything too fancy. I'm just wearing my denim jean capris and graphic tee. I might even bring a light sweatshirt. If it gets chilly, I want to be prepared. Plus, you know how the bugs find me. I don't exactly want a million bug bites all over my arms and legs."

"There is a thing called bug spray, you know?"

"Yeah, even so, they still find me."

"Well, you both know I don't own anything casual. However, with the possibility of sitting in the sand being a high probability, I don't want to ruin anything. I'll probably wear a cotton sundress and flip flops."

I gasped. "You own a cotton dress? Are you sure it's not cashmere or some other ridiculous fabric blend?"

Shelby launched a pillow at my head. "Whatever. I can't help it that my mother doesn't let me purchase certain clothes. As she always says, *A Rowe must be dressed to impress always.*"

"You should get all those sayings printed on something and then burn them."

Shelby giggled. "Maybe. It could be therapeutic."

Riley exited the bathroom with her hair in a cute fishtail braid and her outfit for the fireworks. "I win!"

"You win what?"

"I'm ready first."

I rolled my eyes. "Someday your competitive streak will massively get you in trouble."

She stuck out her tongue and plopped on my bed.

Shelby shrugged and headed to the bathroom next, which worked for me. I still needed to decide on what to wear. I liked my dress with my sandals, but she was right. There was no way I could wear it while being on the beach. I didn't need to twist an ankle and go face first into the sand.

Riley scrolled on her phone and then music erupted. It was a pop tune and had a good beat. She got up and shimmied around the room, then pulled me with her.

I groaned. "I don't want to dance right now. I'm trying to figure out what to wear."

"Your clothes will be there when the song is over. Just dance!"

I shook my head and then gave in.

Shelby came out and joined us until the song ended. It lightened the mood as we finished getting ready. I hoped tonight would be good for everyone.

CHAPTER THIRTY

I glanced up the stairs one last time. "Are we all ready?"

Sophie shuffled down the stairs with Drew following behind her. "I'm all set."

Riley and Randy hovered near the back door and Luke had been the first one downstairs.

"Let's head out then. It's faster to walk on the beach than use the road. Not to mention the road will be congested."

They followed me out the back door and to the beach. Once I hit the sand, I ditched my shoes and held them in one hand as the sand squished between my toes. The sand had cooled from the day as the sun descended into the horizon. We had about thirty minutes until the sun set and then they would start the fireworks.

Most groups were down close to the water sitting in chairs and on blankets. They gathered close together in groups facing the water, waiting for the show. I hadn't been to the fireworks, but I had heard it was beautiful to see. The colors would reflect off the water. My favorite fireworks weren't even the big ones. They always managed to startle me when they burst high above my head. Instead, I liked the sparklers. They let me enjoy the lights without dealing with the massive boom when they exploded.

"Where should we watch?" Riley asked.

I pointed to an empty spot high up on the beach. "This area works here." I eyed Luke. I hadn't told the girls of my plan to watch the fireworks separately. I wanted to enjoy this holiday with him. Just us. "I think I'll keep walking the beach though."

Riley's face drooped into a frown but nodded.

Sophie on the other hand winked.

Luke pulled his hands from his pocket. "Do you want company? I can walk with you."

"Sure."

We waved at the group as we walked away. They laid blankets on the ground and were settling in before they disappeared.

I weaved around the groups of people on the beach as I headed for the spot I had in mind—the rocks.

Luke's arm brushed mine as we walked.

"What do you usually do on July fourth?"

"It depends on if my parents are home or not." Luke moved around another group. "Most of the time we sit on our back deck at home and watch the fireworks from town. We can usually see the big ones. Or we would go on vacation and look up firework displays there."

"That sounds nice. What's your favorite place to see fireworks?"

"Hmm, can I tell you tomorrow?"

I scrunched my face. "Why tomorrow?"

Luke's expression changed to a grin. "Because tonight hasn't happened yet."

My stomach lurched and twisted at the thought. How sweet was that?

Luke shoved his hands in his short's pockets. "How about you?"

"Well, like with most holidays, my father is usually on a business trip and Mother goes to sleep early. When my Aunt Delilah visits she would make it special, but otherwise I wouldn't do much at all. Chef Frank would make me barbecue or something different for dinner."

"I'm sorry, Shelby."

"For what?"

"Your family doesn't realize the special person they have around them. I'm sorry they don't acknowledge that."

I bowed my head and focused on the sand. "Thanks."

He stopped and lifted my chin. "I mean it. How incredibly lonely. It's no wonder you were lost last winter. How can you trust anyone when your family barely spends time together?"

I shrugged. "It used to bother me immensely, but lately not as much."

The rocks were laid out before us. Luckily, no one else had wandered this far down the beach. We were at least fifty feet from the nearest group.

Luke outstretched his hand to help me up on the rock. I sat on a large one with a flat top, warmed from the sun. Luke sat close to me.

The silence filled the air, but not awkwardly. It was more of an understanding between two people. We didn't need words to communicate. The silence told a story of its own.

Silence like this would have unnerved me with some people, but with Luke it felt comfortable. It was like our souls were old friends and were catching up. I turned to face him and caught him staring at me. The gesture made my stomach flip again. If I looked into his eyes too long I was afraid of what it would tell me.

Sure, we had made progress by stating we felt like there could be something between us, but we hadn't burst the dam of feelings yet. I wasn't exactly sure when that would happen, but I didn't want to get my hopes up only to have them crushed. I learned a long time ago that if I had no expectations, I couldn't be disappointed.

We sat like that for a long time. The dark blue drove across the sky as it blanketed us in darkness. At some point the area in front of me had gotten dark enough I could barely see my own hand. Then a spark of light soared into the sky and burst. I could see the colors of red, white, and blue before I could feel the energy or smell the smoke in the air.

Of course, I startled.

"Are you okay?" Luke asked, his body moving closer. It was this pulse that emanated from him. The closer it got, the harder my heart thudded in my chest.

"It startled me," I screamed over the next wave of booms and crackles.

From the light of the fireworks, I turned to study Luke's expression. Just like me, he stared at my face—not the fireworks.

Our gazes locked and it tethered me to him. I could barely blink, let alone shift my gaze away. Each of us moved toward the other, until our noses were mere inches apart.

The electricity in the air was more than just from fireworks, but from all our feelings sizzling between us. I only hoped at that moment that he could sense it all, too. It was like running to the top of a mountain, looking out at the view and knowing that when it was time to descend, things would be different.

We inched even closer. His breath caressed my cheek—

a waft of mint mingled with his cologne, creating the scent I considered to hold the essence of him.

My eyelids fluttered close as if they held the weight of the world and couldn't be forced open. And then his lips brushed against mine.

Then his hands were around my waist holding me closer to him. His breath was hot and heavy against my neck, as he trailed kisses to my earlobe.

Sensations exploded all over. The fireworks shattered and the cascade of lights dimmed the shadows as he kissed me. I could feel the slight pressure of his fingertips on the small of my back as his lips brushed mine.

When we separated, we were breathing heavily.

Clearly the kisses had affected us both and in that moment, with the lights traveling across his face, I couldn't stop myself from saying it. "I *really* like you, Luke."

He grinned, pulled me back to him, and kissed me again. Then barely moving away, so that I could feel the words on my cheek he said, "I *really* like you, too, Shelby."

Was this the moment? Was this when I should ask him to be my boyfriend? Did I need a set number of dates to know that what I felt in this moment wasn't some frivolous and fleeting emotion?

"Luke, do you want to be my boy—"

An eruption of fireworks, signaling the end, shot into the sky, drowning out the second half of that important word.

CHAPTER THIRTY-ONE

The sky lit up with a dozen or so fireworks to finish the finale. Colors of all kinds dotted the night in intricate designs. There were so many bursts of color it was like the sun hadn't quite set just yet. And then just as quickly, they fizzled out with their crackles and sparks.

"That was amazing," Sophie said.

"Right? I can only imagine how much it must have cost for all those big ones."

"Based on a fight my parents had once for the fireworks my dad had bought, several thousand at *least*."

"Yeah, but it was always so cool the ones he could find," Drew said.

"Yes it was, but Mama's face was as red as her hair that one time. He never bought quite so many the next few years. Even still, he made it work."

"I could watch hours of that," I said.

Drew and Sophie muttered something out of ear shot, while Randy sat close, but not as close as I had thought he would have. He was always finding ways to let me know his presence with little touches here and there, but instead, he had stayed quiet, keeping his gaze trained on the sky.

I had hoped to catch him looking at me, but it didn't happen. Not even a glance was thrown my way.

Drew stood and then Sophie followed.

She stretched her arms high above her head and shook her dress. "Drew and I are returning to the house. Do you want to come with?"

I looked between them and Randy. "It's okay. I'm not ready to go back just yet."

"I'll stay with her," Randy said, even though his voice had the wrong edge to it. Normally his voice would be light and laced with the hope of being alone to talk, to be close, or to just sit embraced together, but this was different.

Sophie's gaze pleaded with me, but I shook my head. I knew she and Shelby could sense the tension, but tonight was now or never. We needed to talk about what happened before and I needed to be honest. I couldn't wait any longer in limbo.

Drew placed his hand on Sophie's back. "See you two later." Then he walked with her until they disappeared in the dark.

My stomach flopped and not in a cute butterfly kind of way; it was like when I had been caught doing something I shouldn't by my mom.

"Are you okay?" I asked. I wasn't even sure if he would answer me. His mood seemed to have infiltrated everything.

"I'm fine."

Sure he was, and I was a mermaid.

"You don't seem like yourself. Not since before I left to see my dad."

He shrugged. "I just have a lot going on with the festival stuff."

"Okay …" This was going horribly. What kind of response did I hope to have when he already seemed less than open? I wiggled on the blanket, the sand shifting unevenly so that my butt was too high on the right and too low on the left. "I was hoping we could talk."

"We're talking now."

My eyebrows drew together. This was not how I pictured this conversation going. "I wanted to talk about *us*."

Randy visibly shifted his weight away from me.

What was it they said? When someone closed off their body language it wasn't a good sign? Or was it when they moved away?

Either way, the vibe was not light.

"I know when we talked a couple weeks ago you said you still didn't feel like the timing was right. That you wanted things to be better with your family first. Can I ask what you hope is better?"

He eyed me warily. "I want things with my dad to be on a better, more stable path."

"What does that look like?"

"Sobriety."

"So, you want to wait until your dad is completely sober before we date officially?"

He wouldn't look at me but gave a little shrug.

"Why?"

Randy sighed and fiddled with the sand at the edge of his blanket. "I've said before that my family stuff shouldn't be a burden to anyone else. It wouldn't be right."

"How would us dating put that burden on me?"

"Riley, I saw how you reacted before."

My nose crinkled. "How I reacted? To what?"

"To Sophie's drinking."

My eyes widened. "What does that have to do with your dad?"

"You were upset. I saw your worry and your anxiety when you talked about those nights. My dad's drinking is ten times worse than Sophie's. If that's how it impacted you, then how could I put you in that situation again?"

Was this really his hold up? Sophie and his dad were in totally different situations. I reacted the way I did to Sophie's drinking because she was my best friend. I was watching her spiral and she wouldn't let me in. I hadn't even met Randy's dad.

"Do you not consider us close now?"

His face was puzzled. "Of course, I think we're close, Riley. How can you ask me that?"

I reached for his hand and entwined our fingers, happy that he didn't pull away. "Then how exactly would dating change anything if we are already close? We spend all our time together. We are living in the same house this summer. Most people at school assume we are already together. I don't see how dating is supposed to negatively affect me anymore."

His fingers slid from my grasp. "It just would, Riley. I can't explain it. You'd have to live it to understand. I won't do that to you."

My hands laid in my lap, picking at the frayed string on my capris. "So, you're saying you still don't want to be my boyfriend? That even now with this summer and all that has happened between us, that we should remain friends? Kissing, but not together? Holding hands, but not together? Making memories, but not together?"

Emotions crossed his eyes and then fleeted before I could read them all. The one he settled on was resignation. "Yes. I'm saying we can't be a couple right now."

I stood as my eyes burned. "Then maybe we need

space because I can't stay in limbo anymore. I *love* you, Randy, but I don't love this situation anymore."

He stood. His gaze bored into mine. "Are you sure that's what you want?"

I nodded.

He reached out but let his hand fall. Then, he turned and walked away.

I crumbled back on the blanket. My breath came in jagged waves as I bawled my eyes out. The tears flowed so quickly down my cheeks it felt like it was raining. I looked ridiculous, curled up on a picnic blanket, sobbing, but I didn't care. I didn't care anymore, because I told him I loved him, and he willingly walked away. He *walked* away. How could he do that?

I replayed his exit repeatedly. Each time the sobs poured out of me, until my eyes were puffy, and I had no more moisture left in them for me to cry. I balled the blanket up and stuffed it under my arm. I trekked to the house slowly, since it was much darker than our trek down, not to mention I didn't want to run into Randy like this. I had made my plea and he answered it. Now I just had to find a way to fill the Randy-sized hole that had taken residence in my heart.

CHAPTER THIRTY-TWO

The fireworks finale was beautiful from what I could tell of it while still staring into Luke's eyes. Of course, the stupid finale would happen when I had gotten the courage to ask him the most important question in our relationship.

Luke leaned closer and cupped his hand to his ear. "I'm sorry, what did you say?"

The air was quiet, nothing but muffled voices as people left and the rhythmic sound of the waves as they crashed into the rocks.

Luke grabbed my hand and turned it palm side up. He traced the lines of my hand with his finger. The movement was delightful but did nothing to help me ask the question again.

He waited. He didn't rush me. He just traced my hand repeatedly. It was like he knew I needed time to say whatever I had asked before. He didn't want to push me, he just … waited. It was that waiting that let the feelings build again.

"I-I asked if you wanted to be my boyfriend." And

then the words flowed from my mouth like water bursting through a dam. "I know we've only gone on two dates, and maybe that isn't enough, but I know what I want. I want us to be a coup—"

Luke's finger moved over my lips. "You are seriously cute when you babble and I was prepared to let you continue, but I thought you might want to hear my answer."

My eyes widened.

"I want you to be my girlfriend, too. I was going to plan this elaborate date and ask you then, but I agree, why should we wait when we know what we want now?" His finger moved from my lips.

"You mean it?"

Somehow in the darkness, he found my lips with his and kissed me. It was different from before, fast and with more force, but it felt right in the moment.

When we pulled apart, he asked, "Does that answer your question?"

I giggled. "Yes. Should we head back? It's getting late."

"Sure." He stood first and moved from the rock. He shined the light from his phone onto the rock I sat on then proffered his hand to help me down.

We walked in the sand back to the house with my arm wrapped around his waist and his arm wrapped around my shoulder—a perfect fit.

"So, what was this big, planned date you had in mind?"

He chuckled. "Nope. Not telling."

"What? Why not?"

"If I tell you, I can't use it in the future."

"Psh. Are you saying I must *wait* for this date to happen at some point? How would I even know when it happens?"

He curled a strand of my hair around his finger. "Do you really want to know?"

I nodded against his body.

"Well, I would take you into town back to Over Easy's. It was the time I felt a different spark between us. I realized I could really like you and be friends with you there. I would have them duplicate our order. You with your hot chocolate and me with my black coffee and cowboy burger."

He remembered what I had?

"And then I would have them bring out dessert with whip cream on the plate asking the question. I know it's corny."

It was straight out of a romantic comedy, but I should have expected it because it was his favorite movie genre. "Not at all. I think it's cute. I think your plan would have been flawed though trying to use it in the future. You can't exactly decorate dessert with something you already have."

"Fair point. I know I'm supposed to be this confident alpha male who has an ego the size of a house, but at the risk of breaking that façade down, I can't believe this is happening."

I giggled. "Me either, and I like that you aren't egotistical and arrogant, that would deflate the whole thing."

"Duly noted."

Our walk back to the house ended quicker than I had wanted. As we ascended the porch stairs, Drew was on the sectional … alone.

As I studied his expression, he looked rattled. Drew was never anything more than calm. Something was wrong.

When Drew glanced up and saw us he stood. "Shelby, you might want to head up to your room. I think Riley needs you and Sophie right now."

I glanced at Luke. How was I supposed to run now?

We just became a couple. Shouldn't I spend more time with him before the night was over?

Luke must have been able to read all those thoughts in my gaze. "Go. I'll stay down here. Come find me when you're done."

Drew shook his head. "I don't think she will be back down tonight. Riley was upset when she arrived back. Her makeup was smeared, and Randy wasn't with her. His stuff is missing from the room."

My jaw slackened.

Luke nudged me toward the door. "Go. I'm fine. She needs you right now. I'll see you in the morning."

I nodded, kissed his cheek, and rushed toward the stairs. This sounded bad, like next level bad. The door was closed, but the light poured out from the gap at the bottom. I turned the knob and pushed it open. Riley sat on Sophie's bed, her head in her hands as Sophie rubbed her back up and down repeatedly.

"What happened? We just got back. Drew said you might have been crying?"

Sophie's head snapped to my gaze, and she mouthed, *Randy left.*

My eyes widened. He left? Like left for the night? For the summer? What had happened on that beach?

I walked toward my bed and sat.

Riley had yet to look up and say anything. Sobs erupted from her, and her shoulders shook.

This was bad. Really, really bad. How could he do this? I didn't even know what happened, but he had to have a part in it. Why would he hurt her like this? He cared about her so deeply.

Riley snuffled and wiped her eyes with the back of her hand. She gazed into my eyes but remained silent.

"What happened?"

"I told him I couldn't be in limbo anymore. I said I loved him but not this situation," she said through hiccups.

My eyes widened.

"He said we couldn't be a couple and I said then maybe we needed space. So, he left."

"Like *left*, left?"

"I don't know. He walked away when I was sitting on the beach. I haven't gotten the courage to see if he's in his room or if his truck is out front."

"Drew … Drew said his stuff isn't in the room anymore."

A new wave of sobs erupted from Riley, she stood and ran to the bathroom.

"Oh man," Sophie said.

"You can say that again. What was he thinking?"

"I have no idea, but I could kill him right now. She is absolutely devastated."

"He's so stubborn. I would bet anything he said things were still not right with his dad. He doesn't get it. He acts like he must keep her at arm's length with the whole thing. Some of the weight could be lifted from him if he just let her in."

Sophie huffed. "Well, getting that through his head will be impossible. Not to mention how would we even tell him that. If I saw his face right now, I'd be tempted to hit him, and I know Riley doesn't want that either."

"Maybe he was just blowing off some steam tonight and will be back tomorrow?"

"Do you really think so? She asked for space. I think Randy plans to give her all the space she wants."

"Ugh, you're probably right. He will stay away because he thinks that is what she wants."

Sophie laid back on her bed. "This is so screwed."

"You can say that again."

"This is so screwed."

Despite myself, I giggled. "This is not the news I expected us to be sharing tonight."

Sophie jerked up and wiggled her eyebrows. "What do you mean? Do you have news?"

I averted my gaze.

"You do!"

"Yes, but now hardly seems like the time."

Sophie gave me a stern look. "Riley wouldn't want you to stifle what is happening with you just because she's upset."

"I know, but it seems wrong to say it to her right now."

"So, tell me."

The corners of my mouth turned up into a slight smile. "Luke and I … We made it official!"

Sophie grinned. "You two are a couple?"

I nodded.

"Ahhh! That's so exciting." Her mouth drooped. "But I see what you mean. Give her a few days and then tell her. She will be happy for you two no matter what. You know that."

I did know that, but I didn't want to rub salt in the wounds. How could I rejoice in my new relationship when hers just ended before it started? Sophie was right, this was *so* screwed.

CHAPTER THIRTY-THREE

SOPHIE

My bookbag sat next to the front door. My theater shift was in two hours, and I had to leave for town soon. This was the lightest my bag had been since I stayed at the cove house. I would only be gone for the day, coming home after dinner.

I couldn't leave Shelby alone with Riley too long. Currently, she still sat on the couch, sprawled in front of the TV watching endless shows and barely eating. She got up to go to bed and to go to the bathroom, but otherwise, she didn't bother leaving the couch.

The last three days had been beautiful outside, making it by far the best week at the house. She would have no clue, however, because she had yet to go on the sand since the Fourth of July.

Shelby and I had hoped that Randy was just taking the night to cool off and then would be back the next day, but that had not happened. And with every passing hour, Riley continued to sink into herself. It was becoming ridiculous. She couldn't be a vegetable on the couch for the rest of her life. She either needed to act on what had happened or move on, and she wouldn't do either of them.

I plopped on the couch by her feet. "How ya doing?"

She shrugged, never taking her eyes off the TV.

"So, I must go to the theater for a shift. Do you want to come with? You could watch some movies, my treat?"

"No."

"Okay, how about I drop you off at your mom-mom's?"

"No. There's a marathon of old DIY shows on today."

"You'd rather watch TV than go for a road trip? You haven't been in my Jeep for a few days."

"I want to see the renovation projects. Maybe next time."

This was impossible. How was I supposed to get her off the couch if she wouldn't even look at me? "Are you sure? It will be fun."

"I'm positive. Now shh the show is back on."

I stood and walked through the French doors to the back porch.

Shelby sat in a dark-green Adirondack chair with Luke sitting in a deep-royal-blue one next to her.

"It's dark in there. Like medieval times during the plague dark."

Shelby nodded as she took a sip of her tea. "I've tried everything I can think of to get her off the couch. She's been stuck in that same spot for so long that there will be a Riley impression on the cushion."

"Normally I would laugh, but it's seriously the truth. I tried to convince her to come back with me during my shift, but she didn't want any part of it. She wants to watch the DIY marathon."

"At least she talked to you. I only had mumbles and groans earlier."

"What can we do?"

"I have no idea. On the one hand, I feel like we should leave her alone to sort it out. On the other hand, I think I want to injure them both."

Luke chuckled. "Uh oh. We've stirred up the feistiness."

Shelby rolled her eyes and swatted at him. "I'm serious. I'm mad at him for leaving. I'm also worried about him because I know how much he cares for her. Then when I see her on the couch, I get mad again."

"I know what you mean. I guess we give it more time and then reevaluate. She should pull herself together soon. Maybe I can get her to go for a run when I get back. It'll be after dinnertime. I'm planning to stop by Mama's to eat, then drive back."

Shelby nodded. "Is Drew leaving, too?"

"No. His shift isn't today. Mr. Martin has barely scheduled us together all month. So, he will be here."

Shelby faced Luke. "Maybe you two can go do something and I'll try to pry her off the couch?"

"I can try to help, too," Luke said.

She patted his hand. "That's sweet, but you don't have to. To be honest, I don't know that I'll be successful myself anyway. You two go enjoy the day.

"Drew is up in your room. Or at least he was when I said bye."

Luke stood, then bent to kiss Shelby quickly, before he headed inside.

I smiled. "You two look cozy."

Shelby's cheeks reddened. "He has been so adorable I almost don't think it's real."

"I'm glad it's working out. Two out of three of us is a start."

Shelby grimaced.

I checked the time on my phone. "I need to head out. Text me if you need me to come back right after my shift. I'm done at six."

Shelby waved me off. "I'll be fine. Nothing will happen, except she might sink farther into the couch."

"Let's hope not." I headed back inside. Riley hadn't moved whatsoever on the couch. "Bye, Riley."

She raised her chin in a slight nod and remained trained on the TV.

I walked to the front door, picked up my bag, and headed to my Jeep. It would take a miracle to get her off the couch at this point, but hopefully Shelby had one up her sleeve.

***

"Mama! I'm home," I called as I dropped my bag and kicked off my shoes.

She peered from around the kitchen wall. "Hey, Soph. How was work?"

"Not bad. Sasha is getting better, so that's a start."

"Everyone takes their own time to come around. I'm glad she is getting the hang of things. It's hard when you have no clue what you're doing."

I raised an eyebrow. "Is this about sage advice from someone more experienced or are you feeling that now in your new job?"

Mama had applied for a promotion amid my chaos this past spring and had gotten it. She couldn't start for over a month until they found a replacement for her, and she was able to train them. Now she was in her second week of the new position.

"Maybe a little of both. I love the new opportunities at work and the schedule, but there are aspects of my job I haven't done before." She shrugged. "I'll get the hang of it. I must keep trying and be persistent."

I walked to the kitchen and plopped down in one of the chairs.

Mama stood at the stove stirring something in a large pot.

My eyebrows knitted. "Are you making chicken noodle?"

"Yep."

"In the summer? Why?"

"Caleb has a cold. I figured it would help open his air passages."

"Oh, gotcha."

The stove timer dinged, and Mama pulled a tray from the oven. "Don't worry. We aren't eating soup. I thought it would be nice to have some fried chicken and mac n' cheese."

My stomach grumbled at the thought and my mouth salivated. "Ooh yes, please. I have missed your fried chicken. You used to make it so much more."

Mama smiled, but sadness seeped from her eyes. "Your dad loved my fried chicken. I always made it for him." She swiped at her eye. "Not to mention, I would be as big as the house if I always made it. That kind of food goes straight to my thighs."

I giggled. "You wouldn't be that big, Mama."

Mama placed the pan of mac n' cheese on the table over a trivet. She caressed my cheek and pushed a piece of hair behind my shoulder. "Thank you, but not the truth."

"How was your Fourth of July?"

"It was simple. I had to work earlier in the day and then I watched TV with Rowan."

"What'd Caleb do?"

"He went out with friends."

"And then he got sick? You better make sure he wasn't kissing some girl."

Mama laughed. "Your brother doesn't have a girlfriend. It's just one of those summer colds. You know how it happens sometimes. It just comes from nowhere."

"Mm-hmm. That's what he says."

She shook her head. "You're a mess. Should I be monitoring *your* kissing habits? I mean you are living with your boyfriend."

My cheeks reddened. "No, Mama. And yes, he's in the house, but the boys stay down on their end at night. I haven't even been in their room much. Only to say bye to Drew, like this morning. Trust me, the boys don't want to be anywhere near our room right now."

Mama's nose crinkled in confusion. "Why's that?"

Was it going against girl code to tell Mama about Riley's situation? Or maybe she would have good advice. "Riley and Randy had a big disagreement. He left the house on Fourth of July and Riley has glued herself to the couch."

Mama's eyes widened. "Oh no. What was the disagreement?"

"He still didn't think they should be a couple. She did."

"Yikes. That's hard." Mama took two plates from the cabinet and placed it on the table. Then she moved the fried chicken, too. "Having feelings for someone can be complicated, and fighting feels the worst."

"What do you mean? You and dad didn't *fight*, fight."

Mama burst out laughing. "Oh yes we did, honey. We may have hidden it from you and Caleb well, but we definitely fought. All relationships will have conflict. What's important is how you handle it."

"What did you two fight about?"

"Oh, plenty of things. Some were stupid and silly and

didn't last long. Others were a bit more drawn out." Mama ladled soup into a bowl. "I'll be right back."

I nodded and watched as she carried the bowl back to Caleb. While I waited, I piled food on my plate and ate.

"So, your dad and I fought when we moved into this house."

"You did?"

"Yep. We had put every bit of our savings down on this house to help lower the mortgage payment. I had said it was a stupid idea because who knew what hidden expenses we would have or what would happen. He thought it made sense to lower the amount of interest we would pay overtime."

"Who was right?"

Mama smiled. "We both were. I was looking short term, which was important because we were soon pregnant with you and had many bills. Having a child is expensive before they're even born. All the lab work and ultrasounds, it certainly adds up. But he was also right because we will end up paying less on the house than if we hadn't lowered the overall loan."

"How did you guys stop fighting?"

"We eventually realized that we agreed to disagree, and it wasn't worth being mad just to be right."

"I don't know that Riley and Randy will work this out."

Mama made her own plate. "They may not, but if you care about someone, as I suspect those two do, then it hurts to know that person is hurting. Not to mention, you kids are young. Life is short, why waste a second of it being apart?"

She had a point. We would head to college soon and then what? Would they miss their chance because they had been stubborn?

"They aren't even near each other right now. What if

they don't fix things before school starts again? It'll be awkward at lunch."

"If they don't make up, then I'm sure lunch will change, but what's sadder is that they aren't trying to work it out. Like I said, if there is someone in this world that you care about and they care about you, that is worth everything. It's hard to find those people and when you do, you want to hold onto them with everything you have." She patted my hand. "Trust me."

I nodded, but realized it felt less about Riley and Randy and more about Rowan and Mama. Was he that kind of person for her?

Of course, he was.

I had seen it with my own eyes. He doted on her. He helped us and genuinely would do anything if she asked. And even though he wasn't my dad, I knew he had grown to that same level for her. He might not have given her us, but I could tell she would help him if he needed. She was balanced somehow by being around him.

Did I need to put my own stuff aside to let them be happy? I didn't want to cause the kind of unhappiness that Riley and Randy felt for Mama and Rowan by standing in their way. Maybe it was time I stopped.

CHAPTER THIRTY-FOUR

RILEY

It had been a week since Fourth of July and there had been no communication from Randy. He left that night and I hadn't heard from or talked to him since. It was strange. He was part of my everyday life for months. I either saw him in person or had texted him.

And now to be devoid of that, it was like someone had cut off a piece of my body and expected me to now function. I heard phantom chimes from my phone, as if he had texted me. I heard phantom calls of my name as if he was in the room.

And when those phantom sensations didn't haunt me, I fought with myself if I should text him or not. I had asked for space. He clearly was giving me that space. But it was the last thing I wanted. When I had said that I had expected him to say, *No, Riley. I'm not going anywhere. Let's talk this through.* But instead, he walked away.

I barely slept, even though I was sure Sophie and Shelby thought that's all I did. I focused on the TV because living inside my head was worse. That scene replayed repeatedly, followed by scenes of worse things—

Randy saying he never cared about me or that he had made a mistake to say he ever had feelings for me.

Each one was worse than the one before it. So instead, I laid on the couch consuming every HGTV show possible. I knew the pattern of the shows at this point and somehow that pattern comforted me. At least something remained predictable in my life.

I should have confided in Shelby and Sophie, but it hurt. To confide in them made it real. Each and every feeling that bubbled to the surface made it more real that Randy had left. That the last thing we said wasn't what I wanted. And how was it possible that we may never get back to being in the same room as one another again?

Shelby and Sophie lurked at the corners of the room, watching me and trying to get me to go outside on the beach, but I just couldn't do it. The beach was where it all went wrong. How was I supposed to look at it without thinking of that night?

I stuffed the pillow over my face. This endless cycle of thoughts made me exhausted. I wanted to get off the hamster wheel and feel like myself again. I hadn't even gone for a run in a week. I was surprised Sophie hadn't pushed me out the door at this point, but I had no energy to run. The *want* to run was gone and not even when my parents had separated did that ever happen to me. Running helped me feel better, except in this situation.

Drew and Luke knew what was going on, too. Luke would occasionally watch HGTV with me and comment about the renovations. He had told me that his mother was big into renovating every few years and that her most recent project had been their kitchen.

It was nice that he tried to get me to think of other things and to endure my own silence.

At food times, Drew would appear with a sandwich or

something else that was easy to eat. I had no idea if Sophie and Shelby put them up to it or they simply did it on their own.

I also suspected something had shifted between Shelby and Luke, even though she hadn't mentioned anything yet. I supposed I wouldn't want to tell her my own relationship news if she looked like I did. I hoped she knew I would be happy for her no matter what was going on with me, but once again I had no energy to even bring it up.

I wiggled farther into the couch cushion, closed my eyes, and prayed for sleep. I had thought about things enough for the day … and besides, it was time for my afternoon nap. One of the only times I slept soundly—for a little bit anyway.

CHAPTER THIRTY-FIVE

The walk to Over Easy's was short from my founders' meeting. The next time we would all meet, the summer festival would have happened, and we would be looking at the profit margins and other success percentages.

The festival was headed in the right direction. Things were on track and the to-do list was getting shorter by the day, yet my stomach was queasy as I walked to Over Easy's.

It had been two weeks since Fourth of July and nothing had improved between Riley and Randy. Sophie and I were at our wits end with her. She still barely moved from the couch, and I was convinced at this point my parents would have to either fumigate it or get an entirely new set for the house when she peeled herself from it.

The door chimed above my head as I entered the diner.

Randy sat in a booth toward the back, his head bent over a cup of something. He had missed the founders' meeting, the first one in a long time. I had expected him to be there to help present our progress, but he had texted saying he couldn't make it and could we meet after.

I tossed my purse onto the booth seat and then shuffled to the middle, trying to avoid my bare legs sticking too much to the cushion.

When he looked up, his hair was a mess, sticking out in different directions. He had bags under his eyes and the skin below was a darkened purple hue. And the strong aroma of coffee floated toward me from his mug.

"How was the meeting?"

I crossed my arms. He may have been hurting, but he should have shown up. "You would know if you had been there."

He averted his gaze to the mug. "I know. I'm sorry. I just … I just couldn't go."

"Well, with the way you look, it was a good thing you didn't show up. You look like you've been on a bender, Randy."

He gripped the mug tighter. "Were they all on board?"

"Yes. No one is holding up the progress."

His shoulder relaxed a tad. "Good."

"But if you miss other things, people will notice, Randy. It was clear that the Walkers were missing at a *founding* meeting. The two empty chairs stared at us all."

"I know. I just—"

"Couldn't come. Yeah, I got it."

Randy studied his mug before he lifted his head to look me in the eyes. "How is she?"

My eyebrows rose. I honestly didn't expect him to talk about her. "How do you think she is?"

Pain flashed through his expression. "Honestly? I have no idea. Part of me hopes she is as miserable as I am, but the other, bigger part hopes she is good because I don't want her hurting."

What did I do with that? "She's not great. She has been on the couch since it happened."

Randy's expression twisted. "You mean after you all spend time on the beach and she runs, right?"

"No, Randy. She hasn't run since that day and all she does is sleep on her bunk bed or lay on the couch."

His eyes widened. "She loves to run."

"She loves you, too."

He winced. "She asked me for space, Shelby."

"And why is that? She also told you she loved you but not your situation anymore."

"We can't be a couple. It wouldn't be right. I can't bring her home. My dad still isn't fully sober. He has nights where he slurs at the dinner table or falls asleep, beer in hand in front of the TV. It's bad enough I can't shield my sisters from it, but I won't do that to her, too."

"You aren't *doing* anything to her, Randy. She knows things aren't perfect with your dad. She doesn't care. She wants to be with *you*."

"She says that now, but she hasn't seen it with her own eyes. I know what it does to my sisters and my mom. I can't bring her home to see them and how can I not bring my girlfriend home to meet the family? They are part of who I am. Couples share that part of their lives with each other."

"Okay, sure. Things at home aren't the greatest and she might see that. But is it less about her feelings and more about how *you* feel if she does see it?"

Randy looked away.

"You aren't less worthy because you have an alcoholic dad. Not that long ago, you told me I had to choose who I wanted to be. Would I be who my parents wanted me to be or who I did? You need to take your own advice because their actions don't define *you*, but how you react to their actions does."

"She doesn't need my family's drama in her life. She's better off."

"Really? Is this alternative better for you? You look tired. You have bags under your eyes. You miss her! Don't lose her or you're dumber than I thought you were."

"I can't change what happened. I still don't know if I even should. Being a couple would be a selfish thing to do."

I grabbed my purse from the cushion. "Randy, let me ask you this. Do you want to be with her? And I don't mean this half friend, half boyfriend situation you have now. I mean, really be with her?"

His eyes were glassy, and the pain radiated from him. "Of course, I do. She's everything to me. If I didn't want to be with her, I wouldn't let my family stuff get in my head so much."

"Then do something about it. You can't change your dad. If he chooses to get better, that's on him. But are you okay with wasting your chance with her because of *him*?" I stood. "Because when that girl decides she is done wallowing in her feelings for you, there is one thing I am certain of; you won't get her back. It will kill her to move on, but if she does, she won't come back to how things were. So, think about whether you can live with that."

I turned toward the door and walked away. If he didn't move past this there was no hope for them. The street was busy as I crossed to where I parked my BMW. I silently hoped that he saw reason and did something to change their trajectory.

CHAPTER THIRTY-SIX

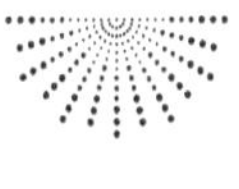

SOPHIE

The rhythmic circling of Drew's finger on my hand steadied my heart rate. July twenty-sixth was one of those days that I would never ever forget; it was the day my dad had officially died. Six years ago, we found out late that night that he would never come home.

Drew glanced in my direction. "How are you doing?"

I offered a weak smile. "I'm better while you do that."

"Then I won't stop." He kept circling my hand but faced the road. We were headed back to Mama's house for our annual dinner to celebrate his life and spend time together as a family. This was the first year Drew would accompany us, but it felt right to have him here by my side.

I was thankful that he had offered to drive. I would have been okay to do it, too, but this was better. I didn't have to fight my brain from the thoughts that lingered to drive safely.

"Thank you for coming with me."

"Of course. I told you, if you ever need anything, I'm there. Always."

I smiled. "You are seriously the best; do you know that?"

"You make it easy."

I placed my other hand over his and squeezed. I didn't know how I had spent so much time away from him or even avoiding him. All that wasted time, I wish I could have taken it back.

"What's your favorite memory of him?" I asked.

"Hmm. Probably when he would do those cartoon impressions at the barbecues. He was always making me laugh and those impressions were spot on."

I laughed. "He practiced them on us for the entire year, until he got them perfect. So, by the time he performed them at the barbecue, we were so tired of them."

"I never knew that."

"No one did. He swore us to secrecy. He wanted it to seem spontaneous when he broke out his routine. He was determined to get those laughs."

"That makes sense, though. It's definitely like him. He succeeded. I always thought he was funny and came up with it on the spot."

"He would have loved to know that."

"I'm sure he does, wherever he is now."

We turned into the neighborhood, and he parked in the driveway. Only Mama's SUV was there. I hadn't been sure if Mama would invite Rowan or not, but I guess for now it would just be us.

Drew exited the car and opened my door. He proffered his hand to help me out and then we walked arm in arm toward the house.

I took a deep breath and opened the door. "Mama, we're here."

"I'll be right out!" Mama shouted.

Caleb sat on the couch. "Hey, Drew. I didn't know you were coming."

"Is that okay?" he asked.

Caleb scrunched his nose. "Why wouldn't it be? You two are still dating, right?"

I snatched the pillow from the couch and launched it at his head. "Of course, we are. He was making sure you didn't mind him at our *family* event, dweeb."

Drew chuckled. "Well, clearly he doesn't mind." He leaned in close to my ear. "Be nice."

I rolled my eyes. "You sound like Mama."

Just then Mama walked into the main room. "Why does Drew sound like me?"

"He told me to be nice to Caleb."

Mama laughed. "Nicely done, Drew. You saved me from having to do that." She hugged him and then faced me. "And you better be nice." She hugged me, too, and settled her hands on my shoulders as she studied my face. "You okay?"

I nodded. "I am right now. It's bittersweet."

She rubbed my back with her right hand. "I know it is. Why don't you come help me in the backyard? I have a table set up but need to put on the tablecloth. Drew can hang out with Caleb."

I glanced at Drew, who gave me an understanding look. He sat next to Caleb and chatted about the TV show he was watching.

Mama and I exited using the back door through the kitchen. On the table sat two folded tablecloths.

"If you get one side, I'll get the other," Mama said.

I grabbed the side closest to me and waited for her to unravel her end.

We raised the cloth up in the air and then set it on the table.

Mama smoothed the folds with her hands and then applied the second cloth which was more of a runner than an actual tablecloth.

"I'm surprised to see Rowan isn't here."

Mama straightened and studied my gaze. "I wasn't sure how you would feel about him being here. I still want to be respectful of your feelings and how you choose to grieve your dad. I didn't want to mix it, especially today."

My stomach twisted. How many times had she done this for me at this point? She put me first instead of how he would have comforted her on a day like today. "Oh."

She stopped at my side. "It's okay, no worries."

What got me was that she was completely okay with putting my needs above hers. I supposed that was a mom thing, but was it fair to her at this point? I would be eighteen this year and she deserved to be happy. I couldn't keep her from that anymore. But more importantly, I wouldn't.

"I think I would have been okay if he had come today. Maybe not the whole time, but later would still be okay. He's important to you. It's time I made room for him to be important to me, too."

Mama stilled and looked me in the eye. Her expression morphed between blissful and wary. "Do you mean that?"

I nodded.

She pulled me in for a quick hug and then gazed into my eyes. "That means so much to me, Sophie. I hope you know that."

"I do, Mama. I do."

Mama squeezed my shoulder and then looked at the job we had done. "I think that works, don't you?"

"Yes."

"Shall we go get Caleb and Drew?"

"Yeah, I don't want Drew to run away. Caleb is probably driving him crazy by now."

Mama shook her head. "Someday you'll like having a little brother."

"Yeah, maybe far, far in the future."

Mama chuckled and wrapped me in a side hug as we walked to the back door. She let me walk in first.

When I entered the family room, Drew and Caleb were laughing over something. I rested my hands on my hips. "What's funny?"

"Caleb showed me this video on his phone from his one friend." Drew stood and walked over to me. "You okay?"

I nodded. "I was worried you would be bored to tears."

"Nah. Your brother is cool."

My eyebrow rose. "I don't think I will ever use the word *cool* to describe him, but sure."

"You never know. Give him a year or two and you may change your mind."

Mama popped her head in from the kitchen. "Let's head out back. Everything is all set."

Caleb shut the TV off and we all walked to the picnic table. Caleb sat next to Mama and Drew sat next to me.

Mama waited until everyone grabbed a drink and food before she talked. "Your dad never liked people feeling sorry or sad for him. He always wanted people to rejoice in his life and in what he accomplished through his family. So, I thought this year we could go around the table and share something we think someone else did in this family that he would have been proud to see."

I raised my cup. "Caleb graduating from eighth grade."

They all raised their cups and took a sip with me.

"Mama getting a promotion," Caleb said.

Mama stared into my eyes. "Sophie getting her first job."

"Every one of you opening up your hearts to love," Drew said.

Mama's eyes glistened.

Of course, he would know the deepest thing to say that had impacted our family.

Mama drank to Drew's contribution and gazed at him with love in her eyes. "Thank you, Drew. You are so right." Mama then looked at Caleb and me. "He would have been so proud of you two for finding ways to grow even in his absence. As usual, I made his favorite barbecue food, so grab a plate and dig in!"

My body warmed from the inside out. Sure, it was a hot July day, but this warmth was more about the love from the people who sat with me, than from the temperature of the air around us. I only wished my dad could have spent one more day with us so I could hear his voice one more time and feel his arms around me as he embraced me tightly. But if that wasn't possible, then this was the best alternative I could have imagined.

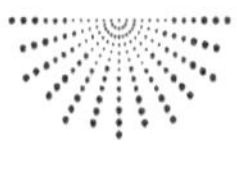

CHAPTER THIRTY-SEVEN

Riley moved from the couch to an Adirondack chair on the front porch. She still hadn't gone running since the incident—a good three and a half weeks later. But Sophie and I were happy for *some* progress.

Sophie eyed the door, glancing every few minutes.

"Why don't we go out and check on her if you're so worried?"

She opened and then closed her mouth. "What makes you think I'm worried?"

"You can't stop staring in that direction."

She crossed her arms. "Fine, but I don't want to scare her back onto the couch. She hasn't been off it this long in weeks."

"Just bring her water and tread lightly."

Sophie nodded, grabbed the drink from the fridge, and met me at the door.

We walked out together.

Riley sat in a dark-green chair, staring at the road and the occasional car that passed by. She didn't even turn when we sat on opposite sides of her.

Sophie held the water out to her. "Want water?"

Riley faced her. "Hmm?"

Had she not heard us?

"I brought you water."

She took it. "Oh, thanks."

Sophie eyed me and then jerked her head toward Riley.

"Beautiful afternoon, isn't it?" I asked.

Sophie exhaled. Clearly that's not what she wanted me to ask. But I wasn't going to touch the elephant on the porch … not yet anyway.

"Yeah, it's okay." She tucked her legs under her and sat the water on the chair's arm. "I need to talk to you two about something."

"Anything," I said and leaned closer.

"I have thought about this a lot and I'm leaving for home tonight."

Sophie leaned closer. "Okay. And then you'll come back this weekend?"

She shook her head. "I'm thinking about just staying at home for the rest of the summer."

I gasped. "What? Why?"

"You know why. I've been one massive Debbie downer. You two are here with the boys you're with or like and I'm ruining it. I see you two watching me instead of going to the beach with them or worrying about your summers. This is all we have left before senior year; I don't want to be the reason why the rest of your summer was less than mediocre."

"You are not ruining our summer," Sophie said.

"Absolutely not. We want you here. We don't need anything crazy. It's nice just living all together in the house."

Riley stared at me. "You and I both know that's not

true. No one wants to spend a summer with someone who acts like a leech on the couch. I barely move. I barely interact. It's not fair." She stood. "I've already packed. I'm not changing my decision."

Sophie reached to pull her back down, but she side stepped it. "Are you sure about this? It won't be the same without you here."

Riley shoved her hands in her pockets. "I'm sure."

"Why don't you have dinner with us before you leave?"

"My mom and Mom-mom expect me for dinner. I'll text you two when I get there, but I'm gonna grab my bags and head out." She walked back inside before we could say or do anything else.

I sighed. "Well, that sucks."

"You can say that again." She leaned forward. "Aren't I supposed to be the pessimistic one? You're usually positive."

"Not sure how to positively spin this one. Those two need to fix this."

"Totally agree."

"So, what do we do? Randy was just as helpless after the founders' meeting."

"Should we even go that far? Won't they be mad we meddled? I know I would be."

I shrugged. "Would you rather they stay like this or be mad and around each other?"

"Fair point."

Riley pushed open the door, carrying her bags over her shoulder. "I'll put it in my car, then come back and say bye." She sprinted down the stairs and back up. "Go have fun. Seriously, I'll be fine at home. I'll text you both."

I hugged her. "You better or we will blow up your phone and come kidnap you."

Sophie nodded and looked like she would do harm to someone.

I stifled my giggle. After knowing Sophie better, I knew her physical threats weren't as scary as they had seemed before.

Riley bounded down the stairs, turned to wave one last time and then got in the car and pulled away.

"So, what do we do?"

"When will you see him again?" Sophie asked.

"I have a meeting with him to do stuff for the festival."

"Then at the meeting you need to convince him to stop being an idiot."

I sighed. "I tried that last time. I used most of what I could think of and already told him I thought he was being dumb."

"Well, maybe more time will change his opinion and he can hear what you're trying to say now."

"Possibly. You know how stubborn he is. He's almost as bad as you are."

She stuck out her tongue. "I can still be persuaded if you do it correctly. He must budge first. She would still be with him if he decided it was time."

"I know that, but what if when he comes to his senses she has already moved on?"

"I don't know. I guess we just hope that hasn't happened yet."

I leaned back in the chair. "Are we doing what's best for her? I mean I think they should be together, but if he doesn't see what he's missing, then should we be campaigning this hard for them to fix things?"

"Yes. They are both being silly. Stopping things before they get started is different than a relationship falling apart because it doesn't work. They both care so deeply about each other."

I knew that. I did, but somewhere it still felt like this was too far. What was the saying? If it was meant to be, it would be. Well, maybe this was a sign it wasn't.

Sophie knocked my elbow off the arm rest.

"Hey! What was that for?"

"You're doubting them."

"I ... How?"

"I can read your faces, too," she said and then stuck out her tongue again.

"I'm going to chop that off if you keep sticking it out."

Sophie's features changed into a devilish grin. "I'd like to see you try."

"Don't tempt me."

Sophie burst into laughter and I laughed, too. It was nice to feel a little lighter, even if I would miss Riley's presence here.

CHAPTER THIRTY-EIGHT

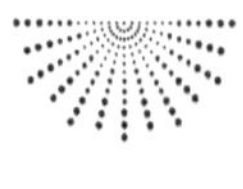

RILEY

I wasn't sure what time it was. My curtains were closed and my phone was off. Shelby and Sophie were probably mad that I had ghosted them since I had gotten home, but I didn't care. I couldn't care about anything except the hole in my life and in my heart that Randy had left.

It wasn't just missing the possibilities of a relationship with him; it was also missing our conversations and our friendship. He was an important person in my life, and he was straight up gone. It had been a month and that fact never got easier.

A slight knock on my door was followed by my mom and my mom-mom barging in.

"Riley Mills, get your butt out of bed!" Mom shouted.

I pulled the pillow tighter over my head. "I'm tired."

Someone pulled the curtains open, the sun streamed through. So, it was daytime, who knew?

"Riley bug, meet us downstairs in ten minutes. Okay?"

They left and cracked the door.

I sighed. If I stayed upstairs there wasn't a doubt in my

mind that they would come upstairs and pull me out of bed. On the other hand, if I went downstairs they would also probably give me a lecture for being holed away. How were these my only options?

In reality, I only had one. So, I grabbed my light zip up hoodie and trudged down the stairs.

Mom and Mom-mom sat on the porch; their voices floated through the hallway through the propped open screen door.

I turned the corner and exited, sitting on the other side of the porch.

Mom-mom's eyebrows knitted.

I knew she had expected me to sit in my usual spot next to her on the swing, but I just wasn't feeling it today.

They exchanged a glance before Mom said, "We are worried about you. It's been a week since you came home from the beach house, and we have barely seen you at all. You haven't gone running and don't join us for meals. What's going on?"

I exhaled. "I know you both know that Randy left and that we aren't going to work out."

Mom stiffened. "What makes you think we know?"

"Because my phone has been off for a week. I guarantee that Sophie or Shelby or both have contacted one or both of you to see what's going on with me. You would have answered, and they would have told you the story. Not to mention it's been a month, and this is Honey Cove. I'm sure the whole town knows by now."

Mom's eyes widened.

Mom-mom pushed harder on the deck floor, sending the swing back and forth, quicker than normal. "You're right, we do know. But more importantly, we are still worried about you. Reason or not, this is a long time to feel like this at such a level. Are you …?"

"Are you depressed?" Mom asked.

"What? Why would you think that?"

"Well, you're exhibiting signs, Riley. When is the last time you have gone for a run?"

"It's not been that long and so what? It's not a big deal."

"It's something you love, and you no longer find joy in. That's a symptom."

"Okay, so one symptom."

"Have you been eating? Showering? Sleeping too much or too little? Your room was a cave. You're usually up early. You don't sleep away a day like this. It's a significant shift in behavior."

I crossed my arms. "I'm not depressed. I don't want to harm myself."

Mom moved closer. "It's not always like that, Riley. I'm glad you don't want to do anything rash, but I think you are still depressed." Mom glanced at Mom-mom, who nodded. "I-We think you should go talk to someone. Maybe your school counselor?"

"It's summer."

"I understand that, but I could call and ask around?"

"I don't want to talk to the school counselor. I'm fine. I'm just sad."

"We understand that you're sad, but we aren't sure how to help you. We don't want you to get stuck in this cycle. What if you moved back to the cove house to be with your friends? Or had them over? You need some normalcy back in your life."

I snorted. Normalcy? Normalcy would be Randy texting me good morning or going for a run and looking for him outside at Morgan's. It would mean seeing him at least once a day and talking on the phone until we were together. None of those things happened anymore. So, how was I supposed to get back to normalcy?

I would pull it together. I would put on a smile and go to school when we started back, but I still had a few weeks and no desire to fix it right now.

"I understand your concern. I'll go for a walk tomorrow, but I'm not talking to anyone. Okay?"

"Okay," Mom said. "How about we order pizza, have some fresh iced tea, and watch one of your shows on the TV?"

I held my breath. This was far from what I wanted to do tonight, but again, if I didn't make this step, they would be more concerned, so I pulled all the happiness I could muster and said, "Sure."

They visibly relaxed and ushered me inside.

Mom-mom went for the phone and Mom nudged me toward the couch. She handed me the remote. "Choose whichever show you want."

I had no idea what I even wanted to watch, I chose something from the now trending list and waited until they sat on the couch to hit play. I could do this for them. It was a few hours, then I could crawl back into my room in peace.

CHAPTER THIRTY-NINE

SHELBY

I checked the to-do list five more times before Randy's truck pulled up outside the guest house. We had several baskets to pull together and this time we only had each other to do it.

I could have asked Luke, Drew, and Sophie to help, because I knew they would, but this wasn't just a festival mission, it was also a mission to get Randy to see the light and stop being an idiot.

Sophie and I had heard nothing from Riley. She never texted us like she said she would have, so Sophie had called her mom. I had no idea how Sophie had gotten Riley's mom's number, but she did, and we had found out that Riley had been locked away in her room since she had gotten home.

So, any doubts that I had had before were gone.

Randy opened the main door to the guest house, carrying a bag and several small boxes, piled above his head.

"I could have helped you bring stuff in."

He set them on the couch. "Good, because I have more in the truck."

We headed back outside, and my eyes widened. "What is in all these?"

"Decorations. Apparently, several stores wanted to donate to the overall atmosphere this time. So, these are full of decorations. I figured we could use them to help with the baskets and then the rest can be used around the different attractions."

"That's awesome, but this is seriously a lot of stuff."

He nodded. "Tell me about it. I had to go around today and pick it all up."

My eyebrows knitted together. "I would have helped with that, too."

He shrugged. "Wasn't a big deal. I could fit more in my truck, and it doesn't take two people to drive around and load it in."

I shook my head. Why must he be so stubborn?

We took several trips until all the boxes were finally unloaded.

"This pile almost rivals the pile in the back room of donations. Although I think we have fewer overall donations this time. Most companies were pickier about what they wanted in the baskets."

"Makes sense. We have a lot more data on what worked and what didn't from the spring festival."

I pried open the first box and sorted through a variety of deflated beach balls. "Maybe for the big water slide and bouncers? We could also fit a few on the wagon ride."

He nodded as he opened a second box full of a large background of a beach, then many masks for a photo booth set up. "This could be cool near the booths. Have people take photos then tag us using our hashtags for social media."

"I agree. Do we have those signs with all the hashtags?"

"Yep. I have those at home. We can set them up all around the big events to remind people. I think this will popularize the festival for the later days."

Several boxes contained little favors with a summer theme and boxes of balloons and a few helium tanks and ribbon. "This is amazing. What businesses donated this?"

"Most are on the scavenger lists. They were thankful for the increased sales and visits, so they wanted to pay it forward."

"Good to know." I surveyed the materials. "So, let's do the baskets and we can use the party favor boxes to help fill around the products."

"Works for me."

We carried the boxes with favors to the back of the guest house where the rest of the products for the silent auction and regular auction were.

Once we got started, I figured this was the best chance to ask how things were going. It wasn't like he could get up and walk away. We had to make these baskets. He was practically a hostage.

"So, have you thought anymore about things with you and Riley?"

He shrugged.

"You know she left the cove house?"

Surprise flitted across his expression, then he buried it, but still said nothing.

I sighed. This would be harder than I thought if he refused to engage in a conversation about it. "Sophie and I are worried about you two."

Still nothing.

"Randy? I mean seriously, how are you doing?"

He sighed. "You aren't quitting, are you?"

"You're my friend, too."

"I'm not great. Is that what you want to hear?"

"No. I don't want either of you are feeling like this."

"But?"

"But you have the control to stop it. So, why don't you?"

"I've told you before, Shelby. My dad isn't on the mend. If anything, my ability to run the company the way I have and to do things in meetings has allowed him to get away with it more. Our profits are up and it's such a habit at this point that he doesn't know how not to drink all day."

"I have no way of knowing what that feels like. I can't imagine being the parent for your parents, but it still doesn't change my stance that Riley isn't the type of person to run away from that. She knows things are difficult with your dad. Why can't you let her in and let her be a part of your life in a deeper way?"

"Because it's not fa—"

"If you say, *because it's not fair to her*, so help me, I will beat you into a pulp. Better yet, I'll let Sophie do it."

"Just because you don't like the answer, doesn't make it any less true. She might be upset now, but she will get over it. She will move on and be fine. She will go to college and be happy. I'm doing what's best for her."

I crossed my arms and used all my willpower not to throw some of the basket confetti at his head. "Did she tell you that? Did *she* say it's what is best for her? Because unless I hear those words come from her mouth, I don't buy it. She is a big girl. She has the right to decide what should happen in her life. If you care about her and want her in your life like that, then let her decide when it's too much. At this rate, you're basically cutting it off before it *possibly* fails. The alternative is that you two could continue to be an amazing duo and make you both stronger as you go through things in life."

"It's easy to say that when you don't see what it's done to my sisters. To my mom."

"That's fair, but, Randy, everyone has something. Are you saying that anyone who doesn't have every aspect of their life together doesn't deserve a partner? If that was the case, then Luke and I shouldn't be a couple, either. My parents are barely around for me; to most therapists, I have had poor models for relationships my whole life. Does that mean Luke and I shouldn't date because I have a greater likelihood of being a crappy girlfriend?"

"No, of course not. You deserve happiness."

"Exactly, and so do you. It's not like you are the one binge drinking and I'm pushing you both to act on the feelings you both clearly have. It's your dad. Is it ideal? No. Is it something to make sure to be aware of in your relationship? Yes. But my god, she can help you shoulder some of that weight. She can be there for *you*! You take care of your sisters and mom and shelter all the burden of your dad's disease, but no one checks in on how you manage it, except her. You both are throwing away a powerful chance to be genuinely happy."

Randy's gaze was trained on the basket he had to assemble.

I couldn't tell if he was mad that I kept pushing or if he was truly contemplating what I had said. Either way, I stayed silent and let him initiate more conversation at his own pace, even if I had to wait until the last basket was finished.

"How would I even come back from walking away? It's been over a month."

Play it cool. Just play it cool.

"Just be honest with her and tell her how you feel. You

know her, and last time I checked in with her mom, she was still isolating herself."

Randy frowned. "You haven't talked to her directly?"

I shook my head. "She turned off her phone."

Randy's shoulders slumped. "So, how will I reach her?"

I tapped my finger to my chin. "Sophie and I can get her to the festival, but then the rest would be up to you."

"The festival? But we have so much to do during the festival. I barely saw her at the spring one."

"You can take some time to go talk to her. I can hold it together. It's the second one and people know what to expect this time. It's a no-brainer. Think of it like a lunch break."

He eyed me warily. "Are you sure? That's a lot to put on you."

"I really don't mind. This is a cause I support. Just don't mess it up this time. Seriously. I can help once, but a second time and I have to slash your tires and let Sophie take a swing at you."

He chuckled. "Deal."

I smiled. Hopefully, he came up with a decent plan because I was serious. If he screwed it up a second time, there was no helping him. And quite honestly, Riley probably wouldn't listen a second time, either.

CHAPTER FORTY

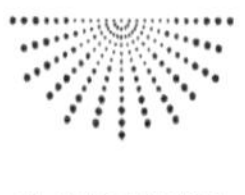

SOPHIE

My hands were clammy as they rested on my Jeep's steering wheel.

"Are you sure this is a good idea?" Drew asked.

"Yes. No. Yes. It's something. At least this will tell us what to do next instead of waiting."

Drew's eyebrows rose, but he stayed silent. He had voted that Riley and Randy work it out on their own, but then again, he wasn't big on meddling in other people's business. It wasn't that Shelby and I were necessarily meddling. We were just aiding and abetting the criminal's plan. It was less obtrusive in my opinion.

I was tasked with picking Riley up, dragging her to the festival, and then giving her to Shelby where Randy would surprise her.

We had no idea how he planned to make things up with her and we didn't ask, but I had enough ahead of me to drag her from the house. Her mom had told us she still hadn't spent time with them even after they talked to her. So, drastic measures were necessary, which is why Drew was sitting shotgun on this adventure.

He had to convince Riley I needed help and had to come outside. Once we did that, then I would kidnap her in the Jeep and drive her to the festival. It had to work.

"Just remind her to get dressed because we must drive to get to me."

"I know. I've heard the plan at least ten times. I just don't think it'll work. Why would I go to her house about you? What could possibly be so horrible?"

"Tell her it's something with Rowan. That will be believable and get her to think about me instead of her. It should work."

"Has she even showered today?"

"Well, if not I'll shove her in the shower at home on the way."

He shook his head. "This plan is a terrible idea. Why don't you go in and be honest with her? If she doesn't want to go, then let that be her decision."

Why must he always be so logical?

"Because she needs to hear what he has to say whether she thinks she does or not. If she doesn't want to listen once he is in front of her, that's on her, but I'm not going to screw up the plan before it's even begun. She needs this to heal."

"I guess. I'll try, but I don't make any promises."

"Just don't tell her the plan is to meet Randy. Just get her out here. Then I'll take it from there."

The long driveway was just ahead, and my stomach lurched. I hadn't been this nervous since Drew had asked me on our first date. So much depended on getting her to the festival. It had to go well. There was no room for failure. Our friend group was in a crisis. If this didn't work, we would have to take sides at lunch. No one could be around Randy, and he had grown to be a good friend. Not to mention it would leave Drew outnumbered.

I parked the Jeep and watched as he lumbered toward the door. With each step, I could tell he wanted nothing to do with this plan. I had to make it up to him later. He supported me no matter what, even in these schemes.

Mrs. Brooks answered the door, peered outside, and waved.

Then Drew disappeared inside.

I tried to settle my nerves by focusing on the song blaring through my speakers. My fingers trailed my steering wheel, beating in the same rhythm. Eventually, Drew emerged with Riley in tow. She was unaware until she stopped dead halfway down her porch stairs.

She crossed her arms, and I could tell from where I sat that she was fuming.

Drew shrugged and I took my cue to bound after her before she fully escaped into the house.

Thankfully, Mrs. Brooks stood at the screen door, blocking her path.

"Riley, wait. Just come to the festival with us."

"Why did you have Drew tell me something was up —," she leaned close and whispered,—"with Rowan? I was all worried about you."

"I know. I'm sorry, but I wasn't sure you would get in the Jeep with me if I had just told you to get dressed."

"Well, maybe not, but I don't like being lied to."

"Okay, that's fair, but we wanted to get you out of your rut. You haven't left the house to do *anything*. What did you expect we would do?"

"Kidnap me." She uncrossed her arms and sighed. "Fine, this is what I would expect you to do, but I still don't like how it happened." She walked toward the Jeep where Drew stood by the passenger door.

He opened it for her, and she climbed in, buckling up in the backseat.

I walked around to my side and hopped in, waving to Mrs. Brooks as I closed the door. "I'm glad to see you at least showered today."

Riley groaned. "Mom-mom practically forced me in the shower. I had no choice."

I chuckled. "I love her."

"Yeah, me, too, usually."

The drive back into town was silent except for the radio playing pop and country songs. Riley stared out the window and Drew scrolled on his phone. Thank god Shelby had to have direct contact with Randy and Riley. This car ride had enough tension to last me a lifetime and the main event hadn't even happened yet.

We used Morgan's Market's parking lot and walked over to the festival's grand entrance. There was a large archway made of balloons in different shades of blue, creating an ombre effect. I supposed the idea was to make it look like water, but either way it was gorgeous.

I had to remember to tell Shelby that once I saw her. Just like from the spring festival, there was a large, tented area which held tables of vendors selling trinkets and handmade items, as well as the companies of Honey Cove selling their products or giving out freebies to attain emails.

I didn't have to work a booth for Rowe Industries, and I was ecstatic. I also wasn't in trouble, so I could do what I wanted this time without feeling like I would ruffle feathers if I didn't agree.

We walked toward the center of the tables. Drew and I were to get Riley to the second Rowe Industries table toward the back by the blow-up obstacle course and water slides. There, Shelby would take over and Drew and I could find my family.

"Shelby went all out this time. It feels twice as large as last time," I said.

Riley nodded. "Yeah, it looks good."

"Soph, it feels larger, because it is. Don't you remember her saying there are like thirty extra vendors?" Drew asked.

Of course, I did, but I was trying to make conversation.

"Oh right. That must be it." I nudged Riley's arm. "Let's go check in with Shelby. Okay?"

She shrugged.

Drew eyed me warily. Apprehension rolled off him in waves. I wanted to tell him it would all be worth it once they made up, but there wasn't time before we arrived at Shelby's table.

Shelby was dressed in a white pencil skirt and a flowy, purple tank top. She wore high, wedged, brown sandals. How she planned to walk or enjoy any of the festivities in that outfit was beyond me.

"Hey, Sophie and Drew." She clasped a hand over her mouth. "Riley! I'm so happy to see you."

I rolled my eyes. Her so-called surprise reaction wasn't believable. She sounded as fake as I used to think she was.

Riley arched an eyebrow. "Am I to believe you weren't in on the kidnapping plan? There's no way Sophie concocted this scheme alone or even with Drew. He practically screamed anxiety at this whole ordeal when he walked into my mom-mom's house."

"Well, Sophie mentioned she would try to get you here, but I didn't know for sure if she would succeed. My surprise is genuine."

I stifled a giggle. When she wanted to, she laid it on thick.

Shelby shuffled a few pamphlets on the table. "Want to help recruit new customers for Rowe Industries?"

"Oh, ah, no thanks," I said and linked arms with Drew. "We must go find my family. Mama is expecting to meet us. You know how moms are. Riley can totally help you, though. Gotta go." I pulled Drew away from the table before Riley could object and suck us back.

Shelby's gaze narrowed as we fled the scene but recovered quickly.

Once we were several tables away, I peered back. Riley's shoulders were slumped, and her stance was less than enthusiastic to help Shelby. I felt bad leaving her there, but Randy should be around shortly, and Shelby wasn't *really* making her work. It was just a ploy.

I raised my chin to view the top of the large, wet bouncy slide. The slide was at least thirty feet in the air and one of the ones that deflated once the pump stopped. "Are you sure about this?" I asked Drew.

Drew smirked. "Is someone scared of going on this little old slide?"

Caleb crowed in my ear. "Sophie's a scaredy cat. Sophie's a scaredy cat."

Mama scowled. "Already? Honestly, you two are worse than people fighting over politics. It's been five minutes!"

Rowan chuckled. "They'll grow out of it eventually. My sisters and I used to be the same exact way. Now we are much closer."

"Lord, I hope so. If not, I'll have an ulcer."

Drew nudged Caleb's arm. "Why don't you go first and show her how it's done."

Caleb beamed. "Gladly. Sis, keep your eyes open."

I glared at Drew. "What'd you do that for? Now he thinks he won."

"It got him to go away, didn't it?"

My eyes widened. "Oh."

Mama laughed and patted Drew's shoulder. "You can

come referee anytime you wish. That was diffused in seconds. You must show me your ways."

Drew laughed. "Can do."

Rowan winked and put his arm around Mama's shoulders. He gazed at her when she wasn't watching. It was sweet. This was the right thing to do. I needed to give him my blessing. And I needed to do it today.

Caleb stood at the top of the slide waving. He cupped his hands around his mouth and shouted, but the noise from the crowd drowned him out. He jumped onto the landing and slid down on his belly, water gushing out the sides of the slide. At the bottom of the slide, he punched his fist into the air and shouted, "Wahoo!"

Mama shook her head. "Lord help me when he goes to school this fall."

"Yep. I'm not telling anyone he's my brother. He is going to be a hot mess."

"Sophie!"

"What? I'll be a senior. I don't need his freshman butt ruining any of that."

Mama covered her face with her hands. "You'll be driving him to school. What do you think people will assume? You can't deny relation to your brother."

I shrugged. "I'll make him get out and walk before the parking lot."

Mama gasped.

"Kidding!"

Drew chuckled. "I'll make sure she doesn't do that."

I arched an eyebrow. "Oh yeah? How's that? You'll be driving yourself. How will you know what I do?"

He crossed his arms. "I think I'll know."

"Well, thank you, Drew," Mama said. "He will be in good hands with you around."

Drew smiled, but I stuck out my tongue at him and mouthed, *butt kisser.*

He smirked and pretended nothing had happened.

Caleb bounded toward us. "That was awesome! I'm going again."

"At this rate, we'll never see the whole set up today."

"You two can go off on your own if you want," Mama said.

"No, that's okay. We'll stay with you. We will just have to yank Caleb from the slide once he gets down before he can say he wants to go again."

Mama's smile reached all the way to her eyes, causing crinkles in the corners. That smile was always reserved for the best of moments, which only meant that she was happy we were all spending time together.

Once again, Caleb shouted something from the top, then slid down. Once he ambled over to us, Mama snatched his elbow and directed him toward the tables.

Caleb propelled us forward at the front of the group, while Mama and Rowan walked in the middle, leaving Drew and me to close the rear.

Many of the booths were like those from the spring festival, but some of the designers made adjustments for the summer theme and weather. There were anklets in addition to bracelets. There were more sun protectant products from the major companies of Honey Cove, too.

Drew linked his arm with mine. "How are you feeling?"

"More relaxed. I was worried about getting Riley here and all. I wonder how it's going."

"I'm sure you'll find out once it all happens."

"Hopefully, otherwise my curiosity will kill me."

Drew chuckled and then leaned close to my ear. "Are you going to do it today?"

I nodded. "I must find a way to get him away from Mama and Caleb."

"Why don't I help you?"

I raised an eyebrow. "How will you do that?"

"I'll get them on the wagon ride and you and Rowan can stay off."

"Mama will be suspicious that Rowan didn't want to go on."

"Maybe, but he will figure out a way to smooth it over."

"Okay."

Drew moved up toward them. "Mrs. … I mean Faye. Have you checked out the wagon this time yet?"

Mama's smile widened. "I haven't. I wanted to though."

"Me, too. Want to go with? Caleb you, too?"

Caleb nodded.

Mama looked toward me and Rowan.

"Sophie was going to hang back. Rowan, maybe you can wait with her?" Drew suggested and then winked before Mama noticed.

Rowan's eyes widened and then understanding flitted through his gaze. "Oh, absolutely. You three go enjoy. Sophie and I will look at this booth over here."

Mama's nose crinkled. "Are you sure?" She gazed between Rowan and me, hesitant about this arrangement.

Rowan grinned. "Absolutely. I know how much you love those wagon rides. Go have fun. We'll be right here."

I smiled and nodded. "Yeah, you'll have to let us know how it was compared to the spring festival."

Drew, somehow, successfully herded them toward the wagon. They climbed aboard and headed around the path.

Rowan crossed his arms and leaned in their direction. "That boyfriend of yours is subtle."

I laughed. "Thank goodness he is, because I'm not."

Rowan chuckled. "So, what's the endgame for this large elaborate plan to get your mom away and me to stay here?"

"You caught on pretty quickly."

"I'm not totally senile just yet."

I smirked. "Well, Drew helped me because he knew I needed to talk to you."

"About what?"

"I thought about what you had asked me. Recently, I've seen some of my friends be without the person they like, and I don't want to stand in the way of you and Mama anymore."

Rowan's gaze softened as he peered into my gaze. "Are you sure, Sophie?"

I nodded. "You love her. That's been clear from the beginning. At first, I thought that the love I had for my dad could only be reserved for him. That we all had to keep his spot open to show him how much we loved him. I thought that we had to sacrifice any other love. I was wrong. I was so wrong. I can still love him and make room for other people. It doesn't have to be one or the other."

"I would never try to take his place. I hope you know that."

"I do. Now, at least. Mama has gone through a lot losing my dad and I know you'll take care of her."

"That means a lot to me to have your blessing, Sophie."

"Just one condition."

"Anything."

"You must help Caleb through his high school years. He's a mess."

Rowan chuckled. "I will be here for you both … If you ever need it."

I smiled.

The wagon arrived back at the start. Mama peered over the edge and eyed us warily.

Drew and Caleb filed out the back with Mama in tow.

I gave Drew a thumbs up as he got closer.

His shoulders relaxed and he nudged his glasses farther up his nose.

"How was it?" I asked.

"It was fun. They took a different route this time." Mama eyed Rowan and me. "And were you successful at the booth?"

"Nah, I ended up not liking the designs. I'm glad you had fun."

Rowan pulled Mama closer.

Mama didn't stop glancing at me. I knew she was confused and didn't believe our story, but she didn't say anything. I had managed to give Rowan my blessing. The rest was up to him.

CHAPTER FORTY-ONE

SHELBY

Sophie and Drew disappeared into the distance. That little butthead had scampered away the second she had brought Riley to me. I had hoped she would wait with me until Randy arrived, but she had other ideas.

"So, what do you think of the decorations?"

She probably didn't care.

"I loved the archway in the front. Was that your idea?"

I nodded. "Thanks. I wasn't sure what people would think about the ombre blues."

"Makes me think of the water."

I smiled. "Good. That was my goal." I shuffled the papers on the table and checked the free samples still available on top.

"How's it going?"

"Busy. This is the smallest line our booth has had all day. I was surprised we still had such a turn out after the spring festival. Many families have come in from neighboring towns. It's working."

Riley smiled. "That's amazing, Shelby. I'm glad you guys are doing so well with it."

It was nice to hear that others recognized the success of the festivals. It was hard to believe that less than a year ago festivals weren't even on anyone's radar.

"Me, too." I stepped a little closer and lowered my voice. "How are you doing?"

She shrugged and looked off into the distance.

"We've missed you at the house. It's not the same without all three of us there."

"I miss you all, too. I just couldn't deal with being there around all the feelings, even though they followed me home, too."

"I can understand that. Do you think you'll come back to see us before the summer is over? We only have a few more weeks before we go back to school."

"Honestly? I'm not sure. It's hard." Riley twisted the string on her shorts.

The crowds were more dispersed than earlier in the day. Everyone must have been getting lunch and taking a break before exploring more. Either that or they were on the other end of the park with the blow-up slides and bouncers.

"I never got a chance to tell you something … before."

Riley lifted her gaze to meet mine briefly. "Oh? What's that?"

Just tell her.

"Luke and I became a couple. He's now my boyfriend."

Despite everything Riley had been going through, her expression lightened. She stood and bombarded me with a tight hug. "Yay! I'm so happy for you. Did you ask him? Or did he ask you?"

"I asked him, but we were both thinking about it. I don't know how we will do the long-distance thing while he's at school, but I feel giddy all the time."

"I'm happy for you. That's wonderful news. You two will be just fine during school. You can FaceTime, text, call on the phone. You'll be fine. I just know it."

I beamed. "Thank you. I wasn't sure …"

Riley shook her head. "Don't do that. I will always be happy for others, regardless of what's going on in my life. We aren't in competition. I'm not threatened because I'm not in a relationship and you two are. You two deserve to be happy and it has been clear that you both would do that for each other."

I was seriously the luckiest person in the world. I had no idea how I managed to go from fake friends like Tabitha and Priscilla to loyal friends and a boyfriend in less than a year. People said someone couldn't change, but I didn't believe that. Anyone can change if they're willing. It was my time and I'm so glad I did.

Someone cleared their throat from behind and I turned around.

Randy stood a few feet from the booth, holding a brown bag. His head hung low as he glanced repeatedly at Riley. He didn't look confident in this plan whatsoever.

Riley's shoulders slumped as she registered our visitor. She nibbled on her lower lip and trained her gaze on the ground.

They both seemed wracked with nervous energy and unease.

"Hi, Randy. How are things on your section of the festival?"

Randy's expression shifted into business. "Looking good. We have more people at the booth than before. Many businesses are reporting an increase in sales as well as more people participating in the *scavenger hunts* with businesses and their punch card."

"Excellent." I peered over Riley's shoulder and

squinted. Then I pretended to see someone I needed to speak with. "Oh, shoot, Riley. I must run. I see Mildred and I must speak with her." I dashed off to a few booths away. I was far enough away to hear absolutely nothing of their conversation but I could still watch in case she needed me to intervene. Not to mention I couldn't abandon the Rowe booth completely.

Randy would enact his plan and then I would saunter back. I just hoped his plan was perfect, nothing short of perfect would end well.

My nails tapped for the hundredth time on the counter as I waited for Luke. He had promised to meet me at our guest house once the festival for the day was over. I had been so busy running around checking in on people and pulling off what I hoped was a miracle between Randy and Riley, that I had had zero time for Luke.

I forced my attention back to the remaining baskets in the hallway. For the summer festival, we had two waves of baskets. First day baskets were filled with summer items and a few company products, but the baskets for the final day would be more company products centered around a theme. So far everything was going well, but I just had to finish packaging one basket and then my to do list would be done for the night.

I tied the ribbon tight as my phone beeped, alerting me to a new text, *I'm here.*

I walked to the door and reached for the doorknob, when it turned first. On the other side of the door stood Luke in a coral T-shirt and black khaki shorts. The color brightened his hazel eyes and set off the tan he had worked on all summer.

He smiled. "Hello, gorgeous."

I blushed. Since we had made it official, he complimented me anytime he had the chance. It was sweet, but so hard to get used to. "Hey."

I moved to the side so he could come in and then closed the door behind him.

"My sources tell me that the festival is crushing it."

I frowned. "Your sources? Didn't you go today?"

Luke chuckled. "Of course, I did." He moved closer and wrapped his arms around me. "I had to see my *girlfriend* at work."

I looked up into his gaze. Girlfriend was also hard to get used to. "And?"

"And you were on fire. Seriously, I walked around, and everyone seemed so happy and having a good time. You guys nailed it."

I beamed. "Thank you."

He lowered his face until his lips were only inches from mine. He gazed into my eyes, until his eyelids flitted closed. He caressed my face with his hand and then kissed me, sweet and gentle. After the kiss, he leaned away, but still kept his arms around me.

"Have you eaten yet?" I asked.

"Nope."

"Good. I want you to meet Chef Frank. He's seriously the best."

Luke cocked his head. "The best huh?" He rubbed his hands together. "Then my stomach can't wait."

I giggled. "You're silly."

He shrugged then laced our fingers together as we walked from the guest house toward the main house. He paused before we went in. "Where are your parents?"

"Not home."

His eyebrows rose. "Neither of them?"

"Nope. Mother went to visit Aunt Delilah, which is still a shock to me. This summer has changed her in some way because I had never expected to hear that come from her mouth. And my father is at work, like usual. Even when he does get home, he will probably go straight to bed."

Luke wiggled his eyebrows. "So, we're here all alone?"

I slapped his arm, shaking my head. "No, there are plenty of workers in the house, including Chef Frank."

Luke's serious expression broke into a smirk. "I'm kidding, but it makes sense why you wanted to go to the cove house. It's got to be lonely being in this massive house and never having anyone else be near you except the workers."

I shrugged. "I got used to it."

He lifted my chin. "Well, that's still a travesty. If I'm around, you don't have to get used to the empty space."

That tugged at my heart. I knew he meant it, but what sucked was he wouldn't always be around, and not in a *we will eventually break up sense*, but he went to boarding school and sooner than I wanted to think about, he would be headed to Georgia again. I would be alone in this massive house and no amount of FaceTime, texting, calls, or video chats would change that.

I twisted the door handle and held it open for Luke as he entered through the dining room and waited. He surveyed the room. I wondered how different he thought it was from his house. I had only been there that one time for New Year's Eve, but his house had been full of pictures with his parents, from when he was an infant and toddler, up to that year.

Our dining room, like the rest of our house, was devoid of photos, except the few I kept in my room and the one large portrait my parents had created for the front hallway when they became engaged.

I shuffled around the corner and nearly smacked right into Chef Frank.

He gasped. "Oh, my word, Shelby. You scared the life out of me. I'm going to die three years earlier now."

I couldn't help but to giggle. "I'm sorry, but you scared me, too."

"I thought I heard a noise, but I didn't expect anyone to be home, so I had to check." Behind his back he held a frying pan.

"Were you going to beat me with it?"

He moved it to the front of his body. "You? Never. An intruder? Absolutely."

"Good to know." I pointed to Luke, who stood off to my side. "This is Luke. He's my boyfriend."

Chef Frank's eyes widened. "Hello, Luke. It's nice to meet you." He didn't ask about the story, although his eyes twinkled with curiosity.

Luke extended his arm to shake hands.

"Are you kids hungry?"

I nodded.

"Fabulous. I'll whip you up something special. Any requests?"

I looked at Luke, who shook his head.

"Any allergies, Luke?"

"Nope."

"Okay. Why don't you two hang out in the entertainment room? I'll let you know when it's done."

I squeezed his arm. "Thank you."

He winked then shooed us from the kitchen.

I led Luke to the couch in the entertainment room, then plopped onto the cushions.

He sat next to me, our legs barely touching. "How did the plan with Riley and Randy go?"

"Not sure. I figured Riley would text me to let me know, but I haven't gotten anything."

"I'm sure they'll figure it out. Randy is a stand-up guy."

It was strange to hear Luke talk about them like that, but we had hoped they would get closer living together. Who knew what they spent nights discussing in their bunk room?

"Let's hope so."

Luke scooted closer on the cushion and rested his hand over mine. He used his thumb to circle the mole between my thumb and index finger. The motion was entrancing, sending shivers down my arm. He gazed into my eyes as he continued to swirl his finger on my hand. Between both actions, my chest felt like it could barely expand to let oxygen into my lungs.

The air between us crackled as the tension increased the longer we stared into each other's gaze, with nothing to say. His eyes shifted from my gaze to my mouth and back again, each time increasing the intensity in his gaze.

The tension pulled us closer together, until I practically sat in his lap and his arms held me as we continued to gaze at one another. He broke eye contact first to plant his lips on mine. This time his lips were filled with passion and a need, as if kissing me was the only way to keep himself alive. His hands roamed across my back and shoulders, until his right hand rested against the bottom of my hairline and neck as he cradled my head in his hand.

His touch tickled me, sending goosebumps across my skin.

A loud throaty cough sent us flying apart. "Dinner is ready," Chef Frank said. His eyes twinkled with amusement before he turned back toward the kitchen.

Heat consumed my cheeks as I realized what a scene

that had to be to walk in on. We both breathed heavily as we regained control and the fire settled in our gaze. I had never felt an intensity like that for someone. It was intoxicating.

On the dining room table, Chef Frank had placed two plates, both had filet mignon, a caprese salad, and Fettuccini Alfredo as a side dish. The plates were beautiful—the way he would plate our meals when we had visitors or generally how he plated for Mother, who expected the most elegant looking meals no matter when it was.

"Wow, this looks amazing, Chef Frank."

He bowed. "I'm glad you're pleased. If you both finish this, I also have a little surprise dessert, too."

I mouthed, *thank you*, as he winked and exited the room.

Luke pulled out my chair, then took a seat at the plate across from me. "You guys eat like this all the time?"

I shrugged. "Not all the time. He's showing off for you. I usually eat something simple or have him make Fettuccine noodles a lot."

"Well, I'm jealous. I wish we had these kinds of meals at boarding school. For an expensive tuition, we have basic foods like chicken nuggets, hamburgers, or meatloaf."

My eyebrows rose. "Really? I'm surprised."

"Trust me, if more of the families knew, I'm sure they'd have to change it. I don't usually mind, but I could get used to this."

I giggled and twirled the pasta around my fork before taking a bite.

Luke wasted no time cutting off a piece of his filet and stuffing it into his mouth. He looked like he was about to melt from happiness.

"I take it you like the filet?"

"It's *so* good. I must know how he made it. I need to replicate this."

"He might share it … if I ask him."

Luke groaned as he took another bite.

I bit the inside of my lip to keep from giggling. Boys were weird about their meat. Although, I guess I couldn't blame him because I definitely felt that way about my pasta dishes.

We both had been hungrier than we let on because we stayed silent as we polished off our food. Both of us barely came up for air, let alone to talk as we shoveled each bite into our mouth.

The tinkling of the silverware onto the plate must have signaled Chef Frank who peered in the doorway. "All done?"

Luke patted his stomach. "Yes. That was amazing. I so need to steal you."

My eyes widened. "Oh no. You can't have Chef Frank."

Chef Frank chuckled. "I'm sorry, Luke. I simply can't be bought. Shelby is my favorite client."

Luke crossed his arms and sighed. "Well, crap. I'll just have to spend as many meals here as possible."

Did he mean that in the way I had hoped? Could he still visualize himself here as much as possible? I wanted nothing more than that, but maybe he just enjoyed the food.

Chef Frank cleared our plates then returned. "Shelby, would you and Luke want dessert?"

I nodded before I even looked at him, but he, too, was nodding.

"Dessert coming right up."

Luke leaned in close. "What do you think he made?"

"Honestly? No idea."

He returned, holding a ramekin with chocolate soufflé

and vanilla ice cream. He placed two spoons on the table, then exited the room.

"Damn he's good," Luke said.

"What do you mean?"

He shook his head. "I'll have to take pointers from him. This is a genius dessert."

"Genius how?"

He wiggled his eyebrows. "I can't reveal all the secrets right away."

I raised an eyebrow as he handed me a spoon. We scooped a small bite to test it out. The chocolate was rich and decadent, while still being light and airy. Luke must have enjoyed it as much as I did because he dipped back into the dessert and had a much bigger portion this time.

"What do you think?" I asked.

"It's so good."

We ate in silence until the ramekin was empty. When Chef Frank came out to grab the dish we thanked him. I had to remember to thank him in private later when Luke left. He created a magical meal for us, just like he always did for my family. I had meant what I said. Chef Frank was an amazing cook, and I was glad our family had found him.

I glanced at the time on my phone—9:00 pm. As much as I didn't want the night to end, tomorrow would be early on the second day of the festival.

Luke seemed to recognize that I was torn between ending the night and staying up later. He pushed the chair away from the table and stood. "It's getting late, I should probably head home."

"Are you sure?"

He nodded. "I'll come find you at the booth tomorrow. How does that sound?"

I looked up into his hazel eyes and smiled. "Sounds

perfect." I led him back through the back door and out to his car in the driveway.

He hesitated before he leaned in and kissed my cheek. Then he climbed into his car and drove away.

I locked the door on the guest house after I double checked the rooms and the baskets and headed for my bed. I had to wake up at 5:00 am the next day to beat the vendors to the festival. It would be an early start, but I knew it would be beneficial for our company.

As I climbed the stairs, I thought about my evening with Luke. We may not have gone anywhere fancy, but it had been the perfect night. I could still feel his lips on my skin as my fingers hovered over them. We had been a couple for a little over a month and it had been better than I had expected. What would I do when he left for school?

CHAPTER FORTY-TWO

The familiar scent of mint and honey wafted into my nostrils while the overwhelming feeling of someone watching me took over. I knew without turning around it was Randy and not in the imaginative way my brain had been playing tricks on me these last few weeks, but in the real he was standing behind me way.

Too many times to count I had thought he'd said my name or that I felt his presence as I entered a room, but it hadn't been real, just a sick twisted game my senses kept playing on me.

So, now that I had what I wanted, my body felt like it would shut down. I couldn't lift my gaze to meet his eyes and I couldn't process anything other than the deliberate escape Shelby had just pulled on me.

The pieces clicked into place as I realized I had been had. Sophie and Shelby hadn't wanted me to come to the festival so much as they wanted me to run into Randy. Had they conspired with him to make it happen? Was he merely monopolizing on an opportunity that he could see me?

I shook my head. This was predetermined. I could feel

it in my bones. Everyone else knew this would happen today, except me. And to be honest, I had no idea how I felt about it, which is why Randy had yet to speak.

He could always sense my moods and if he was sensing them right now, then he knew my insides were a curled-up mess. Half of me wanted to jump over to him and hug him and never let go. The other half of me wanted to turn and run away. What would he say? Would he apologize? Would he say he meant what he said but was sorry I hurt? Did he hurt?

I peeked and regretted it.

He had been watching me, with those big blue eyes full of regret and sadness. I had never seen that expression on his face, not even when he talked about his dad. If his appearance was accurate he looked as miserable as I felt.

Which was the *only* reason I talked first.

"Nice job on the festival," I said.

"How are you?"

My fingers lost its grip on the loop in my shorts. Apparently small talk was not on his agenda. I sighed and said, "I'm not sure what you want the answer to be."

"I want you to tell me the truth."

He wanted the truth? The only way that was possible was if I focused on the grass, so that's what I did. "I feel gutted. I feel like someone took a spoon and scooped out my insides and replaced it with nothing but insects that eat away at my body. I feel like I don't recognize my life anymore. That someone who was supposed to be in my life every single day isn't at all. I spend my days worrying about you. I wonder what you're doing. I wonder how you are, and then I feel shame and guilt because instead of focusing on what I need to do all I can think about is you."

"I don't run anymore. My mom and my mom-mom think I'm depressed, and who knows, maybe I am. But even with all those feelings it's like I'd rather have them than feel nothing because at least I'm still connected to you in some way." I picked at the nail polish still left on my fingers. "And as I say these words to you I feel silly. How could I let someone get so far inside me that I fall apart when they're gone?"

Randy inhaled slowly and deeply. I didn't know if my confession hurt his feelings or if he didn't care anymore, but in some ways, it felt good to release it all.

My gaze dropped back to the grass. "You asked for honesty."

"That I did. Would you walk with me?"

Did I want to go with him? Did I want to say anymore or hear what he was thinking? I supposed it was at least a start that he wanted to even be around me any longer after telling him all of that, but what else could there be to say?

Despite myself, I said, "Okay."

This walk was different. Before we would always be inches from each other almost to the point that the heat from his body radiated toward me. This time, however, there was no heat, and his body was not close enough for me to sense. Was he keeping his distance because of what I said or because of how he felt?

He shoved one hand in his short's pocket, while the other hand, held a brown bag he had yet to open. "I heard you left the cove house."

"Yep. It didn't seem right to stay anymore after you left."

"I never wanted to ruin your summer."

I shrugged. "You can't control how people will react to what you say. You can only speak your truth and hope that their reaction matches yours. This time our reactions weren't in sync."

"That may be true, but I want you to know I never

wanted to hurt you or ruin your summer. Just like you, I was optimistic of what this summer could be."

What did that even mean? He was *optimistic*? Clearly his *optimism* wasn't about making us an official couple, or the last month would have gone differently.

He led us to *his* bench. The same one he brought me to after going to Over Easy's for our English project. He gestured toward the bench as if he wanted me to sit, so I obliged.

"Do you remember when we came here after working on English and you asked me what I came here to think about?"

I nodded.

"That day I told you I came to this spot to think about everything. My family, my parents, you. This past month hasn't been easy for me either and I know that it's my fault. And it affects me more than you know to hear that you haven't been doing well. On the Fourth of July I thought I was doing what was best for you and for me. My family is a mess. My father still drinks. He acts like his drinking is forgivable and our family will come together and ignore what has happened. But what he doesn't see is my mother trembling as he enters our house every night, wondering if he's been drinking. And my sisters locking themselves away in their room and crying themselves to sleep when they can hear the slurring in his words."

The hurt in his voice made it hard to breathe.

"And even me. I barely recognize who I am when I'm at home. I don't do anything but go to school and work. And other than you, Sophie, Shelby, and now Drew and Luke, my friends from school are nonexistent. It's not that I expect my life to bounce back to what it was before. I know things will never be the same again, but I guess I wanted to shield you from it. I saw how upset you were when Sophie drank this spring. I didn't want to be the cause of that same kind of hurt again for you and yet I did it anyway. By keeping us from being a couple, I hurt you anyway and I hate myself for that." His voice broke and his eyes were glassy.

I reached for his hand. His raw emotion broke any barrier I had attempted to build to protect myself from this gaping hole in my chest. No matter what he had said to me, I still loved him, and I couldn't bear the pain.

"Don't hate yourself. I don't hate you. I could never hate you. I told you I loved you and I meant it. I think I will always love you, Randy." I held his face in my hands as I stared into his eyes. "I can't imagine the pressure you feel in your family to make things right and to do what's best for them. You're holding it altogether for them. I've always noticed that and am in awe of the strength it takes to do that. All I've ever wanted is to be your partner in your life to help you with those struggles and to get *you* through them. I can't begin to guess how I will react if I do see your dad drunk at your house, but I want our chance to be together."

"I don't want his actions to hurt you or us."

"You can't know what will happen in the future. We are either in pain now because we never attempt what could be, or we become a couple and maybe things don't work, but maybe they do. All relationships are a risk."

"Would you even still want to be with me if that was an option?" His gaze met mine, hesitant to hope that we could even be a couple at this point.

I didn't know how to answer. I loved him and I knew I loved him, but was I willing to open myself up to him in the likely chance that he couldn't do the same?

"I don't know. I guess I would have to know you really wanted to try. You were pretty adamant before."

He took a shaky breath. "I can understand that." His gaze bore a hole straight through my heart. "I've missed you."

"I've missed you, too."

He held my hand for a minute before he squeezed and then brought the brown bag between us. He pulled out a bag of peach rings and a small jewelry box.

My heart fluttered from the anticipation. What would he possibly give me?

He cracked open the box to display a silver necklace with a heart shaped pendant. "I had it engraved." He handed me the necklace.

The engraving said, *To be, RW.*

My heart rate kicked into high gear like when I ran at a track meet. I hadn't felt it soar so much in so long. "It's beautiful, Randy."

He smiled weakly and placed the necklace back in the box before he handed the bag over. "It's all yours. I'll give you time to decide what you want to do with it." His gaze settled onto the festival in front of us.

People milled about, laughing and enjoying their afternoon.

"To be clear, what are you suggesting? Are you saying if I wanted we would be a couple?"

"Yes. I'm saying that to the extent I can make it possible, we would be a couple. I have no idea what the future would be like with how my family is, but I would let you be by my side in the deepest sense there is."

I gripped the bag tighter. It was everything I had wanted more than a month ago. It was everything I wished we could be, and now that he had offered, I had no idea what to do. Had he really changed his mind, or did he just feel bad? Had he been guilted into talking to me in the first place? I needed time to sort it out, to make sure he was sincere.

"Thank you for giving me time to decide." I peered into the bag and yanked open the peach rings, popping one into my mouth. "I think I might take a run home. Clear my head."

He stood still gazing at my expression. I couldn't tell if he was memorizing my face or just afraid to look away, but he wouldn't take his eyes off me. "I hope to see you soon."

I pulled him close for a hug, wanting it to last forever, but knowing I had to pull away. I gazed into those blue eyes for one last look, then walked toward the park entrance. When I was far enough away, I looked back; he had returned to the bench and was looking forward.

For the first time in six weeks, I wanted to run, and that's exactly what I did, all the way home.

CHAPTER FORTY-THREE

SOPHIE

Ever since Drew and I started dating we entered Over Easy's multiple times in a month, but I never expected to go there with Rowan again. After I gave him my blessing, we had decided to meet to discuss his ideas for a proposal. I could tell he was nervous. Every detail was important to him, all the way down to the ring.

"Are you hungry?" he asked.

I nodded. "Should we get lunch while we talk?"

"I think that sounds like a great idea." He perused the menu after Roger took our drink order.

I was fond of the staff at Over Easy's. Betty was a regular waitress, but usually had dinner hours, except on weekends. Roger was on whenever Betty wasn't. Both were always welcoming and took our orders with a smile. The more I came here with Drew, the more I felt like this place had a little bit of our relationship woven into the egg décor.

Rowan peered over his menu. "Any ideas on what you want?"

"I was thinking about their cowboy burger or their homestyle baked mac n' cheese."

He stroked his chin as he squinted. "There are so many choices. You would think that with how long I've lived here, I would have tried everything by now, but I can't bring myself to try new stuff when I just love their chicken pot pie and all."

I laughed. "Well, try something new, then next time get your usual."

"Hmm. That's sound advice. I think I'll take your idea and go with the cowboy burger to mix it up."

Once Roger had taken our orders, the air between us seemed filled with tension. We may have made great strides in our relationship when I gave him my blessing for Mama to get married, but it didn't mean that we were best friends. I could barely even remember what he had told me months ago about himself. At the time, all I had wanted to do was eject myself from his vehicle and our conversation, so cataloging the details of his life wasn't a high priority on my list.

"So, how's the cove house? Your mama had said you seemed like you were all having a wonderful time."

"It's been great. The beginning half more than the second half."

"Worried about the summer ending?"

I shook my head. "Just some tension with two of my friends."

He arched a brow but didn't pressure me for the rest of the story, which to be honest, I was thankful for. It was weird to talk to him about Riley and Randy when I hadn't even told Mama about it much yet.

"So … I have a confession."

Rowan leaned forward. "Okay."

"I was wondering if you could tell me about your

family again. I-I wasn't exactly in the best headspace at the time to listen to what you said."

Rowan chuckled and rested his hands behind his head. "I can respect that. What do you want to know?"

"I think you said you had sisters, right?"

He nodded. "I'm actually from Illinois, not far from Chicago, but not in the city, either. My two eldest sisters, Rebecca and Jeannie, still live there. My youngest sister, Katie, lives in California."

"Why did you move?"

"For a job. I had been recruited out of college for a job in Mississippi. That plant eventually transferred me to their Georgia office seven years later. Almost a decade later, Mr. Rowe had heard me speak at this company's convention on marketing. He liked my pitch so much that he decided he wanted me at Rowe Industries and now I've been there for five years."

"Was it hard to move away?"

"At first, absolutely. Technology wasn't as easy. My sisters were married with families; they didn't have time to send an email or call me during the week and I stayed up late on the weekends, our schedules never synced. Eventually we started a group text and then I made a vacation once a year to Illinois."

"I can't imagine living so far away from Mama and even Caleb. Although he is still a dweeb."

Rowan laughed. "Someday he won't seem quite so annoying."

"Let's hope that's tomorrow."

Rowan smirked. "He's not that bad. Jeannie was annoying. She used to tell my mom when I snuck out of the house to hang out with my friends. My mom would be waiting right in the doorway for me to stumble in. Jeannie would smugly smile from the corner of the room as I received my punishment of being grounded for a week, then two weeks, until eventually it was a month."

My eyebrows rose. "She tattled on you?"

"Yep."

"Did you retaliate?"

"Heck no! She would have made it worse. My mom wouldn't have known about half the stuff I did in high school if it wasn't for her."

"Wow. I would kill Caleb."

"See? Not so bad."

"Maybe."

Roger placed our cowboy burgers on the table.

Rowan had decided to get broccoli—*yuck*—and a baked potato.

I, on the other hand, wanted double fries. I mean who got a baked potato *and* broccoli?

A comfortable silence settled over the table as we dug into our food. A pang of guilt settled in my stomach. I had prejudged Rowan harshly. It wasn't his fault that he had fallen in love with Mama. He shouldn't have paid for my leftover grief about Dad. He was a decent person, and more importantly, he made Mama happy. My biggest regret was that I had waited so long and had stood in her way for so many months before I realized that.

I finished chewing my bite and then placed the hamburger on the plate. "I want to apologize."

Rowan froze as he held his burger and sauce dribbled down his chin. He chewed and then gulped loudly as he swallowed. "For what?"

"I shouldn't have been so closed off this past spring—"

Rowan raised his hand to stop me. He shook his napkin from under his plate and dabbed his chin. "You don't have to apologize to me, Sophie. You're allowed to feel whatever you felt. There's no judgment from me and I hold no resentment from that."

"But I was rude … several times."

He shrugged. "Something I failed to mention before is that my parents divorced when I was ten. My dad was the first to remarry and I can tell you that I understand what it feels like to gain an adult in my life that I hadn't expected to make room for. I will never know or pretend to know how it feels to lose a parent, especially at your age, but I understand what it feels like when a parent replaces their significant other. Granted there are different circumstances here, but you are well within your right to feel how you feel. Everyone is allowed to acknowledge and accept how something makes them feel."

"I don't know how you do that."

"Do what?"

"Be so forgiving and move past it."

"I've had many more years on this planet and in some cases, I've learned the hard way. But, Sophie, I didn't have any expectations going in except one. That I care for your mom, and I wanted to get to know her children, however they'd let me."

"Well, then we have a ring and a proposal to discuss."

He grinned and took another bite of his burger before saying, "That we do."

CHAPTER FORTY-FOUR

RILEY

I turned off my Impala and stared at the vehicles in the driveway. I hadn't expected to see these stairs and this driveway again this summer. When I left the cove house over a month ago, I didn't want to see it again. I wanted to close the door on the house and that chapter.

But now I had a decision to make, and I needed my friends to do it. Shelby's BMW and Sophie's Jeep were parked in the front spots of the house, so at least they should be there. I only hoped I didn't interrupt any dates or dinners with their special guys.

I jogged up the stairs two at a time and turned the knob as I pushed open the door.

Drew, Sophie, Luke, and Shelby sat at the kitchen table, laughing as I entered.

Sophie saw me first. Her eyes widened and then she screeched as her chair went flying.

Shelby snapped her head in my direction and followed Sophie.

They nearly knocked me over in an embrace, which lasted a minute before they let go.

Drew and Luke had stood and moved toward the back door.

"We're taking a walk down by the shore," Drew said.

"We'll be back in a little," Luke added.

I smiled as they left. I needed to remind myself to thank them for letting us talk in private.

Sophie stared at me, waiting for me, as if any sudden noise or movement might have scared me away.

I giggled. "I won't blow away, Sophie. I'm doing better."

Shelby gazed into my face. "Are you sure?"

"Yes."

Sophie grabbed my hand and pulled me toward the couch to sit. "So? We've been dying to find out what happened."

I raised an eyebrow. "Are you two admitting you planned it prior to the festival?"

Sophie waved me off. "That's not important."

Shelby poked my leg. "Well?"

I sighed dramatically and rested on the couch's back cushion. I wanted to drag it out to torture them for meddling. When Sophie's gaze turned to a glare, I said, "He didn't waste any time. He asked me how I felt and wanted me to be honest. So, I was. I told him I was miserable and torn between wanting to give him what he asked for and wanting to know how he was doing, too. He asked me to take a walk. We stopped at his bench and then he basically said we could be a couple." I pulled the jewelry box from my back pocket. "Oh, and he gave me this."

I handed the box to Shelby, who opened it and then passed it to Sophie.

Sophie clapped. "So, you're together then?" She cheered. "We can—"

"You are together, aren't you?" Shelby asked.

I hesitated.

Sophie's gaze turned suspicious. "He asked you out and what did you say?"

"That I needed to think about it."

Sophie stood and paced the rug in front of the couch. "You need to *think* about it?" She threw her hands in the air. "Why?"

"Because it has been over a month, and I need to figure out his motives." I sat a little straighter and looked between their gazes. "Did either of you put him up to talking to me at the festival?"

"No. He asked about you at our meetings and I told him to figure out what he wanted," Shelby said.

"So, you didn't put the idea in his head?"

She shook her head. "I merely read his expression. He looked tired and defeated. He obviously still cared if he was asking about you, so I said if he didn't make a decision, he could lose you permanently. If that's not what he wanted, he had to do something about it."

"We didn't do anything, except promise to get you to the festival," Sophie said.

"He wanted this then?"

They nodded in unison.

"Is that all you're worried about? That he felt pressured to ask you out?"

I shrugged. "Yes and no. He just seemed so determined for us to be friends for now. He kept repeating that it wasn't the right time. I didn't expect him to change his mind in a little over a month. I don't understand what made him change it. He still seems hesitant because of his dad. Why now?"

Shelby tapped my arm. "He was miserable. I know you didn't see him at the meetings, but it tore him up to walk away from you. I think since the moment he made his decision that he regretted it."

"How can you be so sure?"

"It's just the way he talked about you and asked about you."

"Okay, so we both missed each other, but what happens when his dad drinks the first time? Is he gonna break up with me? Are we going to fall apart? I know I told him that any relationship is a risk, but it feels like if I give us a chance now that there's a higher risk that we won't make it. I just want it to feel right. All the anticipation puts so much pressure on our relationship and what it could be that I don't want that to get in the way of how we truly feel about each other."

"You said it yourself, Riley. There's no guarantee. So, why now are you worried about it not working? Are you scared he'll hurt you again?"

"Maybe?" I sighed.

Shelby's eyebrow rose. "What do you want? When you wake up tomorrow morning before all your thoughts can be filtered, when how you feel is uninhibited, what do you want?"

"I want what we had before. I want to talk to him every day. I want us to laugh together. I want to know that he's in my corner."

Shelby smiled. "That sounds a lot like a relationship."

I tilted my head to the side. "I guess you're right."

Sophie nudged my arm. "So, you should be happy then."

"I know. My self-doubt just keeps getting in the way of everything."

"You don't have to rush your decision. He took over a month to make his mind up about what he wanted with you. I think you're entitled to as much time as you need."

"But isn't it weird? I finally get him to ask us to be a couple and I put the brakes on. I've been hoping all summer and at the end of the school year that we would get together. Isn't this a sign it isn't right, if now things feel different?"

"Not necessarily," Shelby said. "You both felt what it was like to lose each other. For him I think it woke him up. It made him realize what life would be like without you and what he had with you. For you, you already recognized what you both had, so when you went your separate ways, the reality of what could happen if things go badly became more apparent to you."

She snorted. "Actually, it's kind of funny. The things each of you worried about before it happened are kind of switched. He never wanted to hurt you and lose you because he knew how important you were to him. So, when that happened you realized what it would be like to lose that which was his fear. And you understood how important your relationship was and wanted more and when you guys walked away he realized how important that was and what you wanted. Walking a mile in each other's shoes and all that …"

"Yeah, maybe." I patted my leg and stood. "I didn't just come here to talk about Randy though."

Sophie's eyebrow rose above the other.

"I wanted to thank you both. You have been so supportive of me as I figure out what I'm feeling. I want you to know that I value that. I feel like I haven't been awake for too long and I want that to change. Regardless of what happens, I'll make an effort to be there for you both, too. I barely know how things are going with you two and that's my fault."

Sophie nudged my arm. "We understood."

Shelby nodded.

I pushed them closer to me so I could hug them again. "You guys are seriously the best."

"We know," Sophie said as she plopped on the couch. "But you have some catching up to do."

Now it was my turn to be curious. I sat and listened as they caught me up on things that had happened to them. It felt good to be around them again. I needed to remember that even without Randy, I would always have them to pick me up. I just needed to let them.

CHAPTER FORTY-FIVE

SHELBY

The wind rustled my hair as I waited on the front porch of the cove house for Luke. He had decided after the good news from Riley showing up that we needed a date night, but I wasn't supposed to know any of the details.

Luke closed the door and walked to me. His cologne occupied all my senses and I loved it. Just like his cologne made my stomach flop in anticipation of his kisses. He had combed his hair and used gel to keep it in place. He wore dark washed jeans and a pale orange button up shirt. Wow, did he look amazing.

"Hey, beautiful."

I blushed. It was still hard to get used to the pet names. "You're looking pretty handsome yourself."

He tugged on the edges of his button up shirt and smiled. "Why, thank you." He proffered his arm and I interlocked my own in the crook of his elbow. We walked down the stairs to his Audi. He opened the passenger door and waited until I climbed in, before going around to the driver's side. "All set?"

"As ready as I can be without knowing where we're going."

He winked. "You'll like it. I promise."

I shook my head. "Do all guys think the surprise-the-girl-with-a-date thing works every time?"

His eyes widened and then he smirked. "No, but it works with you."

"Is that so?"

"Yep," he said smugly as he backed out of the driveway.

I crossed my arms.

He glanced over and then poked me in the side.

A giggle escaped from my mouth, and he smirked again. "You think you're so clever don't you?"

He shrugged. "Nah, but I'd like to think I know you pretty well at this point."

I pinched his pinky as it rested on the shifter. "Maybe."

"Ouch!" he said as he snatched his hand back. "Someone is feisty."

I stuck out my tongue, which made him chuckle.

"Are you worried about Riley and Randy?"

"Nice conversation switch, but no, not as much as before. Riley seems to be coming around. I'm glad she stayed at the house last night. She seems better even if she is confused about what to do."

Luke glanced from the road. "She isn't sure?"

I shrugged. "I don't think it's that. I think she's worried about him disappearing again after she's gotten even closer."

"Relationships are always a risk."

"That's kind of what we said."

"They deserve to be happy."

I patted his hand. "They do, but let's talk about us. Like where are we going?"

"Nope. It won't work. You'll see when we get there."

I sighed. "You can't give me a hint?"

He chuckled. "Nope." He interlocked our fingers and drew my hand to his mouth. His lips lingered on my hand, then he squeezed, before resting our hands on the shifter.

I stared at the road as we drove farther and farther from Honey Cove and closer to the border of North Carolina and South Carolina.

Where on earth was he taking me for our date?

Once we entered South Carolina, he took the second exit.

I scanned the sign to see if I knew any of the stops, but none seemed right for a date.

"What are you thinking about?" Luke asked.

"Where we're going."

"You'll find out soon. We're almost there."

I twisted my shirt around my finger. If we didn't show up soon, I would lose my mind.

He turned off the main road, down a long lane, until we drove under a sign for a horse ranch.

My head tilted as I looked through the field. Horses were everywhere. He had brought me to a ranch?

Luke shifted his gaze to my side. "What do you think?"

"It looks beautiful. Whose ranch is this?"

"A friend from school. His family owns the ranch. He said I could come by sometime and I finally took him up on his offer."

"That's so sweet. We could have ridden at my house, though."

"I wanted it to be a getaway date."

"Ah, and for what?" I asked as I wiggled my eyebrows.

"You'll see." He parked then walked around to my side before holding open my door.

I used his outstretched hand to step onto the driveway

and then waited as he grabbed a large basket from the trunk. I arched an eyebrow. "Another surprise?"

He shrugged as he wrapped his arm around my shoulder.

I rolled my eyes.

A large, black stable with green metal hinges loomed in front of us. It was more like a home than a stable but was mesmerizing. I couldn't stop looking at each ornate detail until the horses loomed closer. I gasped. A few stunning Appaloosas were near the front.

"Are we riding?"

He nodded. "But not the Appaloosas. I have a few Arabians inside the stable that should be saddled for us."

This was so thoughtful. I hadn't been on a ride with Rio in weeks. Something I needed to fix. He was such a sweet companion and with everything going on with the festival and the cove house, I had neglected spending time with him.

Luke pushed open the stable doors and strolled to two Arabian horses standing as he mentioned all saddled. He patted the gray Arabian. "This is Storm." He rubbed his mane as I surveyed the horse next to Storm. He was a chestnut Arabian, and he was magnificent, even tempting. He looked strong and fast.

"That's Tracker. He likes to lead on the trails."

I approached Tracker. It was important to me that he knew I was trustworthy. There was nothing worse than a spooked horse on a trail ride, and since I had no idea of the terrain around here, that was not a good combo.

I let him sniff my fingers before I rubbed his nose. He exhaled loudly and settled his head on my shoulder. I smiled and whispered, "I like you, too, Tracker. By the way, you are a handsome boy, aren't you?"

He whinnied as if he knew exactly what I had said.

Luke strapped his basket over his horse and then guided him out the back of the stable and to the closest trail. He hopped up in the saddle and waited for me to do the same.

"You ready, boy?" I asked Tracker.

He moved forward toward Storm.

Luke waited for me to mount before he instructed his horse to walk.

"This is a lot different from our last horse ride."

Luke chuckled. "You mean when you galloped through the whole field trying to lose me?"

My eyes widened. "You knew that?"

"It wasn't that hard to figure out. You clearly didn't want me to be there, and your pace is a little abnormal if you're trying to have a conversation with someone."

I giggled. "I'm sorry."

"No reason to be sorry. We didn't really know each other then. If I hadn't been on orders from my own mom, I probably would have left the second you galloped away." He winked. "I guess my persistence paid off, though."

"Oh, is that so? That's not what won me over."

"No? Then what did?"

I stared into his beautiful hazel eyes as the sun brightened them. There were many things I liked about him. I liked his loyalty to those he cared about. I enjoyed his humor, even when it was directed toward me. He was handsome, but none of that did the trick.

"New Year's Eve."

His smile grew, making the skin crinkle. "It was a good night. I had wanted to kiss you so badly."

"You did."

He shook his head. "I kissed your head. I wanted to

kiss your lips. The whole movie I couldn't believe you were in my family's theater watching a romantic comedy. I wanted to lean over and kiss you senseless."

"Why didn't you?"

"I chickened out. I wasn't sure how you felt and didn't want to mess up our progress." His horse moved a little closer. "It would have been too soon, right?"

I shrugged. "Probably. I don't really know. I thought you were about to until you went for my head instead, but I needed more time to process everything else."

"That's what I had figured. So, it was a good thing I waited."

We kept a steady pace on the trail. It was mostly flat, with tall grasses on the sides. Occasionally, the grass would brush my leg, sending goosebumps everywhere, followed by the urge to scratch. The trail broke away from the grass and opened into an expansive view of the land. Larger hills loomed in the distance, but what caught my eye was the white gazebo and benches surrounding a large pond.

Our pace slowed even more, until Luke jumped down and tied up his horse on the fence post. I followed suit and then waited as he grabbed the basket from the horse. He walked to the gazebo and then took out a thin blanket from the basket. He splayed it out on the ground and then sat. Container after container emerged from the bottom. He had planned a picnic.

I sighed with delight. It may have felt like one of his romantic comedies, but it was perfect. The sky was erupting with golden hues of orange and purple as the sun set. We still had time to eat before dark, but the scenery was breathtaking.

We settled on the quilt he brought for us and filled our plates with food. We ate in comfortable silence, sparked by occasional glances that screamed with emotion. At one point I thought Luke would discard his food and shorten the distance between us, but instead he stayed in one place and ate. Our dates just kept getting better and better.

Our picnic ended and we sat as the sun dipped below the hill before we mounted our horses and returned to the stables. Parting with Tracker was harder than I expected, but he had wriggled his way into my heart, the same way Luke had.

"Do I need to get you two a room?" Luke joked.

"Ha ha. He's a good boy," I said as I rubbed his nose.

"They were definitely good hosts. I'll have to pass it on to my buddy when I go back to school."

At the mention of his school, my stomach sank and threatened to expel all the yummy food I had gorged myself on. I wasn't ready for him to go back to school yet.

"It'll be okay. We will make it work."

My eyes widened. "How did you know what I was thinking?"

"I saw your face change when I said school. It was like someone stepped on your puppy."

"I just … I just hate that you must go. Things are so good. What if it changes when you leave?"

Luke strode closer and rested his hands on my shoulders as he bent his head to look me in the eye. "My feelings for you won't change. They didn't change this past year, and they won't change now."

I twisted my shirt in my fingers. "How are you so certain?"

"Because I believe in us."

I smiled. I didn't know how he stayed so positive when our long distance seemed like the worst thing, but if he was certain, then I needed to be certain, too. I had to fake it until I made it, right?

CHAPTER FORTY-SIX

"Time's up. Put your pencil down."

I shifted uncomfortably in my Adirondack chair. This was my final practice test for the SAT. The next time I sat to take it, I had to take it for real and the score would count.

I peered over Drew's shoulder as he took the practice test and started to score it. Nibbling on my bottom lip, I asked, "So? How'd I do?"

He waved me away. "I'm not done. Just relax and I'll let you know when it's scored."

I groaned. "This feels like a new level of torture."

"Don't be so dramatic. I'm almost done."

The anticipation was killing me. I was running out of time to improve my score.

He clasped the paper to his chest. "Are you ready?"

"Yes! Just tell me."

"Fifteen hundred."

"What? Are you serious?" I yanked the paper from his grasp and stared at the big red number he had circled. Just like he had said, a big red fifteen hundred was on the top.

"I did it!" I jumped with the paper tight to my body. "I can't believe I actually did it."

Drew nudged his glasses farther up his nose. "Well, believe it. You earned that score. I knew you always had it in you."

"Because of you."

"No, because of you. I didn't do anything."

I snuggled close to him, wrapping my arms around his midsection. "You did so much to help me. You pulled me out of my hole."

He bent down and kissed me slow and deep, his hands shifting into my hair as he cradled my head. When we pulled apart he looked straight into my eyes. "You pulled me from mine, too." He grabbed my hand and tossed the practice test on the chair. "Let's go to the beach and celebrate."

I nodded.

We sprinted up the stairs and separated at the top before going to our ends of the hallway.

I ransacked my bathing suits, trying to pick one that fit the occasion and our celebration. I settled on my dark purple one piece that had cut outs throughout the back. It didn't give me the best tan lines, but it wasn't like I planned to sit out and sunbathe, either. Plus, it hugged my curves and I wanted to make Drew drool. He deserved a reward for spending his summer helping me study and deal with the whole house drama.

Most of my towels were in a heap on the floor. I needed to do laundry, but after sniffing a few of them and settling on one that smelled clean enough, I bolted back downstairs to wait for him.

He came down the stairs a few minutes after me wearing his black and white striped bathing suit and an orange T-shirt.

I took the time to look at him. We had been so busy that I hadn't noticed he was much tanner since the beginning of the summer. His hair was much lighter in spots, especially on top where it was almost white from the sun.

He noticed my staring and checked his shirt. "What? Do I have something on me?"

I giggled and brushed his hair from his eyes. "Nope. Just admiring how tan you are now."

He wriggled his eyebrows. "Oh?"

"Yep." I kissed his nose then sprang out the door, bounding down the steps and halting my pace as I hit the sand. It was much hotter than I expected as it found its way under my foot between my sandals. Once I got closer to the shoreline, I toed off my shoes and launched into the water, wading out until I was at least waist deep.

Drew had kept up with my pace, but it still took him a few minutes before he joined me. He stared at me incredulously. "What was that all about?"

I shrugged. "Just wanted to get to the water."

He chuckled. "Spending all that celebratory energy?"

"I guess so. I suppose it hit me all at once that we only have a couple weeks left of summer. Then senior year will take over and the summer's spell will break."

"True, but this year will have so many adventures, too." He swam closer to me. "Plus, we haven't spent all fall together yet."

"You're so corny."

He gasped. "Am not."

I splashed him. "Are, too, but I like it."

He gazed into my eyes and just stared, then closed his eyes and leaned toward me until our lips met. The kiss was gentle at first and then deepened as his arms wound around me and I moved my hands up and down his bare back. The pockets of skin exposed from my bathing suit had goosebumps as he found them with his hands. The heat of his skin warmed me in a different way than the weather, like our bodies couldn't be close enough, even as I seemed to fit perfectly in the curves of his own body.

When we pulled apart, my lips felt puffy and swollen. His gaze looked hazy as we both tried to recover and slow our heart rates.

He caressed my hair as he moved it over my shoulder and gazed into my eyes. "I love you."

My eyes widened. I hadn't expected him to say it, but when he did, I knew I loved him, too. I couldn't imagine my life without him in it at this point. He made it all better and helped me to grow at my darkest moments. "I love you, too."

He smiled and embraced me, not letting go as the water crashed into us from the waves. Today couldn't get any better.

CHAPTER FORTY-SEVEN

Over Easy's seemed busy from the outside. People kept opening and closing the door.

I sat in my Impala staring at the people coming and going, wondering what their stories were. Had they picked up food on a Sunday after church? Or were they here to make an important life decision, too?

I knew on instinct that Randy would be in our booth already sipping on his coffee waiting for me, and yet I couldn't make myself go inside.

This decision, well, to put it simply, would change everything. If I agreed to be a couple, we would have the chance I had been begging for, for months. If I said no, I'd be giving in to fear of being hurt again and was it fair to wreck both of our lives over fear?

I sighed and turned off the car, pushed open my door and walked to Over Easy's entrance. I peered inside and sure enough, Randy sat in our booth, waiting for me. He seemed preoccupied as he stared at the table. Was he as nervous as I was?

I couldn't help remembering all the times we met right

here in the last year—after he had ditched me in school, when he never came to homecoming, and for countless English projects. And here we were again, after a big obstacle, trying to find our way through the mess.

No longer able to wait, I pushed open the door and walked to our booth.

He raised his head as my feet signaled my entrance. His smile was slight. I hadn't told him my answer, only that I wanted to meet to discuss things. For all he knew, our worst nightmare was about to become real.

I plopped on the booth seat, letting that familiar vinyl move underneath me. Soon it would be stuck to my legs and feel like getting waxed when I tried to stand, but for now, it was cool against my skin.

"Thanks for texting," he said.

I glanced up. He had bags under his eyes and his hair was wavy in an unkempt way. He looked terrible, which gave me a mixture of feelings. It made me happy that he felt miserable without me, but I also felt a pit in my stomach that he was hurting.

Betty eyed us both as she approached our table. Even she could tell something was off kilter with us. "Want your sweet tea, Riley?"

I nodded. "Thanks, Ms. Betty."

"Anytime, sugar."

I picked at my nail polish. Why was it so hard to talk to him?

He sipped his coffee, giving me the time and space to talk when I was ready.

I had thought making this decision would be easy. It's what I wanted, but as I sat here and watched him, everything felt more complicated.

"Gun to your head, not sure you'd make it, would you want to be a couple?"

Randy frowned. "Of course." He placed his hand halfway between us, like an offering if I was willing to accept it.

"Your dad still drinks?"

He nodded, his forehead wrinkling.

"Nothing has really changed with your family since July then?"

"No."

"Then why a change of heart about us?" I sighed. "Randy, I don't doubt you have feelings for me; I know they're there. I can feel it when you look at me, but if nothing's changed I can't help worrying you'll be upset with me or resent me for being a couple when you didn't want it."

"Aw hell." He pulled my hand into his and held tight. "Yes, it's true that my family dynamics haven't changed and that my worry was hurting you if we were together. But these weeks without you opened my eyes to how much you already *are* in my life. People at Morgan's ask about not seeing you around and my sisters even asked if something happened with us after seeing how I've been. I've been delusional to think that we weren't already more than friends."

I sucked in a deep breath.

"I have missed you with every breath that I take. I've missed your smile, your incessant need to run, and your laugh. I've missed how you make me feel just being in your presence." He sighed. "I was a moronic idiot on the Fourth of July. I wish I could take back what I had said every day since then, and if I was given that chance, I would change it all."

I reached beneath my shirt to clasp the heart-shaped necklace that nestled over my chest.

His eyes widened. "Are you … are you wearing the

necklace?"

I nodded.

"Does that mean?"

I released the necklace, letting it fall over the top of my shirt, sitting prominently on my chest. "I have gone back and forth so many times. I love you, Randy Walker. I don't expect that to change, but I have been terrified of getting hurt again. I fell apart after you walked away. I am worried how I would survive if we broke up after being a couple."

"I completely underst—"

I placed my finger over his soft lips, which nearly derailed my entire train of thought. "But ultimately, I would be a moronic idiot, too, if I didn't try."

He grinned beneath my finger, before he moved from his side of the booth to mine. His nose came close to mine before he stopped and looked into my eyes.

The gesture caused my heart to beat so fast, I thought it would leap from my chest.

"So, you'll be my girlfriend?"

I nodded.

He pumped his fist into the air before his lips slammed into mine.

I giggled at the gesture before his kiss had distracted me from all possible thoughts. His kiss was full of emotion as his lips poured over mine and his hands settled on my waist, moving up and down in a rhythmic pattern.

He pulled away only to nod at someone I couldn't see.

Puzzled, I stared. "What was that?"

He grinned. "You'll see."

Betty brought over my sweet tea in one hand and a peach cobbler made for two in the other. Poured over the top in whip cream was the message, *I love you.*

I blushed, sending heat crawling up my neck and cheeks. "What if I had said no?"

"I hoped you wouldn't. I mean it, Riley. I love you and I'll make it up to you for this summer."

I leaned against his shoulder and wrapped my arms around his body as I melted against him. "This is definitely a good start."

He rested his chin on my head and we sat, entwined together until we had to split apart to eat the cobbler. He didn't move to the other side though. He stayed with me, and I can't say I was upset. I didn't want him to go that far from me for a *long*, long while.

CHAPTER FORTY-EIGHT

SOPHIE

My hands gripped the wheel tighter as I pulled into our neighborhood. I was driving home to help Rowan surprise Mama with his proposal. I had no idea I would feel this nervous.

My palms were sweaty, and my heart was beating fast, I was waiting for it to break out of my chest. This was the right person for Mama after Dad, but it was still nerve wracking. She didn't expect anything, except a family dinner with Rowan.

I parked down the street to give plenty of room for their vehicles if they wanted to leave and be alone after. I would watch Caleb although he was old enough to be alone. I didn't want Mama to worry about anything.

Rowan had ordered Mama's favorite Italian food from a fancy restaurant a few towns over and went to pick it up. According to him, Mama didn't understand what the point of all the fuss was, but he said he wanted something different for me when I came home from the cove.

I locked the Jeep and tightened my purse across my body. I had to pull this off for him and especially for her after all I put them through. They deserved a special night to remember, always.

I opened the door and was immediately struck with an awful smell. I scrunched my nose before plugging it with my fingers. "What is that *smell*?"

Caleb pulled his gaze away from the TV long enough to say, "What smell?"

I walked closer and braved the smell for a second to sniff. It was definitely him. It smelled like rotten eggs and moldy cheese. "Caleb, what did you do?"

He eyed me warily. "What are you talking about? I don't smell anything."

"You reek. Seriously, what have you done today?"

His expression was blank and then shifted. "I had football tryouts."

"Did you roll around in the locker room? Seriously. It smells bad. Get off the couch and go get a shower. Rowan will be here any minute."

"Since when do you care about what I am like when Rowan is here? He doesn't care."

I glared at him and pointed at the hallway. "Go get a shower!" When he didn't budge an inch and instead stared at the TV, I yanked him off the couch by the shirt.

"All right, all right. Keep your pants on." He rolled his eyes and sauntered down the hall, leaving a putrid smell in his wake.

Boys are so weird! Ick. I launched myself into the kitchen to scrub the smell from my hands before I attacked the couch with Febreze spray we kept in the laundry room. Of all days, he had to be such a boy today. Luckily, Mama was either oblivious or hadn't smelled it yet.

Coughing like crazy, I put away the Febreze and hoped I had drowned out the wretched scent enough. Then I grabbed plates from the cabinet and placed four of them on the table.

Once the table was set, I went looking for Mama. I paused in the hallway staring at the even more additions to the wall of Mama and Rowan or Rowan and Caleb. Mama still had up the ones with Dad, but now the wall had equal amounts of both—another compromise she made in her relationship with Rowan.

"I'm home, Mama."

"In my room, Soph."

I followed her voice into her bedroom and found her in front of the full-length mirror, flattening out her maxi dress.

When she saw me, she smiled. "I was surprised you'd be home tonight. With only one more weekend left, I figured you'd be soaking up all your time at the beach as you could."

"I will be heading back tonight, but I just wanted to eat dinner with you all."

Mama walked to me and embraced me. "I'm glad you came, sweetie. It seems too soon that you are old enough to be at a beach house. Next time, I'm saying no, because I miss you too much."

I giggled. "I missed you, too, Mama. But I'd still go."

She laughed. "You probably would." She then wrapped her arm around my shoulder and walked us toward the family room. She sniffed the air, like a hound dog on the trail. "What is that smell?"

I grimaced. "Is it bad?"

"It smells like a whole bottle of Febreze got knocked over."

I relaxed against her arm. "Oh. Caleb smelled like a dead animal, so I made him go take a shower. It reeked in here when I walked through the door."

Mama raised her eyebrows. "Well, next time light a candle. The Febreze is giving me a headache."

I winced. "Maybe we can open the front door and air it out?"

She smiled. "Good idea. We can open the door in the kitchen too for a cross breeze. It shouldn't take too long once the air is flowing."

"Okay. Trust me when I say the Febreze smells better than Caleb did."

Just like clockwork he exited his room and walked down the hallway, toweling off his hair. "What did I do?"

I crossed my arms. "You smelled disgusting. Who wouldn't shower after tryouts? That's just gross."

He shrugged. "Didn't bother me any."

I cringed and walked past him toward the door.

"Your sister is right, Caleb. You should shower after that. It's just good hygiene and respectful of others."

He groaned. "I guess."

I giggled as I propped open the door and let the screen door's windows fall open. Rowan walked up the sidewalk at the same time.

When he saw me, he winked as he peered over the bag of food he carried.

I had opened the door just in time for him to stroll inside.

"Thank you," he said.

I nodded as he walked past to put the food on the counter.

Mama kissed his cheek and helped him unpack it all onto the table.

They moved seamlessly around each other—an orchestrated symphony in perfect harmony.

I couldn't help but to smile. How hadn't I noticed how in sync they were together? Except, I did know how. I had always worried about my baggage with their relationship, instead of what I should have focused on, how happy Mama was. Tonight was all about changing that.

If Drew had been here, he would have told me to stop beating myself up about the past, but it was so hard to listen to him.

Mama grinned as Rowan pulled out her chair for her. "Thank you." She pointed to the chairs. "Come sit. Caleb, dinner's ready."

Caleb bounded around the kitchen corner, nearly knocking me over and sending droplets of water from his still damp hair toward me.

"Ugh. Watch where you're going," I said as I gritted my teeth. I didn't want to get in a fight with him on Mama's proposal night.

Breathe, Sophie, breathe. Ten, nine, eight …

"Go ahead and pass around the bread and salad." Mama slapped Caleb's hand as he went to stuff a roll in his mouth. "Wait until everyone has their food, Caleb."

Rowan chuckled.

I hoped he knew what he was getting himself into. This would be his family soon, too, and then he had to deal with Caleb. Personally, I wouldn't want that job, but he was my dweeby little brother, so I couldn't blame everyone for not having the same distaste toward him.

"So, how were tryouts?" Rowan asked.

"I did what you suggested, and I caught the coach watching me. He seemed impressed. I won't know until Monday, though, if it all worked out."

Rowan grinned. "I'm sure you did. Your last practice with me was on point. They'd be dumb not to snatch you up."

"Thanks. I guess we'll see."

Mama turned to me, as they continued to chat about the tryout. "How was this week at the cove house?"

"Good. Riley came to visit us. She said she might talk to Randy to work things out."

"Oh, that's wonderful. They are so cute together."

I smiled. "Yes, they are."

Rowan hadn't told me the entire plan, only that Italian food would be for dinner and then once we ate, he would ask. I had no idea if he had shoved it in dessert, or would bend down on one knee during the cleanup, but with all our plates empty and sitting as if we couldn't shove one more bite into our mouths, it had to be soon, didn't it?

My leg jiggled. I needed him to do it soon, or I would give it away. If Mama didn't see my leg bobbing up and down as if I was a bobber on a lake, she wouldn't make too much of it, but if she did see it, she'd know something was going on.

Rowan eyed me from across the table and slightly jerked his head toward the hallway. "I'll be right back, just heading to the bathroom."

My eyebrows knitted. Was I supposed to follow him? Or was he really going to the bathroom? Not sure what else to do. I stood as well and scurried from the room before Mama noticed. Even though Mama noticed everything, soon it wouldn't matter.

I found Rowan halfway down the hallway looking fidgety. "You did want me to follow you, right?"

He nodded. "I need you to hold this, and when I get on my knee, pass it to me."

"Are you sure? What if she sees it before you kneel? I don't want to ruin it."

"I'm sure. You've got this."

I gulped. "Okay." I grabbed the red satin box from him

and hid it in my back pocket, then went back to the kitchen.

Mama was in mid conversation with Caleb and for once didn't eye me warily when I returned to my seat.

Rowan returned a few minutes later and cleared the table of our plates, while Mama relaxed. It was nice to see her so comfortable, one more reason to show me this was the right thing.

Rowan reached for Caleb's plate, but Caleb stopped him.

"Oh wait. I'm not done. I want more."

My stomach sank. He wanted to have everything cleared before he asked.

I kicked him hard in the shin. He winced, but I didn't care. "You're done," I said and glared.

Mama had missed the kick, but not the comment. "There's plenty more, Sophie. He can have more."

Rowan was frozen mid-step.

"I wanted to take the leftovers to the cove house. He can't have any more."

Mama's eyebrows drew together. Normally she was all for sending the leftovers away, but with Caleb wanting more, it put her in a weird spot.

Caleb stuck out his tongue, which irritated me further. Why did I have to be stuck with a brother who didn't have a clue?

"Caleb, you're done. Remember? You have that dessert you asked me to bring."

Caleb's expression was puzzled. "What—"

"Go check the freezer in the garage. You'll see it."

Rowan cocked an eyebrow.

I shrugged.

He continued cleaning up, which was the point. When Caleb returned, I'd shut him up somehow so Rowan could have his moment, but at least he would stop for now. After the proposal if the never-ending garbage disposal wanted to keep eating, he could.

Mama stood at this point to help Rowan clean up; I headed for Caleb on his path back inside.

"There's no—"

"I know, you moron. I needed you to chill. I'll take you to Charlie's after. Just say you're done or found it when you go back in."

He crossed his arms. "For one measly ice cream cone you want me to do all that? As if."

"Fine!" I shouted as I yanked him back in front of me. "Ten ice cream cones, whenever you want."

"Ten?"

"Yes, ten."

He outstretched his hand. "Deal."

I slapped away his hand. "Now get back in there and be good."

He rolled his eyes, but at least he listened.

Mama and Rowan sat on the couch; his arm wrapped around her as she sat snuggled into him.

Rowan winked as Caleb and I sat on the opposite side of the long sofa.

Mama was entranced into the TV show—a new Hallmark summer movie. I had no idea what the new movie was, but if it had to do with Hallmark then Mama would watch it.

Rowan grabbed the remote and paused the TV.

"Hey what did you do that for?" Mama looked from the TV to Rowan as he stood. "Where are you going?"

Rowan looked at me and nodded. Then he bent down on one knee. "Faye, when I met you this time last year at a corporate event I didn't realize that I could ever give someone my heart as much as I gave you. I remember seeing you across the room and thinking *that woman would never give me the time of day let alone go out with me*, but I tried anyway. Boy am I glad I didn't let fear stop me from asking you out. When I found out you had children, I thought there was no way I could manage them, especially teenagers, and yet you welcomed me into your family. Caleb and Sophie feel like they could be my own children, and I'm forever grateful that you were able to give me that." Rowan waved me over.

I handed him the box and stared at Mama's face. She was in shock. I couldn't tell if it was because she didn't expect to be proposed to or because she wasn't ready, but I hoped it wasn't the latter.

"Faye Antoinette Graham, would you do me the honor of being my wife?"

Mama gasped and covered her mouth with her hand. She looked from Caleb to Rowan to me and back again. "I-I don't know what to say."

"Say yes, Mama."

Mama faced me with tears in her eyes. "You knew about this?

I walked over to her and took her hands in mine. "Rowan asked me this summer what I thought if he proposed to you. At first, I was a little apprehensive if I'm being honest, but he's the one for you. I know you had daddy and losing him had to have been unimaginable. But someone was looking out for you and Rowan is your person. If this is what you want, then I'm all behind it."

Mama sniffled. "Are you sure?"

"Absolutely." I released her hands.

She turned back to Rowan, who waited apprehensively for her answer.

"Well?" he asked.

"My answer is yes," she said and then squealed.

He picked her up and twirled her around.

Caleb, who had never been so quiet in his entire life, had stayed silent during the proposal.

I elbowed him in the ribs for rolling his eyes earlier and nodded toward the outside.

Surprisingly, he followed.

"He didn't tell me."

What I wanted to say was, *ha ha*, but in this moment, I realized I needed to act like the older sister. "He only didn't tell you because he knew that you wouldn't have a problem. And in some ways that's better because he asked me knowing that there was something going on with how I felt about them together."

"But I could have helped him."

I nudged him with my hip. "You'll have plenty of time to help him plan the wedding with Mama."

Caleb, who had never held a grudge to anybody except me, grinned at that.

"Wanna go get that ice cream now?"

He nodded.

We walked to my Jeep and hopped in.

I took one last look at our house before pulling out of the driveway. Soon this would be a house of four not three, and to my surprise I was excited.

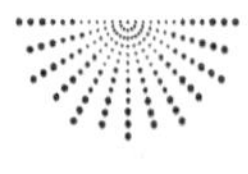

CHAPTER FORTY-NINE

My marshmallow dripped off the end of my stick and crackled as it hit the bonfire. I groaned. "That's the fourth one in a row."

Randy scooted closer to me and chuckled. "Want me to make you another one?"

"Yes, please." I crossed my arms as I relinquished my stick. "This is ridiculous. I should be able to make a s'more, for crying out loud."

Sophie tossed a marshmallow at my face. "You should, and yet those attempts are pathetic."

Shelby giggled as she nestled into Luke.

Drew nudged Sophie's arm. "Be nice. Not everyone is used to bonfires and s'more making."

I crossed my eyes and stuck out my tongue. "I'll still smoke you at tryouts in two weeks. You can keep your s'more making skills."

Sophie's eyes widened. "Is that so?"

Shelby stood and held out her hands. "Enough. You two have plenty of time during tryouts and the season to trash talk. This is our last night here. I want to enjoy this feeling. Got it?"

We all saluted Shelby as she sat back on the chair with Luke. He whispered something in her ear.

She erupted into a fit of giggles and then laid her head on his shoulder. They looked adorable.

I was so happy for her. As I looked around the bonfire, we all were coupled up. Sophie and Drew had come through the summer stronger than ever. I couldn't believe Sophie had said I love you to Drew *and* helped Rowan propose to her mama.

Even Luke and Shelby had figured things out and managed to tell each other how they felt before the summer was over. And now as they snuggled together with the crackling bonfire illuminating their faces in amber tones, I knew they would make the long distance.

And then there was *my* boyfriend. A shiver wracked through my body. I still couldn't believe that Randy was my boyfriend. His chestnut hair and blue eyes illuminated by the fire mesmerized me.

I longingly gazed into his eyes. I would never take this feeling for granted.

Randy caressed my face and returned a loose strand to its place behind my ear. "What are you thinking about?"

I smiled and grabbed the hand he used to touch my face. "You. This. I'm so happy."

His smile returned. "Oh." He pulled me closer to him, then wrapped his arms around me, letting me relax against his chest. His muscles flexed as he settled into the hug. "It's pretty great, isn't it?"

I nodded against him.

Shelby raised her glass of soda toward the fire. "I think we need a toast."

Sophie rolled her eyes. "For what? That's so cheesy."

Shelby glared, which only made Sophie laugh. "We need a toast to celebrate this occasion. We're all here, together, on this last night before we must return to our homes and soon to school."

Luke cleared his throat. It had almost looked like something hit his cheek, but as soon as I had thought I saw it, it disappeared.

Shelby raised her glass of soda higher. "To all of us, this summer, and the year ahead of us. May we always rely on each other to get through anything."

"Here, here!" Luke called.

We all raised our own glasses and then sipped our drinks.

It was crazy to think that a year ago, I had just moved to Honey Cove. My parents' marriage had crumbled and I felt so lonely leaving everyone I knew and loved in New York City. Now, I had a boyfriend, two best friends, and I couldn't be happier.

Randy leaned closer and kissed the skin under my earlobe. The sensation sent shivers down my neck as the heat from his breath mingled with the cool breeze from the water. His kisses trailed down my neck to my collarbone, then to my lips, gentle and soft. He paused. "I wanted to ask you something."

"Hmm?" I asked, still cloudy from the sensations.

"Do you want to come to my house this weekend? Officially meet my sisters and parents? I can't guarantee what state Dad will be in, but I'd still love you to come see them."

My eyelids sprang open. "Really?"

He grinned and kissed my forehead. "Really."

"I'd love to." I gasped. "Wait, what do I wear?"

"Clothes?"

I shoved his arm. "This is not the time for jokes. I'm serious. I want to make a good impression."

"You're Riley Mills and my girlfriend. That's the only impression you need to make."

I smiled and let him shut me up with another kiss. He wasn't entirely correct, although I let him believe he was. Later, I would have Shelby and Sophie help me pick out an outfit. Until then, he could believe what he wanted, because this night was perfect, and I didn't want to ruin it with my worries.

CHAPTER FIFTY

SHELBY

It was time. I had to pack my stuff and escort everyone out of the house. Somehow the past three months had flown by. We were tanner or burnt in some cases—evidence of our summer touched by the sun at the cove house. On top of that, two new relationships, a breakup, a proposal, and countless laughs filled our summer. And yet, even with all that had happened, I wished we had more time. More long summer days, more time together without the overbearing gaze of our parents.

It wouldn't feel the same not being able to wake up all under the same roof and in the same room as my two best friends. I had to admit, as someone who had grown accustomed to the loneliness of being an only child with no boyfriend and parents who took hands off parenting to a new level, I didn't know how I would fit back into my old life, even if it was only for one more school year before college.

Sophie bumped me with her hip. "Stop overthinking everything. Your frown lines are getting frown lines. And personally, I don't want to be blamed for your mother's rant about good skincare and not creating wrinkles."

I giggled.

"There we go! Although, be careful. You can get wrinkles from laughing too much, too."

I elbowed her playfully. "I'm packing, just cool it out."

"Don't let her fool you. She's focusing on you so she doesn't have to focus on herself. I heard her sniffling this morning in the shower," Riley said as she zippered her bag.

Sophie gasped. "What? How …? Why were you even able to hear me in the shower?" she asked, her hands firmly placed on her hips.

Riley smirked. "I had to get my blow dryer from the drawer and I could hear you. So, leave Shelby alone. We're all sad to be heading home. This has been a summer none of us want to leave behind."

I held my arms out. "One last hug before we head downstairs?"

Sophie rolled her eyes but still came close, while Riley didn't need any coaxing.

I squeezed them as they wrapped their arms around me and each other. Riley was right. I would never want to forget this summer.

Sophie inhaled a deep breath and then pushed away. "All right, all right. Let's get moving. You know traffic will be horrendous if we don't hurry up."

Riley sighed, then nodded.

Sophie pulled her pillow off the bed and then picked up her bag and exited the room.

Riley piled her stuff on the floor. "Need help?"

I shook my head.

She grabbed her stuff and followed behind Sophie.

I surveyed the room, looking for anything left over. I

then went to the bathroom and did the same. When I was satisfied that everything we had brought had been taken, I walked out. I checked the boys' room too, which was in a neater state than dare I say it, our room was, but with no personal belongings.

A cleaning service would be in to scrub it all down from the top to the bottom. They would pull the sheets and launder them, then make it all back up in preparation for whomever would use it next.

I grabbed my stuff from the hallway and hopped down the stairs.

Riley and Randy stood together near the kitchen, while Drew and Sophie sat on the couch.

I scrunched my eyebrows. "Where's Luke?"

Sophie rose from the couch. "He was out on the back deck. He said something about checking for towels by the pool."

"Oh, okay." I sauntered toward the deck door and pushed the glider open, letting the humid beach air soak into my hair and pores for a little longer. Just as Sophie said, Luke was by the pool, checking all the nooks and crannies. I stood and just watched him for a few minutes before he realized I was there.

When he saw me, he smiled. "I was just checking everything outside before we left."

I walked toward him and grabbed his right hand. "Thanks, that's very thoughtful of you."

He smirked and leaned close. "I'm a very thoughtful person."

"That you are."

He swooped his arms around me and pulled me close to his body. I didn't want him to leave and go back to school. It was so unfair that we couldn't spend every day together attending classes and hanging out after school.

"Don't do that."

I pulled my lips into a smile, even though I felt nothing close to that. "Do what?" I yanked him forward. "Come on. We better head back in and finish checking the house before we pile in."

He nodded and walked behind me.

Everyone stood by the door.

"I checked the fridge. Everything is either packed into these three bags to take home with us, or I threw it away. No way would anyone want to find a pack of moldy food in the fridge several weeks from now," Riley said.

I giggled. "Thanks."

She nodded and scuffed her foot on the floor. "Randy and I are heading out. Let us know when you all get home, okay?"

I nodded and hugged Randy and Riley.

They hugged Sophie, Drew, and Luke, then waved as they walked through the door.

"And then there were four," Sophie said.

I nodded and swallowed down the sadness that crept into my thoughts and chest. If I let it build, I would never be able to let Luke go.

Sophie nudged Drew, who fake coughed.

"Well, Shelby, thank you for having us this summer. It was a blast. I should head out, too," Drew said.

"If you don't need anything else, I should head home, too. Mama is helping Rowan move in tomorrow. I'll need my sleep later if I want to be ready to help."

"Okay," I said and then hugged them.

Drew helped Sophie with her stuff, loaded it into her Jeep, then got in his own car.

They pulled away separately, leaving me alone with Luke.

Luke wrapped his arms around my waist from behind,

pulling me closer to him. The heat from his chest was against my back. A lump landed in my throat and no matter how many times I tried; I couldn't clear it away.

Luke pulled his one arm away to check the time. "As much as I hate this, I need to head out, too."

I turned to face him, his arms still around me. I laid my head on his chest and listened to his heartbeat. I didn't want him to leave. He would be home tonight and then early tomorrow morning, he would leave for school.

The steady beating of his heart did nothing to soothe mine. If anything, it merely caused my heartrate to kick up into high gear in comparison.

Luke lifted my chin.

I gazed into those beautiful hazel eyes as his dimple appeared and then disappeared.

I sighed.

"I don't want to go, either. I would love to stay, but I've stayed all I can. I must head home to get ready and finish packing for school."

"Okay."

"We can do this."

I smiled. "I know, but I'll miss you."

He pulled a small charm bracelet from his pocket. "I will miss you, too, but I got this for you when you're having a tough day and I can't answer your call right away."

I held out my wrist as he placed the bracelet around it and secured the clasp. I shook it gently and then looked at the charms.

"The horses are for our first ride." He winked then continued. "Then there's a picnic basket, waves for the beach house, and finally a firework. All my top five moments."

"Five?"

"The fireworks represent New Years and Fourth of July."

My heart clenched. "This is the sweetest gift ever."

He kissed my nose. "You deserve it, Shelby." He hugged me one more time, then grabbed his bag and headed for his Audi.

He placed his luggage in the trunk and headed for the driver's side door. "I'll text you when I get home." He blew me a kiss and then got in.

A small tear escaped and trickled down my cheek. I wiped it off and waved as he turned out of the driveway. I sat on the top stair as his Audi got smaller and smaller until it disappeared. Then, I headed back inside.

The silence was deafening. It reminded me of all the good and tough times we had here this summer and how empty it would be until we returned.

I grabbed my bag from the floor and shut off the lights. I fished my keys from my pocket and bounded down the stairs toward my BMW. Once everything was loaded, I jogged back up and locked the doors, then walked back down.

I stared at the beach house. Memories from this summer flooded me as well as the love I had been a part of in this house. It was the end of the summer, but it wasn't the end of our journey together. We still had our senior year … who knew what would happen next.

THE END

If you enjoyed this book, please consider leaving a review on Goodreads and Amazon.

ACKNOWLEDGMENTS

Book five and the ending to my Honey Cove series is a strange combination. When I first dreamt up this series, it was merely an idea. To see it come to fruition is bittersweet. I have enjoyed spending the last three years writing in this small town full of charm, but everything must come to an end.

I have had the honor of working with many wonderful people for this novel. First, I want to thank my publisher Creative James Media. Their continued support makes me forever grateful.

I also want to thank Kereah Keller for her edits of this novel. Diana TC for her amazing cover work.

To my beta readers: Sarah, KOBM, DM, and DKM. All your notes and feedback are invaluable to me. Thank you for putting your effort into helping me.

Finally to my family for supporting me, even when I split my time between them and my characters.

Please consider leaving a review after reading.
Goodreads Review
Amazon Review

For the latest news and updates, please check out Marie McGrath on her social media pages. Exclusive content and sneak peeks can be found in her FB Fan Page.

Twitter: @Marie_McGrath_
Instagram: marie_mcgrath_
Facebook: MarieMcGrathAuthor
Website:
https://mariemcgrathauthor.wixsite.com/books

New standalone novel – The Fate of a Crush- releases October 11, 2022! Check out this YA romance of a best friend's brother.

ABOUT THE AUTHOR

Marie McGrath lives in a small rural town in Maryland. She hopes to inspire others with her stories. When she isn't listening to her own characters, you can find her deep in any novel she can get her hands on, especially YA and contemporary fiction. She loves the color turquoise, lions, and listening to music.

www.ingramcontent.com/pod-product-compliance
Lightning Source LLC
Chambersburg PA
CBHW061040190726
48286CB00006B/1537